Sign up for our newsletter to hear
about new and upcoming releases.

www.ylva-publishing.com

Other books by Jae

Standalone Romances:
Falling Hard
Heart Trouble
Under a Falling Star
Something in the Wine
Shaken to the Core

The Hollywood Series:
Departure from the Script
Damage Control
Just Physical

Portland Police Bureau Series:
Conflict of Interest
Next of Kin

The Vampire Diet Series:
Good Enough to Eat

The Oregon Series:
Backwards to Oregon
Beyond the Trail
Hidden Truths

The Shape-Shifter Series:
Second Nature
Natural Family Disasters
Manhattan Moon
True Nature

Perfect Rhythm

JAE

Acknowledgments

A big thank-you to my awesome behind-the-scenes team that helped me make *Perfect Rhythm* into the book you now hold in your hands:

To my alpha reader, Melanie, for the prompt feedback and the delicious salads.

To my invaluable team of beta readers: Anne-France, Claire, Christiane, Danielle, Erin, Mariah, and Tricia.

To Tricia—for her insights into life in Missouri, the daily cat photos, and her friendship.

To Mariah—for composing a beautiful song to go with Leo and Holly's story.

To Christiane, for again providing me with medical information.

To Gabby, for her gaming advice.

To my developmental editor, Lee, who did a wonderful job with the content edits and who came up with a name for Sasha's bakery.

To my meticulous copy editor, Michelle, for lending me her eagle eyes.

To my sensitivity readers, Alex, Constance, and Evie. You are *ace* in every sense of the word!

To my readers, for giving this book a chance. I hope you'll enjoy it. If you'd like to listen to some music while you read, check out "When Our Hearts Collide," which Mariah Glasscock wrote for *Perfect Rhythm*.

Dedication

To anyone who has ever felt different, left out, invisible, or not "normal."

Chapter 1

CHANTS OF "JENNA, JENNA, JENNA!" echoed through Madison Square Garden. Even after a ninety-minute concert, the crowd apparently couldn't get enough of her. Goose bumps erupted all over her body as twenty thousand people were cheering, clapping, and shouting her name.

Well, not really her name—her stage name.

No one had called her by her real name—Leontyne or Leo—for more than a year. When she was on tour, she became Jenna Blake, pop icon.

Other voices added screams of "Butterfly Kisses," the title of her top hit, to the cacophony.

From his place next to her in the wings of the stage, Ray groaned. "If I have to play that song one more time..." He lifted one of his drumsticks and pretended to stab himself. "It's part of our playlist already. Why do they want to hear it again?"

Leo sighed. After performing the song in one hundred and eighteen concerts during the past thirteen months, she was pretty sick of it herself. "If that's what the fans want, that's what they'll get. Come on." She clapped Ray's shoulder. "One last encore and we can all go home."

She took a sip of her lukewarm water before putting the bottle down and lifting her hand to signal the tech crew.

The lights in the arena went out, leaving just the glow of thousands of cell-phone screens. Smoke-machine fog billowed out from behind the amplifiers.

Leo handed her guitar to her guitar tech, stepped out from the wings, and felt her way up the few steps to the dark stage.

Who the hell thought this was a good idea? She mentally cursed her knee-high stiletto boots and the skintight halter-neck jumpsuit as she made her way blindly along the catwalk connecting the main stage to a smaller platform.

As soon as she reached it, a lone spotlight flared on, bathing her in purple, and the huge video screens behind her exploded with colorful fireworks.

The crowd erupted in cheers.

Derek played the opening notes of "Butterfly Kisses." The bass notes mingled with the beat of the drum, and her body shifted into the song's upbeat rhythm as if on autopilot.

When Leo pulled the cordless microphone from its stand, her pop-star persona slid into place as easily as the mic slid between her fingers.

Her sultry, husky voice filled the arena as she dove into her hit song and gyrated to its seductive beat. She strutted across the platform and paused tantalizingly close to its edge. Within touching range of her fans, she dropped her voice to a sexy croon and sang directly to them.

Hands reached out for her.

Before anyone could make contact, she drew back with a playful flick of her hair and belted out the chorus.

The lights were hot on her skin, but she ignored the sweat soaking her costume and focused on her dance moves and the lyrics.

The crowd below her writhed, clapped, and sang along.

When she got to the chorus again, she held out the microphone to have them sing it. Blinded by the stage lights, Leo couldn't make out faces. All she saw were hands holding up cell-phone flashlights. Every now and then, when spotlights panned over the crowd, she caught a glimpse of someone wearing a T-shirt with her face or name on it.

Even after more than a dozen years in the music business, she still hadn't gotten used to that.

Gazing out over this undulating sea of people, knowing they were there just to hear her, and having them sing along with her… For a moment, she felt a flash of the old excitement as the crowd's energy flowed over her.

Finally, the song came to an end.

Her fans stomped and clapped, making the stage tremble beneath her feet.

"I love you, Jenna!" a girl in the first row shouted. Others echoed the sentiment.

"I love you too, B—" She caught herself just in time. Nope, not Boston. That had been yesterday. Today, they were in New York. Home. "Beautiful." She somehow managed to make it sound as if that was what she'd meant to say all along.

"Thank you, everyone, and good night." The mic seemed as heavy as an anvil as she placed it back onto its stand. With a bow and a few quick waves in all directions, she sauntered offstage as fast as her stiletto boots would allow.

A black-clad security guard led her through the winding corridor and past techs, backstage-pass holders, and pictures of artists who had played Madison Square Garden before her.

She kept her Jenna Blake smile pasted to her face as crew members and fans called out "congratulations" or "great show." Only when the door of her dressing room closed behind her did she allow herself to relax. For the first time in what felt like forever she was alone, without anyone vying for her attention. She took out her ear monitor and set it on the dressing table. Her gaze fell on the large, lightbulb-framed mirror.

Damn. She looked like shit. Maybe there was something to be said for the heavy makeup they made her wear for the show. It concealed the dark shadows beneath her eyes, at least from a distance. If she wasn't careful, the usual rumors would start—that she was doing drugs or spending her nights at wild parties.

As if. She plopped onto one of the three chocolate-colored leather couches. Within seconds, she had wriggled out of the instruments of torture adorning her feet and buried her bare toes in the plush carpet.

Her eyes fell closed. *Heaven.* As the adrenaline high of being onstage ebbed, exhaustion crashed down on her. She could have sat there forever, just enjoying the peace and quiet, but the creaking of the door caused her to open her eyes.

Saul, her manager, entered the dressing room and pushed past wardrobe stands with a wide grin on his bearded face.

His assistant and one of the makeup artists followed him in.

"You were great out there." He gestured toward the huge flat-screen TV showing the stage. "They loved you."

Leo said nothing. They loved the carefully constructed image of sexy pop star Jenna Blake, not her. Without getting up, she bent over her bag and rummaged around for a sweatshirt. She couldn't wait to get out of the jumpsuit that stuck to her damp skin—and to get rid of the makeup.

Saul pulled the bag out of reach. "That'll have to wait. You've got to go to the meet-and-greet in a sec and then make an appearance at the after-party."

"I'll change for the after-party, but do you honestly think my fans care what I'm wearing when I'm popping in to say hi for a second?"

"They care," Saul said. "I doubt they paid extra to meet the butch version of you."

As a kid, Leo had practiced raising one eyebrow in front of the mirror for hours, and now that skill came in handy. "Since when are jeans and a sweatshirt considered butch?"

"Have I ever steered you wrong?"

She sighed. Saul had gotten her where she was today; she knew that, but she was no longer so sure that was where she wanted to be. "I'm tired, Saul."

"I know. It was a long night."

"A long year," she murmured.

"But it's over now." He waved a hand as if that could wipe away the stress of touring for more than a year and traveling from city to city until they all blurred together. "And you'll cheer right up when you hear what great new opportunity I secured for you." He bounced over to her, and she could practically see the dollar signs popping up in his eyes.

Great. What did he have in store for her now?

"I got you a spot as a judge on *A Star is Born*." He spread his arms wide, clearly expecting an enthusiastic response. "The auditions start in January. That gives you six months. If we get Irene and the rest of your songwriting team together, that should be enough time to put together fifteen songs and then go back into the studio to—"

"No. I told you I'm tired," she said, louder this time. "I mean it. I need a break."

Saul glanced at the makeup artist. "Could you give us a minute?" He waited until she'd left the room before he faced Leo again. "Fifteen minutes with the fans and a little chitchat with the record label execs at the after-party, then I'll have a driver take you home. A good night's sleep, a nice breakfast and you'll feel much better."

"No, Saul. You're not listening. I need more than eight hours of sleep and an egg-white omelet." She shoved a damp strand of hair out of her face. "I'm tired. Tired of it all."

Deep lines etched themselves into Saul's forehead. "You don't mean that."

She held his gaze. "I do. Maybe I'm getting old."

His lips twisted into an amused smile. "You're thirty-two. Not exactly old."

"It is when you're supposed to be a sexy pop star. I hung in there until the end of the tour, but I can't keep doing it. I'm this close to burnout." She held her thumb and index finger a fraction of an inch apart.

"All you need is a little pick-me-up." He pulled a sterling-silver pillbox from the inside pocket of his custom-tailored suit jacket and snapped it open.

Leo jumped up without taking a look at what was inside. She didn't want to know. On her way to fame, she'd seen what that stuff had done to other musicians. "You know I don't allow drugs on my tours. If you don't get that shit out of my dressing room this instant, I'm gonna—"

"Who said anything about drugs? I'd never give you anything illegal. This is just a pill to help you—"

"I don't need that kind of help. How often do I have to tell you? I need a goddamn break." Her bare foot hit one of the stiletto boots, kicking it across the room.

Saul's new assistant winced. He probably thought she was some kind of diva throwing a tantrum, but she didn't care.

"Suit yourself." With a shrug, Saul put the pillbox away. He sank onto the couch and patted the space next to him.

She glared at him for a few seconds longer before pointedly choosing to sit on the other couch.

"Listen, Jenna." He put his elbows on his thighs, leaned forward, and regarded her across the glass-topped coffee table. "I know you could do with a week of sipping cocktails on some tropical beach. By God, we all could. But you haven't had a number-one hit in more than three years."

A low growl rumbled in her throat. "I've spent half of those years on the road to promote my last album."

"I know." He held up both hands, palms out. "I'm not accusing you of being lazy. But this is not the time to take a break. You were lucky you didn't lose your entire fan base when you came out to the public—against my advice, I might add—but you won't be that lucky twice."

"Lucky?" Leo echoed. "I worked hard to—"

"Hard work isn't enough. You know how fickle fans are. If there's a new hottie on the horizon who can hold a note for more than a second, they'll forget about you faster than you can say *career slump*."

Leo sighed. As much as she hated it, he was right. Before she could think of something to say, a phone rang.

Saul fumbled for the ever-present cell in his pocket, but it wasn't his.

The tones of Aretha Franklin's "Call Me" drifted over. Few people had Leo's number. She hadn't heard her own ringtone in so long that it took her a few seconds to react. Thankful to escape the discussion and get a moment to think about how to answer Saul, she moved to get up.

But he was already waving at his assistant. "Get that, will you?" He turned back toward her. "We're in the middle of an important discussion. This can wait."

She sank back down. He was right. She had told him she needed a break before the world tour she had just wrapped up, but apparently, she hadn't gotten her point across. This time, she had to get through to him. She needed one month away from it all, or she'd go crazy.

The assistant put down his clipboard, picked up her cell phone from the dressing table, and slipped out of the room to take the call outside. But before she could get anywhere with Saul, the young man was back, holding out the phone with a helpless expression on his face.

Saul glared at him. "That better be the president of the NFL, wanting her to sing the national anthem at the Super Bowl!"

The assistant gulped audibly. "Uh, no, it's some woman. I didn't catch her name. She says she wants to talk to a Leontyne." He pronounced it to rhyme with Valentine, as if he hadn't paid any attention to the way the woman on the phone must have pronounced it.

"Le-on-teen," Leo automatically corrected.

"Um, yeah, I think that's what she said. I told her she's got the wrong number, but she insists—"

She waved her fingers at him. "Give me that phone."

The assistant hurried around the glass table and handed it over.

A woman asking for Leontyne could only be one person. She braced herself. "Mom?"

Saul's assistant gaped at her.

What? Had he thought she had been grown in a lab, with no parents?

"Leontyne?" It was her mother's voice.

A lump lodged in her throat. They hadn't talked in five years, so if her mother was calling her now, something must have happened. "Yes. What's wrong?"

"I was wondering if... Do you have...?" Her mother gulped in a breath of air. "I would really like you to come home."

"What? Come home?"

Saul's eyes widened. He urgently shook his head. "Absolutely not," he said, probably loud enough for Leo's mother to hear. "This isn't a good time for family visits. You're supposed to lay tracks for your next album."

Leo stuck her finger in her ear to drown him out. "Maybe I can come visit next—"

"I really think you should come see your father now," her mother cut in. "He had a stroke."

Chapter 2

HOLLY LEANED AGAINST THE EXAM table and glanced from her mother—the only vet in Fair Oaks—to Mrs. Mitchell and the cat carrier in her hand.

If Holly had ever seen an aptly named pet, it was this one.

As soon as Mrs. Mitchell put down the carrier on the stainless-steel table, Diva twitched her whiskers as if in disgust, turned around, and presented them with her butt.

Mrs. Mitchell chuckled. "Please excuse her manners, Beth. She doesn't like going to the vet."

"I'll try not to take it personally." Holly's mother grinned wryly.

Now that Mrs. Mitchell's hands were free, she walked toward Holly.

For a second, Holly was afraid that her former math teacher would pinch her cheeks as if she were still a child, but instead, she gave her a hug.

"I haven't seen you in a while, dear. I guess taking care of poor Gil keeps you busy…or have you decided to take over your mother's practice after all?" Mrs. Mitchell swept her arm in a gesture that included the exam room and the rest of the vet's office.

Holly laughed. "Oh no. I'm a nurse, not a veterinarian. I'm just helping out for a few hours because Susan called in sick." As she helped her mother get the hissing, growling cat out of the carrier and onto the exam table, she congratulated herself on making her own career choice instead of following in her mother's footsteps. Her human patients were usually much more compliant—and they didn't have needle-sharp claws.

Diva let out a deafening shriek, as if she were being tortured, and puffed up her fur until she appeared to be twice her already-impressive size.

Holly started to sweat as she tried to hold on to the cat without getting clawed to death.

"Hey, hey," her mother crooned. "No one's gonna hurt you."

That promise seemed to be pretty one-sided. Diva flicked her tail, which at the moment looked like a bottle brush, and tried to bite.

Holly's mother took the cat's neck in a gentle yet firm grip. With practiced ease, she palpated Diva's abdomen, listened to her heartbeat and lungs, and then checked her ears. Holly struggled to hold on to the spitting cat, who sent her an unhand-me-this-instant-you-brute glare.

Finally, her mother stepped back. "Everything looks just fine, Thelma. But Diva could stand to lose a little weight."

A little? That was the understatement of the century. The cat was at least twenty pounds of attitude. She wouldn't turn into the feline version of Kate Moss anytime soon.

"Didn't you give her the special diet food I recommended when you brought her in for her shots last month?" Holly's mother asked.

"I tried, but she won't touch it."

"Try again. She will once she realizes her usual food isn't coming, no matter how much she pouts. Trust me. It worked with this one too when she was a kid and didn't want to eat her green beans." She nudged Holly.

"That's what you think," Mrs. Mitchell said. "In the school cafeteria, she always traded her apple for Amber Young's cookie."

As her cheeks heated, Holly cursed her fair complexion. At least Mrs. Mitchell didn't seem to suspect that she and Amber had also traded their homework: Holly had done all of Amber's science and math while Amber had written her English papers. "Hey, leave me out of this, you two."

Her mother and Mrs. Mitchell chuckled. Diva hissed again, and they returned their attention to the cat.

"What if she refuses to eat?" Mrs. Mitchell directed a concerned gaze down at Diva. "Isn't it dangerous for cats to go on a hunger strike?"

"I don't think that'll happen. Let's try another flavor of the diet food. You can mix it with her usual food and then shift the ratio a little more every day."

Mrs. Mitchell nodded. "I can do that."

"Great." Her mother's white coat rustled as she turned toward Holly. "You can put Diva back in her carrier now."

The cat had calmed down a little under her steady grip, but as soon as Holly's mother let go and Holly lifted her off the table, Diva lashed out with one front paw.

Holly flinched back but wasn't fast enough. One sharp claw caught her jaw. Pain flared, making her stumble and nearly drop the cat.

Resolutely, her mother took over, and within a few seconds, Diva was back in her carrier. "Are you okay?" Her mother's usually steady hands trembled a little as they flew over Holly, as if she were dealing with a saber-inflicted wound.

Since her dad's accident, her mother tended to freak out over the smallest injury. "I'm fine, Mom. It's just a little scratch." Although it burned like crazy. She fished a tissue from her jeans pocket and pressed it against her jaw.

"Let me see."

"It's fine. I'll put disinfectant on it in a second. No big deal."

"Let me see," her mother repeated in her no-nonsense-mom voice.

Sighing, Holly lowered her hand with the tissue.

Both her mother and Mrs. Mitchell crowded closer, fussing over her.

Holly's cell phone rang to the tune of Aretha Franklin's "A Natural Woman."

Saved by the bell. Thanks, Aretha. She gently warded off her mother's hands and glanced at the display. The name flashing across the small screen sent her pulse racing. "It's Sharon. I have to take this."

Instantly, her mother and Mrs. Mitchell backed away and started to exchange the newest town gossip about Sharon's famous daughter, Leontyne.

Holly didn't listen. She quickly lifted the phone to her ear. "Sharon? Is Gil okay?"

"Oh, yes, dear. He's napping. I hope I didn't worry you."

"No," Holly said, but they both knew it was a lie. It took a few seconds for her heart to settle into a calmer beat.

"Listen," Sharon said after a moment of silence. "Is there any way you could come in a little early today? Leontyne is coming home, and I'd love to make a strawberry-rhubarb pie. It's her favorite, you know? Well, at least it was when she was growing up, but I bet she still likes it."

Holly barely heard the rambling about the pie, her mind still stuck on one thought. "Leontyne is coming home?"

Behind Holly, her mother and Mrs. Mitchell fell silent. Even the cat stopped grumbling.

"Yes," Sharon said quietly, joy and worry mixed in her tone. "I don't know for how long, but…yes. She's coming."

"Oh, how wonderful," Mrs. Mitchell whispered, clutching her hands together.

Holly scrunched up her face. As much as she tried, she couldn't share that sentiment. Leontyne should have come home much sooner—last year, when her father had suffered his first, milder stroke, or even in May, after the second stroke, when he'd spent weeks in the hospital and then in a rehabilitation facility. She should have been there when her mother had broken down and cried on Holly's shoulder.

But, of course, Leontyne—or rather Jenna Blake—had been too busy traipsing all over the world, enjoying the limelight, to care about what happened to her parents. She hadn't even called, as far as Holly knew.

"So?" Sharon said when Holly remained silent. "Can you come?"

Holly turned a questioning gaze on her mother, knowing she had listened in on her conversation. "Do you still need me to…?"

"Go," her mother said. "I'll handle things here."

"If you can't, it's fine too," Sharon said. "I know you're already doing much more for us than is covered in your contract."

"Sharon, I'm not some hospital nurse you barely know. I consider both of you friends. Heck, I'm basically living with you. So forget the contract and just ask for help whenever you need it, okay? Now, would you like me to go by the store on my way over, or do you have what you need for the pie?"

Sharon exhaled audibly. "Holly Drummond, you're a godsend. I hope I'm telling you that enough."

"It's okay, really. I don't mind." Holly chuckled. "Plus I still owe you and Gil for what you had to endure when he tried to teach me how to play the piano."

Sharon's laughter reverberated through the phone—a sound that had become much too rare in the past two months since Gil's second stroke.

Smiling, Holly jotted down the shopping list, ended the call, and said goodbye to her mother and Mrs. Mitchell.

"What about your scratch?" her mother called after her.

Holly waved over her shoulder. "I'll live." At least after handling Diva, the demon cat, dealing with a spoiled pop star should be a piece of cake, right?

Leo sped north on Highway 169, glad to escape the airport and its crowd of people asking for autographs and pictures. *Slow down.* She eased her foot off the gas and set the cruise control. It wasn't as if she was in a hurry to return to Fair Oaks, the place she had fought so hard to get away from fourteen years ago. There was nothing left in that small town for her, certainly not a great relationship with her father. Hell, he was probably glad she'd stayed away all those years, and she wasn't so sure he'd want her around now that he was sick. Her father had never been one to show any weakness.

She sighed and gazed through the windshield.

The hills of northwest Missouri rolled like gentle ocean waves, and the white wind turbines dotting the landscape like masts of ships only added to the feeling of being far out at sea. The farmhouses and silos sprinkled along the highway seemed like isolated ports, their long driveways with mailboxes at the end extended toward the road like jetties.

She had forgotten how beautiful this part of the country could be.

Fields stretched on both sides of the road—golden wheat almost ready to be harvested, green rows of soybeans, and stalks of corn that looked to be already taller than Leo's five foot ten.

It reminded her of summers, twenty years ago, when she had earned some extra money by "walking beans" on the farms in the area. Cutting out weeds in the summer heat, up to her waist in soybeans, hadn't been her idea of a fun summer break, but her father believed in teaching her good work ethics. "If you want some spending money, Leontyne, you've got to earn it," he'd said.

Wow, she had forgotten all about that. She snorted. *More like repressed it.*

Walking beans was exhausting. She'd always ended up dew-soaked up to her waist, with a sunburned neck and her hands covered in blisters and cuts.

She lifted her left hand off the steering wheel and glanced at it. No blisters and cuts now, just calluses on her fingertips from the strings of her guitar. Saul would kill her if she came back with mangled hands, unable to play. Not that she intended to help out the local farmers again. She would stay just long enough to make sure her father had what he needed. Mingling with the locals wasn't on her to-do list.

As if on cue, her cell phone rang through the rental car's speakers, and her manager's name flashed across the dashboard display.

For a few seconds, she considered ignoring him, but if she did, he'd probably be on the next flight to Kansas City to hunt her down. Sighing, she pressed the phone button on the steering wheel to stop the music on the radio and accept the call.

"Are you there yet?" Saul never bothered with a *hi* or *how are you?*

"Not yet. It's a ninety-minute drive from the airport." She turned right onto the state highway that would connect her to Highway 136.

Saul clucked his tongue. "I still can't believe you're doing this. Going to Bumfuck, Kansas, when you should be laying tracks on your new album."

"It's Missouri, not Kansas, and trust me, it's not my idea of a fun vacation either."

A tractor appeared in front of her, hauling a trailer piled high with hay bales.

"Great," Leo muttered. She wasn't in a hurry to arrive in Fair Oaks, but that didn't mean she wanted to crawl along the highway at ten miles per hour. "Welcome to small-town America."

"Excuse me?" Saul said.

"Nothing."

The tractor driver pulled onto the shoulder of the road a little more so she could pass.

Leo stepped on the gas and gave a grateful wave as she passed.

"This sudden family emergency…it's not just an excuse to get away for a while, is it?" Saul asked.

She clutched the steering wheel as if attempting to throttle it. "Jesus, Saul! You were there when my mother called. You think I would fake something like that?"

For several moments, only silence answered. "Well…"

Thanks a lot, asshole! She swallowed the words before she could utter them. It already felt as if her career was teetering on the brink, so there was no use in alienating her manager.

"It's just that the few times you talked about your father, it sounded as if he were already dead," Saul said.

No. It's more like I'm dead to him. But she didn't feel like getting into it. "I have to go, Saul. I'll be there soon."

"All right. Please try to work on a couple new songs while you're holed up with the family, okay?"

"I'll try," Leo said, even though she had a feeling she wouldn't be in the mood for composing upbeat pop songs.

When she ended the call, the radio came back on, playing the last notes of some country song. She pulled off the highway onto a narrow two-lane road riddled with potholes. To the right, a large, white sign announced *Welcome to Fair Oaks, hometown of Jenna Blake.*

Leo snorted. Fair Oaks hadn't been her home in many years, and no one there had ever called her Jenna.

Next to that sign, a smaller one said *City limits of Fair Oaks, population 2,378.*

City limits? Her lips twitched. *That's stretching it.*

Just as she passed the two signs, the opening lines of "Butterfly Kisses" drifted through the car's speakers. Groaning, she turned off the radio and drove through town in silence.

It had been five years since she had been back for her grandmother's funeral. Fair Oaks hadn't changed much, but somehow it felt foreign—so different from the skyscrapers and bright lights of New York City. The water tower carrying the faded high school mascot appeared on the left, while the red brick spire of the courthouse towered over the town on the right. Several buildings at the edge of town appeared to be abandoned, their windows boarded up.

Leo halfway expected a tumbleweed to blow through. She encountered only a white pickup truck that pulled into Ruth's Diner. The guy behind the wheel stared at her, probably because he didn't recognize her car, which gave her away as an out-of-towner.

Her fingers around the steering wheel grew damp as she approached her childhood home. It was right across the street from her old high school. The sight of the brick building with the brass bell displayed on the front lawn didn't make her feel any better. She hadn't fit in with her small class any better than she fit into town now.

Gravel crunched as she turned into her parents' driveway. When she turned off the engine, the sudden silence felt strangely loud.

Reluctant to leave the sanctuary of her rental car, she stared through the windshield toward the house. Like the town, her childhood home was almost exactly the same as Leo remembered. Despite the money she had sent her parents over the years, they hadn't added to their two-story house. It was only after a few minutes of silent staring that she detected some changes: The weathered windowsill on the dormer window jutting out from the roof had been replaced; the house had gotten a new paint job, and the trees shading the front lawn had grown taller.

She took a deep breath, as if about to go underwater, and opened the driver's side door. The July heat slapped her in the face, but she couldn't hide out in the air-conditioned car for the rest of the day, so she braced herself and climbed out. The sound of the car door slamming shut was like a rifle crack, making her flinch.

Leo opened the trunk and lifted out her suitcase and her battered guitar case.

The porch swing creaked in the breeze as she walked up the path toward the house. The lawn she had mowed every Saturday throughout her teenage years was neatly trimmed, and she wondered who was taking care of it now.

On the porch, she set down the suitcase but kept gripping the guitar case. She needed its familiar weight to calm her down. Ringing the doorbell felt strange, but even if she still had a key, she couldn't imagine just walking in, especially since she had no idea what would greet her inside.

Bleak mental images of her father being attached to beeping machines assaulted her, and she shoved them aside. If he were that bad off, the doctors wouldn't have released him from the hospital.

Her father had never been sick. In his forty-year career as a music professor and concert violinist, he had never missed a single day of work or a Sunday playing the organ at church. Mind over matter; that was what he always said.

Whatever had happened, he would make a full recovery. Before she knew it, he would drive her crazy with his opinions on her songs and popular music in general, his disparaging glances at her guitar calluses that would mess up her violin playing, and his none-too-subtle nudges for her to go out with one of the Wilson boys, no matter how often she told him she was a lesbian.

With a hand raised toward the doorbell, she hesitated. *Come on. You've sung in the biggest arenas in the country—you can do this.* Her heart beat a crazy staccato as she rang the bell. Her knuckles on the handle of the guitar case turned white while she waited for her mother to answer.

Footfalls approached, and the door swung open, but the woman standing before her wasn't her mother. A stranger in her late twenties stared back at her.

Her nerves frazzled, Leo said the first thing that came to mind. "Who the hell are you?"

"I'm Holly." At Leo's blank stare, she added, "Holly Drummond."

The name sounded familiar. "Drummond? Wait, you're Zack's baby sister, aren't you?"

Holly grimaced. "He likes to tell people that, but I prefer the term *younger* sister."

Yeah, she definitely wasn't a baby anymore. Leo remembered her as a skinny, awkward teenager. Now she was all grown up, with generous, feminine curves. Her faded T-shirt only hinted at full breasts, though, not flaunting them as the women in Leo's world did. Over the years, Holly's carrot-red hair had darkened to a rich auburn, which framed her pretty face in a soft pixie cut and formed a striking contrast to her pale skin.

Leo was used to people looking her up and down, but Holly's vibrant blue eyes never moved from her face. Definitely not a lesbian or bi or pan, she concluded.

Instead of welcoming her home, Holly hovered in the doorway like a pit bull guarding a bone.

Leo felt like an idiot as she stood on the porch, clutching her guitar case. Who the heck had appointed Holly guardian of the house? She hadn't even been aware that Holly and her mother knew each other. But then again, everyone in Fair Oaks knew everyone else.

"Um, may I?" She gestured at the house behind Holly.

"Oh, sorry. Of course." Holly shuffled backward, making room for her to enter.

An avalanche of memories hailed down on Leo as she picked up her suitcase and stepped inside. The house smelled of mouthwatering pie and her mother's lavender perfume. Classical music drifted through the main floor. After a moment, she recognized it as Pachelbel's "Canon in D," one of her father's favorite pieces.

"Your mother is in the kitchen," Holly said.

Leo set down her suitcase, propped the guitar case against the stairway curving up to the second floor, and moved past Holly, glancing back to see if she would follow. Maybe having someone else there would make the reunion with her mother less awkward.

But Holly stayed behind as Leo walked toward the kitchen.

Her mother stood with her back to Leo, wiping down the same gray-and-white-speckled Formica countertop they'd had fourteen years ago.

Leo paused and stared across the bar separating the kitchen from the dining room area. When had her mother gotten so old? Her hair, formerly the same honey shade as Leo's own, was now streaked with gray, and she seemed thinner than Leo remembered. Her mother had always prided herself on her youthful appearance, but now she looked much older than her sixty-five years.

As if sensing Leo's gaze on her, she turned around. Her mother gasped and dropped the rag she'd been holding as if surprised to see her, which was strange because she must have heard the doorbell. Had she doubted that Leo would actually come and assumed it was a neighbor?

Leo stood frozen, not sure how to greet her. The bar between them wasn't the only thing separating them.

Finally, her mother took the initiative. She rushed over and engulfed her in a tight embrace.

After a moment, Leo's arms came up to hug her back. Had her mother felt as fragile in the past? She didn't think so.

Her mother stepped back but kept her hands on Leo's shoulders, holding her at arms' length to look her over. "Your hair… It looks so different."

Leo tucked a strand of her tousled, shoulder-length mane behind one ear. "The label thought it was a good idea to add a few golden highlights for the cover of my last album, and then we decided to stick with it." It occurred to her that even now, as an adult, she wasn't the one who got to make the decisions about how to wear her hair.

"It looks good," her mother said.

"Thanks."

Silence fell like a suffocating blanket between them.

"How was the flight?"

"Fine."

"And the drive up?" her mother added.

"That was fine too." Leo heaved a sigh. She was too tense to muddle through the usual small talk.

Her mother finally let go of her shoulders and bustled back into the kitchen. "Did you eat? I've got a pie in the oven, but it still needs twenty minutes before I can take it out. I could make you—"

"No, Mom. I'm not hungry." She wiped away a bit of flour her mother's hug had left on her tank top and wished the awkwardness would be as easy to shake off.

She let her gaze roam the kitchen. Everything looked the same here too: the glass-fronted oak cabinets with their brass handles, the four-burner stove, and her mother's spices neatly lined up on a shelf. Then her gaze fell on the back door, and she spotted something new through the screen. A wooden ramp had been laid over the three steps leading to the patio.

A lump lodged in her throat. Was her father so bad off that he was bound to a wheelchair or had to use a walker? She hadn't asked a lot of questions on the phone, not sure if she was ready to deal with the answers.

Her mother followed her gaze and walked back around the bar. "Why don't you go wash up before you see your father?" she asked quietly, the forced cheerfulness gone from her tone. "He's taking a nap in the downstairs bedroom."

"Downstairs bedroom?" Leo croaked out through the lump.

"We converted the music room into a bedroom for your father since he can't manage stairs anymore," her mother said.

"Oh."

"Holly will help you get your baggage upstairs."

Leo waved away the offer. "I can manage, Mom."

"Nonsense. Holly doesn't mind, do you, dear?"

When Leo glanced over her shoulder to where her mother was looking, Holly stood in the dining room, her arms crossed over her chest. She watched Leo with the wariness other people reserved for a growling Doberman.

Please don't tell me she's one of the locals who think lesbians should be burned at the stake. Leo already had enough to deal with; she didn't need this too.

"No, of course I don't mind, Sharon." Holly's cheeks dimpled as she smiled at Leo's mother.

Sharon? Not Mrs. Blake? Why the hell were these two suddenly acting as if Holly were part of the family?

"Come on." Holly turned and walked toward the staircase without waiting to see if Leo would follow.

Sighing, Leo marched after her. She hadn't even been back for ten minutes, but she already couldn't wait to get the hell out of Dodge.

Before Holly could reach out to pick up the guitar case, Leontyne shouldered past her. "Let me take that."

Holly gritted her teeth. If only Leontyne had been as worried about her parents as she was about her precious guitar. *Don't say anything. If you chase her away, it'll break Sharon's heart.* So she bent and picked up the lone suitcase instead—just one, which sent a clear message. Leontyne didn't intend to stay for long.

She never had. Holly's brother Zack, who'd gone to school with Leontyne, had often joked that she'd been born with two things in her hands: a guitar pick and a map out of town.

They started up the stairs at the same time, nearly bumping into each other.

Holly waved at her to go first. Neither of them spoke a word as they climbed the stairs and headed down the hall.

When they got to the second of the upstairs bedrooms, Leontyne opened the door. But instead of entering, she leaned a trim hip against the doorframe and took in her old room. Was she reliving her youth or comparing her childhood home to her luxury condo on Park Avenue?

Holly couldn't tell. She put down the suitcase and watched her.

It was strange to see the face that was plastered on billboards all over the country. In a gray tank top, well-worn cowboy boots, and a pair of jean shorts that clung to a slim waist and left her long legs bare, she looked more like a country singer than a pop star—minus the big hair. She wasn't wearing makeup, so the dark smudges beneath her olive-green eyes were easy to spot.

Had she spent her last night in New York partying, or had she lain awake, worrying about her father?

If the fresh citrus smell was any indication, Sharon must have cleaned the room to make her daughter feel welcome. With its posters of pop stars, the room looked like a shrine to Leontyne's youth, but she still eyed it as if it were the anteroom of hell. It reminded Holly of the way animals looked entering the waiting room of her mother's practice.

Finally, Leontyne set one of her booted feet into the room, followed by the other. She put the guitar down, turned toward Holly, and took the suitcase from her. Belatedly, she muttered a "thanks."

Clearly, Ms. Pop Princess was used to being treated like royalty and having her baggage carried for her.

The door clicked closed between them, leaving Holly to stare at the wood.

Slowly, Leo let the suitcase sink to the floor. She'd been so sure that her parents would turn her old room into an office or a guest room the moment she'd left town, eager to erase the existence of the daughter they didn't approve of.

Instead, they had kept her room exactly as she remembered it—except a lot tidier. It felt as if she'd stepped into a time capsule. Her old desk was perched in the niche beneath the dormer window, next to the rocking chair in which she'd spent countless hours learning to play chords. The bookshelf still held her novels and CDs. She flopped down onto her single bed and stared up at the posters of Pink and Destiny's Child pinned to the sloped ceiling.

The pillow beneath her smelled of clean cotton and fabric softener. Not a hint of dust in the entire room. Maybe it should have made her feel good to have her mother clean the room so thoroughly, but instead, it made her feel trapped. It was just one more indication of how much her mother wanted her to stay.

Suddenly, the room felt even smaller and more stifling than it actually was. She jumped off the bed and nearly ripped the door off its hinges as she tore it open.

Holly, who had reached the bottom of the stairs, turned and stared.

Heat rushed into Leo's cheeks. Was she actually blushing? It had been a long time since that had happened. She shrugged it off. It was probably being back in her childhood home that made her more emotional.

She put on her impenetrable pop-star mask and followed Holly down the stairs. Her muscle memory made her avoid the steps that creaked, and she realized that Holly must have done the same since she hadn't heard the stairs creak. *What the...?* How much time had Holly spent in the house to become so familiar with it?

It didn't matter now. She focused her attention on the door to the former music room.

Before she could work up the courage to open it, Holly took hold of her arm and held her back. "Wait!"

Leo glanced down at the hand on her arm.

Quickly, Holly let go. "Did your mother tell you what to expect?"

She shook her head. Her mother hadn't told her much beyond recounting that scary moment when she'd found him on the floor, unable to move or speak. Or maybe she had, and it just hadn't penetrated through the fog that had filled her head after hearing the word *stroke*.

"After the stroke, his right side was completely paralyzed," Holly said. "He's getting some function back in his leg, but it's a very slow process. The physiotherapist thinks he can eventually get him to where he can get around using a walker."

Her proud father shuffling around with a walker... She didn't want to believe it. "What about...?" She had to clear her throat before she could finish the sentence. "What about his arm?"

"It might get a little better too, but right now, he can't use it at all, so he needs help with everyday tasks like getting dressed."

Which meant he wouldn't be able to play his beloved violin. Leo curled her hands into fists as she imagined how it would feel. As much as she wanted to get away from music for a while, the thought of never touching an instrument again was as foreign to her as never breathing again.

"If he's that bad off, why isn't he in a hospital or in a rehab center?"

"He was," Holly said. "That's where he spent the last two months."

Last two months? Leo's head spun. Her father's stroke had happened two months ago, and no one had thought to call her until now?

"Recovery will be a slow process, and there's not much a rehab center could do for him that we can't do at home," Holly cut into her thoughts.

"We?" Leo repeated. Why was Holly talking as if she were part of the family?

"I know I don't look like it..." Holly glanced down at her jeans and the faded T-shirt. "But I'm a home-health-care nurse. Since I'm here on a full-time basis, your mother told me not to wear scrubs. She wants your father to feel like he's at home, not in a hospital."

"You're a nurse? I didn't know that."

Holly shrugged. "How could you? You haven't been home in fourteen years."

Leo ground her teeth at the blatant reproach in Holly's tone. "I was here five years ago, when my grandmother died."

Holly pressed her lips together and said nothing.

"Okay." With a stern nod, Leo reached for the door handle that had replaced the old brass knob, but once again, Holly held her back with a touch to her arm.

"There's more."

Oh hell. With jerky movements, she turned and waited for what else Holly had to say.

"He's got aphasia."

"Aphasia?" Leo repeated. "Does that mean...he can't talk?"

"Not much. He can understand most of what you say to him, especially if you keep your sentences simple, but he struggles to get even a single word out. He knows what he wants to say, but he can't access the words. Most of the time, he refuses to talk to anyone and doesn't like being around people. I think he's embarrassed."

Leo could imagine that. Her father had always hated for anyone to think he was less than perfect. "But he wants to talk to me?"

Her mother joined them in front of the bedroom, and Leo turned toward her. "He knows I'm here, right?" If he unexpectedly came face-to-face with his lesbian pop-star daughter, he might have another stroke.

"He knows," her mother said.

That didn't answer her other question, but flying back to New York without seeing him was not an option. She gripped the door handle with sweaty fingers and opened the door inch by inch. The doorway had been widened, probably to accommodate the wheelchair that stood by the hospital bed in the middle of the room.

Even Holly's explanation couldn't have prepared her for the sight of her father in that wheelchair, his body slumped to one side and his right arm resting limply in his lap. He absentmindedly kneaded his fingers with the other hand. His face, which had always looked as if chiseled from a rock, was now drooping on the right. His mustache, formed like an albatross in flight, was gone. With his bare upper lip, he looked strangely vulnerable. Instead of the pressed trousers and the starched shirt she was used to, he wore sweatpants and a creased short-sleeved button-down.

Her stern, unyielding father appeared human—mortal—for the very first time.

Leo paused in the doorway. What was she supposed to say to him? She'd never known how to talk to him in the past, and now it certainly hadn't gotten any easier.

She felt her mother step up behind her. Her hand on Leo's shoulder cemented her in place, as if her mother was afraid she would turn and flee otherwise.

That actually sounded like a pretty good idea. She swallowed, and it sounded much too loud in the silent room. "Um, hi, Dad," she finally said.

He stared at her but didn't answer or nod to acknowledge her presence. Did he even recognize her?

"Come on, Gil," Holly said. "I know you want to talk to Leontyne."

Gil? To her knowledge, no one had ever called her father anything but Dr. Blake or Gilbert.

He looked from Leo to Holly and then back. The muscles in his jaw worked. He opened his mouth, and after two seconds, a simple "hello" came out. It sounded more like "a-no," so Leo hoped it was a greeting, not his way of saying *no way do I want to see you, much less talk to you.*

She took a hesitant step into the room. "How are you doing?"

Again, he looked as if he needed to search his mind for the right word. "Fine," he finally said. The corners of his mouth, even the side that wasn't drooping, didn't lift into a smile.

At least that one thing hadn't changed. His expression had always been naturally disapproving when he'd looked at her.

He jerked his chin at her.

Was he trying to return the question and ask how she was doing? "I'm fine too," she said.

He nodded once.

They stared at each other from opposite ends of the room.

What else could she tell him? She shifted her weight. Great. Now she was struggling just as much as he was for something to say.

To her surprise, it was her father who broke the awkward silence. "Music…" He paused and seemed to search for the right word. The kneading of his fingers became faster, more agitated. "Um…music no."

She had no idea what he was trying to say, so she took a guess. Maybe he was asking about how her career was going. "Yeah, no more music for a while. I just wrapped up a world tour. Mom caught me right after the last concert in Madison Square Garden."

Her father didn't look impressed.

What did you expect? He had a stroke, not a personality implant. Nothing short of a concert in Carnegie Hall could ever impress him.

He shook his head. "No, no. Music bedroom. No listen." He waved his good hand at something Leo couldn't see.

God, this was like charades, and Leo had never been good at guessing games. She realized that she didn't know her father well enough to guess what he was trying to say.

"Music. Put." He tapped his fingers on the wheelchair's armrest in a demanding rhythm.

"Oh." Holly stepped next to her. "You want us to turn the music back on. Is that it?"

Her mother had turned off the classical music that had been playing in the background.

The tapping stopped, and he nodded.

"But it's hard to talk with the music on," her mother said softly. "You know you can't focus if there's too much background noise."

He tapped the armrest again, harder this time.

Leo pressed her lips together. *Message received.* Clearly, the conversation was over. She was dismissed.

Her mother hooked her hand into the bend of Leo's elbow. "Come on. You can talk more tomorrow. I'm sure you want to get unpacked before dinner." She led her to the door, turning the stereo back on in passing.

Not that Leo needed to be dragged. She was more than happy to get out of there. At the door, she glanced back at her father, who sat with his eyes closed as if wanting to block out the world and focus on the music.

Holly followed them out and closed the door behind herself.

"Is he getting speech therapy?" Leo asked.

"Yes," Holly said. "An hour of speech therapy, occupational therapy, and physical therapy five times a week."

"If his insurance doesn't cover it all, I'll foot the bill. Or if he needs a motorized wheelchair or something. Whatever he needs. Money is not an issue."

Holly's brow contracted. "You know, not every problem can be solved by throwing money at it." She clamped her mouth shut.

What the fuck? Leo turned toward her with her shoulders squared. "That's not what I'm doing, but my mother called me for a reason, so I'm trying to figure out what needs to be done."

"There are other ways to—"

"Now, let's not fight, girls." Her mother patted Leo's arm. "We all want what's best for your father."

Something clattered to the floor in the bedroom.

"I'll go," Holly said and slipped back into the room.

Leo stared after her. "Is she always such a ray of sunshine, or is it just me she doesn't like?"

"Holly is a lifesaver," her mother said. "We couldn't have managed without her. She's a lovely girl, really. I hope you two can get along."

She shrugged. It didn't matter. Whatever Holly's problem was with her, she didn't intend to stay long enough for it to become an issue.

Gil had wanted to be brought back to his room after dinner, and Leontyne had retreated upstairs, but Sharon was still puttering around the kitchen, running the rag across the countertop, even though it was already sparkly clean.

Holly gently took the rag from her and draped it over the faucet. She leaned against the counter and studied the woman she had come to regard as a friend. "Are you okay?"

"Yeah, I'm fine." Sharon sounded anything but.

"I thought you would be happy and finally get to relax a little now that Leontyne is home."

"I am happy. It's so good to see her." For a moment, the old spark returned to Sharon's eyes, but the familiar expression of worry soon smothered it.

"But?" Holly prompted.

Sharon trailed the tip of her index finger over the counter, watching its path instead of looking Holly in the eyes. "No but. I just... I guess I'm afraid she'll leave and I won't get to see her for another five years."

Holly bit down on the inside of her cheek to stop herself from saying what was on her mind. Sharon had been through so much. How unfair of Leontyne to make her worry about yet another thing.

"Hey." Sharon grasped one of Holly's hands and held it in both of hers. "Please don't be mad at her. I really didn't expect her to come home and help out with her father. Her life is too busy and...complicated."

So what? Holly didn't care how complicated Leontyne's life might be. Who else was there to help out Gil and Sharon since Leontyne was their only child? The boatload of money Leontyne sent wasn't really what they needed, even if it could buy help like hers.

But saying so wouldn't do any good. Sharon didn't need to deal with Holly's anger on top of everything else. She squeezed her hands, then let go. "Go get some rest. I'll take Gil to the bathroom and get him settled for the night before I go to bed."

"Are you sure you want to stay the night? I called you in earlier than expected today, so if you want to take the night off and get a good night's sleep without having to keep one eye on the baby monitor..."

"And miss your wonderful breakfast?" Holly grinned. "No way! If you give me a few minutes so I can take a quick shower, I'll be ready to earn my pancakes."

Chuckling, Sharon leaned forward and kissed her cheek. "Thanks, sweetie. I'll go see if he wants some company before bedtime." She squeezed Holly's shoulder and then walked down the hall.

Holly watched her for a few seconds before kicking herself into motion.

A couple of minutes later, she climbed into the shower and sighed in relief when the hot water rained down on her. Taking care of a patient with hemiparesis, helping him from his bed to the wheelchair and back, was hard work. Although he might look thin and fragile, Gil still had forty pounds on her. Her eyes fell closed as she stood beneath the spray and let the heat soak into her aching muscles.

She could have stayed there forever, but she knew Sharon and Gil were waiting downstairs, so she reached for the shampoo and washed her hair.

Just as she rinsed the last suds from her hair, a draft of cool air brushed over her, making her wet skin pebble.

What the…? Spluttering, she lifted her head from beneath the spray and wiped suds from her eyes so she could see.

On the other side of the fogged-up glass, a blurry figure stood in the doorway. "Oh. Uh, I'm sorry." It was Leontyne's voice. She jumped back and pulled the door toward her until just an inch of space remained.

Even though Leontyne could no longer see her, Holly turned off the water, snatched the towel from its place over the glass door, and covered herself with it.

"Sorry," Leo said again. "I guess I was distracted, so I didn't hear the shower running, and I…I…I didn't know you would be…um, here. Are you…staying the night?"

Her stammering was almost cute. Almost.

Holly had been in such a hurry to get back downstairs that she hadn't even thought of locking the door. After three weeks in the house, she had gotten used to having the bathroom to herself and had all but forgotten that the guest room where she stayed and Leontyne's room shared a bathroom.

"Yes," she said. "Your mother was running herself ragged, not sleeping enough, so we worked out a schedule. I stay here three nights a week to keep an eye on your father so she can get some rest."

"She didn't tell me that," Leontyne grumbled.

Was anyone talking to each other in this family? It was so different from Holly's own family, which you couldn't get to shut up even if you tried. Everyone was in each other's business all the time.

The steam surrounding Holly dissolved, and cooling water dripped onto her shoulders, making her shiver. "Sorry. I thought you knew."

"No. But I'm glad she's got some help. I, um, will let you finish your shower now. Again, sorry for walking in on you." The door clicked shut.

Holly slowly loosened her grip on the towel. Well, now she could say that superstar Jenna Blake had seen her naked…kind of. With a shake of her head, she unwrapped the towel from around her body and began to dry off.

Jesus! Leo dropped down on her bed and rubbed her heated face with both hands. For the second time today, she was blushing. *Oh, come on. What's there to blush about?* She had hardly seen a thing through the fogged-up glass, just a blurry outline of Holly's body.

Her very naked, very wet, very curvaceous body.

She had stood there like an idiot while the vanilla-and-coconut scent of Holly's shampoo or shower gel wafted around her.

It wasn't as if she'd never seen a woman naked before. Hell, once, a fan had thrown her top and bra at her during a concert, leaving herself naked from the waist up. But this wasn't some stage. This was Fair Oaks. Being in her hometown and seeing her parents again had obviously thrown her off her game.

She stared up at the poster of Destiny's Child. "Did you ever have to deal with stuff like this?" she muttered up to them.

Of course, neither Kelly nor Beyoncé answered.

"Thanks a lot, girls." Sighing, she climbed off the bed to ask her mother for the Wi-Fi password. She hoped the Internet connection in Fair Oaks had gotten better since her high school days.

Chapter 3

THE CHEERFUL CHIRPING OF BIRDS woke Leo. No traffic noise filtered in from outside. She opened her eyes, pushed up on her elbows, and looked around, disoriented for a moment. Bright sunlight fell into the room through a dormer window. While she was used to waking up in unfamiliar beds, this clearly wasn't some hotel room in London, Berlin, Barcelona, or Sydney.

After a second, she remembered.

She was in Fair Oaks, in her old room.

As much as she didn't want to be here, at least it meant she didn't have to rush to meet the band for rehearsals and sound checks, attend interviews or CD signings, or have lunch with execs from the record company. She let herself fall back against the pillow and closed her eyes.

Footsteps sounded on the stairs, and the scent of frying bacon drifted up. Leo had nearly forgotten that everyone got up at the crack of dawn here. She yawned widely.

A knock came at her door. "Breakfast is ready," her mother called, just as she had for nearly every morning of Leo's childhood.

What a strange déjà vu.

"I'll be right there," Leo called back. She climbed out of bed and listened at the door to the bathroom for a moment to make sure she wouldn't walk in on Holly again. When all remained quiet, she entered and quickly brushed her teeth and washed up. Her clothes were still neatly folded in her suitcase. No sense in unpacking since she had no idea how long she would be staying. She picked a clean T-shirt and got dressed, knowing her father didn't allow pajamas at the table.

Only when she was halfway down the stairs did she remember that her father no longer had a say in what she wore for breakfast.

Holly was already in the dining room, pushing his wheelchair to the table. Once again, she was wearing jeans, a T-shirt, white sneakers, and no makeup. Clearly, she dressed to be comfortable, not to impress anyone. Somehow, Leo found it to be a refreshing change from the women she knew.

"Good morning," Leo said.

Her father didn't return the greeting.

Holly straightened from where she had set the brakes on the wheelchair. "Morning."

Leo walked toward her seat, the chair where she had sat as a child—and promptly collided with Holly, who had taken a step toward it too. Apparently, it was her seat now.

Holly grabbed hold of Leo's arms to keep her balance, and Leo instinctively rested her hands on the nicely curved hips. *Mmm.* Her perfume or shower gel or whatever it was smelled good.

"Sorry." Holly quickly stepped back and chose another chair.

Her mother entered the dining room with a stack of pancakes. "Good morning." She kissed Leo's cheek, but all Leo could feel were the ghost imprints of Holly's hands on her arms. She shook herself out of her strange daze and sat too.

The table in front of her was loaded down with buttermilk pancakes, hash browns, fried eggs, and bacon—a far cry from the egg-white omelets, granola, and grapefruit she usually had for breakfast. The mug of coffee with cream her mother set down in front of her was usually a big no-no too since coffee irritated the throat and dairy produced phlegm that could affect her voice.

"Yum." Holly rubbed her hands. "Breakfast heaven."

Leo's mother beamed at her from across the table before turning toward Leo. "When was the last time you had a homemade meal?"

"It's been a while." After eyeing the food for a few more seconds, Leo pierced a pancake with her fork, lifted it on her plate, and squeezed a dollop of maple syrup on it. Her nutritionist would have a heart attack if she could see her. The first bite nearly had her moan out loud. The taste immediately evoked memories of her childhood, and she had to admit with some reluctance that not all of them were bad.

"Quiet night?" her mother asked Holly.

"Pretty much. We got up once. I think it was around three, right, Gil?"

Leo's father grunted something that could be interpreted as a confirmation.

She sat at the table, as quiet as her father, while her mother and Holly chatted about the weather, town gossip, and all the good players the Kansas City Royals had lost this season. Their small talk was so far removed from Leo's world, where the only topics were album sales, sexy costumes, and concert attendance numbers.

It occurred to her that Holly appeared much more like a family member than she did. Holly cut her father's pancake into small pieces that he could eat more easily, while her mother stirred just the right amount of cream into his coffee. They worked together like a well-established team, as if they had done this exact thing hundreds of times already and no longer needed to speak or even think about it. In comparison, Leo felt discordant, like a badly tuned guitar.

The pancake sat like a ball of lead in her stomach, and she wasn't sure if it was all the sugar and fat or the out-of-place feeling she couldn't shake.

She was glad when everyone else finally cleared their plates and breakfast was over.

Her mother started to stack the dirty plates, but Holly stopped her. "You made breakfast. Let us clean up."

Jeez, was she trying to be on her best behavior because Leo was here, or was she always like this? In Leo's experience, no one was this nice without wanting something in return. She just hadn't figured out yet what it was that Holly was after. Was she trying to get into her parents' good graces so she would one day inherit some of the money Leo had sent them?

While her mother wheeled her father into the living room, Holly and Leo cleared the table and carried the breakfast dishes into the kitchen. She rinsed the plates and handed them to Holly so she could load the dishwasher.

Their hands brushed. Warmth climbed up Leo's arm and flowed through the rest of her body. She looked up, but Holly continued to put the plates into the dishwasher, completely unaffected.

"What?" she asked as if sensing Leo's gaze on her.

Leo quickly directed her attention to the dirty forks and knives. "Nothing. You just…um… You've got a scratch on your chin."

"Oh. That." Holly fingered the inch-long, scabbed-over scratch that stood out against her fair skin. She closed the dishwasher and leaned against it. "Kitty love bite. I was helping out my mother yesterday, and one of her feline customers didn't appreciate it."

Feline customers? Oh, right. Beth Drummond was the only veterinarian in town.

"You helped out your mom yesterday?" Leo's mother said as she stepped into the kitchen. "Holly, you're working too much. Why don't you take the day off?"

"No, I—"

"I insist." Her mother's glance traveled from Holly to Leo. "In fact, why don't you two head into town? Holly could show you around and point out what has changed, and you could have a nice lunch at the diner—my treat."

Yeah, right. Sightseeing in Fair Oaks. That would take all of two seconds.

Holly didn't look any more enthusiastic than Leo felt. "I don't think I'll want lunch anytime soon after all those pancakes, Sharon."

"Mom, I hardly think Fair Oaks has changed that much. I can get around on my own. Holly doesn't need to play tour guide on her day off."

"Nonsense. She spends too much time with sick people and not enough with people her own age." Her mother spoke right over both of their protests. "Go and have fun. Maybe you'll meet some former classmates."

That wasn't Leo's idea of fun either. What could she still have in common with her classmates who had never left their small town?

Relentless, her mother shooed them out the door.

When it clicked closed behind them, Leo clutched the porch rail. *Damn.* Even her manager usually couldn't steamroll her like that. She turned toward Holly. "You don't need to babysit me. I can find my way around town just fine without a guide."

A wry smile brought out Holly's dimples. "Has it been so long that you forgot how things work around here? If we go our separate ways, how long do you think until word gets back to your mother that I abandoned you?" She shook her head. "No, thanks. I want to keep eating those delicious pancakes."

Pancakes. Holly didn't really expect her to believe that was all she wanted from the parents of filthy rich superstar Jenna Blake, did she?

"I have to run some errands anyway." Holly tugged on her arm. "Come on. I'm driving."

"Why are you the one who gets to drive?"

"Because I fall asleep within a minute of getting into a car if I'm not the one driving." Holly strode toward a red Jeep Liberty parked at the curb. It was an older model but looked well cared for.

Leo stared after her, then jogged down the stairs to catch up. "You're kidding, right?"

As Holly parked her Jeep in the small town square, the canopy of gray clouds hanging over Fair Oaks parted, and the July sun cast shadows across the pockmarked asphalt of Main Street and its cracked sidewalks.

Downtown consisted of a single row of stores, all housed in old brick buildings: Ruth's Diner, a little mom-and-pop grocery store, a beauty salon, a hardware store, the grain and feed, a tiny pharmacy, Johnny's Bar & Grill, a bakery, and a body shop with tires piled up in front.

On the other side of the square, behind the courthouse, were the library; the post office; Casey's gas station; and the Fair Oaks Ledger, the town's tiny newspaper.

"Wow," Leo muttered as they crossed the street. "I forgot how small this town really is. It's claustrophobic."

"It's endearing," Holly corrected.

Leo shot her a disbelieving glance. "If you say so."

As they strolled through town, memories played through Leo's mind like snapshots in a photo album. There was the bar—the only one in town— where she'd had her first gigs. Not that the locals had really appreciated her guitar riffs or her choice of music. People here mostly listened to country, not pop. But maybe that was a good thing. Here, she wasn't a big star; she was just the Blakes' daughter who had returned because her dad was sick.

A gray-haired man waved from behind the counter of the hardware store.

Leo stared. Was that Mr. Gillespie? He'd already been older than Methuselah when she had graduated from high school. *Must be the fresh country air.*

Holly waved back. That was what people did here.

When Leo had first moved to New York, it had taken some time to get used to people not nodding or waving at each other in passing.

Just when Leo thought they might actually make it to the grocery store without anyone stopping them, two women in their mid-twenties rushed toward them. "Excuse me... Are you Jenna Blake?"

For a moment, Leo was tempted to tell her she wasn't, but lying to someone who might be a fan wasn't her style, so she flashed her well-practiced pop-star smile and nodded.

One woman elbowed her friend. "See! I told you it was her. I'm a big fan. I have all of your albums. They're so awesome. Could we get an autograph?"

"Sure. Got something to write on?"

The two women rummaged through their purses and then held out a pen, a magazine, and a scrap of paper.

Leo signed the autographs and then handed pen, paper, and magazine back.

"Hey, Holly, would you mind? I'd love to get a picture with Jenna." The two women held out their cell phones.

Holly patiently snapped pictures.

"Thank you so much!" One of them gave a little hop like an excited teenager.

Two retirees on a bench across the street watched as if they couldn't understand what was so exciting about the return of the Blakes' daughter.

"You're welcome. And thanks for listening to my music." Leo continued down the street, walking at a faster clip. If they didn't make it out of here, other autograph hunters would follow. "You said you had errands to run?"

Holly smiled as if she knew exactly why Leo had reminded her of the errands. "I just need a few things from the grocery store. Want to come or wait out here?"

If she stayed outside, she would draw attention. "I'll come with you."

The bell above the door jangled as Holly pushed open the store's front door.

Two middle-aged customers blocked the aisle, little shopping baskets hanging from their arms. "Did you hear about Lizzy Wilmers?" one of them said. "Her dog pooped on the front lawn of the courthouse."

"Again?" The other one laughed.

Leo struggled not to roll her eyes. What Fair Oaks lacked in size, it made up for in gossip. It was one of the many things she didn't miss about the place.

"Hi, Sheryl. Cora." Holly gave them a bright smile.

Leo could feel their gazes burning into her as they squeezed past. The whispers started before they even made it around the corner. She tried to ignore them as she followed Holly down the aisle.

Thankfully, Holly seemed to know exactly what she needed and was done within minutes.

The woman behind the cash register stared at Leo while she rang up Holly's purchases. Just when Leo thought she would ask her for an autograph, the woman said, "Oh my God, Leo, is that you?"

Truth be told, Leo had no idea who the woman was. Her blonde hair seemed to be bleached, so maybe she had looked a lot different fourteen years ago. "Um, yeah. It's me."

"So you're back?" the woman asked.

Leo rocked on the heels of her boots. "Just for a little while."

The woman's gaze raked over her. "Yeah, you look like you could use a break. I guess being a superstar and touring all over the world takes a lot out of you." She giggled like a teenager.

Great. People in small towns weren't any better than tabloid reporters who felt free to comment on the way she looked.

"Everyone's going to be so excited to see you." The woman clapped her hands. "A bunch of us get together every Saturday at the bar. You should come and catch up."

Holly had bagged her own purchases while the cashier had been busy talking to Leo. "She'll make sure to do that," she said and pulled Leo from the store.

Leo exhaled sharply. "Thanks for the rescue."

"You have no idea who she is, do you?" Holly laughed.

They effortlessly fell into step as they walked toward Holly's Jeep. For a moment, Leo faltered, amazed to feel in sync with someone from Fair Oaks, even for a few seconds.

"Nope. Should I know her?"

"I'd think so," Holly said with a grin. "You and Jenny were in the same class all the way from kindergarten to high school."

Leo stared back toward the grocery store. "Jenny? That was Jenny Keller?" *Great.* Jenny had been the town busybody even back when they were teenagers. *So much for staying under the radar. By lunch, everyone will know I'm here.*

"It's Jenny Bonnett now. She and Travis got married right out of high school."

No surprise there.

"You know, Jenny meant it." When they reached the Jeep, Holly unlocked it and placed her purchases in the back, next to neatly sorted medical supplies. She closed the rear hatch, turned, and leaned against the car. "You really should come have dinner with some of your old friends."

Leo managed not to grimace out of politeness. "No, thanks."

"What? Now that you're a star, you're too good to hang out with us little people?"

"It's not that. I just… Jenny and I have never really been friends. She and her girlfriends never gave me the time of day when we were in high school…unless they could gossip about me." When she had come out to Ashley, her best friend back then, Ash had told Jenny. The next day, the entire town had known—including her homophobic father.

"I didn't exactly have a lot of friends in high school either, but people can change, can't they?" Holly said softly.

"In my experience, they usually don't."

"After your father's stroke, Jenny brought over her famous green-bean casserole. She and the rest of town made sure your mother ate. They were there for her."

And you weren't.

Holly left it unsaid, but the unspoken words hung in the air between them.

God, she was so sick of the reproach coloring Holly's voice and the looks she'd been giving her since the moment she had rung the doorbell.

She abruptly turned and marched away from the Jeep and its owner. But, of course, she knew she couldn't escape her in this small town. Holly was her father's nurse, so she needed to deal with her.

"Come on," she called over her shoulder. "I need some coffee." What she really needed was something stronger, but it was too early for a drink. Besides, she didn't want to start any rumors about Jenna Blake having an alcohol problem. For now, coffee would have to do.

The familiar smell of grease and brewing coffee teased Holly's nose as she followed Leontyne into the diner.

"Morning, Holly," Ruth said from behind the long counter. She adjusted her glasses and stared. "Leontyne Blake, is that you?"

Leontyne's shoulders heaved beneath a silent sigh.

What the heck was wrong with her? It couldn't really be so horrible to be back in Fair Oaks and talk to the locals for a while, could it? Or was it because she was just Leontyne here, Sharon and Gil's daughter, instead of superstar Jenna Blake?

Somehow, Holly had a feeling that wasn't it.

"How's life treatin' ya in the big city?" Ruth asked.

"Can't complain too much," Leontyne said.

Ruth smiled. "That's what your father always said when I asked him how he's doin'." Her smile waned, and she glanced from Leontyne to Holly. "How is he, honey?"

"Hanging in there," Holly answered. "And he says thanks for the pie you sent home with me last time."

He hadn't really said that, and they both knew it, but Ruth grinned and nodded anyway. "I'll get you a piece to take home with you—blueberry, his favorite. Take a seat anywhere you like. I'll be right with ya."

Leontyne stepped past the glass-enclosed pie case without giving the displayed desserts a glance.

The other patrons of the diner watched as she settled into a booth along the back wall. Holly nodded a greeting in passing before sliding into the booth opposite her. She leaned her forearms on the table, and it took her a moment to realize that Leontyne had done the same. They were unconsciously mirroring each other.

She slid one arm off the table and leaned back.

The swirling of the ceiling fan overhead and the chatter in the background were the only sounds interrupting the silence between them.

She was grateful when Ruth stepped up to the table, pulling a small notepad from her apron pocket. "What can I get you, honey?"

"Just coffee," Leontyne said.

"For me too, please."

Ruth pressed her notepad to her ample chest. "No breakfast? But, honey, we've got biscuits and gravy as our daily special today."

The mention of her favorite breakfast made Holly's mouth water, even though she wasn't hungry at all. "I know, but I already had breakfast with Sharon and Gil...and Leontyne."

"Are you sure?"

Holly nodded and patted her belly. "I'm still stuffed to the gills."

"All right. Just holler if you change your mind." Ruth marched away and returned with their coffee. She flipped over the white mugs on the table and poured coffee from a glass pot.

Leontyne doctored her coffee with creamer, took a sip, and then grimaced. Probably not the low-fat decaf latte she was used to. She put down the mug and looked across the table at Holly. "Leo."

"Um, excuse me?"

"You called me Leontyne. Other than my parents, no one calls me that. If you're going to judge me, you might as well call me Leo."

Blood rushed to the surface of her skin. "I...I'm not judging you."

"Oh yeah? Totally feels like it."

Holly opened her mouth, but before she could answer, someone stepped up to their table.

Chris, who worked in the kitchen, shyly grinned at her and placed a chocolate milkshake onto the table in front of her. "Your mother mentioned you were on night shift when she dropped by earlier. I thought you could use this."

"Uh, thanks."

"I made it extra-thick."

What was she supposed to say to that? She didn't want to hurt his feelings, but she had no desire whatsoever to go out with him—or anyone else. Even without glancing up, she could feel Leontyne's...Leo's grin. "Thank you, Chris. That was very, um, nice of you."

He smiled broadly and lingered next to the table for so long that she started to fear he would ask her out again, but then he tipped an imaginary hat and went back to the kitchen.

Holly slumped against the back of the booth and stared at the extra-thick milkshake.

"That was Chris?" Leo asked, staring after him. "Chubby Chris with the braces?"

"Yes, that's Chris. He lost the braces—and forty pounds." Which didn't make her any more interested in him.

"You know," Ruth commented as she passed their table with a couple of dirty dishes, "you should really give him a chance. That boy is crazy about you. A pretty, young thing like you shouldn't be alone."

Holly bit back a groan. Not that again. She ignored Ruth and stirred her milkshake with the straw. "Want some?" she asked Leo.

"Nah. He's so not my type. Wouldn't want him to think I want a piece of his extra-thick anything."

Holly's first sip of milkshake nearly shot out of her nose. She sent her a glare but couldn't help chuckling. Leo might be a spoiled egomaniac, but she had a great sense of humor. "He's not mine either...my type, I mean."

"No?"

Leo studied her, clearly waiting for her to elaborate, but Holly didn't want to get into her complicated love life—or lack thereof—with Leo, so she shook her head.

"Maybe you should tell him that...him and Ruth."

"I did—repeatedly—but..." Holly shrugged.

"Don't you mind that half of the town is poking their noses into your business?" Leo ran one hand through her honey-blonde hair. "It used to drive me crazy."

"I'm not a fan of their matchmaking attempts, but that's their way of showing they care."

Leo snorted into her coffee. "That's their way of satisfying their curiosity."

"Wow." Holly regarded her with a shake of her head. "You really hate this town, don't you?"

"Let's just say the feeling's mutual. There's not much love lost there for me either. I never fit in."

That wasn't the way Holly remembered it. She knew what it felt like to be an outsider, and she had never thought of Leo as one. The locals talked about her with pride.

They drank their beverages in silence for a while.

From behind the counter, Ruth lifted the coffee pot invitingly. "How about a refill? Or some breakfast after all?"

"No, thanks. I think we should get going. Looks like we're going to get wet if we don't hurry." Leo waved her hand toward the diner's large front windows.

A curtain of dark gray clouds loomed directly overhead, blocking out the sun.

Holly's eyes widened. *Oh shit.* How had she missed that? If they didn't make it to the car within the next minute, they'd get drenched.

They put some money on the table, scrambled out of the booth, and rushed to the door.

"What about that piece of pie for Gilbert?" Ruth called out.

"Next time," Holly shouted back before the door closed behind them.

Side by side, they hurried toward the Jeep. Leo slowed a little so she wouldn't leave Holly with her shorter legs behind.

The air was thick with the threat of impending rain. A gust of wind rolled a Coke bottle down the sidewalk. Thunder rumbled not too far off in the distance.

As they crossed the street, the first drop splashed on her head and then trickled down her scalp. Leo winced. Then the second droplet hit her nose. Within seconds, the sky opened up, and rain pelted down on them.

"Run," Holly shouted.

They sprinted the last few yards toward the town square. Holly blindly pressed the button on her key fob, and they tore the doors open and dove onto the Jeep's front seats.

Breathing heavily, they sat in the car. Water dripped down Leo's hair and trickled into her shirt. Not that it mattered. She was soaked to the bone anyway.

Holly hadn't fared any better. Her wet T-shirt clung to her full breasts.

Leo tried not to stare. She really tried. But Jesus… No wonder good, old Chris was so smitten. Holly might not look like a runway model, but there was something about her that captured Leo's attention—and it wasn't just her breasts.

Unlike Leo, Holly didn't seem to have a problem keeping her eyes to herself.

Her poor gaydar, which normally was very reliable, was having some kind of early midlife crisis since she had met Holly. At first, she had assumed Holly was straight, but when they had talked about Chris in the diner, Leo's gaydar had insisted that Holly wasn't interested in him because she was attracted to women. But then why didn't she even glance in Leo's direction? *Maybe she's just got better manners than you do.*

Holly started the Jeep and carefully backed out onto the street, where large puddles were quickly forming.

The windshield wipers slashed back and forth across the glass, set to top speed. Holly's knuckles turned white as she clutched the steering wheel. She leaned forward and squinted through the rain-smeared windshield.

Leo hoped Holly could see more than she could. She could barely make out the road in front of them.

A flash of lightning burst through the clouds, and thunder boomed above them.

No way would they make it home in this weather.

"Why don't you pull over?" Leo raised her voice over the thunder and the low music playing on the radio. "You can't see a thing. We're going to end up in a ditch!"

Holly stopped the car at the side of the road. She waited a few seconds, but when the thunderstorm showed no signs of letting up, she turned off the engine.

They sat in silence, which was interrupted only by the drumming of the rain on the Jeep's roof.

Under different circumstances, it would have been a strangely romantic moment. *This would make a good song.* The thought surprised her. She hadn't written a new song—a least nothing worth recording—in what seemed like forever.

Holly ran her hands through her short hair, which now stuck to her head in sodden, dark auburn strands. She shook herself like a dog, showering Leo with raindrops.

"Hey!"

"Oops." Holly flashed her a mischievous smile. "Sorry." She still had barely glimpsed in Leo's direction, instead watching the play of lightning outside.

Leo peered down at herself. Her white T-shirt was nearly see-through now, revealing the outline of her bra and her hardened nipples. The paparazzi all over the world would have paid a fortune for a snapshot like this, as would her fans, men and many women alike.

But Holly wasn't interested in her involuntary wet-T-shirt contest. It was a refreshing change from being ogled twenty-four/seven, but it stung that Holly didn't seem inclined to help pass the time by talking to her.

"What exactly is it that you don't like about me?" The words burst out of her almost without conscious thought.

Holly turned her head and stared at her. "What? I don't…"

"Is it that I got out of here," she swiped her hand in a gesture that included the entire town, "and you didn't?"

"Who said I didn't get out—or that I wanted to?" The thunderstorm nearly drowned out their voices, so they had to shout at each other to be heard. "I got my bachelor of science in nursing at Mizzou. I *chose* to return, as hard as it might be for you to understand that."

"What is it, then?" Leo shouted over another bout of thunder. "My music? My sexual orientation? My—?"

"Nothing. I like you just fine."

"Could have fooled me."

Holly's knee bumped into the middle console as she whipped around to face Leo. "If you really want to know… I hate the way you abandoned your parents."

"Abandoned? I'm here, aren't I? Stuck in Fair Oaks, in this car. How is that abandoning them?"

Holly let out an unladylike snort. "Yeah, you're here, but for how long? I bet my meager paycheck against your millions that you haven't even unpacked your suitcase so you can hightail it out of town all the faster."

Leo had already opened her mouth for a snide response, but what could she say without lying?

"Come on, admit it." Holly's gaze pierced Leo, her vibrant blue eyes relentless. "This is just another one of your drive-through visits."

"So what if it is? You don't know anything about me. Did it ever occur to you that I have my reasons for not wanting to stick around? What makes you think you can judge me?" Leo thumped her fist against the middle console. She was shouting at the top of her voice now, even though her manager would have told her to cut it out. Shouting could harm her voice. But to hell with Saul. And to hell with Holly too. If she wanted to shout, she would, goddammit.

"I wouldn't need to judge you if you finally got your head out of your ass and got over whatever it is that irks you about this town or your parents!"

"My relationship with my parents is none of your damn business!"

"The hell it isn't! Your parents are good people. They deserve better than having to find out what's happening in your life through the tabloids because you never visit. You never call."

"Why would it even matter to you?"

"Because…" Holly blinked as if she hadn't seen that question coming. "Because I care, dammit!"

That shut Leo up, but only for a moment. Her manager and her ex-girlfriends had said the same thing, but most often, it turned out that all they cared about was her money and her fame. Why would Holly be any different? She was after something; Leo just hadn't figured out what it was yet.

"I care enough about your family to have been at your grandfather's funeral last year—unlike you," Holly added.

"I was in the middle of a concert tour in Australia. What was I supposed to do? Cancel it?" This time, it was Leo who sprayed Holly with droplets of water when she wildly shook her head. "It wouldn't have done my grandfather any good. I get that you think I'm an egotistical bitch, but people depend on me. My band, my manager, the crew, the label, my fans… I can't just drop everything and cancel a tour willy-nilly."

"Willy-nilly?" Holly blew a drop of water off the tip of her nose. "It can hardly be called willy-nilly if you'd wanted to be there when your grandfather died or when your father had his first stroke."

Another lightning bolt flashed, and Leo felt as if it had hit her right in the chest. She gripped Holly's hand, which was resting on the middle console. "W-what did you just say?"

Holly stared down at the hand on hers. "I know it's not really my place to—"

"No." Leo cut her off with an impatient wave of her free hand. "Did you just say…this wasn't the first stroke my father had?"

Thunder crashed. Holly's forehead creased into a frown. Her lips moved, but Leo couldn't understand a word.

"What?" she shouted.

"No, it wasn't," Holly said so quietly that Leo could hardly hear her, even though the thunder had faded away. "Didn't you…didn't you know?"

"I didn't know a goddamn thing!" *Because I never visited. I never called.* Guilt penetrated the armor of her anger, but she shook it off. The phone worked both ways. Her mother could have called her at any time. "When… when did that happen?"

"Last year in the spring. It was a mild one, compared to the stroke he had in May. He had some physiotherapy, and I came in a few times a week to help him with his exercises, and he seemed to fully recover."

Leo sank against the back of the passenger seat and stared straight ahead, through the windshield. Outside, the rain became lighter and the thunder stopped. A ray of sunshine broke through the dense bank of clouds. Jesus. She'd had no idea.

"Leontyne," Holly said quietly. "Leo…"

Leo didn't turn her head to look at her. "Just drive." After a second, she added, "Please." She realized she was still clutching Holly's hand and quickly let go.

Holly turned the key in the ignition. The engine came to life, along with the radio. She switched it off, and they made their way home in silence.

Chapter 4

WHEN LEO MARCHED INTO THE kitchen, her mother did a double take. "Oh my God, Leontyne! You are soaked to the bone!"

Water dripped from Leo's hair and clothes onto the kitchen floor, but she didn't care. "Why didn't you tell me Dad had a stroke last year?"

A wooden spoon slipped from her mother's hand and clattered to the floor. "I…I… Please don't be angry. It wasn't anything like this one. They only kept him in the hospital for a few days. There was no need to upset you."

"No need? I'm your daughter!"

"There was nothing you could have done."

"It's not like I can do much now either. I still would have liked to know."

The phone started to ring, and her mother picked it up quickly, as if she was glad to escape the discussion. "Oh, hi, Julia." She flicked her gaze toward Leo. "Um, yes, she's here. Oh. That's a wonderful idea, but you'll have to ask her." She held the phone out to Leo and whispered, "It's Julia from the mayor's office. They heard you're home and would like you to sing at the county fair. Wouldn't that be—?"

"Tell her no." She was here to escape, not to give more concerts. "I'm going upstairs to take a shower." Without waiting for her mother's reply, she stalked out of the kitchen.

Everyone and their dog was calling her, yet her mother couldn't manage to pick up the phone to let her know her father had suffered a stroke.

No wonder Holly had acted so judgmental. She had assumed Leo had known and not cared enough to come home.

It rankled her that Holly would think that, but at the same time, she couldn't help being impressed with her. Back in New York—in any city anywhere in the world, really—people fawned over her and fell all over themselves to please her. Holly's down-to-earth bluntness was refreshing. Maybe, just maybe, Holly really was who she appeared to be, someone who wanted to help without any ulterior motives. She certainly wasn't a starstruck groupie; that much was for sure.

By the time Leo had showered and changed, she had calmed down a little, but she still wasn't in the mood to go downstairs and face her mother or the callers who all wanted something from her—or rather, from Jenna.

She stepped up to the bookcase and ran her index finger over the top shelf. No dust. Her mother had gone out of her way to make her feel at home here, but Leo was too angry with her to focus on that right now, so she randomly picked books off the shelf to distract herself.

A hardcover copy of *Harry Potter and the Sorcerer's Stone*. Tattered paperbacks of *Tipping the Velvet, Stoner McTavish*, and other lesbian novels. She had bought them in a bookstore in St. Joe and displayed them proudly, knowing her parents wouldn't recognize those titles as lesbian.

Next to her copy of Tina Turner's biography, she came across her old high school yearbooks. She slid her senior yearbook off the shelf, sat cross-legged on the bed, and leafed through it.

Her senior picture made her cringe. Good thing she had a stylist and a hairdresser now.

The text beneath her headshot said she had been voted *most likely to succeed*. She traced the line of words with her fingertip. *Guess they were right.* Back then, she would have given anything to achieve fame as a singer, but now that she had it, she felt as if she had lost herself in the process.

Sighing, she thumbed through the rest of the yearbook, in search of Holly's picture. She was only a few years younger than Leo, so she had to be in there somewhere.

The headshots of the underclassmen were smaller and arranged in alphabetical order within each grade. There she was, in the freshman section.

Holly's hair had been longer and more reddish than auburn, pulled back into a ponytail, but the look in her startling blue eyes was the same. She was smiling into the camera, and the dimples framing her lips made her seem friendly, even a bit mischievous, as if she was about to crack a joke. At the same time, she somehow appeared to be above all the high school drama. In an *X-Files* T-shirt, she clearly hadn't dressed up for photo day.

Leo leafed through the group photos of various sports teams, the drama club, and the school's jazz band. Holly hadn't been in any of those. Had she been an outsider, like Leo?

A knock on the door made her flinch. She quickly closed the yearbook and slid it beneath the blanket before taking a deep breath, preparing to face her mother and have a more civilized talk. "Come in."

Holly opened the door a few inches and peeked in, wanting to make sure Leo was decent before she entered. No sense in repeating that little encounter in the bathroom, just in reverse.

Leo sat cross-legged on the bed. Her hair, still slightly damp, fell to her shoulders in untamed waves. With her long, elegant limbs and her golden tan, she resembled a lioness.

Shaking her head at the strangely poetic thought, Holly opened the door more fully. "I'm about to go home for the day, but first I wanted to… um… Can I come in for a minute?" This was something that she didn't want to talk about in passing.

Leo unfolded her legs and put both feet on the floor. "Sure. Come in and have a seat."

Her wet clothes were draped over the only chair in the room, so Holly had to perch on the foot of the bed. A hard corner dug into her butt. Frowning, she reached beneath the blanket—and pulled out a thin hardcover. It was a high school yearbook.

"Um, I was just…uh, looking at some old pictures." A flush climbed up Leo's throat and into her cheeks.

Holly couldn't help grinning. Leontyne Blake, stammering and blushing like a teenager. It was almost cute. The thought gave her pause. *Oh no. You know better than this. Thinking people are cute usually leads to wanting to date them, and that leads to them wanting sex.* She wouldn't go down that road again—and certainly not with Leo. But somehow, it had been easier to ignore Leo's good looks when she'd been angry with her.

Not that she wasn't still angry. She was, but now she was beginning to realize that maybe things weren't quite as black-and-white as she had believed. Maybe she had misjudged her.

Leo sat at the other end of the bed and watched her curiously. Her blush slowly faded away. "So? You wanted to talk or something?"

"Um, yeah. I..." Holly glanced down at the golden numbers embossed on the cover of the yearbook. "I wanted to apologize." She looked up. "I thought you knew about your father's first stroke. I shouldn't have jumped to conclusions." Leo opened her mouth to say something, but Holly held up her hand. "To be completely honest, I still think you could have called or visited a little more often. But I'm your father's nurse, so it's not my place to tell you off the way I did. That was completely unprofessional."

Now Leo just stared at her without saying anything.

"You know, this is the place where you either say 'I accept your apology' or 'Go to hell.'"

A smile tugged on the corners of Leo's lips. She shook her head, a pensive expression on her face. "I just don't get you."

"Is that the 'I accept your apology' or the 'Go to hell'?" Holly asked.

Leo's smile blossomed into a full-out laugh. "I accept your apology."

The tension fled from Holly's body. She blew out a breath, only now noticing how much it meant to her. "Thank you." She put down the yearbook and stood.

The rich voice with the smoky edge Leo was famous for stopped her before she reached the door. "I really didn't know. About my father's first stroke. And I only found out about the most recent one a couple of days ago."

Holly believed her. She turned around and studied her. "Would you have come if you'd known?"

Leo glanced down to where her fingers traced figure eights on the covers. "I...I don't know."

Well, at least she was honest. Holly could appreciate that.

"I think so," Leo said after a while. "My father and I... Things between us are..." She waved her hand in an unsteady line.

"Complicated?" Holly supplied.

Leo barked out a laugh, but the sound held no humor. "You could say that, yeah. We haven't had even one civilized conversation since I left home. Strike that. Even before, we never talked much, and whenever we tried, we usually got into an argument. And now...now we can't talk, even if we wanted to—and my father made it clear as day that he doesn't. So I don't know why I should stick around."

"You could still talk to him, you know?" Holly said softly. "He understands what you're saying, even if he has trouble answering."

"I don't know what I would say."

"And maybe that's why you should stick around—to find out." When Leo didn't answer, she opened the door. Maybe she had said too much. She was Gil's nurse, not Leo's friend who was free to comment on her personal life. Forgetting that had gotten her into trouble, and she vowed not to make the same mistake again.

Just before she could pull the door shut behind her, Leo called, "I'll see you tomorrow."

Holly looked back and met her gaze. "See you."

Chapter 5

HOLLY BALANCED THE LAPTOP ON her thighs, her feet resting on her coffee table. Her fingers flew across the keyboard as she updated Gil's medical records and documented the work she'd done during the week. Her mother would have scolded her if she'd known she was working on a Sunday, but she didn't like doing her documentation while she was with a patient. The laptop created a barrier between them that she'd rather avoid.

The patient continues to require…

The Skype ringtone coming through her laptop's speakers interrupted her midsentence.

She rolled her shoulders, grateful for the break, and clicked over to the Skype window. A grin spread across her face, and she hit the green icon to accept the video call.

Her friend's beaming face filled the laptop screen. "Hey there, Nerdy Nurse." Meg's voice boomed through the speakers.

Grinning at the use of her Tumblr nickname, Holly turned the volume down a notch. "Hi, Mordin."

"I saw you online and thought I'd catch you before you disappear again," Meg said. "Is this a good time?"

"Yeah, sure." Holly clicked over to her documentation, saved it, and closed the window. Work could wait. It had been a while since she had caught up with her friends. "How are you doing?"

"Great. Organizing the next ace meet-up keeps me out of trouble."

Holly chuckled. Sometimes, she envied her friend a little for living in a big city where she could meet other asexual people. As far as Holly knew, she was the only ace in Fair Oaks. "And how's Jo?"

"She's right here."

Jo, Meg's queerplatonic partner, stuck her face into the webcam's field of vision and waved. She pressed a quick kiss to Meg's head before disappearing again.

"Talkative as always," Meg said with an affectionate smile.

The open affection between them often confused people. Holly remembered assuming the two were a romantic couple when she'd first seen them interact. An easy mistake to make, considering Meg and Jo cuddled, lived together, and shared finances. It had taken Holly a while to understand that this level of commitment between two people was possible without it being a sexual or romantic relationship. Now she hardly thought about it anymore. As far as she was concerned, love was love, no matter what type of love it was.

"What's new with you?" Meg asked.

Holly shrugged. "Not much."

"Are you still working overtime? You really should take some time off and come to Chicago so we can finally meet face-to-face. We'll spoil you rotten, and we could finally kick some butt together in the same room when playing *Borderlands*. Maybe it'll help, and I won't have to save your ass all the time." Meg hopped up and down on her chair, her face bouncing out of camera range for a second before reappearing. "Hey, you could come to the ace meet-up!"

"I'd love to, but this isn't a good time. There's too much going on here right now, so I can't get away."

Meg squinted at her. "Does this have anything to do with Jenna Blake being in town?"

Holly sat slack-jawed for a moment. "How do you know that?"

"So she's really there? In your itty-bitty zero-Starbucks town?"

No use in denying it now. "Yeah. She's here. How did you know?"

"One of the guys I play with online has a cousin who's friends with her guitar tech, who apparently heard her manager talk about it."

Holly's head was spinning to keep up, but it didn't matter how Meg had found out. The aluminum edges of her laptop dug into her hands as she clutched it. "You have to keep quiet about it. She's dealing with a lot right now, and I'm sure she'd rather do it without the paparazzi swarming around her like a flock of vultures."

Meg mimed zipping her lips. "Not saying a word to anyone."

"Thanks."

"Do you think you could get me an autograph?" Meg asked.

"You want an autograph? You? Since when are you a fan?"

"I'm not. Not really." Meg's grin flashed across the screen. "But you have to admit she's hot."

Holly's feet nearly slid off the coffee table. She stared at her friend.

"What?" Meg laughed. "Just because I don't want to jump her bones doesn't mean I'm blind. She fits all the commonly accepted criteria for hotness."

Now Holly laughed along with her. "Did you survey your friends and colleagues to put together a list?"

"Kind of," Meg said. "Back in high school, when I was still trying to fit in and play the pretend-I'm-straight game, I tried to figure out what my friends were talking about when they called someone *hot*."

Holly had done the same. It had taken her a while to understand that *hot* wasn't quite the same as *beautiful* for most people. There was a level of sexual attraction involved in finding someone hot that she had never experienced—and likely never would. It had taken some time to come to terms with being different, but now she accepted that being asexual was a part of her, just like being a nurse or a redhead.

"So," Meg said, "have you met her?"

"Yeah, of course. It's a small town." She trusted Meg, but she couldn't tell her that Leo's father was her patient.

Meg leaned toward the screen. "Aaaand?"

"No *and*. She's just a woman, despite all the fame." It surprised her how defensive she sounded, and she hoped Meg wouldn't notice and ask even more questions.

Her friend studied her for a moment before nodding and moving on to another topic. Soon, Meg had her in stitches, recounting the latest incident at the coffee shop where she worked. Before she knew it, the alarm on her laptop went off.

"Oops. Sorry, Meg. I have to go. I'm having dinner with my family, and my mom will have my hide if I'm late."

"Go," Meg said. "I don't want to be responsible for you being disinherited."

"I'll call you next week to hear how the meet-up went." She ended the call, closed Skype, and within two minutes was on her way to her mother's house.

After Holly had spent most of the week sharing meals at the quiet Blake household, Sunday dinner with her family was an adventure. She watched her mother, brothers, sisters-in-law, nieces, and nephews reach across the table in a crisscross pattern to pass around the pulled pork, mashed potatoes, green beans, and coleslaw.

Noah, her youngest nephew, was hording the cornbread at his end of the table, and her niece Harper was trying to wrench the breadbasket away from him, nearly toppling over her glass of juice in the process.

The noise level was comparable to a medium-sized airplane during takeoff.

She wondered how Leo might fare in such a chaotic family setting.

"So," Zack said, ignoring his offsprings' ruckus, "how's Leo doing? I haven't seen her in town. Has she changed a lot since high school?"

Holly stopped her mother from heaping more of the mashed potatoes onto her plate. "Haven't we all?"

"Not me," Zack said. "I can still fit into my football uniform from back then."

Lisa, his wife, leaned over and pinched his belly. "Yeah, but you won't need the pads in some places anymore."

The table erupted into laughter.

Zack swatted her hand away but then lifted it to his lips and kissed it. "Come on, admit it. You love my pads."

Holly, her brother Ethan, and several of the kids made gagging sounds.

"Stop it," their mother said.

Everyone fell silent. Their mother was the undisputed boss of the family. She could glare even Holly's adult brothers into silence.

"Seriously, Holly." Zack paused with the fork halfway to his mouth. "I've heard talk around town. I didn't see Leo at church with her mom this morning, and Peggy said she has a pretty big chip on her shoulder now that she's famous. Any truth to that?"

Holly pushed her plate away, knowing she wouldn't get to eat a single bite before she'd satisfied their curiosity. "I thought so at first, but now that I've gotten to know her a little…"

"Ooohooo!" Ethan let out a wolf whistle. "So the two of you have gotten closer? Did she charm you with her 'butterfly kisses'?"

Holly grimaced at his bad pun. She tossed a piece of bread at her smirking brother. He of all people should have known there was nothing going on.

"Kids!" Their mother raised her voice.

It worked, even now that they were grown up. *At least physically,* Holly mentally added and grinned.

"I never said we were close," she told her brother. "I'm over at the Blakes' to work, not to get to know their daughter."

"You could do both, couldn't you?" her mother said. "You need to get out more, meet up with friends…"

"I just talked to Meg and Jo before I came here."

Her mother waved her fork. "I'm talking about real friends."

"Meg and Jo are my real friends, Mom. Just because we talk online doesn't mean it's not real."

Their mother and the Internet went together like dill pickles and apple pie.

"Yeah, Mom," Ethan threw in. "Cait and I met online too, and now look at us—very real."

"Thanks," Holly mouthed to him and then added, "Jerk."

They grinned at each other.

"Yeah, but the Internet can't give you a hug after a bad day, can it?" their mother said. "It can't cook you dinner, take you out dancing, or marry you and give me more grandkids." Her eyes twinkled.

Holly groaned. "Mom, please. I don't want kids. You know that."

"Yeah, but what about a relationship?" her mother asked. "Don't you want to find a nice…" She hesitated, then continued, "…woman and settle down?"

Holly gave her a grateful smile. It had taken her mother a while, but she had finally come around and accepted her orientation—at least the part she knew about. "It's not that easy, Mom."

"If you're staying alone because you're worried about what people will say…"

Zack put the bowl of green beans down with a thump. "To hell with people!"

Harper gasped. Four little faces turned to stare at him.

"What?" Zack said. "It's true. People shouldn't get a say in how you live your life. If anyone's got a problem with you, they can—"

"Thanks, Zack," Holly said before he could get himself into even more trouble with their mother. A warm feeling filled her from head to toe. "But that's not it. I just… I don't want to date right now, okay?"

"Don't worry, Mom," Ethan stage-whispered. "She won't be lonely. We'll get her a cat or twenty for her next birthday."

Their mother sent him a glare that made him shut up.

"Who said I'm lonely? I'm perfectly happy on my own. And it's not like I'm turning into a hermit. Meg invited me to come visit her in Chicago, and Zack talked me into meeting with the old gang at Johnny's on Saturday."

Her mother cocked her head. "Oh? Will Leontyne be there? She's a lesbian too, you know?"

The sip of water Holly had just taken nearly went down the wrong pipe. Her ears started to burn. "Jesus, Mom. Don't start. I'm not going to date Leo."

"Just saying." Her mother looked around. "So, who wants dessert? I made bread pudding."

At the chorus of "me" that echoed around the table, Holly sank against the back of her chair, glad that the obligatory topic of her relationship status was closed for now.

Chapter 6

AFTER BEING BACK HOME FOR a little more than a week, Leo had gotten used to her mother and Holly having lively conversations over breakfast. But apparently, Holly didn't work weekends, so on Saturday morning, breakfast in the Blake household was a rather quiet affair.

"So," her mother said, for the third time trying to draw Leo into a conversation, "how is your career going?"

Leo took her time chewing and swallowing a bit of biscuit. Her anger at her mother had faded, but not being told about her father's first stroke still hurt. "Pretty well."

"Yeah?" Her mother's gaze revealed that she expected her to elaborate on that.

"Yeah. Most concerts of my tour were sold out." Leo peered over at her father to see if that got a reaction out of him, but he continued eating without showing the slightest interest in the conversation.

"Oh. That's good," her mother said. "So you're happy?"

"Well, there's always room for improvement. We didn't quite fill the Manchester Arena, but my manager says the Brits can be a tough audience for an American singer."

"No, I mean…are you happy…not just with the last tour, but with your life overall?"

"I guess so. I'm living my dream, aren't I?" Was she asking her mother or herself? Leo no longer knew.

A smile spread over her mother's face. "You certainly are. Your father always said music is in your blood. I remember your first concert when you were eight. The violin looked so big in your little hands, but you stood on the stage with an earnest expression, and you blew them all away. Your father was so proud, weren't you, Gilbert?"

He grunted.

Yeah, proud. Right. Her father had no longer been proud when, a few years later, she had wanted to get a guitar and play pop instead of classical music. For him, the guitar was not a serious instrument, and he had refused to come to any of the gigs she and her band played.

Even though she'd lost her appetite, she shoved the rest of her biscuit into her mouth, just to be done with breakfast.

But her mother took her time. She broke open another biscuit and ladled gravy over it. "I haven't heard you play since you've been home."

"I played one hundred and eighteen concerts in the past thirteen months," Leo answered. "It's time for a break."

Her mother reached across the table and squeezed her hand. "I'm glad you're taking a little time off. You're welcome here for as long as you want."

Leo nodded, but if her mother was looking for some indication on how long she intended to stay, she couldn't give her one, because she didn't know either. Part of her wanted to leave Fair Oaks as soon as possible, but where would she go? If she returned to New York, she would be sucked back into the never-ending maelstrom of concerts, interviews, and recording sessions. Maybe spending a little more time in Fair Oaks was exactly what she needed to clear her head and figure out why her life felt more and more like a straitjacket.

Her mother swiped a piece of biscuit through a puddle of gravy. "What are you going to do tonight?"

"Do?" Leo repeated.

That was the thing about Fair Oaks: there was very little to do on a Saturday night. As teenagers, their only entertainment had been hanging out at the diner until they were kicked out because Ruth wanted to close or cruising up and down Main Street once they were old enough to drive.

"Yes. It's Saturday after all. Do you have any plans?"

Actually, yes. But Leo wasn't sure her mother even knew what Netflix was. Her plans for tonight involved holing up in her room with her laptop and binge-watching her favorite TV show, *Central Precinct*. At least the writers of the crime show knew better than to kill off their lesbian characters or to have one of them cheat on the other. "I'm probably just going to stay in and watch some TV. Touring made me miss a lot of episodes I need to catch up on."

Her mother waved dismissively. "You could watch TV now and go see your friends tonight. Holly said some of them are getting together at the bar."

"In half an hour, I'm meeting with the guys putting in the new sink in Dad's bathroom, and I want to look into a less-steep ramp for him. Besides, I don't have any friends here, Mom."

Her mother shoved her now-empty plate back. "Nonsense. Of course you have friends. There's Jenny and Travis and—"

"Jenny!" Leo snorted. "We've never been friends. Don't you remember? She was the one who outed me in front of—"

"I remember." Her mother held up her hand like a shield against the spoken words. "What about Ashley?"

There was no denying that she and Ash had been friends—or maybe more. The jury was still out on that, and Leo didn't want to linger on what-ifs. Still, she couldn't deny that the mention of Ash's name stirred old feelings deep inside of her. "Does she still live around here?"

"Oh yes. She never left. Didn't you keep in touch?"

Leo shook her head. "No, we… I guess our lives were just too different. Is she married?"

"No. There were rumors a while ago, but…" Her mother compressed her lips into a razor-sharp line. "I don't think she's in a relationship. She bought the old Smotherman place a few years back. You remember that little red house at the edge of town? The one with the white shutters?"

Ash's shutters weren't what interested her. "Rumors?" she asked instead.

"It's nothing. You know how people can be." Her mother rose and started to clear the table.

"Let me do it," Leo said. On Holly's days off, the burden of taking care of her father was mostly on her mother. Guilt scratched at her conscience, but she couldn't imagine taking over his daily care. Not that her father wanted her to. He had rejected any help from her so far. But helping out with household chores was something she could do.

"Thank you." Her mother set the dishes back down. She released the brake on the wheelchair and started pushing him toward his room. Over her shoulder, she asked, "So, are you going?"

"Guess I am," Leo said. Her mother wouldn't be satisfied until she agreed to meet her classmates, and, admittedly, she was curious to see what had become of Ashley.

As soon as Leo got out of her rental car, she felt half a dozen pairs of eyes on her.

Most of the stores along Main Street were already closed, but a few locals were still out and about, and now they watched her every move as she crossed the street.

A young man hastened his steps to catch up with her. "Ms. Blake?"

She turned, expecting to be asked for yet another autograph.

"My name is Billy Neff. I'm a reporter for the Fair Oaks Ledger." He flashed his press card. "I normally wouldn't stop you on the street, but I tried to reach you all week, and I, um, was wondering if you would be willing to give me an interview."

He barely looked old enough to write for anything but the school paper. Clearly, he was hoping a homecoming story about Jenna Blake would boost his career.

She suppressed a sigh. "Listen, I was hoping to fly under the radar as much as I can while I'm here. But if you promise not to print anything about me for the moment, I'd be willing to sit down with you and answer any questions before I leave."

His eyes lit up. "Oh, sure. We could—"

Her phone rang, and she wasn't surprised to see Saul's name on the display. He had e-mailed her the contract for *A Star is Born* a few days ago, and now he probably wanted to know why she hadn't looked at it yet.

"Do you have a card?" she asked the young reporter. When he handed it over, she put it away before giving him a nod and picking up the phone. "Hi, Saul. I've been meaning to call you, but the cell-phone reception in town is really shitty."

"Have you looked at the contract?"

"Not yet. I'm still not sure a show like that is something I want to do."

"Are you kidding? It's targeting your key demographics!"

"But the show is not about the music. It's more like a popularity contest with fake drama and—"

"Who cares?" Saul said. "It'll get you in front of millions of viewers."

"I know. Sorry, Saul, but I've got to go. I'm meeting with a reporter." It wasn't a total lie, and Saul didn't need to know the interview wasn't today. She ended the call.

A few more steps brought her to the door of Johnny's Bar and Grill, where she paused.

Already she began to regret letting herself be talked into coming. Was it too late to turn back?

Without warning, someone ran into her from behind, knocking her forward. She turned her face at the last moment to avoid having her nose smashed against the bar's front door. "What the—?"

When she turned around, the curse died on her lips, and her annoyance faded.

Holly stood in front of her, red hair adorably mussed as if she had been running her hands through it. "Oh God, I'm so sorry. I was looking down at my phone for a second, to make sure I didn't miss any calls from your mom, so I didn't see you. I didn't mean to run into you—literally."

"We seem to be making a habit of that," Leo said with a smile, remembering how it felt to hold on to Holly when they had collided on her first morning back home.

"Yeah. Are you here to meet the gang too?"

Leo nodded. "My mother practically kicked me out of the house. Apparently, there's a quota of locals I have to meet before she'll let me back in."

Holly chuckled. "My family is the same. They insisted that I tag along with Zack, even though I wasn't in your class."

"Where *is* your brother?"

"Probably already inside, halfway through his first beer. I was running a little late." A hint of a blush colored her cheeks.

Peering through the glass, Leo scanned the bar. "Is it too late to turn back?"

"It won't be so bad. Come on." Holly reached around her and pushed the door open. Her arm brushed Leo's shoulder, and her perfume teased Leo's nose as Holly stepped past her.

Now there really was no escape.

As soon as she followed Holly in, a chorus of shouts erupted from the back of the room, where her former classmates had commandeered the corner booth. Jenny and her husband, Travis; Zack; Chris; and Ashley were crowded around the table.

"Well, well, if it isn't Leo Blake," Travis called. "Or is it Jenna Blake now?"

Lately, she had begun to ask herself the same question. That was the one good thing about being back in Fair Oaks: she got to reconnect with the part of her that was just Leo. "Leo's fine."

Ashley and Zack, who sat at the ends of the horseshoe-shaped booth, scooted to the side to make room at the table for Holly and Leo.

Even though Ashley was closer, Holly chose to sit next to her brother.

Leo glanced back and forth between Ash and Holly. Was there some bad blood between them? As far as she knew, they hadn't hung out in high school.

"So good to see you," Zack said. "Sit down and tell us all about the glorious celebrity life."

"Jeez, Zack!" Holly elbowed him in the ribs. "Let the poor woman order first!"

Yeah, Leo definitely needed a beer or ten to survive this evening. After a moment's hesitation, she squeezed in next to Holly. While she was curious about how Ashley had fared since graduation, keeping her distance might be a good idea.

Speaking of distance...or lack thereof... She was very aware of the way Holly's breast pressed into her arm. Well, in these close quarters, it couldn't be avoided.

"What do you want?" Chris asked. "Looks like Johnny is busy, so let me get your drinks, or it'll take forever."

"I thought you work at the diner?" Leo asked.

"I do, but I help out at the bar every now and then too. So, what can I get you?" His gaze lingered on Holly, not on her. It should have been a relief—she got enough attention anywhere she went—but his puppy-eyed look got on her nerves.

"Thanks," Holly said. "A Bud Light for me, please."

"Do you have Blue Moon?" Leo asked.

He shook his head. "No, but we have Boulevard Wheat on tap."

"Sounds good. Thanks."

Ashley stood to let Chris out of the booth, and he marched off toward the bar.

Everyone at the table stared at Leo, so she had ample opportunity to study them too. Well, there really was only one person she was looking at—Ashley Gaines.

Usually, when people said someone hadn't changed a bit since high school, it was a bold-faced lie. But Ash really looked like the gorgeous girl she'd had a huge crush on. Her curves had filled out, but her hair, the same color as the wheat on her father's fields in summer, still reached down to her waist, and she still exuded that farm-girl innocence. Back then, she'd been class president and homecoming queen, and Leo wouldn't be surprised if she became the mayor of town one day—or ended up being married to the mayor.

Ash looked up from the label of the beer bottle she'd been scratching at with her thumbnail. She smiled at Leo, but it was the polite smile you gave an acquaintance you hadn't seen in more than a decade. Maybe Leo was nothing more to her after all those years. She couldn't read Ash anymore.

"I can't believe you're back," Ash said.

"I'm not back. I'm just visiting for a while." She wasn't here to stay, and she wanted to make that clear from the get-go.

"You look stunning," Travis said, drawing her attention away from Ash.

A deep frown settled on Jenny's face, and she dug her elbow into her husband's ribs.

"Thanks." Leo gave him a stiff grin. "I've been eating my vegetables."

Chris returned with their beers, and everyone moved together to make room for him, bringing Leo into even closer contact with Holly's body to her left. It distracted her so much that she even looked away from Ash.

"No need to ask what you've been up to for the last dozen years," Zack said. "We've all been following your career. Must be pretty exciting to jet all over the world, get to see Paris, Rome, and all those fancy places."

Leo snorted. "All I usually get to see are the airports, my hotel room, and the backstage area, and trust me, they look the same all over the world. Nothing exciting about that."

"Oh, yeah, you lead such a boring life. As if I'd believe that for a minute." Travis slid to the edge of his seat and leaned across the table. "Is it true that pop stars like you have groupies that throw themselves at you in every city?"

"Only in your fantasies." Leo took a sip of beer and then wiped a bit of foam off her upper lip. "Whatever you read in the tabloids, it's hopelessly exaggerated."

Travis eyed her over his beer bottle—probably not his first one of the evening, she suspected. "Nuh-uh. You're holding out on us. Come on. Tell us. What's your craziest groupie story?"

"I don't have one." Sure, there were always groupies around, but she wasn't interested in the men, and after her first few months on tour, she had learned to stay away from the women too. They didn't really want her; they wanted the idea of her and the bragging rights of being able to say they had slept with Jenna Blake. It got old real fast.

"No juicy stories?" Travis was almost whining now.

"Cut it out, Travis. She said no." It was Holly who had come to her rescue.

Even though she was the youngest, Travis seemed to listen to her. He finally shut up and focused on his beer.

Leo raised her glass to Holly and nodded a thank-you. "Let's not talk about me all night. My life isn't half as interesting as you might think. So, what have you guys been up to since graduation?"

"Would you believe I'm an insurance agent?" Zack said.

"Sounds, um, interesting."

"It pays the bills. I've got a family to feed." He whipped out his phone to show off photos of his wife and kids.

"I'm pumping for a living," Travis said with a smirk and some provocative hip movements.

God, this guy was really getting on her nerves. He hadn't gotten any more mature since their high school days.

"He means he's working at the gas station at the edge of town." Holly rolled her eyes.

"And I own the flower-and-gifts store across the street," Ashley said. "It's small, but it's all mine."

"Are you still playing the keyboard?" Leo asked.

Ash peered down at the table, then back up. "No. I gave that up."

Along with women? But then again, if you didn't count that one kiss on prom night, Ashley had never allowed herself to become involved with a woman, at least not as far as Leo knew.

Jenny started to talk about her part-time job at the corner grocery store. Leo nodded in all the right places, but her mind was on the past.

"Tell us more about yourself," Ashley said after a while. "We all know each other's stories, but we only know what the tabloids are writing about you. Not that it's much about your private life, mind you."

Leo shrugged. "Being on the road for most of the year doesn't leave much time for a private life."

"Is there a man in your life?" Ash asked.

Oh please. "You mean woman." Leo looked her in the eyes. Ashley had been the first person she had come out to and the first girl she had kissed. Why pretend that Leo was interested in men, even though the entire world knew different?

Ash fiddled with a loose corner of the beer label. "Um, yeah."

"Not right now. Not for some time, actually. Like I said, life as a recording artist doesn't lend itself to a successful relationship. How about you?"

The label nearly ripped off the bottle as Ash's fingers slipped. "Me? Um, no, I'm single."

Chris sighed into his beer. "Me too."

The others at the table laughed.

"Yeah, and we all know who you're holding out for." Travis thumped him on the back. "Forget it, man. You don't have the right appendages for Zack's little sister."

Blushing to the roots of his crew cut, Chris lowered his head. "Seems to be a lot of that going on around here." He peered from Holly to Leo.

"And let's not forget our perfect Ms. Homecoming Queen," Travis threw in.

For several seconds, everyone at the table froze and sat in silence. Someone's shoe squealed across the floor.

"What's that supposed to mean?" Jenny asked.

The others muttered in confusion, while Leo stared at Ashley, who looked as if she were facing a serial killer who came at her with an ax.

"Oh, come on! Didn't anyone notice?" Travis looked at each of his friends in turn.

"Notice what?" Chris asked.

"A couple of years back, Holly's car was sometimes parked in front of Ash's place—all night long. What did you think they were doing? Braiding each other's hair?" Travis slapped the table and roared with laughter.

Leo stared along with everyone else. Holly and Ashley? *Holy fuck.* She hadn't seen that coming. So her gaydar hadn't been off—Holly was a lesbian or bi...and so was Ashley, the crush of all her teenage years.

Zack had gone pale. "You'd better watch your mouth, buddy. You're talking about my sister."

"I'm only telling the truth that the rest of you are too blind to see," Travis muttered.

"Ash?" Jenny whispered. "Is it true? Do you...? Are you...um, like Holly and Leo?"

Ashley let out a nervous chuckle. "He's imagining things. It's called wishful thinking. You know, that thing guys have about two women together. If one woman as much as hugs another, it gets their little fantasies going."

Holly didn't say anything. She sat without looking at Ashley, her back ramrod straight, and took a big swig of her beer.

"Holly?" Zack said. "That's all it is, right? You and Ash weren't...? I mean, if you were, you would have told us, right?"

She focused her glacier-blue gaze on him. "I've already got enough on my plate dealing with my own sexual orientation. I can't speak for anyone else. If Ash says she's straight, you'll just have to trust her."

"Yeah," Chris said. "She should know, right?"

The others laughed, but the lighthearted atmosphere from before was gone.

Leo sat with her head turned toward Holly, still watching her. They didn't really believe her, did they? Had no one else seen that flash of hurt in her eyes when Ash had denied being involved with her?

"So, is anyone up for a game of pool?" Zack nodded toward the lone pool table in the back.

Ash finished her beer with one long pull. "Not tonight. I'd better head home. I have to get up early tomorrow."

"Oh, come on, Ash. Tomorrow's Sunday."

"Well, you know how it is. A store owner's work is never done. I'll beat your ass at pool next week." Ash tucked two bills beneath her empty bottle and stood. She was out the door before anyone else could protest.

Holly's gaze followed her. She looked as if she would have loved to leave too—either to confront Ashley or to go home and nurse her wounds. But she didn't. She let herself be dragged to the back of the room and proceeded to clear the pool table.

Leo leaned on her cue and watched her. She couldn't help admiring her—and it wasn't just because of the way her jeans pulled tight over her butt whenever she bent over the table. Would she have held up so well if she and Ashley had gotten together and Ashley had denied her in public?

"Earth to Leo," Zack called.

Leo wrenched her gaze away from his sister. "Hmm?"

"You're up. Unless, of course, your dainty little celebrity fingers are only good for holding a mic, not a cue stick these days."

Leo strode to the head of the table and racked the balls. "Watch these dainty little celebrity fingers beat your ass, Drummond."

"Drive carefully," Zack called as he unlocked his car.

"I've had one beer, and it's not like I'll have to drive halfway across the state." Holly appreciated his concern, but sometimes, his big-brother routine was just too much. Or maybe she had run out of patience after the stunt Ash had pulled.

He held up his hands. "Just saying." He got in and drove off.

Travis and Jenny waved goodbye and climbed into their pickup.

Chris shuffled his feet and jingled his keys. "Guess I'll see you next Saturday."

She nodded, too tired to make small talk.

When he got into his car and pulled away from the curb, the only one remaining behind was Leo.

"Come on. I'll walk you to your car."

"You don't need to," Holly said. "I'm parked right across the street."

"Then we're headed the same way anyway, because I'm parked right behind you."

They crossed the street in silence. Holly unlocked the Jeep and opened the driver's side door before turning back around.

In the light of the single streetlamp, the golden highlights in Leo's hair looked like silver. She shoved both hands into her jeans pockets and tilted her head. "So you and Ashley, hmm?"

And here she had hoped she would be able to make her escape without anyone bringing it up again. But of course Leo wouldn't let it go. Holly clenched her fist around the car keys. "Leo, I…"

"Don't bother denying it. It's really not fair of her to force you to lie for her."

Holly's defensive posture deflated. No, it wasn't fair at all. She had taken a huge risk by coming out to her family and living her life openly, despite the small-town mentality some of their neighbors held toward anyone who wasn't straight. Leo's coming-out, years ago, had paved the way, but it still hadn't been easy. Finally, after a couple of tense situations, she felt as if she had weathered the storm—only to be forced back into the closet by Ash's insecurities. "Yeah. I don't like it, but if she ever comes out, it has to be her decision. I can't force it on her."

"So you're still dating?"

"God, no. That's old news. We only saw each other for a few months after I got back home from college. I have no idea why Travis brought it up now."

"I take it, it didn't end well?"

Holly grimaced. "You could say that."

"No wonder. Ash seems to be so deeply in the closet, she's finding next year's Christmas presents."

Despite her tension, Holly couldn't help chuckling. "Yeah. But it wasn't that. Well, not just that. Of course, her reluctance to even be seen with me didn't help, but there were other issues as well."

Leo nodded but didn't ask what they were, as if sensing that Holly didn't want to talk about it.

Holly was grateful for that silent understanding. "You didn't seem very surprised when Travis said… Well, you know what he said about me and Ash."

"Oh, I was surprised. Somehow, I can't see the two of you making a good couple."

"Then you're wiser than me," Holly said, suppressing a sigh. "Wait a minute... That's what surprised you? That Ash and I got together, but not that we like women?"

"I had a feeling about you."

"And about Ash too?"

"Um, you could say that."

There was something in her voice—that voice that could effortlessly express a range of emotions in her songs. Holly squinted at her. "You don't mean...?" No, she couldn't possibly mean that, could she?

Leo sighed. "Let's just say you and I have more in common than our awesome pool skills."

"You and Ash?" Holly's voice cracked like that of a teenage boy, so she paused and cleared her throat. "You've been together?"

"No. It never went that far. All we shared was one kiss—one pretty hot kiss," she added with a crooked grin, "on prom night. Didn't she ever mention it when you were together?"

"No. She never talked about you, period. I thought you and she had some sort of falling out, so I didn't force it."

"Falling out," Leo murmured. "Yeah, I guess you could call it that. She didn't have the courage to face what had happened between us. After that night, I only saw her one more time. I asked her to come to New York with me, but she told me it was just one kiss and didn't mean anything. She was straight. Or so she said."

Holly snorted. "Yeah, right." Only one of them had been eager to have sex—and it hadn't been Holly. She leaned on the open car door and watched Leo. "I still can't believe we kissed the same woman."

Leo gave an exaggerated shiver. "Pretty weird, right? But I guess that's what happens if you grow up in a small town with only three lesbians."

Strictly speaking, it was two lesbians and one asexual who was romantically attracted to women, but that distinction didn't matter at the moment. "Yeah, things can get messy when your dating pool is the size of a puddle."

Leo's laughter rang out into the night. "More like the size of a shot glass."

That reminded Holly that she really wanted a drink after the debacle with Ash. For a moment, she wondered whether she should ask Leo to come. *Haven't you learned anything? That's so not a good idea.* Inviting a woman home for a drink could easily lead to her jumping to conclusions, and she had reached her limit of drama for the night.

She lifted one foot to climb into her Jeep.

"See you on Monday," Leo said. "Drive carefully."

For some reason, it didn't annoy her when Leo said it. "Will do." About to close the door, she remembered something. "Oh, wait. What do you want for breakfast?"

"Uh, breakfast?"

"Yeah, you know, the meal people usually eat in the morning." Holly added a smile so Leo would know she was teasing.

"Thanks for the expert definition, Ms. Merriam-Webster. I know what it is. Are you buying?"

"Yes. I bring breakfast most Mondays so your mother doesn't always have to make it. So, bagel, croissant, blueberry muffin…?"

"Are you going to Slice of Heaven?"

Holly nodded. It was the only bakery in town after all. "My baking skills are a bit… Um, let's just say my baking is about as good as my singing."

"So I shouldn't hire you as a background singer anytime soon?" Leo asked with a grin.

"Only if you want to end your career."

Something flickered across Leo's face, but it was gone before Holly could identify it. Probably just an effect of the streetlamp's dim light. "If you're stopping by Slice of Heaven, I'd love to have one of their apricot-orange cream scones. It's one of the few things I miss in New York."

"Yum. Good choice. They're my favorite too." Holly's mouth watered.

"Then it's established. We're women of good taste. Well, maybe except for our taste in women."

They chuckled, and Holly marveled at the fact that she could laugh about it, especially so soon after Ashley had basically called the thought of them together ridiculous.

After a quick wave, she closed the door and started the engine. She waited until Leo had gotten into her rental car before she pulled away from the curb. *Leo and Ash.* She shook her head. *Who would have thought?*

Chapter 7

WHEN HOLLY ENTERED SLICE OF Heaven on Monday morning, the scent of freshly baked bread and pastries made her sniff appreciatively.

Her friend Sasha came around the counter and bent her six-foot-something frame to give her a hug. As always, she smelled of cinnamon. "Good morning."

"Morning." Holly looked around the bakery. "Are you the only one manning the fort today?"

"Nah. Auntie Mae is in the back, keeping an eye on my raspberry twists."

Holly chuckled. "Still can't keep her away?"

"Nope, she always says they'll have to carry her out on a gurney one day," Sasha said with a fond smile. She stepped back behind the counter. "So, what can I get you today? The usual?"

"No. Not today." Holly eyed the pastries, cupcakes, pies, and breads on display. "Could you give me two cinnamon rolls, two mini-quiches, two blueberry scones, and three apricot-orange cream scones, please?"

Sasha let out a low whistle. "So Leo actually has my pastries for breakfast?"

"What?" Holly chuckled. "You thought she'd have half a grapefruit?"

"Uh, kind of. I mean, she's so...tiny." Sasha held her hands about half a foot apart to indicate Leo's size.

Holly opened her mouth, then snapped it shut, surprised at the impulse to defend Leo. Admittedly, compared to Sasha's solid frame, Leo might look tiny, even at five foot ten, but Holly liked her lithe, graceful build. "She actually loves your apricot-orange cream scones."

"Really? Auntie Mae will be happy to hear that. It's her recipe, after all."

Most of the people in Holly's life would have made a comment such as "ooh, a woman after your own heart." Her other friends, especially the ones who were married or in a relationship, tended to ask about her love life all the time, constantly nudging her to find *the one*. But not Sasha.

Sasha was happily single and proclaimed herself far too busy for a relationship. Hanging out with her was like a mini-vacation from all the pressure and the expectations her well-meaning family and friends put on her.

That and the fact that they both worked unusual hours had cemented their friendship.

They made plans to go to St. Joe for an early movie on Sunday, while Sasha put the baked goods into a white paper box with the bakery's logo, handling them carefully, as if they were precious pieces of art.

Holly put some money on the counter and carried the box to the door. "I'll pick you up after lunch with the family."

Sasha wisely didn't even try to suggest that she should drive. "See you Sunday."

An hour later, Holly nearly wished it was the weekend already. Despite having the mini-quiches he loved for breakfast, Gil had been grumpy all morning.

When she came into his room to help him with his exercises, he told her no—the only word he could speak clearly and without having to search for it.

For a moment, Holly thought that Leo might have told her parents about Holly's relationship with Ashley and that had put him in such a bad mood, but she rejected the thought immediately. No one in town had any idea about the kiss the two had shared fourteen years ago, so Leo knew how to keep her mouth shut. She didn't seem the type to indulge in gossip or out other people.

"We had a bit of a rough night," Sharon said as she joined them. "He had to get up three times, and the last time, I was a bit too slow to wake up, so he, um…"

Oops. Holly didn't comment so she wouldn't embarrass Gil any further. He was already glaring at his wife.

Leo peeked into the room but didn't enter. "Why didn't you call me? I could have helped."

"It was fine. I didn't want to disturb you. But if you want to help, why don't you go over and play something for your father?" Sharon pointed to the living room, where an antique-looking baby grand stood. "You could play some Pachelbel. That always cheers him up."

Leo leaned in the doorway, looking as grumpy as her father, and made no move toward the living room. "I haven't played that in ages. Probably forgot how to."

Gil let out a snort. "Sports," he got out while glaring at them all. "Go. Um…alone."

Leo's gaze flicked toward Holly as if she were a translator.

"He wants you to leave us alone so we can do his leg and arm exercises."

Without comment, Leo turned and walked away.

Holly listened, thinking that maybe she would change her mind and play some music for her father after all, but everything remained quiet in the living room.

Leo lay in bed, arms folded behind her head, and listened to what her father had always called the *country song*—the chirping of crickets and cicadas filtering in through the closed window. Every now and then, an owl hooted in the pine tree next to the house.

It was as soothing as an all-time favorite song, but Leo still couldn't sleep. It was three o'clock, and she was wide-awake. Her brain wouldn't shut up. Thoughts of her career, her father, Holly, and Ash tumbled through her mind in a chaotic swirl.

She stared across the room, at the shadowy contours of her guitar case in the corner.

In the past, holding her guitar, feeling the familiar strings beneath her fingers, had always calmed her, but lately, her music had lost its soothing effect on her—maybe because it was no longer the one sure thing in her life. Now it just added more questions that she didn't have answers for.

The owl hooted again.

"Woohoo to you too," Leo muttered. She swung her legs out of bed and padded downstairs for a glass of water, barefoot and wearing only a tank top and a pair of boxer shorts. Since she still knew each step to the kitchen by heart, she didn't bother turning on the light.

In the hall, she collided with something warm and soft.

Cursing, she stumbled back and crashed into the wall. *Ouch.* She rubbed her hipbone. That would leave a nasty bruise. She reached for the light switch and squinted against the sudden flare of light.

One hand pressed to the opposite wall, Holly stood in front of her and shaded her eyes with the other.

They stared at each other.

"God!" Leo's heart hammered against her ribs. She blew out a breath and rubbed her hip. "You scared the crap out of me."

"Ditto." Holly pressed a flat palm to her chest. Unlike Leo, she was fully dressed.

"What are you doing up?" they asked at the same time.

"Your father needed to use the bathroom, and I didn't want to wake up the entire house by turning on the light in the hall," Holly said.

"Same here. About the light, I mean. I wanted a glass of water."

"That sounds good," Holly said. "Could I have one too?"

"Of course. You don't have to ask. You practically live here, and I'm just visiting."

They tiptoed to the kitchen—not that it was doing any good after the ruckus they'd made. They were really making a habit of colliding, Leo thought with a grin.

Instead of filling a glass with water from the tap, Leo spontaneously took a carton of milk from the fridge. "Want some milk instead?"

"Sure, thanks."

Leo poured both of them a glass of milk. "Oh, I think there are some scones left over from this morning."

"Scones? Now?"

"Is there ever a bad time for scones?" Leo asked.

A smile dimpled Holly's cheeks. "Good point."

Leo climbed onto a stool next to Holly. "What's that?" She nodded down at a cordless receiver that Holly had placed on the breakfast bar.

"A baby monitor."

Baby? Leo stared at her. "Don't tell me you've got a kid!"

Laughter burst from Holly's chest, and she muffled it behind her hand. "No. It's for your father. He's got the transmitter in his room, and either your mother or I keep the receiver with us at all times. That's how we know when he needs us."

Leo felt a little stupid for not knowing that. But then again, why should she?

They shared a blueberry scone and the last apricot-orange cream scone, creating a mess of crumbs all around them as they broke them in half.

Holly tore off little pieces and put them in her mouth.

For the first time, Leo noticed that she was wearing a black ring on the middle finger of her right hand. *Isn't that...?* She stopped chewing and stared. One of her dancers wore the same type of ring, and when she had asked him about it, he had explained that it was a symbol for his swinger lifestyle. Did that mean Holly was a swinger too?

Somehow, she couldn't imagine it. Holly probably just liked how it looked and had no idea what it could mean. She thought about enlightening her, but then decided against it. No one in a small town like Fair Oaks would know what it meant either, so it wasn't as if the ring could cause any problems for Holly.

Neither of them said much besides "yum" until the scones were gone.

Finally, all that remained was a single crumb that clung to Holly's bottom lip. As Leo watched, she flicked out her tongue and licked it away.

Had it suddenly gotten hotter? She resisted the urge to press the glass of ice-cold milk to her forehead.

Luckily, Holly didn't seem to notice where Leo's mind had drifted. She nibbled on her full lip and looked back and forth between her glass of milk and Leo's face.

"What?" Leo asked.

"Um, I have a favor to ask, but I'm not sure if I should..."

Leo stiffened. *Great.* Just when she had started to relax. She tried not to let her dismay show. "Ask."

"I was wondering... I feel silly asking, but..." Holly bit her poor lip again. "Would it be okay to ask you for an autograph?"

Leo nearly started laughing. An autograph? That was all Holly wanted? The way she'd been stuttering and stammering, she had been prepared to be asked for money or for a favor such as introducing a wannabe musician friend to an exec from her record label. That was what people usually asked her for.

"If you'd rather…"

"No, no, it's okay. I just… It just surprised me."

Holly looked at her over the rim of her glass. "You're surprised to be asked for an autograph? Come on. I've seen people stop you for an autograph several times. You must hear that question a dozen times every single day."

"Yeah, but… Forget it." She didn't want to admit her assumption. Slowly, it was getting through to her that Holly was different from the mooches who asked for money or other favors. Holly could have asked to be paid extra for all the additional things she did for Leo's parents, but she had never brought up the topic of money. Even though Leo had learned not to trust in appearances, she was starting to believe that Holly was exactly what she seemed to be: a genuinely nice and decent person.

"So? Do you have something to write on?" Leo quirked a grin. "Unless you want me to sign your boob, like some of my fans."

A hint of red crept into Holly's cheeks. She laughed, maybe a bit too loudly, as if the thought made her nervous. "No, thanks. Paper will do. Otherwise, it would be a little hard to hand over the autograph to my friend."

"Oh, so it's not for you?"

"Um, no."

"Not a fan?" Leo managed to give the question a teasing inflection, but she had to admit that the answer meant something to her.

"I liked your first album. 'Odd One Out' in particular really struck a chord with me. I listened to it on auto repeat for a week when it first came out."

That pleased Leo immensely, maybe because it didn't sound like the usual flattery. *Hmm, she said the first album…* "What about the rest of my work?"

"You want an honest reply?"

"Ouch." Leo grimaced. "That bad?"

"No. No, please don't think that. It's just… I don't like your newer stuff as much. I mean, the songs are all trendy, and they fit a certain…um, format, but…" Holly paused as if searching for the right words. "Well, it might sound stupid, but they have no real soul."

Wow. Leo was stunned speechless. No one had come right out and told her something like that—ever. She was used to being fawned over. People usually told her what they thought she wanted to hear, or maybe they really liked her newer songs.

Leo didn't. She had told her manager the same thing Holly had just commented on, but he had insisted that this kind of music was what her fans and the record label wanted.

"God." Groaning, Holly buried her face in her palms. "I'm sitting here in the middle of the night, having milk and scones with you in your parents' home, and to top it all, I insulted you."

"No," Leo said forcefully. Without pausing to think about it, she grabbed one of Holly's hands, pulled it away from her face, and squeezed it. "I'm not insulted. It's just pretty rare that anyone talks to me so openly."

Holly dropped the other hand to her lap and looked at her. "I'm sorry. I—"

"Don't you dare apologize." She became aware that she was still holding Holly's hand and quickly let go. "I like it."

They sat in silence for a moment, with only the humming of the refrigerator as background noise. It wasn't an awkward silence, though.

Leo got up and snooped through her mother's kitchen in search of something to write on. Finally, she found an unused greeting card in a drawer full of recipes and household tips her mother had cut out from magazines. "Will this do? For the autograph?"

Holly chuckled. "It says *happy birthday.*"

"Yeah, well, maybe you can give it to your friend for their birthday."

"Good idea. Her birthday is actually coming up next month."

Leo slid back onto her stool, clicked on a pen, and gave Holly a questioning look. "So, who am I making this out for?"

"Her name is Meg, but could you make it out to Mordin? We met each other on Tumblr, and that's her username, so the nickname stuck."

"Mordin?" Leo asked. "After the Salarian in *Mass Effect*?"

Holly looked at her as if she had suddenly grown a pair of horns, like the Salarians. "You know *Mass Effect*? Does that mean you're a gamer?"

"I wouldn't go that far, but I play every now and then. My bassist got me hooked during our first tour, when we were stuck on the tour bus for hours every day, going from one city to the next."

"Wow. Meg will be so excited when I tell her." Holly paused. "Is it okay to tell her that?"

When was the last time someone had been so considerate of her privacy? Leo couldn't remember. Even some of the people she had considered friends had blabbed details about her private life to the tabloids. "Oh yeah, that's just fine. So your friend, she's a gamer?"

"Hardcore." The corners of her eyes crinkled as Holly laughed. "She says Yennefer from *The Witcher 3* is the only crush she's ever had."

"Yen? Really? I mean, she's hot and all, but I like Triss much better." With a crooked grin, Leo added, "Guess I'm more into—" *Oh jeez.* She'd almost gotten herself into trouble. If she had finished that thought, Holly might have thought she was coming on to her. As nice and attractive as Holly was, getting involved with someone from Fair Oaks was the last thing Leo wanted.

"Into what?" Holly asked.

Redheads. "Um, healers." As soon as she'd said it, she could have slapped herself. Holly was a nurse, so she could have been considered a healer too.

Luckily, Holly didn't seem to think anything of it. She continued sipping her milk.

After secretly blowing out a breath, Leo picked up the pen again and wrote *happy birthday and many butterfly kisses* onto the birthday card and then signed it. As an afterthought, she added, *P.S. Triss is way cooler than Yen.* When she was done, she held the card out to Holly, who took it carefully.

"Thank you." She studied the card. "Why did you pick a stage name? Why not just go with Leontyne Blake?"

"It was my manager's idea. Leona Lewis had her debut album out shortly before I did, and he thought the names were too much alike. So we decided on Jenna, my middle name."

"Bummer," Holly said. "I've always thought Leontyne is such a beautiful name."

The tips of Leo's ears began to burn. Man, was she blushing now, just because Holly liked her name? She ignored it. "Um, yeah. I didn't like it much when I was growing up, but now I've come to appreciate it."

"You didn't?"

Leo shook her head. "Just one more thing that made me stick out like a sore thumb in this town."

"Ah." Holly nodded as if she understood exactly what she meant.

"Plus my father named me after his favorite opera singer, Leontyne Price, and I wasn't into classical music at all."

Before Holly could answer, the baby monitor on the breakfast bar came to life with a demanding grunt from Leo's father. "Bath," he called out.

Even Leo could guess what that meant—he probably needed the bathroom. For a second, she considered offering to help him so that Holly could go to bed.

But Holly squeezed her arm as if knowing what she was thinking. "It's okay. I'll go." She slid from the stool and walked to the door. "Good night. And thanks again for the autograph."

Leo stared at her retreating back. "You're welcome," she said into an empty room.

Chapter 8

WHEN LEO HAD BEEN GROWING up, her father's Steinway baby grand had always stood in the music room. Now it dominated the living room the same way her father had always dominated the house. Sunlight gleamed off its shiny surface, making Leo wonder if her mother still dusted it every day.

Drawn to it almost against her will, she put her hand on the lid. It felt warm and smooth. She hesitated, glanced over her shoulder, and when she saw that no one was around, she sat down on the piano bench. As a child, she had spent so many hours on this bench that it probably had grooves from her backside. After another glance over her shoulder, she lifted the lid and settled her fingers on the keys.

She sat there for a long time without playing. Hesitantly, she tapped out a single note and then played a D major scale to limber up her fingers.

The piano was kept in good tune. Not that she had expected anything else.

She knew her mother wanted her to play something classical, but she wasn't in the mood to cater to her parents' expectations. If they didn't accept her the way she was, that was their problem, and that included her sexual orientation and her choice in music.

Almost without a conscious decision on her part, her fingers slid over the keys, coaxing the first notes of "Odd One Out" from the instrument. God, it had been some time since she'd last played. None of the songs she had performed during her world tour had her at the piano—"Who do you think you are? Alicia Keys?" her manager always said whenever she wanted to include a piano piece in her song list. So these days, her guitar and her voice were her main instruments. *And my body,* she mentally added and let out a sigh. More and more, it was all about the flashiest show, the sexiest costumes, and the most erotic dance moves.

Here, in this house, it had always been just about the music, even if it was her father's style of music, and Leo had to admit it was very freeing.

"Odd One Out" hadn't been one of her greatest hits, so she hadn't played it in years, but the melody and the lyrics quickly came back to her. With every note, the movement of her fingers became more controlled and nimble.

Holly had been right. It was a good song. One of the last Leo had written on her own, without the input of her songwriting team.

She let the emotions wash over her.

When the last note faded, she sat there for a few minutes longer. This was it—this was how she wanted to feel playing her music. Too bad it couldn't always be this way.

Why not? a voice in her head piped up.

Before she could address the question, a creaking floorboard made her look up.

Her mother stood in the doorway. The apron tied around her hips indicated that she'd been cooking. "Don't stop. It was lovely."

The piano lid she'd been about to close almost slid from her fingers. Her mother thought one of her songs was lovely? But then again, she had always been the more tolerant one of her parents. "Nah. I'm done for the day. Just wanted to stretch my fingers a little."

She got up and squeezed past her. Her mother's disappointed gaze followed her, but Leo ignored it. After thirteen months on stage, she wasn't in the mood to play for an audience, even an audience of one.

The door to her father's room, which was closed most of the time, stood open for a change. When Leo went to walk past it, a sound from within the room stopped her. It was her father's voice. Had he called her name? She wasn't sure, so she stuck her head into the room.

He was in his wheelchair, facing the window.

"Was there something you needed?" Leo asked.

"Old," he said.

She wished Holly was there to translate, but as far as Leo knew, she was upstairs somewhere, taking a break before lunch. Hesitantly, she circled the wheelchair so she could see his face. "Um, what?"

He didn't turn his head to look at her but kept staring out the window. "No. Rust. Rusty." He lifted his good hand and pointed over his shoulder in the direction of the living room.

"What do you...? Oh!" Understanding hit her like a bucket of ice water. "You mean my piano playing is pretty rusty?"

He nodded.

Great. The first time he really talked to her in ages, and it turned out he was criticizing her. She shook her head at herself. *Why did you expect anything else?* It had been like this for as long as she could remember.

"Bush...um, cleaning. No. Um, pruning. Remember?"

Oh yeah. Leo remembered only too well what he had always told her in the past: Playing the piano was like pruning hedges. A little and often was the key. That was how he had urged her to practice every day.

"Maybe if you live in a tiny little town with nothing else to do, you've got all the time in the world to prune your hedges every day. But when am I supposed to do that? When I'm on the road, it's a constant whirlwind of practice, dance rehearsals, sound checks, concerts, interviews, and after-parties."

He turned his head in her direction and made an impatient motion with his left hand, probably to cut her off, but she continued. She had been silent for much too long already, and now it burst out of her with the force of water that had been freed from a dam.

"You don't understand my life. You never did. You never made the slightest effort to. Can't you be even a tiny bit proud for once instead of criticizing everything I do?"

He just stared at her, either unable or unwilling to answer.

"Why am I even talking to you?" she muttered and marched to the door.

No sound came from behind her. She realized she was straining her ears, waiting for him to apologize or to say something more positive, and a wave of anger at herself swept over her. Why had she even come here, risking her career? Had she really expected things to change, that he might tell her how proud he was or how much he loved her? She might as well expect him to get up and walk across the room all on his own.

Taking the stairs two at a time, she rushed to her room and slammed the door shut behind her.

The door to Leo's room rattled in its frame.

Holly peeked out of her room, but there was nothing to see except for the closed door. Exhaling, she sat back down on her bed, reached over to her nightstand, and turned the volume on the baby monitor back up.

When Gil had strained to get out the first words, Holly had rushed to the door, thinking he needed some help. But then she'd realized that he wasn't talking to her—he'd been talking to his daughter.

As far as she knew, they hadn't talked since Leo was back. She would have loved to know what they were saying to each other, but she didn't want to disrespect either of them by listening in, so she had turned down the volume on the receiver until she couldn't understand their words anymore.

Judging by the way Leo had slammed her door, the conversation hadn't gone too well.

Should I…?

She hesitated, remembering her resolution to act like a professional nurse and nothing else toward Leo. But her compassion urged her up from the bed. Whatever had happened between Leo and her father, Holly knew instinctively that Leo wouldn't talk to her mother about it.

She slid the receiver into her back pocket, tiptoed across the hall, and paused in front of Leo's door.

Just as she was debating with herself whether she really should knock, the door opened and Leo came storming out.

Once again, they collided with each other and ended up in an almost embrace, clutching each other to keep their balance.

"Are you okay?" Holly whispered, tightly holding on to Leo, who in turn rested her hands on Holly's hips. Leo's perfume—orange blossoms, almond, and a barely there touch of musk—teased her senses.

"Yeah." Was it just her imagination, or was Leo's voice even huskier than usual? Leo forced a smile. "It's not like you're a three-hundred-pound defensive tackle."

"No, I meant… I heard you slam your door. Did something happen?"

For a moment, Leo's expression was completely vulnerable before it closed off. She let go and stepped past Holly. "I'm fine. I just need some fresh air." When she reached the stairs, she turned back around. "Want to come?"

"I wish I could," Holly said and found that it was the truth. After their conversation in the kitchen last night, she had a feeling they really could talk to each other. "But I'm working right now…" She pointed downstairs to where Gil's room was.

"Oh. Yeah. Of course. See you later, then." Leo bolted down the stairs.

Holly leaned on the banister and stared at her back. When the front door closed behind Leo, she put the baby monitor back on her nightstand and went to get Gil ready for his appointment with the speech therapist.

The walk had helped clear Leo's head, and a stop at Slice of Heaven for two apricot-orange cream scones had improved her mood considerably. She had eaten hers on the way home, and now she was holding on to the paper bag with the other like a hunter proudly carrying home her prey.

As she stepped into the house, Holly's voice came from her father's room. It dampened her mood a little since it meant she couldn't hand over the scone right now. Then she realized that Holly wasn't talking to her father—she was singing.

If you can call it that. Sounds more like a cat that had its tail stepped on. Leo winced a little at the off-key singing, but mainly, she found it adorable. What Holly lacked in musicality, she made up for in enthusiasm.

She smiled and kept listening as she slowly climbed the stairs.

It took her until she was halfway up to recognize the song. *Hey! That's one of mine!* In fact, it was "Odd One Out," the song she had played just this morning. Holly seemed to know the lyrics by heart.

Leo grinned and hummed along.

When she reached the top of the stairs, she could still hear Holly singing, this time not directly, but through the baby monitor on Holly's nightstand. She stood in front of the open door to Holly's room for a moment, listening. God, how she enjoyed the irony that her father, who had criticized her piano playing, now had to listen to Holly singing one of her songs.

Her grin faltered as another realization hit her: if she could hear Holly through the baby monitor, Holly had probably heard every single word she had said to her father earlier too.

Goddammit! She could have warned me. Her fingers tightened around the paper bag. Instead of warning her, Holly had pretended she hadn't heard a thing. It was like being spied on in her own home, the one place on earth where she thought she was free of the tabloids and fans constantly observing her.

Great. And I even brought home a scone for her! Now she felt like a fool. She hurled the paper bag through the open door. It landed on the bed, but it didn't feel satisfying at all.

With a growl, she went to her room and shut the door behind her.

After only a minute or two, a knock sounded. It was probably her mother, demanding to know where she'd been and why she had missed lunch. "Yeah?"

The door swung open. Instead of her mother, Holly peeked into the room, a broad grin on her face and the paper bag in her hand. "Is it from you?"

"What, you think it was the scone fairy?" It could have been a funny remark, but Leo's anger gave it a sharp edge.

A frown replaced Holly's smile. She pushed the door open more fully and entered. "Is everything okay? You sound kind of…I don't know…angry with me. Did I do something wrong?"

Holly had gone even paler than usual, and her clear, blue eyes were squinting at Leo in confusion.

Boy, she's good. Possibly even better than Leo's latest ex, who had lying and manipulating down to an art. She had managed to look affronted even when Leo had caught her stealing money from her. "I thought you were different, not one of the lying, scheming people who'd do anything to get into my good graces and think nothing of violating my privacy for the right price."

Holly blinked several times. "Violating your privacy?"

"Oh, come on." Heat bubbled up inside of her at the faux-innocent expression on Holly's face. Did Holly really think she was that stupid?

"Don't pretend you didn't hear every single word I said to my father through your little spy instrument."

"You think I'm spying on you?" Holly's voice ended in an incredulous squeak.

God, she was almost convincing. Leo found herself wanting to believe her, but she tamped down on the impulse. She'd been stupid like that before, and it had never ended well. "How else would you have known I was upset when I got back upstairs earlier?"

"Maybe because you were banging your door like a sulking teenager—exactly like you're behaving right now, making stupid accusations."

They faced each other in a silent stare-down. Holly didn't give an inch. Her blue eyes, usually twinkling with good humor, now looked like arctic ice. Leo, used to flatterers and yea-sayers, couldn't help respecting her for not backing down.

"My word might not mean much to you, but I promise I didn't listen in on your conversation," Holly said. "As soon as I realized the two of you were talking, I turned down the volume so I couldn't hear you anymore."

Over the past fourteen years, Leo had learned not to trust blindly. People had made promises and had sworn to tell the truth while lying through their teeth too many times. But somehow, she believed Holly. She *wanted* to believe her, no matter how foolish it might be.

When Leo didn't answer, Holly walked out and closed the door behind her, pointedly not banging it but closing it in a civilized manner.

Leo winced. *Message received.* She really hadn't been on her best behavior today.

Holly's footsteps faded away while Leo wrestled with herself. Maybe she should just let it go. It didn't matter if she had wrongly accused Holly, right? At some point, Holly would end up betraying her in some way.

But another part of her didn't want to believe that.

With a curse, she jumped off the bed, raced across the room, and tore open the door. "Holly, wait!"

Holly had reached her room and opened the door. Now she turned and looked at her with a wary expression.

"Wait, please," Leo said more softly. "I want to… I need to…" It was hard to get out the word, partly because it had been a long time since she'd had to say it. "…apologize."

Holly's tense stance loosened. "I really didn't listen in on your conversation."

"I believe you," Leo said—and she did. What a weird feeling. It felt like standing on a shaky footbridge over a deep canyon. "I just… Knowing you could have listened in without me realizing… It made me feel very vulnerable. That's why I behaved so…"

"Like an ass?" Holly supplied.

Leo winced. "You're not cutting me any slack, are you?"

"Why should I? Because you're Jenna Blake?"

"No. I don't want to be Jenna Blake." She considered that statement for a moment. There was more truth to it than she wanted to acknowledge. "Well, at least not here. That's the one good thing about Fair Oaks. I get to be just Leontyne here."

"All right, Leontyne Blake. I accept your apology." Holly cracked a smile, and the humorous twinkle was back in her eyes. "Considering you brought me a scone. Or did you poison it?"

"Well, we could share it, just to make sure," Leo said. "I'll eat half, and if I don't fall over in mortal agony, you'll know it's safe."

Holly clutched the paper bag to her chest. "Oh no, you don't get my scone. I bet you had one already."

For a moment, Leo stared. Did Holly really know her that well already? "Okay, okay, you can have it all."

"You could keep me company while I eat." Holly waved the paper bag in the direction of her room. "Maybe tell me what's going on between your father and you."

"I need more than half a scone for that conversation," Leo muttered.

Holly playfully held the bag with the scone out of reach. "I thought we established that you're not getting any of my scone?"

"What kind of friend are you to deny me in my hour of need?"

Friend… The word seemed to echo between them. It was a little too soon to call them that, but Leo realized that it was what she wanted. She hadn't had a true friend in forever—someone who appreciated her for herself, not for her fame, her money, or her body—and she had a feeling Holly could be that kind of friend.

Finally, Holly shrugged. "A hungry one."

"All right. You eat. I'll tell you the sad story of my life." She followed Holly into the guest room.

It had changed since Leo had last lived in the house. The four-poster bed and the sunflower wallpaper of the past had been replaced with more modern furniture and cream-colored walls. Either Holly had left her personal touch on the room, or her parents had renovated it to make her feel welcome.

They sat on opposite ends of the bed. Holly pulled the scone out of its bag and tore off a piece for Leo. Their fingers brushed as she handed it over.

Leo had always thought that tingly feeling at the touch of hands was a thing that only happened in sappy romance novels. Well, apparently, she was wrong about many things today.

But Holly bit into her scone as if she hadn't noticed, so Leo ignored it too. No sense in ruining a new friendship before it even got started.

"So?" Holly asked around a mouthful of scone. "Want to tell me what happened with your father this morning?"

"Nothing out of the ordinary. I played the piano. He didn't approve."

Holly licked a crumb from the corner of her mouth, and Leo had to look away.

Man, being friends with Holly would be so much easier if she didn't look so sexy while eating.

"What's not to approve of?" Holly asked. "I heard it. It was beautiful."

The praise tasted sweeter than the scone. It was almost enough to make her forget her father's reaction. "My father doesn't think so. He's convinced that I'm wasting my life and my God-given talent—his words, not mine—by focusing on pop music."

"Maybe it's a generational thing. My mother doesn't like the music I listen to or the movies I watch either."

"I think it's a little more than that with my father. He never approved of a single thing I did. Short of being accepted at Juilliard, like he was, nothing I accomplish will ever be good enough for him. After I won my first Grammy and called home to share the good news with him, he told me that my namesake—Leontyne Price—had won nineteen of them, so one was nothing to be proud of."

Acid burned in the pit of her stomach. After all these years and two more Grammys that she hadn't shared with her father, she'd thought she was over it, but that old wound still hurt.

Holly stared at her, the last piece of scone seemingly forgotten in her hand. Was she just imagining it, or had Holly's eyes become damp?

"You know," Holly said, then had to stop to clear her throat, "at the risk of sounding unprofessional again… Your father might be a highly gifted musician and a great teacher, but when it comes to you, he's an idiot."

Her bluntness stunned Leo. No one had ever talked about her father like that. She burst out laughing, and the old pain eased. "I agree." She made a playful grab for the last piece of scone.

Holly pulled her hand away and hid it behind her back but then held it out to Leo.

"Are you sure?" Leo asked.

"Yeah. You could write me a song in exchange."

"A song in exchange for an itty-bitty crumb of scone?"

"The *last* itty-bitty crumb of scone," Holly said.

"Deal. How about…Scone Woman." She sang it to the melody of "Moon River."

Holly threw the crumpled-up paper bag at her. "Wider than a mile?" she quoted a line of the song. "Is that a dig at my…um, curvy figure?"

"No." Leo waggled her eyebrows, which probably looked silly rather than seductive. "I happen to like your curvy figure."

Holly put the last of the scone into her mouth and crunched it happily.

"Hey! I thought we had a deal?"

"I didn't like the payment." Holly licked her thumb. "Plus I need all the calories I can get to maintain the curvy figure you like so much."

Was she flirting?

But Holly looked entirely oblivious, so it was probably all just in her head.

Leo flicked a few crumbs off her thighs. "So, you mentioned movies. Which ones do you enjoy?"

Later that day, Leo was in the backyard, taking measurements for the new ramp she wanted to have installed, when her mother opened the screen door.

"Holly's Jeep isn't starting. Can you give her a ride home? I would do it, but the pie still has another fifteen minutes to go before it's done."

Leo put down the tape measure and jogged up the three steps to the kitchen. "Sure."

Holly stood on the other side of the breakfast bar. "That's really not necessary. I can walk home and call Travis to take care of the Jeep."

"It's no problem. I'm done out there anyway." Leo grabbed her keys from the counter. "Come on."

"Um, can I drive?" Holly asked. "Otherwise, I'll fall asleep."

Leo shook her head. "Sorry, but the rental car insurance doesn't cover another driver." She couldn't imagine that anyone could fall asleep on such a short drive anyway.

"I don't know why you keep driving the rental and don't just take your father's car," her mother said. "It's not like he can drive it anymore."

"Dad's old Buick is really not my style, Mom." It wasn't the real reason she kept her rental car, though. Having the rental car ensured she could leave town any time she wanted.

Her mother stood on the porch and watched as they got into the car.

"It's the small house across the street from the elementary school," Holly said as she clicked the seat belt into place.

Leo nodded, started the engine, and drove in the direction of the school. A song on the radio caught her attention for a moment. When it ended, she asked, "So, what's wrong with the Jeep?"

No answer came from the passenger seat.

Leo glanced to her right.

Holly's head leaned back against the headrest. Her eyes were closed and her lips slightly parted.

Leo chuckled quietly. So Holly hadn't been joking. She turned down the radio volume and kept glancing at Sleeping Beauty while she navigated the nearly empty streets.

When she reached the house across from the elementary school, she parked at the curb and shut off the engine.

Holly was still fast asleep.

Boy, she's cute. Leo almost didn't want to wake her, but what was she supposed to do? Sit next to her in the car all night?

Before she could make a decision, Holly sat up and rubbed her eyes. She looked around blearily. "Oh. We're home already. I warned you I would fall asleep."

"You did. I just didn't think you were serious."

"Oh yeah. My father used to tease me about it, even though he's probably to blame for my *carcolepsy*. When I was a baby, I had colic, and the only thing that would calm me was when he was driving me around." Her smile was wistful and didn't bring out her dimples.

Leo grinned. "I bet he's trying the same technique on Ethan's and Zack's kids nowadays."

Holly pressed her lips together. "I wish. He died five years ago." She unbuckled her seat belt and got out of the car.

Damn. Leo quickly followed her.

With her back to Leo, Holly fumbled for her key in the messenger bag slung across her chest.

Leo stepped next to her and put her hand on Holly's arm for a moment. "I'm sorry, Holly. I had no idea."

Holly sighed. "It was a car accident, just a few months after your grandmother died." She unlocked the front door and entered the house as if wanting to leave the memories behind. "Want to come in?"

"Um, sure." With a lump in her throat, Leo followed. Now she understood a little better why Holly had been so angry with her about not coming home and not talking to her parents—at least Leo still had both of her parents.

"How about I give you the nickel tour?" Holly asked.

"Sorry, I don't have a nickel." Leo turned the pockets of her shorts inside out.

"Well, it's not worth a nickel anyway. The place is really small."

The living room, with a tiny eating area at one end, opened up into the kitchen, making the house seem larger than it was. The light of the evening sun gleamed off the hardwood floor. Warm colors and comfortable-looking furniture filled the living room: a tan couch, a worn easy chair, a dark red area rug, and a bookshelf crammed full of books and family pictures. A tattered paperback sat next to a half-full bottle of water and a scented candle in a glass jar on the coffee table. An Xbox was hooked up to the flat-screen TV in one corner of the room, while the opposite corner held a stereo.

Leo walked over to take a look at Holly's CD rack. Among Etta James, Aretha Franklin, Ella Fitzgerald, Amy Winehouse, and Tina Turner, she discovered three of her own albums.

"Does it meet your approval?"

Leo glanced back and caught the flicker of a smile on Holly's face. "Oh yeah. Clearly, you're a woman of great musical taste."

Holly led her upstairs. A queen-sized bed took up most of the space in her bedroom, and a walk-in closet claimed the other wall. The bed was neatly made, a quilt pulled tight over it.

The tour ended in the second bedroom, which Holly had set up as an office with a small desk.

The entire house was lived in, but neat—a warm, comfortable home rather than the luxury show places Leo usually got invited into.

"Nice house. Really cute," Leo said as they went back to the first floor. "Very you." *Damn.* She'd basically just called Holly cute. "Uh, I mean, is it yours?"

If Holly noticed her little slip, she didn't react to it. "No, I rent."

They paused at the front door.

"Do you need a ride tomorrow morning?" Leo asked. "I'd be happy to pick you up."

"No. Thanks for the offer, though. My Jeep probably just needs a new battery, but if it's something Travis can't fix, I'll walk. I could use the exercise."

Leo eyed her skeptically. Holly looked just fine to her. "I don't think you need to lose any weight. But if you want, we could go for a run together sometime."

"A run?"

Leo playfully arched her brows. "Yeah. Unless you don't think you can keep up with me."

Holly snorted and gave her a swat on the arm. "You wish. Day after tomorrow, right after work—you're on."

They exchanged challenging grins; then Leo said goodbye and left with a wave. When she got into the car, her gaze fell onto the passenger seat, where Holly had taken her little after-work nap. Smiling, she started the car.

Chapter 9

GRAVEL CRUNCHED BENEATH THEIR RUNNING shoes as they jogged along the creek that ran through the entire length of Fair Oaks's only park.

Leo sped up so she gained the lead on Holly. "Come on, slow poke!"

"We're not...in...New York," Holly puffed out behind her. "Slow down...and...enjoy the...scenery."

Oh, I'm enjoying the scenery a bit too much whenever we're running side by side.

As the sun slowly made its descent toward the horizon, the summer heat receded a little, but it was still hot enough to work up a sweat. The way Holly's damp tank top clung to her had caused Leo to stumble over a root earlier, so running ahead of her was much less dangerous for her health—and their still-new friendship.

As far as she could tell, Holly didn't have the same problem. She might be attracted to women, but either she was much better at ogling her without getting caught or Leo wasn't her type.

On the one hand, it was refreshing to be around a woman who couldn't care less about the way she looked, but on the other hand, it was tough on her ego.

Forget your ego and just enjoy her company. Leo lengthened her stride, taking advantage of her longer legs. "The last one to the bridge buys the scones!"

They raced toward the bridge with Holly hot on her heels, gravel spraying left and right.

By the time they reached the bridge, they were both gasping for breath. Leo didn't even have enough air left in her lungs to brag about winning the race. They leaned on the wooden railing next to each other.

Holly's face was flushed from the exertion, and her short hair stuck to her head in damp strands, but she was grinning as if she was the one who'd won the race.

Footsteps on the other end of the bridge made Leo straighten and look up.

Ashley walked toward them, leading a Golden Retriever by a leash.

Leo stifled a groan. Of all the people in Fair Oaks, they had to come across the person she least wanted to run into. Next to her, she felt Holly stiffen too, and Leo instinctively reached out to place her hand on the small of her back. As soon as her fingers touched the damp shirt, she became aware of what she was doing, but withdrawing her hand now would only call attention to it, so she left it where it was.

When Ashley saw them, her steps faltered, but then she plastered a smile to her face. "Out for a run?"

No, we're going to the opera. That's why we're wearing running clothes. Leo bit back the words and just nodded.

The dog was wiggling its tail, whining and straining against its leash to get to Holly.

When Holly bent to greet the dog, the contact between her back and Leo's hand was interrupted. Finally, she straightened and returned to Leo's side.

Ash's gaze flicked back and forth between them. "So you two...?"

"Are out for a run, like you just said," Holly finished the sentence with a too-broad smile.

"Well, then, I don't want to keep you. You could pull a muscle or something if you cool down." Ashley tugged on the leash to get the dog away from Holly, and they continued on their way.

Leo watched her walk away before turning back toward Holly. "You know she thinks you and I are burning calories together in ways other than running, right?"

"Nah. I doubt she thinks that."

Leo gave her an incredulous look. "Of course she does."

"Would that be a problem?" Holly asked.

"Not for me. But what about you? The tabloids have been suspiciously quiet since I got here, but what if they start writing bullshit about me returning home for a little fling with a local woman?"

Holly shrugged, and Leo had to ignore the way the movement made the damp shirt stretch across her breasts. "Rumors about a hot affair with you could only help my reputation. I've been called a cold fish by some people."

Leo nearly choked on her own spit. "Excuse me?" Holly was friendly and compassionate. Why the hell would anyone call her that? "Who said that?"

Holly kicked at a piece of gravel, which landed in the creek with a plop. "You know what? Let's not spoil a perfectly nice evening by talking about them. I think I owe you a scone, so let's go get it." She jogged across the bridge without waiting for a reply.

Leo caught up with her. "Didn't Slice of Heaven close hours ago?"

"Yeah, but being friends with the owner has its advantages. I'm sure she's got a few left over for me."

They ran side by side for a while, neither of them saying anything else. When they reached the edge of the park, Leo held her back with a hand on her arm. "Just for the record... I think they're idiots."

Holly put her hand on top of Leo's for a moment and squeezed. "Thanks."

When they reached Slice of Heaven, the front door was locked, and a *closed* sign dangled at eye level.

"Looks like we won't be getting any scones." Leo's stomach grumbled in disappointment.

Holly peered through the glass, and after a second, Leo leaned forward and followed her example so that their heads were nearly touching.

Even after their run, Holly smelled amazing.

Leo tried to ignore it and turned her attention to the bakery. It was empty, and so was the display case.

Holly knocked on the glass.

It took a moment, but then footsteps approached, and someone unlocked the door. When it swung open, Sasha Peterson filled the doorway.

Leo rarely had to look up at other women, but she remembered that Sasha, who had been two years behind her in school, had already been her height back then.

The bandanna Sasha wore instead of a baker's cap held back her braided hair and emphasized her strong features. When she saw Holly, a warm smile lit up her face and immediately made her look less intimidating. "Hey. Let me guess. You were in the neighborhood and wondered if there were any scones left."

"Um, something like that." Holly hugged her without seeming to care about the chocolate streaks on her apron, and Leo marveled at the affectionate way she interacted with her friend.

She sure as hell didn't have any friends like that. Air kisses and pats on the shoulder were much more common in her circles.

Holly gestured toward Leo. "Sasha, you remember Leo?"

"Of course. Come on in." Sasha invited them into the bakery with a sweep of her arm. She seemed entirely unaffected by being in the presence of a celebrity, and Leo was grateful for that. "I saw you when you came in a couple of days ago. Sorry I didn't have time to chat."

"Yeah, it looked busy."

"Sasha has done really well for herself since she took over the bakery." Pride colored Holly's voice.

"Now if only I could get my aunt to stay out of the bakery and enjoy her well-deserved retirement."

Holly and Sasha laughed as if it were a running joke.

Sasha led them into the back of the bakery, where a bread machine was whirring and several of the ovens were still running, heating up the room.

"You're still working?" Holly raised her voice a little to be heard over the noise.

"Just trying out a new recipe. Give me a second, then I'll get your scones." Sasha put on oven mitts, pulled a sheet of what looked like chocolate cookies from the oven, and scooped them onto a cooling rack.

The heat from the ovens tinged Holly's cheeks with an attractive flush as she leaned closer and stole a cookie. She blew on it and then took a bite.

"Uh, Holly, those are—"

Holly froze mid-chew. With a gulp, she swallowed the bite of cookie. "I don't know how to tell you, but you might want to rethink that recipe. I liked your usual espresso chocolate chip cookies much better."

Sasha laughed, a sound that filled the kitchen. "That's because they're not espresso chocolate chip cookies."

"No?" Holly stared down at the other half of the cookie in her hand. "What are they?"

"Um, I call them Beagle Bites." Looking at Leo, Sasha added, "I want to branch out and offer treats for our four-legged friends too."

"You gave me dog treats?"

The wide-eyed look on Holly's face made Leo join in Sasha's laughter.

"Gave you? You snatched it up before I could stop you." Still laughing, Sasha handed her a bottle of water. "Don't worry. It's full of ingredients that are good for you."

Holly drank half of the water in one big gulp. "Will it make my hair all shiny?"

"If it does, let me know, and I'll sell them as the latest health food to my human customers. All right, let me get you the scones."

When Sasha left the room, the kitchen seemed much larger.

Holly made a face and emptied her water bottle.

Leo leaned against the counter and watched her with a smile.

"What?" Holly asked.

"Nothing." Leo reined in her grin.

"Here you go." Sasha returned and handed over a paper bag.

"What do we owe you?" Leo pulled out the ten-dollar bill she kept tucked into the pocket of her running shorts.

Sasha shook her head. "Nothing. A friend of Holly's is a friend of mine."

Being called Holly's friend warmed Leo more than the residual heat from the oven. Usually, Leo hesitated to accept gifts because in her experience, they always came with strings attached, but Sasha's brown eyes didn't seem to hide anything. She put the money back into her pocket. "Thank you."

When they stepped back out onto the street, the air seemed cool in comparison, and Leo shivered a little. She nodded back toward the bakery. "She seems like a good friend."

"Yes," Holly said. "I'm lucky like that."

Leo marveled at how happy Holly was with what she had. She seemed to already have figured out who she was and what she wanted from life. *Unlike me.* Maybe it was part of why Leo enjoyed being around her so much. It had a grounding effect on her.

Holly handed her one of the scones. "Come on. Let's head back before your mother reports us missing."

Their steps were perfectly aligned as they strolled through the park, scones in hand. The setting sun bathed Leo's face in an orange glow that softened her usually guarded expression. Or maybe she was more relaxed now that it was just the two of them, away from her parents' house. Whatever it was, Holly enjoyed that new, at-peace expression on Leo's face. It made her look even more stunning.

"You know," Holly said as they stopped on the bridge to enjoy the way the sun shimmered on the water, "getting scones after going for a run kinda defeats the purpose."

Leo grinned over at her. "Does that mean you don't want your scone and I can have the rest?"

"Nope." Holly took a big bite of her scone.

They sprinkled crumbs into the creek and watched small fish snatch them up.

The ringing of Leo's cell phone interrupted the peaceful silence.

With a grin, Holly realized that Leo was using an Aretha Franklin song as a ringtone too, just that it was "Call Me" instead of Holly's choice of "A Natural Woman."

Grumbling under her breath, Leo fumbled the phone from the waistband of her running shorts.

Holly didn't want to listen in, especially since she knew how sensitive Leo was about any violation of her privacy, but as she started to walk away, Leo put her free hand on her arm and nodded at her to stay.

That show of trust warmed Holly as much as the rays of the setting sun.

"Hey, Saul," Leo said into the cell phone. "Yes, I know. Tell them I'm working on material for a new album. That should keep them off your back for a while." She ran her free hand through her hair while she listened to the reply. "Yeah, kind of. You know creativity can't be forced or hurried along."

She let out an aggravated sigh. "Don't you think I know that? You've told me that a million—Jesus, Saul. Give me a break. Sometimes, you and the label really seem to think I have the IQ of a coconut!"

The corners of Holly's mouth twitched, but she quickly hid it, not wanting to annoy or hurt Leo. The way she sounded, whatever was going on wasn't a laughing matter for her.

"What? Saul, you're breaking up. I'll call you when I've got something for you." She hung up without saying goodbye and hurled the rest of her scone into the creek, looking as if she would have rather thrown in the phone instead.

They watched the piece of scone drift downstream. It bobbed up and down a few times before either dissolving or being dragged down by fish.

The peaceful expression on Leo's face was gone.

"You sounded pretty upset," Holly said quietly. "Is there anything I can do to help?"

"No. Unless you have a second job as an assassin."

Holly rubbed her chin as if considering it. "Hmm, maybe I should. It certainly would pay better than nursing. Who's the person you want me to off?"

"My manager." Leo leaned both elbows on the railing and stared into the water. "He hates me dropping off the grid."

"But he knows where you are, right? That's not exactly dropping off the grid."

"Try telling him that. He wants me in a recording studio in New York, not in Bumfuck, Missouri." When Holly winced, Leo added, "His words, not mine. The only reason he hasn't dragged me back is because I told him I'm working on new songs while I'm here."

"Are you?" Holly asked, even though she already guessed the answer. As far as she could tell, Leo hadn't opened her guitar case since she'd been home, and she had only played the piano once.

A crooked smile flashed across Leo's face. "Well, yeah...if you count 'Scone Woman.'"

Holly couldn't help chuckling. "Um, I can't really see that going platinum."

"Probably not." Leo sighed. "And that's all my manager and the label seem to care about these days—how much money they can make with my music."

"How about you? What do you care about?"

Leo kicked a pebble into the creek. A school of fish swam over, obviously hoping for more scone crumbs. When they found their hopes disappointed, they quickly scattered. "I'm not so sure I know that anymore."

Holly turned to face her and leaned one hip against the bridge's railing. Instead of peppering Leo with more questions, she waited because she sensed that Leo needed to work through her thoughts in her own time.

"In the beginning, everything was great. I finally had what I always wanted. Being up on stage, having the fans go crazy over my music... It was electrifying." She grinned a little. "Better than sex."

"That's not hard to top," Holly murmured under her breath. When Leo sent her a questioning look, she shook her head. "Nothing. So, what changed?"

"I think I got swept up in everything—the fame, the money, the fans shouting my name." Leo half-turned too so that they were facing each other. "But after a while, I started to feel like I was losing my music... losing myself."

"But you're still writing your own music, aren't you?"

"In theory." Leo wrapped her arms around herself as if she were getting cold. "But in reality, my songwriters do it for me because I no longer have the time to compose. The more popular I became, the more time the promotion part of my career took up."

Holly hesitated. She was a small-town nurse, so giving advice to a superstar felt strange, but she wanted to help, so she forged ahead. "I don't know a thing about the music industry, so please tell me if I'm totally off, but can't you cancel a few interviews and instead have time to write new songs?"

"Yeah, maybe. But it's not just that. Saul—my manager—thinks I'm better off sticking to singing and leaving the songwriting to someone else. According to him, he knows exactly what my fans want."

"Which is?" Holly asked.

"Basically, his concept is *sex sells*, pretty much like every other pop singer. So I'm stuck working out, shooting sexy music videos, and practicing provocative dance routines every day while my songwriters crank out one song after another about breaking up and making up."

"I might not be a good representative of your fan base, but you know what I think about that?"

"What?" Leo asked.

Holly pretended to stick her finger down her throat and made gagging sounds.

Laughter burst from Leo, chasing away the shadows on her face.

Holly smiled in reflex. It felt unexpectedly nice to be able to cheer her up.

"Thanks. I really needed that."

They crossed the bridge and moved back the way they had come, this time walking, not running.

"What about you?" Leo asked after a while. "Are you happy with your job?"

Holly nodded without hesitation. "Oh yeah. I wouldn't want to do anything else."

"Really?" Leo arched her eyebrows. "With patients like my father, it can't be easy. Wouldn't you rather work in a hospital, where there are other nurses who can help out?"

"I worked in a hospital for two years. Trust me, home health care is a much better fit for me. I don't have to hurry from patient to patient. I can take my time getting to know the needs of just one or a few and really establish a relationship with them."

"But doesn't it make it much harder when one of them...well, dies?" Leo asked.

Holly blew out a breath through her nose. "Yeah. It does. But I think it's worth it. It's incredibly rewarding to know that I'm making a difference for someone, allowing them to be in their own home instead of a hospital."

Leo reached out and lightly brushed her forearm with her hand, making tingles scatter across Holly's skin. "For what it's worth, I think you're really making a difference for my dad. I couldn't do for him what you're doing."

The praise made Holly's cheeks heat. "Thank you."

Leo sighed. "In comparison, it makes my job seem even more meaningless. I haven't admitted it to anyone, not even to myself, but maybe my father is right."

"Right about what?" Holly asked.

"About me having sold out. That woman up on stage…that's not me. I'm just going through the motions and playing the part. It's gotten to the point where I don't even want to pick up my guitar anymore."

"Why don't you go back to the roots, then? Make it just about you and the music again." Holly remembered hearing her play at school events and summer festivals fifteen years ago—just Leo and her guitar. The experience had left her with goose bumps.

Leo shook her head. "It's not that easy."

"No, I guess it isn't."

They walked side by side without speaking for a while. When they turned onto Jefferson Street, Leo asked, "Are you on baby-monitor duty tonight?"

"No. It's your mother's turn."

"Oh." Leo marched a little faster up the street, so Holly couldn't see her expression anymore.

She sped up too. Was that disappointment in Leo's voice? A smile stole onto Holly's face. "Um, did you want to do something tonight?"

"No, no, that's fine. I just… Well, I could have kept you company, but of course you don't want to hang around on your night off. You probably have plans."

Yep, Leo was definitely disappointed—and not hiding it very well. She was nearly pouting. *God, she's cute.* Holly's steps faltered. *Stop it. You've never been one for celebrity crushes, and you certainly won't start now.* But deep down, she knew it wasn't Jenna Blake she admired; it was Leo.

"Yeah. I've got something special planned for tonight."

"Have fun, then," Leo said in a carefully neutral tone. She took two more steps before peeking back at Holly. "Hot date?"

Holly gave her a mysterious smile. "Something like that. Want to come?"

Leo stopped at the corner of the street where she had to go right while Holly needed to turn left. "You want me to tag along on your date?"

"You'll see. I'll pick you up in an hour." Holly started to jog down the street. Leo's gaze on her back was as intense as the setting sun. Without turning her head, she shouted back toward her, "Make sure to wear something you don't mind getting slobber on."

"Slobber?" Leo called back. "Who the hell are you dating?"

Holly just laughed and waved. She was already looking forward to introducing Leo to her date—or, rather, to her dates, plural.

"Don't I get a hint?" Leo asked for the third time since Holly had picked her up.

"Quit whining. No hints." Holly waved at a couple that had just left the gas station at the edge of town and then turned right onto the highway.

When they passed the Hy-Vee supermarket, Leo finally started to suspect where they were going. "Ah. You're taking me to the Maple Street Deli for a burger?" Her mouth watered. "Is that why you mentioned drooling?"

Holly laughed. "No."

"Damn," Leo muttered. "I could have gone for a double-bacon cheeseburger now that my nutritionist and my personal trainer aren't watching my every move."

"Jeez, that has to be hard."

"It's not the fun part of fame, that's for sure, but, well, sex sells, or so my manager says. So I have to stay in shape." Leo patted her belly. "But that doesn't stop me from craving a burger."

"If you want, we can get one before we head home, but for now, I've got something else in mind."

"What is it?"

"You'll see in a second." Holly pulled onto a narrow gravel road next to the deli and parked in front of a one-story building with a sign that said *small animal clinic*. She turned off the engine and made a ta-da motion with her hand.

"Uh, that's Beth's clinic. Isn't it a little too soon in our relationship to introduce me to your mother?"

Holly blinked. "What? No, I…" She growled and backhanded Leo's shoulder.

It had been some time since Leo had last experienced an interaction like this. Everyone else walked around her as if on eggshells, as if she were fragile or needed to be revered. She liked the way Holly treated her, like an equal, not a celebrity.

"You already know my mother," Holly said. "Besides, she probably went home hours ago."

"What are we here for, then?"

"My, my, aren't we impatient?" Holly unbuckled her seat belt and got out of the Jeep. "Come with me and find out."

Leo followed her.

Holly unlocked the door to the vet's office and held it open for her.

"You've got a key?" Leo asked as she squeezed past her.

"I sometimes help out by checking on the animals in the holding area or cleaning the kennel in the back."

Their steps echoed on the tiled floor. Without any pets or people around, the reception area seemed strangely empty, despite the racks of pet food, flea collars, and dog shampoos.

"I've got to tell you, you've got strange ideas of a fun evening," Leo said. "Must be because you've lived in Fair Oaks for too long."

Holly bumped her with one hip. "Let's see if you'll still say that in a minute." She led her toward the back of the building. "Um, this question might come a little late, but…you're not allergic, are you?"

"Allergic to what?"

"To them." Holly opened a door and motioned at something at the other end of the room.

A low whine greeted them as they entered.

Cages were stacked along one wall, but what drew Leo's attention was a large wooden box that took up one corner of the room. A blanket was spread out in the box, and on it a yellow Lab lay on its side, nursing a bunch of squirming, whining puppies.

Leo's heart melted. "Puppies!"

"Look more closely," Holly whispered so as not to disturb them and guided her closer with one hand on Leo's back.

The warm touch distracted her, so it took her several moments to make out what Holly was trying to show her. Five of the fur babies were indeed Labrador Retrievers—three yellow and two chocolate ones, but mixed in between them were three tiny kittens, nursing along with the puppies. All of them were well nourished, with fuzzy little pot bellies.

"Oh my God. That's incredible. Where's the momma cat?"

"We don't know. Tom Gaines found the kittens in his barn, abandoned and nearly starved, so he brought them in. We were hoping the animal shelter might have a nursing cat who would adopt them, but Happy here took one look at them and decided they were hers."

"Happy?" Leo raised one brow.

Holly pointed at the momma dog, who looked pretty happy indeed, tongue lolling out of her mouth in a doggy grin and her tail thumping against the side of the box. "She had to have a C-section. That's why she's here. She and her pups will probably go home soon."

"And the kittens?"

"They'll go with her until they're old enough so we can find new homes for them."

As Leo watched, the dog ducked her head down and licked their furry butts, cleaning puppies and kittens alike. "Amazing. She adopted them just like that?"

"Yeah. I don't know if she thinks they're strange little dogs, or maybe she doesn't care what they are at all."

Leo sighed. "Wouldn't it be nice if humans were like that too?"

A wistful smile curved Holly's lips. "Yeah."

They looked at each other, and a silent understanding passed between them.

One of the puppies stopped nursing, wriggled out from beneath the pile of its siblings, and tottered toward them on its too-big puppy paws. One of the kittens followed its canine litter mate.

Their mother gave an anxious whine, but Holly produced a doggy treat from somewhere and petted her until she settled back down and continued to nurse.

The puppy tumbled over the low edge of the wooden box and skidded to a stop at Leo's feet.

Leo bent down, then hesitated and peeked over at Holly. "May I?"

"Go ahead. I didn't bring you just to look at them."

Not caring how cold the floor was, Leo settled down on it and held out her hand to the puppy.

It yipped once, sniffed her, and then proceeded to lick her hand.

Laughing, she scratched behind its velvety soft ears with one finger. When the puppy settled down along her leg and started gnawing on the laces of her sneaker, leaving her other hand free, she picked up the kitten.

It let out a squeak of a meow that made them laugh.

Leo cradled the kitten in both hands and touched her nose to the cat's. Its tiny whiskers quivered, tickling her and making her smile. She buried her face in its fur, which was soft and warm. Her eyes fluttered closed. She felt Holly's gaze on her, but for once, she wasn't afraid to let her guard down—not when it was just her and Holly surrounded by a pile of puppies and kittens.

She felt and heard Holly settle on the floor next to her.

"Mine," Leo mumbled without moving her face away from the little fuzz ball. "Get your own kitten."

Holly's laughter mingled with the soft purring of the tiny cat.

Leo's smile felt as if it were about to split her face. "All right," she murmured into the kitten's fur. "I admit this is much better than a burger."

"Even better than a double-bacon cheeseburger?" Holly reached over to pet the kitten too.

The brush of their fingers against each other set off a sensual enjoyment of another kind. Leo opened her eyes. "Yeah." Her voice came out a little raspy, so she stopped and cleared her throat before adding, "Way better." She cradled the kitten against her chest. "Right, kitten?"

As if in response, the tiny cat began to knead against her chest.

"Ouch." Apparently, kittens at that age already had claws—and they were needle-sharp. "Careful there, that's my boob." She tried to move the kitten away from her chest, but its claws were tangled in the fabric of her T-shirt.

Holly reached over and helped free the kitten's paw. In the process, her fingers brushed the side of Leo's breast.

A shiver raced through her, and her nipple instantly hardened. She lifted the kitten to provide some strategic cover and struggled to calm her breathing. When she peeked over at Holly, she didn't seem to have noticed the accidental touch, but Leo's breast was still tingling.

They sat so close together on the floor that their legs touched all along their lengths.

"Ready to go?" Holly asked after a while.

"No." Leo wasn't ready to have this experience end so soon, and it wasn't just because of the kittens and puppies.

Holly chuckled and picked up another puppy that toddled over to them. "Then let's stay a little longer."

As they left the Maple Street Deli and got back into the Jeep, Holly peered over at Leo, who had chatted about the kittens and puppies pretty much nonstop since they'd left the vet's office. She still had the broadest grin on her face that Holly had ever seen. Her sneakers were covered in dog slobber, and cat hair was stuck to her T-shirt, but to Holly, she was even more beautiful than she was in her music videos.

This wasn't the reserved woman who had arrived in Fair Oaks two weeks ago or the famous singer she had seen on TV. She liked this side of Leo. Getting to see the puppies and kittens was always a highlight of her day, but sharing it with Leo had been extra special.

"I don't know which one was more fun—the puppy or the kitten," Leo said as Holly steered them back onto the highway.

"Why choose?"

"Right. They were both lethally cute." Now more pensive, Leo stared through the windshield. "You know, with all the cities I've been to all over the world and everything I've seen, can you believe I've never petted a puppy or a kitten?"

"Never?" Holly echoed. "Didn't you have a pet growing up?"

"No, never. I always wanted one, but my father thought it would distract me from practicing."

"Practicing?"

"Playing the piano and the violin," Leo said.

Gil had denied her the experience of growing up with a pet so she could spend more time practicing his preferred instruments? *God.* Holly was starting to resent him a little, and that wasn't good. He was her patient after all. She was responsible for his well-being, not Leo's. But she couldn't help it.

"Well, you could get one now," she finally said. "In five or six weeks, Happy's puppies and kittens will be old enough to go to new homes."

Leo brushed a few cat hairs off her shirt and watched them swirl through the interior of the Jeep. "I'll be back in New York by then. Besides, with me traveling for concerts and interviews all the time, it wouldn't be fair to the poor animal."

Both were silent for the rest of the ride, their good mood dampened.

When Leo had first arrived in Fair Oaks, Holly couldn't wait to have her leave again. But now she hated the reminder that Leo wasn't here to stay. She would miss having someone to talk to and share scones with. Sure, she had other friends in town, but somehow, spending time with Leo was different.

All too soon, she stopped the Jeep in front of Gil and Sharon's house and turned off the engine.

Instead of getting out immediately, Leo kept staring through the windshield. Finally, she turned her head, and a hint of the carefree smile from earlier flashed across her face. "Thank you for getting me a burger and especially for taking me to see the puppies and kittens. It wasn't what I was expecting when you picked me up, but it has my usual dates beaten by a mile."

Holly started to smile, but then the full meaning of Leo's words hit home. *Wait a minute! Usual dates...* Did that mean Leo considered their little adventure a date? She knew she should speak up and tell her that it wasn't, that she wasn't into dating, just in case Leo might be thinking in that direction. That was how she had handled her friendships with women during the past few years, and she had found that drawing clear boundaries was always better in the long run.

Then why was she just sitting behind the wheel, gaping like a catfish?

Before she could make her vocal cords work, Leo said "good night" and got out of the Jeep. Only the banging of the car door jarred Holly out of her frozen state.

"Leo, wait!"

But Leo apparently didn't hear her. She was already walking toward the house, her long legs quickly widening the distance between them.

Holly let her forehead sink onto the steering wheel, closed her eyes, and let out a long groan.

Chapter 10

ONCE AGAIN, LEO LAY IN bed and listened to the concert of the crickets drifting in through the closed window. Staring at her childhood posters was starting to become a habit, but this time, it wasn't brooding thoughts about her father or her career that kept her awake.

She kept reliving every second of her evening with Holly, especially the smiles and the little touches—Holly's hand on the small of her back, guiding her into the room with the puppies and kittens; the brush of their fingers; the warmth of Holly's leg against hers; the accidental touch of her breast.

Each contact had set off instant tingles all over her body. There was no denying it: She was attracted to Holly, and it wasn't just a physical thing. Admittedly, she also liked the mischievous twinkle in Holly's eyes, her genuine warmth, and the fact that she didn't let Leo get away with anything. Even the fact that Holly didn't seem to want anything from her—not her money, her connections, and not even her body—was part of her appeal.

But had she meant what she had said earlier, in the Jeep? She had thrown out the comment about her usual dates without thinking. So far, she hadn't consciously considered it. Holly lived in Fair Oaks after all, the town Leo wanted to get away from, and Leo had no time for a relationship anyway.

Relationship? Whoa! How had she gone from one possible date to a bona fide relationship? She really was getting ahead of herself. Maybe she should take it one day at a time.

One date wasn't a marriage proposal, even in small-town Missouri. Holly's brothers would hardly get out their shotgun and drag her to church because she went out with their sister once or twice. It was just a pleasant way to while away the time during her stay in Fair Oaks. Nothing more, nothing less, right?

Right. She nodded into the darkness. That was decided, then. She would ask Holly out to dinner. Nothing to it.

But then why could she still not settle her chaotic thoughts enough to sleep?

A few days later, on Monday afternoon, they went out for another run together…although, admittedly, there wasn't that much running involved. Holly leaned back on her elbows. The flat rock beneath her was still warm from the heat of the day, and the relaxing murmur of the creek lulled her into a peaceful trance. Despite her not-always-easy job, this summer was starting to feel like the endless summers of her childhood, when there had been no responsibilities and no pressures and a new adventure had waited around every corner.

The only difference was that this time, she wasn't spending her summer alone or tagging along after her brothers.

She peeked at Leo, who was reclining next to her. She had kicked off her shoes and socks and dangled her feet in the creek. Every now and then, she wiggled her toes or lazily waved her hand to chase off the bees buzzing around her ice cream. She was starting to get a nice tan from spending more time in the sun than she had in years, and the highlights in her windblown hair were real, no longer out of a bottle. It looked really good on her, Holly decided.

Something cold trickled onto Holly's fingers. She jerked her attention away from Leo and back to her own ice cream cone, which hung forgotten in her grip. Quickly, she licked the melted chocolate off her fingers.

"You know," Leo said without opening her eyes, "you're a really bad influence."

"Me?"

"Yeah, you. First, you get me addicted to the scones. Now you buy me ice cream. My manager, my personal trainer, and my nutritionist will hate you."

Holly shrugged and took another lick of her ice cream. "They're not here now, are they?"

"No, they're not. It's just the two of us."

There was something in Leo's tone that made Holly peer at her again, but she couldn't read the expression on her face.

Leo opened her eyes and took one foot out of the water so she could half-turn and look at her. "Um, talking about food and the two of us..." She lowered her long lashes and picked a piece of clover that grew between the rocks before peeking back up. "Would you go to dinner with me sometime this week?"

Holly's pulse quickened. "Dinner?" she repeated, to give herself time to think.

"Yeah, you know, the meal people usually eat in the evening." Leo's lips curled into a smile.

It was almost the same thing Holly had teased her with when they had talked about breakfast almost two weeks ago, so Holly replied with the same words too. "Thanks for the expert definition, Ms. Merriam-Webster. I know what it is. But what kind of dinner are we talking about?"

Was Leo trying to ask her out, or was she talking about a dinner between friends? For the millionth time in her life, she wished she were better at judging potentially romantic situations.

"Well," Leo said, "there isn't exactly much to choose from in town, but how about Tasty Barn? Do they still serve some Mexican food?"

"Um, yeah, but...that wasn't what I meant." Was Leo deliberately pretending not to understand what she was asking? "Is this about two friends grabbing some food together or...?"

Leo pulled her other foot out of the water too. Her gaze searched Holly's face. "Would it be okay if it was a date?"

She looked so cute, so earnest and vulnerable that Holly answered without thinking. "Yes. I mean...no. No, Leo, I..."

She stopped herself, sat up, and forced fresh air into her lungs. Jesus, how could a simple question turn her inside out like this? It wasn't as if she hadn't rejected anyone before. She tried to convince herself that it was better for both of them in the long run, but saying the words was still hard. "I'm sorry. I can't go out with you."

A flash of hurt crossed Leo's face before it turned into the reserved mask Holly had seen in the beginning. "Can't?" She sounded as if she was speaking through clenched teeth. "Or don't want to?"

That was a question Holly didn't want to examine too closely. "I'm sorry," she said again. "I know it sounds trite, but it's not you. It's me."

Leo let out a groan. "That *is* trite. It's usually what women say when they're either straight or think I'm a conceited, shallow celebrity—someone to lust after from afar, not someone to date for real."

Her voice got rougher with every word.

Impulsively, Holly reached out to squeeze her hand or put it on Leo's knee but then realized it would send mixed messages, so she withdrew and put her hand in her own lap. "I don't think that about you. You know that, right?"

"But you're not straight. You do date women."

"I don't date anyone. That's what I'm trying to tell you."

A frown wrinkled Leo's brow. "Don't tell me you're still hung up on Ashley."

Holly barked out a nervous laugh. "No. Definitely not."

"Then it really is me." Leo lowered her gaze to a tuft of clover. "I'm not your type."

"That's just it, Leo. I don't have a type. At least not the way you think."

"Okay." Leo drew out the word in a way that made it obvious that she had no clue what Holly meant.

Holly sighed. Coming out as asexual hadn't been on her list of relaxing things to do on her afternoon off, but she didn't want a rejection to stand between them. She had come to appreciate their friendship too much to lie, even by omission.

Eating the remainder of her ice cream gave her a moment to collect herself. When the last crumb of cone was gone, she clutched her bare legs to her chest and gazed at Leo over her drawn-up knees. God, why was this so much harder than coming out as a lesbian?

Finally, she just blurted it out. "I'm ace."

She wasn't sure what response she had expected, but certainly not the crooked grin that spread across Leo's face.

"Oh yeah," Leo drawled with the husky voice that had won her three Grammys. "You sure are. Totally awesome."

"No, I mean, I'm asexual."

"Asexual?" Leo repeated it syllable by syllable. "What does that mean?"

Oh boy. Maybe that was what made coming out as asexual so much harder. Telling someone she was a lesbian didn't require a half-hour education session.

"It means…" She glanced down and watched as she turned the black ace ring around and around on her right middle finger. "It means that I'm not sexually attracted to anyone."

Leo stared at her, the last bit of ice cream cone apparently forgotten in her hand. "Wait… Are you saying you don't like sex?"

"Not exactly. I'm saying I don't *want* sex."

A gust of air escaped Leo's lungs in an audible *puff*. "You don't want sex? Never? With anyone?"

The look of disbelief on her face made Holly laugh. "There are more important things in life, you know?"

"Yeah, but when it's really good, sex can be mind-blowing." She rolled her eyes skyward and fanned herself with both hands.

"I'll have to take your word for it."

Leo slowly shook her head back and forth. "Have you always been like this? I mean, this isn't because something happened to you…is it?"

She looked so tortured by the thought that Holly did reach out to squeeze her hand for a moment. "No. The most traumatic thing that happened to me as a kid was when my brothers put a frog into my slippers."

Her exaggerated shudder broke the tension between them, and they laughed with each other.

"Anyway," Holly said after the laughter had faded away, "it doesn't work like that. Asexuality isn't a result of some trauma. It's a sexual orientation, just like being a lesbian."

Leo still looked as if she had trouble wrapping her head around it. Maybe an analogy would help.

"It's a little like chocolate," Holly said.

"Chocolate?" Leo repeated, her tone doubtful.

"Bear with me. So, some people like dark chocolate. Some like milk chocolate. And some like white chocolate."

Leo grimaced. "I don't consider that white stuff chocolate."

"Me neither, but you're destroying my beautiful, well-thought-out analogy."

"Sorry. You were saying?"

"There are also some people who like all kinds of chocolate."

"People with bad taste," Leo muttered. When Holly glared playfully, she made a zipping motion across her lips with her thumb and forefinger.

"And last but not least, there are a couple of people who don't like any type of chocolate."

Leo snorted. "Come on. Who doesn't like chocolate?"

"Me," Holly said quietly and held her gaze.

"You don't like chocolate? Um, excuse me, then what's that?" Leo pointed at something on Holly's cheek, probably a smear of the chocolate ice cream she had just eaten.

"No. I mean, yes, I do like chocolate, but…" She rubbed her eyes. Jeez, she was making a mess of things, confusing Leo even more. "Look, all I'm saying is that this," she waved at herself, "is the way I was born—redheaded, crooked-toed, and asexual."

Leo seemed to consider that for a while. "Your toes are cute," she finally said.

Holly stared down at them. "They're crooked."

"But in a cute way." With a tiny splash, Leo's feet landed back in the creek. She swirled them through the water while she lay back and stared at the sky, her forehead crinkled as if deeply in thought. "If you're not attracted to anyone, why were you with Ash?"

"I said I'm not *sexually* attracted to anyone. There are other types of attraction, you know? For you, they're probably all aligned, but I can fall in love with a woman or appreciate her beauty without wanting to jump her bones."

Leo folded her arms behind her head. "Hmm, that makes sense. Kind of. Is that why you're still calling yourself a lesbian? Because you *are* attracted to women, just not sexually?"

"Yeah." Holly quirked a smile. "Plus calling myself a homoromantic asexual would get me nothing but puzzled looks." Like the one Leo was giving her right now. *Poor woman.*

"So, excuse me if I keep asking stupid questions, but…"

"It's okay," Holly cut in. "I don't mind talking about it." To her surprise, she found that it was true, at least right now. Leo might be confused and struggling to understand, but she wasn't making her feel as if she had to defend her sexual orientation. That was nice, especially after the judgmental reactions she'd had from other lesbians.

"Thanks. So…" Leo kicked up a bit of water. The droplets glittered in the afternoon sun as they rained down on her. "You said you can fall in love with a woman or appreciate her beauty…right?"

Holly nodded.

"Then why won't you go out with me…or date in general?"

There it was: the million-dollar question. "Because dating comes with expectations. A kiss goodnight after the first date or maybe the second, then sex by date number three or five or whatever arbitrary rule you apply." She shook her head. "It never works out for me, so I'd rather stay out of that minefield of expectations."

"Even if it means staying alone for the rest of your life?" Leo asked quietly.

Holly often asked herself the same question, but she still hadn't found an answer. "I don't know."

They lay side by side for a while longer, the gurgling of the creek and the rustling of the wind through the trees the only sounds interrupting the silence.

Finally, Holly sat up and slid her feet back into her sandals. "Come on. We have to get back, or I'll be late for my shift."

Leo shoved her feet back into her socks and shoes, stood, and followed her along the path. "Holly?" she said after a few steps.

Every single one of Holly's muscles tensed. It wasn't that she didn't trust Leo, but most often when she had revealed her sexual orientation to someone, it had come back to bite her in the ass, even if the person had first seemed to accept her asexuality. "Hmm?"

"Thanks for telling me," Leo said. "I know that took a lot of courage."

Holly had been so busy expecting a negative reaction that it took her a second to figure out what Leo meant. As soon as she did, warmth flowed through every inch of her body, melting away the tension. "Thank *you*" was all she could get out.

A smile replaced Leo's serious expression. "Just for the record: I still think you're ace—as in pretty awesome."

Holly's laughter rang over the hill. "Thanks. You're pretty ace too." With a hint of a wink, she added, "At least in one way."

Chapter 11

THE NEXT MORNING, LEO YAWNED so widely that her jaw popped. God, she was getting old. Apparently, the days where she could stay up all night and still get up early to join her band mates on the tour bus were over.

She stumbled down the stairs and into the kitchen in search of coffee. This was what a zombie must feel like, only she was hunting for caffeine, not brains.

Her mother was just putting breakfast on the table—biscuits and gravy, Holly's favorite, Leo remembered.

As if conjured up by that thought, Holly appeared in the doorway, pushing the wheelchair with Leo's father toward the table. "Good morning," she said with an almost shy glance in Leo's direction.

Did she feel a little vulnerable after yesterday's coming-out? Leo couldn't blame her if she did. Last night, she had read dozens of coming-out stories of other asexual people. Many of them had faced intrusive questions about their sex lives or been offered ready explanations of what might have "caused" their asexuality: bad experiences, hormonal or mental disorders, not having found the right person yet, or going through a phase—the same stupid things people had told her when she had first come out as a lesbian.

She hadn't said any of that ignorant stuff, had she? Well, admittedly, asking Holly if she'd been abused had probably fallen into the stupid-questions category, but she cut herself some slack. This was still all so new and confusing to her.

The Internet had helped in one way—and made it worse in others. Simply typing *asexuality* into a search engine had brought up millions of websites, Tumblr pages, forums, and YouTube videos, and each click had confronted her with new terms and concepts that had definitely never been mentioned in high school sex ed: graysexual, demisexual, cupiosexual, aromantic, queerplatonic...

Her head was still reeling. There was this whole complex spectrum out there. Why hadn't she ever heard of any of this?

"...Leontyne?"

Her mother's voice wrenched her from her thoughts.

"Um, excuse me?"

"I said why don't you take a seat? You look like you've been up all night. Have you been working on a new song?"

Leo sat at the table across from Holly and reached for a biscuit. "Um, not really. I just got into something online and lost track of time."

"Anything interesting?" Holly asked while ladling gravy onto her biscuit.

"Oh yeah. That same interesting thing we talked about yesterday."

Holly paused with the ladle halfway back to its bowl. "You googled it?"

Leo nodded.

Her mother looked back and forth between them as if she were watching a tennis game, her forehead forming deep lines.

"I'm still trying to wrap my head around it, but it's very interesting. Did you know that..." Leo peeked at her mother, who was still watching them. "...that, um, people with crooked toes make up one percent of the population?"

The corners of Holly's mouth tipped up into an amused smile. She took a bite of biscuit and nodded while she chewed. When she had swallowed, she pointed at her hair. "About the same ratio as redheads."

Leo's mother put both hands flat on the table and leaned forward to pierce them with a penetrating gaze. "Why are we talking about crooked toes?"

Somehow, Leo managed to keep a straight face. "Because Holly's got them."

Her mother glanced beneath the table. "You do?"

Shuffling sounds came from Holly's chair, probably as she pulled her toes out of viewing range. A flush rushed up her neck and colored her cheeks. "Um, yeah."

"Oh dear. I had no idea. Do they bother you?" Leo's mom reached over and patted Holly's hand in a motherly way.

Holly shot a glare in Leo's direction, but Leo put on her most innocent expression. "They did in the beginning. It isn't easy to be the only one with crooked toes while everyone else's toes are perfectly…um, straight."

She and Leo chuckled at her choice of words.

"Couldn't an orthopedic specialist do something about them?" Leo's mother asked.

God. Leo's nostrils quivered as she struggled not to burst out laughing.

"Nah," Holly said. "It's not a medical issue. It took me a few years, but I've now come to accept my, um, toes as a part of me."

"That's nice, dear." Leo's mother patted her hand again. "No use in agonizing over something you can't change. When I was young, I used to think that my nose was too big." She rubbed the body part in question. "But now I think it's all right…isn't it?"

Leo's father let out a growl. "This," he slapped at his paralyzed arm with his good hand, "problem. Toes and…um, mouth…no…um…*nose*… Pfff!"

Holly put her hand on his and smiled at him. "You're absolutely right, Gil. My toes are not a problem."

The topic of conversation drifted to something else—the pie her mother wanted to make and the article about Leo's homecoming in the local paper, but Leo was no longer listening. Her brain was still busy processing what she had found out about asexuality and what it might mean for Holly.

For one thing, it means she's off limits…and that she's not a swinger. The thought made her struggle to bite back a renewed wave of hilarity.

Apparently, a black ring worn on the middle finger of the right hand signified that the wearer was asexual—unlike one of Leo's dancers, who wore it on his right ring finger to indicate that he was a swinger.

When she and Holly cleared the table and loaded the dishwasher, as had become their after-meal ritual, Holly pinched her waist, making Leo jump and hit her head on the hanging cabinet. "Hey!" She rubbed her head.

"Serves you right, you little shit."

But there was no real heat behind Holly's words or her glare.

"So," Leo said as she put the last plate into the dishwasher and closed it, "since you refuse to go out with me, how about watching a movie or something with me after my dad's in bed tonight?"

"Under one condition," Holly said.

"Don't worry. I know there won't be any making out over popcorn."

Holly pinched her again. This time, Leo managed not to hit her head. "There won't even be any popcorn. That's my condition. For a proper movie night, we need pizza."

Oh God. At the rate they were going, she wouldn't fit into any of her costumes by the time she returned to New York. But it was a price she was willing to pay if it meant she got to spend more time with Holly. "Pizza it is."

A heavenly scent accompanied them as Leo carried the pizza box upstairs, followed by Holly, who had brought a stack of DVDs. Pizza from Casey's was another thing she couldn't get in New York. She hadn't thought there was anything from Fair Oaks that she had missed, but the longer she stayed, the more she started to remember the good things.

Or maybe it was that she got to enjoy these things with Holly now.

She grinned at the way Holly's nose wiggled like that of a beagle following a scent trail. Only when they entered her room did she realize there was nowhere to sit but the bed. Well, there was her old desk chair, but that certainly wasn't a comfy place to watch a movie.

"Um, would it make you uncomfortable if we both sat on the bed?"

Holly set the DVDs on the bedside table and turned to face her. "It's kind of cute how considerate you're being. I appreciate it, but I want to get one thing straight...or not so straight in our case. Just because I'm asexual doesn't mean I don't like physical contact. In fact, under the right circumstances, I can be a certified cuddle bug."

Immediately, an image of cuddling with Holly, holding her close while nuzzling her face against the warm crook of her neck, flashed through Leo's mind. *Cut it out. She didn't say she wants to cuddle with you, just that she doesn't mind casual physical contact.*

"All right, then." She tried to sound completely normal, but her voice was a bit rough. "Let's get comfortable, or the pizza will get cold."

They settled on the bed, leaning against the headboard, and Leo put the pizza box half on her own, half on Holly's lap. She flicked on the TV and opened the lid.

The mouthwatering aroma of pepperoni and melting cheese wafted up.

"Yum," they said in unison and then grinned at each other.

"I never thought I'd find someone who likes pepperoni and pineapple on her pizza too. Ray—my drummer—always says it should be on the list of forbidden food combinations."

Holly huffed. "Hasn't he ever heard of don't knock it till you've tried it?"

Did that hold true for sex as well? Leo had to admit that she was curious. Since finding out yesterday that Holly was asexual, she hadn't been able to stop thinking about it, but no way would she interrogate her about her sex life—or lack thereof.

"Apparently not," she said.

They reached for the same slice of pizza, and their fingers touched.

A wave of heat that had nothing to do with the still-hot pizza rushed through Leo's body. The thought that Holly had never, ever experienced a sensation like this was mind-boggling, but it also helped her tamp down on her own attraction.

She waved at Holly to go ahead, picked another slice, and took a big bite.

The extra cheese seemed to melt in her mouth, and the perfect blend of sweet pineapple and savory pepperoni mingled on her tongue.

They both moaned around their mouthfuls of pizza. The sensual sound raised Leo's temperature another degree, but Holly continued to eat as if completely unaware. Leo didn't know if she should feel sad for Holly or envy her.

A familiar theme music finally came to her rescue, distracting her from the little sounds Holly made as she ate. "Oh hey! I didn't know *Central Precinct* was on. I love this show."

Holly blinked at her. "Really? Me too. I've watched it since the very first episode."

"I missed a lot of episodes, but I'm quickly catching up." If not for their afternoon runs or their evenings talking in the kitchen, she would have probably watched all five seasons by now.

"Have you seen this one?" Holly waved her half-eaten slice toward the TV.

Leo turned her attention toward the screen and watched as the two detectives were called to a crime scene. "Oh, that's the episode where Halliday's father is murdered. Yep, I've seen it. It's a good one."

"Yeah. I think Amanda Clark even won an Emmy for this episode. Want to watch it?"

"Sure." They could watch the DVDs Holly had brought another time. A moment later, the thought caught up with her. Interesting how she took it for granted that they'd spend more time with each other. She had never wanted that with anyone else, at least not to this extent—not since high school and Ashley.

They devoured the pizza while watching *Central Precinct*. The last crumb was gone long before the episode ended with a lip-lock between the show's female detective and the female medical examiner. Admittedly, it was part of why it was one of Leo's favorite episodes.

She kicked the empty pizza box off the bed and turned a little so she could face Holly. Since her bed was a twin, her knee ended up pressed against Holly's thigh. "Can I ask you something?"

The smile on Holly's face said she'd expected more questions all along. "Sure."

Leo chewed her lip for a second before deciding to just come out and ask. "So this…" She waved at the TV. "Two hot women kissing… It doesn't do anything for you?"

Holly shrugged. "They're both very beautiful, and I love having a lesbian couple on one of my favorite shows, but I actually found the scene when they talk in the autopsy room much more intimate than I would watching them do the horizontal mambo."

Leo thought about it for a few moments, all the while very aware of her knee against Holly's thigh. That had been the scene right after Halliday's father had been killed and landed on Dr. Castellano's autopsy table. The two characters had opened up to each other for the first time and shared things that were very personal and painful to them. Leo had never done that in any of her relationships. When she talked about "being intimate" with someone, she usually meant having sex, not sharing her innermost thoughts. She didn't talk about her father, her childhood, or her true feelings about the way her career was going.

Not true. You talked about it with Holly.

Could it be that she was already much more intimate with Holly than with any of her former girlfriends, without even having kissed her?

"What is it?" Holly's lips quirked into a smile. "You look like you just found a frog in your slippers."

"No. I just… I think you're right. That scene in the autopsy room was more intimate. But," she added at Holly's triumphant expression, "that kiss was still hot as hell."

"So you find this hot as well?" Holly waved toward the TV.

Leo turned her head. She'd been entirely focused on their conversation, so she hadn't paid any attention to what was flickering across the screen. It was a commercial. A curvy woman in a bikini was sensually running her tongue along the length of a hot dog. Her body glistened with some kind of oil, and it took Leo a second to figure out what the commercial was for—the hot dogs, not sun lotion or swim wear, apparently. "I take it you don't?"

Holly wrinkled her nose. "Nope. I find it pretty ridiculous. Licking sausages…ugh. How does that work for anyone?"

It took some effort not to burst out laughing. Did Holly realize how ambiguous that statement was? She bit her lip and abstained from making a sexual joke about it.

An adorable flush crept up Holly's neck. She covered her face with Leo's pillow for a moment. When she dropped it into her lap, she was laughing. Her blue eyes twinkled. "Okay, okay, I'm obviously asking the wrong person. Licking sausages probably doesn't work for you either."

Leo stared at her.

Holly chuckled. "What?"

"Um, nothing. I just didn't expect…" Leo shook her head. "Forget it. Want to watch another episode? I've got Netflix on my laptop."

Holly glanced at the alarm clock on the bedside table and then double-checked the receiver of the baby monitor to make sure she would hear if Leo's father needed anything. "Sure. We can watch another one. It's getting too late to watch a movie anyway."

"How about the one where they're on their honeymoon in Vegas and get involved in solving the murder case in the casino?"

"That's the one with Grace Durand as the casino owner's daughter, right?"

"Yep."

"Ah. I see. You just want to ogle her." Holly gave her a teasing nudge with her elbow.

Actually, what Leo really wanted was to keep Holly next to her for a little longer. "Yeah, you found me out. I have met her, by the way, and she's even more beautiful in person. Plus she's a genuinely nice person."

"You met Grace Durand?"

Leo nodded. "She's married to my former PR agent, Lauren. She's the one who helped me navigate my public coming-out and appeal to mainstream pop-music fans despite being gay."

"Well, considering you're still a superstar, she must have done a great job."

"Yeah, she did. Well, my manager didn't think so. My sales numbers dropped by twenty percent, but it was worth it."

Holly touched Leo's knee for a moment. "Good for you. That must have taken a lot of courage."

"Being forced to stay in the closet would have been a lot worse." Leo climbed off the bed and got her laptop. "So, is the episode with Grace okay for you, or would you rather watch one that isn't so…um…romance-heavy?"

Holly's dimples made an appearance. "As long as we're not watching porn, I'm fine."

Leo barked out a laugh. "No porn, I promise."

The smaller screen required them to sit even closer together, so now they were really cuddling, kind of, with their legs resting against each other from hip to ankle and Leo's arm on top of the headboard, which basically positioned it around Holly's shoulders.

It was amazingly nice to sit like this.

Leo chuckled to herself. *Grace who?*

Chapter 12

Holly closed Gil's door behind her. Physical therapy was already frustrating enough for him, so he didn't need an audience to watch him struggle. If the physical therapist needed her help, he'd come get her.

She went over to the kitchen, where Sharon was rooting through a drawer.

"Can I help you with anything?" Holly asked.

"No, thanks. I'm just looking for one of my mother-in-law's recipes. I won't start preparing lunch for another hour." Sharon glanced over her shoulder. "Leontyne is in the living room. I think she's a little bored too. Why don't you girls go up to her room and watch another episode of that show you like?"

If she didn't know any better, she would think Leo's mother was trying to matchmake. She encouraged them to spend time together at every opportunity. Not that Holly didn't want to, but she would have felt weird watching Netflix while she was supposed to be working. "No, thanks. I want to stay downstairs in case Gil and Reid need me."

"All right." Sharon went back to her search for the recipe.

Holly wandered into the living room.

Leo sat in her father's easy chair, her eyes closed and her fingers moving to the rhythm of music only she could hear. For a moment, Holly thought she might be working on a new song, but there was no pen and paper and no recording device nearby. Just as she was about to tiptoe out, Leo opened her eyes.

An instant smile formed on her lips. "Hey. Are you done adulting?"

Holly chuckled. "Just for the moment. The physical therapist is with your father for the next hour." She walked over to the piano bench, which was the seat closest to Leo's easy chair, and sat down.

Leo tilted her head to the side and studied her. "You look good there. Do you play?"

"Oh God, no. I wouldn't call it that."

"So you do play? Why didn't you tell me?"

Holly scrunched up her face. "Because it's embarrassing. The only thing I can play is one piece."

"Which one?"

Holly hummed it.

"Ah. Czerny's Study in C Major," Leo said. "Okay, let's play that."

"Um, I thought you didn't want to play classical music?"

Leo smiled. "I'll make an exception just this once." She came over and motioned at her to slide to the side so she could sit next to her.

It felt nice and warm to have her so close, but playing the piano with her was like painting in front of Pablo Picasso when you could barely draw a stick figure. "I don't know about this."

"Come on." Leo bumped her with her shoulder, bringing their bodies into even closer contact. "Dad is busy with PT. It's just the two of us here."

"Yeah, but one of us is musical genius Jenna Blake."

"No," Leo said very seriously and turned a little on the bench to look into her eyes. "One of us is Leo, not Jenna."

"Right. You know you're Leo to me."

Instead of answering, Leo stared at something farther down.

When Holly followed her gaze, she realized she'd put her hand on Leo's leg, probably to reassure her. It felt natural. *But jeez, talk about sending mixed signals.*

Before she could snatch her hand away, Leo covered it with her own and squeezed gently. "Ready?"

Holly swallowed. "All right. Let's play."

Leo opened the lid with the hand that wasn't still covering Holly's. "How about I play the left hand, and you play the right?"

"Okay."

"Remember where to put your fingers?"

"I think so." She placed her fingers on the keys.

Leo finally took her hand away from Holly's and stroked her fingertips over the hand resting on the piano, from wrist to knuckles. "Relax," she said softly. "Focus on how the keys feel under your fingers."

The last thing Holly was focused on at the moment was the piano. Sharing this with Leo was too confusing. There was something between them; she couldn't deny that. She felt drawn to Leo in a way that might have seemed almost sexual to an observer, but to her, it wasn't about sex. This was all about emotion.

Leo shuffled through her father's sheet music, found the right one, and placed it in front of them.

Holly took a deep breath and then haltingly began to play the first notes, stumbling through the piece. God, this was awful. Her tempo was all off, and she had the dynamics of a robot.

Next to her, Leo's fingers moved gracefully and without effort. It looked as if it came as easy to her as breathing. *Wow.* No wonder women were swooning when they watched Leo's long fingers caress the neck of her guitar during concerts. If she weren't asexual, she probably would too. As it was, her fantasies ended at those talented fingers giving her a massage or caressing her tenderly. Other people might have considered it foreplay, but for her it was the main course, an experience that was sensual rather than sexual.

Holly was so focused on watching Leo that she stopped her own playing.

Leo paused too and looked at her.

"Sorry," Holly said. "I told you I'm not good at this."

"Then let's play it slower. Want to try playing the left hand, and I take over the right-hand melody?"

Holly nodded and started to get up to switch sides, but Leo just guided her hand to the correct keys and then reached across Holly's arm to the piano's right side. Their forearms touched each other lightly, but Holly didn't feel crowded. It actually felt…nice.

They started from the beginning, and this time, Holly played without pausing. She had to admit it didn't sound too bad.

When the last notes faded away, they both left their hands where they were for a little longer.

"Who taught you?" Leo asked as she finally put her hands on her lap.

Holly withdrew too. "Your father."

Leo's head swiveled around. "My father?"

"Yeah. You'd think I'd play a little better with him as my teacher, right?" Holly laughed. "He tried to teach me while he was recovering from his first stroke, but I'm hopeless. No matter how much I practiced, I could never coordinate playing with both hands and the pedal."

"I bet that didn't go over too well. After all, if you're not a perfect student, it means he's not the perfect teacher he thinks he is, right?"

"Actually, he took it pretty well."

"Are we talking about the same man?" Leo asked. "When I was eight, my mother had to intervene because he wouldn't let me stop practicing until I got one of Liszt's pieces right."

"I guess it's different with you."

"Yeah." The one word dripped with bitterness.

"Maybe it's because you're his daughter, and he cares about you," Holly said softly.

Leo snorted. "He's got a funny way of showing it."

Holly didn't know what to say to that, so she just slid even closer on the piano bench and put one arm around her hip. "He probably never learned how to show it. But that's his deficit, not yours. It doesn't mean you're not lovable."

That last word hung between them as Leo slowly turned her head and looked at her.

Their closeness suddenly made Holly a little nervous, but at the same time, she didn't want to move away from Leo's warmth. This close, she could make out the brown flecks in her olive-green eyes. The bitterness in them from before was gone, and now they held only—

A discreet clearing of someone's throat made them both jump.

Reid, the physical therapist, stood in the doorway. "Um, sorry to interrupt, but I could use a second person for one of the exercises. Do you have a minute?"

"Sure." Holly quickly withdrew her arm from around Leo and got up. In the tight space between the piano and the bench, her feet got tangled with Leo's, and she stumbled.

Leo caught her before she could crash into the piano. "You okay?" she asked quietly.

Jeez, she really was a bumbling idiot around Leo. "I'm fine. Thanks."

Slowly, Leo took her hands off Holly's hips and slid the bench back to give her more space.

Holly moved past her. At the door, she turned back. "Thanks for playing with me. Uh, I mean…"

Leo laughed. "I know what you mean. And you're very welcome."

A few days later, Leo stood at the dormer window of her old room. The stars twinkled down on her through the glass. As a child, she had often climbed through this window and up onto the roof whenever she had needed to escape. She slid open the window and paused. *Should I…?* She shrugged. *Why not?* It wasn't as if her parents would ground her even if they caught her.

She climbed onto her desk chair, gripped the window frame with both hands, and had just lifted one leg over the sill when a knock sounded on her door.

Quickly, she swung her leg back down and hopped off the chair since she didn't want to give away her secret spot.

"Yes?" she called out and turned to face the room.

The door swung open, and Holly peeked inside. "Hi. Your father is down for the night. I came up to see if you'd like to watch one of the movies with me that we didn't get to see the other night."

Leo hesitated. Her gaze went back toward the still-open window. The spot up on the roof was one place that she had never shared with anyone, not even Ashley. But now the urge to share it with Holly overcame her, and after all, Holly had shared her feel-good place—the room with the puppies and kittens—the week before last.

"Never mind," Holly said when Leo didn't answer immediately. "If you're not in the mood, we can watch it another—"

"No. I mean, yes, let's watch the movie another day. Tonight, I want to show you something else."

Holly stepped farther into the room and closed the door behind her. Curiosity glittered in her eyes.

"You're not afraid of heights, are you?" Leo asked.

"Um, no. I don't think so. What are you planning to do? Take me parachuting in the middle of the night?" Her smile looked a little timid.

Leo chuckled. "No, nothing that spectacular. I'm taking you to my favorite spot in Fair Oaks."

"That spot at the creek, where we always stop when we go running?"

"Nope. That's my second-favorite spot." Apparently, Holly had guessed how much she liked that place without Leo having to tell her.

"So where's number one?" Holly asked.

Grinning, Leo pointed at the window behind her.

Holly stared past her. "Across the street? The high school? I didn't think you liked that place any more than I did."

"I didn't. I don't mean the high school. Come on. I think it's easier if I just show you. Follow me, and be careful. I don't want to explain to the agency you work for how their employee fell off our roof in the middle of the night."

"We're going up on the roof?" Holly squeaked out.

"Yep." She climbed onto the desk chair, held on to the window frame, and swung one leg, then the other over the sill. After two steps onto the roof, she stopped and turned to help Holly. "It's easiest if you put your hand here and—"

Before she could finish her sentence, Holly was already out the window and up next to her.

A light breeze tugged on their T-shirts as they stood on the roof, side by side.

Leo grinned at her.

"What?" Holly returned the grin. "You thought I wouldn't have the courage to follow you, city girl?"

"I'm not a city girl," Leo said automatically.

"No?"

Normally, Leo was quick to say that she was a New Yorker, but now, up here on the roof with Holly, she was strangely content to be right where she was. She shrugged and climbed up the slope of the roof without answering.

They made their way around the jutting-out dormer window, arms spread out to the sides to help them keep their balance.

"Here," Leo said when they reached the brick chimney. "When I was growing up, I would always sit behind the chimney so I couldn't be seen from below."

They settled down next to each other, both of them leaning against the bricks. The shingles were still warm beneath Leo, even though the sun had set two hours ago, and Holly's body warmed her on one side.

The street below them was empty since most people in town were in bed by ten. The crescent moon painted a silvery path across the shingles. Lightning bugs and stars formed a network of light all around them.

Amazing. Leo stared up into the sky. Another thing she had missed. She had never seen the stars like this in the city.

No traffic noise, car horns, sirens, or booming radios interrupted the peaceful atmosphere. Crickets chirped, and the louder song of a cicada came from somewhere close to the tree line at the edge of town. The scent of honeysuckle and freshly cut grass trailed on the air.

It was so beautiful that it felt almost surreal, and Holly's presence somehow added to it instead of feeling like an intrusion.

Neither felt the need to speak for several minutes.

Finally, an owl interrupted the near silence.

"So this is where you went when you needed to escape," Holly whispered, as if she didn't want to interrupt the peace.

Leo nodded. "My parents never found me. I sat up here for hours, looking at the stars, and dreamed of being a famous pop singer."

"And now you are," Holly said, a smile in her voice.

"Now I am." She sighed. It sure wasn't as fulfilling as she had thought back then, but she didn't want to spoil this beautiful night by bringing that up again.

Holly put a hand on her thigh, which was bare below the leg of her jean shorts.

A tingle climbed up her leg. *Oh Jesus.* Holly had no idea what she was doing to her. She just wanted to provide comfort.

Leo cleared her throat and focused on the conversation. "Sometimes, when the need to get out became too bad, I took a map and a flashlight up here and looked up which roads would get me to New York."

"Is it really so bad here?" Holly asked quietly.

Now that Leo's eyes had adjusted to the moonlight, she could make out Holly's features. She was looking at her with an almost vulnerable expression, as if Leo's negative opinion of their hometown hurt her.

"No," she surprised herself by saying, "it hasn't been so bad this time."

Their gazes met and held. A slow smile spread over Holly's face. In the low light provided by the moon and stars, her blue eyes appeared to be a silvery gray, and Leo imagined that she could see them shining with relief or happiness or both.

Silence settled over them for a bit.

Leo let her thoughts drift, partly to the past, partly to the present, enjoying this moment with Holly. *This is so ridiculously romantic, someone should write a song about it.* She chuckled.

"What?" Holly asked.

"Nothing."

Holly poked her. "Tell me."

"Hey. Don't make me fall."

They paused and stared at each other.

"Off the roof, I meant," Leo said hastily.

"I know what you meant. So why were you laughing?"

"Um, just thinking about the time I scraped my ass bad when I snuck out one night and slid down the roof to go skinny-dipping with Ash." She regarded Holly. "How about you? Did you ever do something stupid like that?"

"No. As you can imagine, I wasn't into skinny-dipping with girls...or boys."

"So you knew you were asexual, even back then?" Leo asked.

"I always knew I was different somehow, but I couldn't say what it was that made me different. I didn't have a word for it for the longest time. I just knew that I didn't fit in."

"It was the same for me."

"Yeah, but I think you figured it out a little faster."

"True. The giant crush I had on Ash was a big clue."

Holly groaned a little. "God, all those high school crushes... My classmates suddenly started to go gaga over someone, and all they wanted to do was hang around the boys or talk about the boys." She shook herself. "It seemed so stupid to me. I felt like I was the only normal one. It took me a while to figure out that it was the other way around—everyone else was normal, and I was the weird one."

"Hey." Leo reached over and took her hand. "You're not weird."

"I know that now, but back then... I was the only one in my class who didn't go on a single date during high school."

Leo entwined their fingers. "I didn't date in high school either." She'd been too hung up on Ash back then. With a rakish grin, she added, "Although I sure made up for that when I moved to New York. I take it you didn't?"

"No. I didn't feel I had anything to make up for. I was too busy with school, friends, and hobbies."

"So Ash...she was your first?" Leo studied their entwined hands, and try as she might, she couldn't imagine the two of them together.

"No. I had a girlfriend before her...and a boyfriend my junior year in college."

Leo stared. "A boyfriend? You?" Somehow, she could imagine that even less—didn't want to imagine it, truth be told.

"It didn't last long, and we only slept with each other once." Holly pulled her knees to her chest and leaned her chin on top.

An almost physical jolt went through Leo, and she jerked their entwined hands. "So you...? I thought... You actually had sex?"

Holly nodded and leaned her cheek on her knees so she could regard Leo while they talked. "That's what you're supposed to be doing in a relationship, right?"

"Only if both people involved want it."

"I wish I'd had a friend back then who told me that. The one college friend I talked to asked me how I could know I didn't like sex if I'd never tried it."

"Jesus." Leo hissed out the word through her teeth. "What bullshit. I knew I didn't want to have sex with men without having to try it first."

"Yeah. I should have listened to my instincts. It was a pretty underwhelming experience. I couldn't believe that was the mind-blowing thing that everyone seemed to be so excited about."

Leo could relate. "My first time wasn't exactly spectacular either. I had no clue what I was doing."

"And the second, third, and fourth time?"

"Well," Leo drawled and winked at her, "let's just say my father was right about one thing: practice does make perfect."

Their laughter drifted through the night air.

"Not for me," Holly said after a while. "When I met Dana my senior year at Mizzou, I fell head over heels and thought I had finally figured it out. Clearly, I was a lesbian and just hadn't been attracted to anyone because I'd been looking at the wrong gender."

"But?" Leo prompted when Holly fell silent.

"It turned out I was confusing sexual and romantic attraction. I really loved Dana, but the sex...meh."

Meh. Leo still found it hard to grasp how anyone could feel that way about sex, especially sex with a person they loved. "Did you...talk to her about it?"

"Oh yeah. We did nothing but talk...or fight about it for most of our relationship. I even ended up going to therapy because I thought something was wrong with me."

"And the therapist didn't tell you otherwise?"

"No. She had never heard of asexuality either. That's the hardest thing about being ace—most people don't know it exists, so you just feel broken."

God, and she had thought she'd felt lonely and isolated when she'd been growing up! Compared to Holly, she'd had it easy. At least she had known other gay people existed. Leo held her hand a little more tightly.

"Finally, Dana and I broke up—or rather she broke up with me. She was convinced that if I really loved her, I'd want her as much as she wanted me."

Leo cradled her hand between both of hers and barely held herself back from lifting it to her mouth to kiss her palm. Never had she wanted to comfort anyone so much. "I'm so sorry."

"It's okay. At least then I finally found out what was going on with me. One night, I went online, typed in something like 'help, I'm not interested in sex,' and came across a description of asexuality. A lot of things suddenly made sense. It was such a relief when I could finally stop trying to be someone I'm not."

"I can imagine." Her head was spinning, and it wasn't because she was up on the roof. She processed what Holly had told her for a while, just listening to the concert of the crickets and the occasional hooting of an owl.

Neither of them let go of the other's hand—or acknowledged the fact that they were still holding hands.

"So," Leo said after a while, "once you knew, did you come out to people as asexual?"

"Not to everyone. With some people, I'd rather let them assume I'm a lesbian—which I am, in a way—than to get into the details with them. I did tell the women I dated, of course." She sighed. "Most of the time, it put a sudden end to any date."

"Is that what happened with Ash?" Leo finally asked the question she had wanted to ask for some time now.

"No. It was different with her. She was completely fine with me being ace—or so she said. But it turned out that wasn't quite true."

A wave of rage gripped Leo so firmly that she started to shake. "Did she...?"

"No," Holly said quickly. "She never openly put any pressure on me, but..." Another sigh escaped her. "She clearly wasn't happy without sex, and I felt like I owed it to her."

"Owed her?" The words nearly blurred together in Leo's haste to get them out. "You don't owe anyone anything if it traumatizes or repulses you!"

Now Holly was the one who took Leo's hand in both of hers so that they ended up in a four-handed clutch. "It's not like that for me, Leo."

"But one of the people in the forum said..."

"Not all people who fall on the ace spectrum are the same, just like not all lesbians are the same. Some asexual people are completely grossed out by the mere thought of sex or even kissing, while others wouldn't mind having sex for their partner's sake, even if they don't get much out of it for themselves."

"Oh." Every time she felt as if she had a good grasp on what asexuality was, she learned something new. "And you're one of those?"

"I'm not repulsed by sex. I just never think about it or crave it. If I hear people groan about how long it's been since they had any, it makes me want to laugh. If I never had sex again in my life, that would be fine with me. But that doesn't mean I find it traumatizing."

Leo scratched her head as she tried to puzzle all the pieces together. They didn't quite seem to fit. "That sounds like it's a take-it-or-leave-it thing for you." When Holly nodded, she asked, "If it is, why would you be willing to give up dating and relationships just to avoid sex?"

Holly looked down at their hands as if trying to figure out which fingers belonged to her and which were Leo's. Or maybe she was trying to find the right words. "It's not sex I'm trying to avoid. Not really. If I'm with a woman I love, I don't mind having sex occasionally. But what I can never give her is a truly passionate response. Women want to be desired. They want to be able to turn me on with just a look or a touch. They want me to take them up against the wall or on the kitchen table because I can't wait until we make it into the bedroom."

Jesus, was it getting hot up here on the roof? Leo freed one hand from their tangle of fingers and discreetly tugged on the crew neck of her T-shirt.

"That's something I can never give them, even if I have sex with them."

At the sadness in Holly's voice, Leo's arousal dwindled away. Her stomach knotted, and she pressed their entwined hands against her belly in an effort to ease that almost painful feeling. "Okay," she rasped out. "I get it now…I think."

"Don't worry if it takes you a while to understand. It took my brother Ethan a couple of years to get it. He was the first person I told after finding out I'm ace, and he promptly told me it was just a phase and I'd grow out of it."

Leo waved her free hand at her. "Hello? You're what? Twenty-nine?"

Holly nodded.

"That would be a mighty long phase. My mother told me the same when I came out to her, but even she seems to get it now that I won't grow out of being a lesbian."

"Well, my brother is a slow learner. He gets it now, for the most part, but after that coming-out experience, and after hearing from a lesbian friend that I just needed to have sex with the right woman, I didn't tell anyone else for a while."

Leo shook her head. "God, people can be assholes."

Holly smiled wryly. "Sad but true. How did your parents react when you came out to them?"

"My mother didn't, for the most part. As I said, she thought it was just a phase, so she didn't take it seriously. My father… He told me he didn't want that kind of lifestyle in his house. After that, we didn't exchange another word. I left the week after."

She hadn't expected to talk about this, but it felt surprisingly good to open up. Holly was so easy to talk to. Why the hell hadn't they been friends growing up? Why had she wasted her time with someone like Ash when she could have spent it with Holly?

Holly gave her a sincere look. "I'm so sorry—sorry that he didn't try to understand and sorry that I judged you for not coming back sooner."

"Maybe I should have. Come back sooner, I mean." At the very least, she would have gotten to know Holly sooner. She looked down at their hands, which were once again cradled together. There was a connection between them that went beyond that visible network of fingers.

Under different circumstances, Leo would have assumed it was attraction—and maybe it was, just one of the other kinds of attraction Holly had mentioned, because it sure seemed as if Holly could feel it too.

Something one-sided wouldn't feel so strong, would it?

"Holly, I…" She tightened her hold on Holly's fingers, struggling for the right words, until Holly let out a quiet groan. Immediately, Leo eased her grip. "I'm sorry. C-can I ask you something?" *Great.* Now she, the woman who'd stayed cool when groupies had thrown their bras at her on stage, was stuttering like a teenager.

Holly nodded, the white of her eyes shimmering in the moonlight as she stared at her.

"If there were no expectations of passion or sex, would you start dating again?"

"There always is—"

"Would you?" Leo asked again with more urgency. She felt as if she couldn't breathe until she had an answer. "Because I really would like to. Date you. No sex. No commitment. Let's just enjoy each other's company while I'm here…and, well, maybe a kiss or two."

A shadow darted across Holly's features. Her brows slammed down as if something Leo had said dismayed her.

"If you enjoy that sort of thing," Leo quickly added. "If you don't, that's fine too."

Holly's tongue flicked out and licked her bottom lip. "I do, but… Leo, we can enjoy each other's company the way we have, as friends."

Leo didn't look away. "Then that's all you're feeling? Just friendly feelings for me?"

Holly's eyes said something else. She squeezed them shut as if she didn't want Leo to see. "No, but..."

"Then kiss me. Right here, under the stars."

An unexpected smile flickered across Holly's face, easing the tension a little. She opened her eyes. "Are you getting poetic, Ms. Songstress?"

"You inspire me," Leo said, and it wasn't a line.

"Leontyne?" Leo's mother called from the window. "Holly? Where on earth are you?"

Dammit. Leo suppressed a groan. Her mother had the worst timing in the universe.

"Oh shit," Holly whispered and huddled against her.

Leo leaned even closer, allowing herself to enjoy the press of Holly's body against hers, and whispered back, "Don't worry. She can't see us."

And she was right. After grumbling something they couldn't understand, Leo's mother closed the window.

"Oh no." Holly's eyes widened. "Now we're trapped out here."

"No. I told you, I know a spot where we can slide down the roof and climb onto the porch."

"The same spot where you scraped your ass as a teenager?" Holly asked.

Oops. She gave her a sheepish grin. "Um, yeah."

Holly sighed. "Yippee-ki-yay. Okay, lead the way. We should get back to make sure your parents are okay."

"Ass-scraping, here we come," Leo muttered and let go of Holly's hands to crawl up the roof and down on the other side.

But Holly stopped her with a quick touch to her shoulder. "Leo?"

"Hmm?" She turned back around.

Holly took an audible breath. "I..." She shook her head as if giving up the search for words and instead raised up on her knees.

Leo didn't dare move or even breathe or blink, afraid to startle Holly away and lose this precious moment.

Holly took her face between her hands and looked into her eyes from only inches away. She leaned forward until her warm breath fanned over Leo's mouth.

Oh God, please...

Then her silent prayer was answered. Holly's lips touched hers in a kiss that was almost chaste: no tongue, no wandering hands, nothing but their lips caressing each other. It was slow and soft, all tenderness and harmony—and it was the most perfect kiss Leo had ever experienced.

Finally, she felt as if someone was kissing her, just her, not her Grammys or her money or her body that had been on display in music videos.

Everything around her disappeared, except for Holly's soft mouth and her gentle hands, which cradled her face, rooting her in place.

The kiss ended, but they lingered with their lips just a fraction of an inch apart. When they finally pulled back, they stared at each other.

A smile spread over Holly's face, and Leo couldn't help mirroring it. She wanted to say so much, but it was as if that single kiss had taken away her ability to speak. All she could do was look into Holly's silvery-blue eyes in the moonlight.

"There." Holly exhaled and slowly took her hands off Leo's cheeks, sliding her fingers away until only her fingertips lingered and then dropped away. "I know that wasn't exactly—"

Leo dipped her head forward and touched her lips to Holly's again, just for a moment, to stop her from saying whatever she'd been about to say. "It was perfect." Her voice sounded raspy. "Thank you."

Holly's smile brightened even more, if that was possible.

They knelt on the roof, facing each other, until Leo remembered that they had been about to climb down. She still felt the warmth of Holly's lips on hers as she guided her down the roof. Her limbs were a bit shaky. *Jesus, this isn't the time to go all weak-kneed!* She could imagine the headlines in the tabloids if she fell off and broke a bone or two.

When she reached the edge of the roof, she turned. "Here's the trick. If you hold on to the gutter and swing inward a little, your feet will be on top of the porch rail. You won't even have to jump."

Holly swallowed audibly. "Um, you do know that I'm a nurse, not a circus performer, don't you?"

You're a magician, Leo wanted to say. She had kissed plenty of women in her life, most of them much more passionately, but somehow, Holly's brief, gentle kiss had managed to get to her in a way that the others hadn't. But she bit back the words. Since when was she the sappy type?

"You'll be fine. I promise. It's not as hard as it sounds."

"Okay," Holly croaked out.

"Don't worry. I'll go first and guide you down." She turned so she was lying on the roof on her belly. "You won't scrape your ass if you do it this way."

Carefully, she slid down until her feet were braced against the gutter. Something scratched along her bare shin, making her flinch. She took a deep breath and let one leg dangle down. Now came the moment that she had to let go with her hands and slide down so she could grip the edge of the roof. Last time she'd done this, she had hesitated forever, but she didn't want Holly to think she was a coward, so she let go.

"Leo!"

She grabbed the gutter with both hands. "I've got it." Slowly, she lowered herself down. *Uff.* Good thing her personal trainer had her do pull-ups. Her bare feet found the top of the porch railing, and she eased herself down until she could jump to the porch.

There she stood, one shaking hand pressed to her chest for a moment. *I'm getting too old for this.* But being up on the roof with Holly had definitely been worth it.

"Okay, I'm down," she called up to Holly. "Now you."

Something scraped over the shingles.

Leo held her breath. This was even more nerve-racking than sliding down the roof herself. "Uh, maybe I should go back up to my room and open the window for you."

But Holly's white sneakers were already appearing over the edge, followed by her bare legs.

Leo gripped them tightly and guided her down.

With a soft thud, Holly slid down, right into Leo's waiting arms. Leo's eyes fluttered shut. The scent of summer, vanilla-and-coconut shampoo, and something that was just Holly teased her nostrils. God, she wanted to kiss her again so bad... *No. Don't spoil it. Wait until she tells you what she wants.*

Holly cuddled against her for a second or two, then squeezed her hips once before letting go and stepping back. "Phew. Okay. We're down." She checked the baby-monitor receiver in her back pocket. "Now how do we get back inside?"

"Easy. My mother keeps a spare key beneath one of the flowerpots. At least she did fourteen years ago." She lifted one of the pots and peered beneath. Nothing. Frowning, she tried another—and this time, she found what she was looking for. "Ta-da!" She held it up triumphantly.

Apparently, her parents still hadn't invested in a motion-sensitive porch light, but now it worked in their favor. No light flared on as they crossed the porch. As quietly as possible, Leo slid the key into the lock.

Holly waited right behind her, one hand on Leo's hip. Her fingers radiated a warmth that wasn't merely physical.

Just as Leo was about to turn the key, the door opened from the inside. Both of them stumbled back.

Leo squinted into the sudden bright light and made out her mother's back-lit shape in the doorframe. *Shit.*

"Heavens, Leontyne! Holly! What are the two of you doing outside?"

"Um..." They looked at each other, then back at Leo's mom, and ducked their heads like two teenagers who'd been caught smoking weed. "Uh, just catching a bit of fresh air before bed," Leo stammered out.

Her mother narrowed her eyes at them.

Before she could ask another question, Leo beat her to it, "What are *you* doing up?"

"I heard some noise up on the roof and wanted to check it out. Now that your father...that he can no longer do it, I'm the weird-noises checker in the family." She lifted the flashlight in her hand with a brave smile.

"Um, I don't think you have to do that, Mom. It was probably just a squirrel or something."

"A squirrel?" Her mother looked at her as if she doubted her sanity.

"Oh, yeah," Holly said. "They can make a lot of noise, especially if there's more than one."

Leo's mother still looked doubtful, but she turned and stepped back inside. When they had returned the key to the flowerpot and followed her in, she closed the door and put the flashlight back onto the hall table. "Good night, you two. Don't stay up too long."

"We won't," Leo said. "Night."

As her mother climbed the stairs to the master bedroom, her quiet mutter drifted back to them. "That must have been an awfully big squirrel."

Leo pressed a hand to her mouth so she wouldn't burst out laughing.

The bedroom door clicked shut upstairs.

"Squirrel, huh?" The dimples in Holly's cheeks made an appearance as she gave her an affectionate smile.

Leo shrugged. "It was the first thing that came to mind. Like I said, I never got caught before, so I'm not used to having to make up excuses."

"Then maybe our second date should be someplace less adventurous," Holly said.

"So we're doing this?" Leo asked, searching her face. "Dating?"

Holly's smile gave way to a serious expression. "If I think about it tomorrow morning, in broad daylight, I'll probably think this," she waved her hand back and forth between them, "is a really bad idea."

"Then let's not do it—overthink it, I mean." She tried to avoid it too. For once, she would just go with her gut feeling. "Let's take it one day at a time."

Holly blew out a breath. "All right."

Leo offered her arm. "Come on. I'll walk you home." She nodded in the direction of the guest room.

Another smile chased away the conflicted expression on Holly's face. She lightly settled her hand on Leo's arm, and they climbed the stairs, both of them skipping the creaking steps. In front of Holly's bedroom, they paused and stood facing each other.

With every other date, Leo would have ended the evening with a kiss, but Holly wasn't like every other woman—and even though Leo couldn't wait to kiss her again, she decided that was a good thing. "Good night. Sleep well."

"Good night." Holly put her hand on the doorknob but then turned back around. "Thank you."

"What for?"

"For showing me your secret spot."

Leo's first instinct was to say, *Stick with me, and I'll show you so much more.* But flashing her sexy pop-star grin and hiding behind lines like that wasn't going to cut it with Holly. "I'm glad I did."

"Me too." Holly's hand lingered on Leo's arm for another moment, then she opened the door and, with one last soft smile, was gone.

Alone, Leo stood in the hall and stared at the closed door. After a while, she gave herself a mental kick and went to her own room. She sank onto the bed but knew she wouldn't get any sleep tonight. Not after that kiss and their conversation.

Was she really doing this? Dating an asexual woman? Hell, dating a woman from Fair Oaks! It was completely crazy. She scrubbed her palms over her face. *One day at a time. No overthinking, remember?*

She dangled one hand out of bed and fished for her laptop, which she'd put on the floor earlier. Time for some more research into the complex topic of asexuality.

Chapter 13

HOLLY ENTERED THE KITCHEN WITH some trepidation. Had she really kissed Leo last night—and even agreed to date her? *What the hell were you thinking? You know this won't end well.*

But try as she might, she couldn't regret it too much. That hour up on the roof had been magical. For once, she had been able to talk about the past without hurting or feeling inadequate. Leo had been so fierce when she had defended her—and so gentle when she'd kissed her. She hadn't spoiled it by trying for more. There had been no hint of demand, as if Leo had enjoyed the kiss for what it was instead of seeing it as just an appetizer.

Thinking about it made her want to kiss Leo again, and that had rarely happened to her in the past.

"Morning, Holly," Sharon said from the stove. "Something wrong with your mouth?"

"Huh?"

"You keep touching it."

Holly stared at her traitorous fingers, which were indeed resting on her lips. She snatched her hand away. "Um, no, just some…uh, toothpaste." God, she was as bad a liar as Leo with her squirrel excuse.

Speaking of Leo… She looked around.

She had gotten Gil dressed earlier, and now he was waiting for breakfast at the table, but Leo was nowhere to be seen.

"Where's Leo?" she asked before she could stop herself.

Sharon turned off the stove with a flick of her wrist and carried the stack of pancakes to the table. They both sat. "She's still sleeping."

"Want me to go up and wake her?" At least it would give them a moment alone, even though Holly wasn't sure what she would say to Leo.

"Oh no. Let her sleep. I'll make her some fresh pancakes later. When I peeked in on her a few minutes ago, she was dead to the world." Sharon poured them all coffee and slid Holly's mug across the table toward her. "That squirrel on the roof probably kept her up all night."

The first sip of coffee went down the wrong pipe. Holly started coughing and gasping for breath.

Gil put his fork down and thumped her on the back with his good hand. "Okay?"

"Yeah," Holly rasped out. "I'm fine. Thanks."

He patted her back again, just for good measure, before returning to his food.

Holly inhaled and exhaled deeply and took a more careful sip of coffee, hoping no one would mention squirrels again.

By the time breakfast was done and they had cleared the table, Leo still hadn't made an appearance downstairs. Holly didn't know if she should be disappointed or grateful. Maybe it was better this way. She needed time to think—time away from Leo and the house. Thankfully, she had the rest of the day off, so she said goodbye to Gil and Sharon and headed out.

But instead of driving home, she ended up in front of her mother's practice for her daily cuddle fix. That, of course, made her think of cuddling up to Leo behind the chimney last night.

Just as she had settled down next to the whelping box, covered from hip to toe in puppies and kittens, the door opened and her mother stepped in.

"Hey, sweetie." She pressed a kiss to Holly's head and picked up one of the puppies. "Susan just told me you came in. What are you doing here? I thought you had the night shift."

"I did."

"Then why aren't you home in bed?"

Holly rubbed her cheek against the orange tabby's soft fur. "Gil had a good night. I only had to get up twice, so I was able to get some sleep." Or she would have, if she hadn't lain awake, reliving that wonderful kiss and each word they had exchanged up on the roof and worrying about where it might lead—and where it wouldn't.

Just because Leo was willing to go without sex for the time being didn't mean she was in it for the long haul. Quite the opposite. She had never made a secret of the fact that she planned to go back to New York. That was why she could so easily agree to dating without sex. It was easy to go without for a while, since Leo knew she would soon return to her more-than-willing groupies.

Clearly, there was no happy ending in store for them, and she would only end up getting hurt if she let herself believe otherwise.

Her mother watched her with a concerned gaze. "You know, you could get one for yourself."

Holly blinked up at her. "A happy ending?"

"Excuse me?"

Heat rose up her neck, and she buried her face deeper into the kitten's fur, hoping to hide her blush. "Um, nothing. I was just thinking of…um, fairy tales."

Laugh lines fanned around her mother's eyes and mouth. "I was talking about a kitten or a puppy—although I'm all for you getting a happy ending too."

Holly shook her head. "I'm gone much of the time, so I don't think that would be fair to the little guy."

"Or girl," her mother added, repeating what Holly had always said when her mother urged her to date.

They smiled at each other.

"Or girl," she repeated, suppressing a sigh. Wasn't it ironic? Now that her mother had finally accepted that her daughter might end up with a woman, Holly had realized that it wasn't going to happen, at least not long-term, and certainly not with Leo.

Two days later, Leo set out on a mission. She wanted to take Holly out on a date, but if she took her to a restaurant, they would be interrupted by people asking for autographs. Plus they wouldn't even make it to the main course before the entire town knew about their date. By now, the Fair Oaks rumor mill was probably already buzzing because they had gotten burgers together last week.

Not that she was ashamed of going out with Holly, but for now, she wanted it to be just the two of them. A picnic at the creek seemed perfect for that.

After putting everything she needed into the shopping cart, she steered it around the corner toward the cash register. She had hoped that Jenny wouldn't be working, but no such luck.

Her old classmate was manning the register. She waved cheerfully. "Hi, Leo."

"Hi, Jenny." Leo focused on unloading her groceries, hoping to escape small talk.

"We missed you the last two Saturdays," Jenny said. "You really should hang out with the gang again."

"Um, yeah, I was...busy." *Spending time with Holly.*

"I totally get it. When my mom got sick, I barely had time to go out too. How are your folks doing?"

"Fine, considering," Leo said.

"Your dad seemed to be doing a little better when I dropped by for a visit last week."

Leo looked up. Jenny had visited him lately? It must have been while Leo had been out on a run or getting scones with Holly.

Oh, scones. She made a mental note to get some for the picnic too.

"I bet he's glad you're home," Jenny said.

Leo gave a noncommittal hum.

Jenny reached for the first item, searched for the bar code, and scanned it painfully slowly.

Great. Leo resisted the urge to tap her foot. By the time Jenny had scanned all the goods, there would be mold growing on them.

"Are you getting settled back in at home?" Jenny asked as she reached for item number two, a bottle of red wine.

"Um, there's not much settling in to do. I'm only staying for a few weeks, remember?"

Jenny scanned the wine, nodded down at the rest of the groceries, and chuckled. "Well, this should hold you until then."

Leo regarded her pile of food. Admittedly, it could feed an entire army, not just two people. Maybe she had overdone it a little, but she had wanted to make sure she bought everything Holly might like. "It's, um, for a picnic."

"Oh, that's such a nice idea!" Jenny clapped her hands. "The weather is perfect for it too."

Leo hoped Holly would think so too.

"You forgot the cheese, though," Jenny said.

"Um, excuse me?"

Jenny waved at the bag of grapes she was scanning. "You've got grapes, but no cheese. They go well together."

Damn, she was right. "Can I run back and get some?"

"Sure, I'll scan the rest in the meantime."

Leaving the shopping cart behind, Leo turned on her heel and jogged toward the aisle with the dairy products.

"Get the smoked Gouda," Jenny's voice trailed after her. "Holly likes that one."

Leo slid to a stop in front of the dairy case. Had Jenny just said...? She found the smoked Gouda, grabbed a Camembert and some tiny mozzarella balls too, just in case, and slowly made her way back to the register. "Who says I'm sharing this with Holly?"

"Well," Jenny shrugged, "you two are the only, um, lesbians in town, so..."

Yeah, if you don't count Ash...and maybe a few others who're too scared to come out.

"And you did buy the smoked Gouda," Jenny finished with a smile that said she was impressed with her own detective skills. "Are the two of you... you know...dating?"

What was she supposed to say now? Leo had always tried to keep her private life out of the public eye. She certainly wasn't about to reveal her brand-new dating relationship to the town gossip queen. She and Holly hadn't talked about telling people. Hell, it was all so new and fragile that they could barely cope with it when it was just the two of them.

But after what Ash had done to Holly, Leo didn't want to outright deny being involved with her either. Holly deserved better than that.

"That's between Holly and me," she finally said.

Jenny squealed. "I'm so happy for you guys!"

Leo blinked. "Hey, I didn't say we're dating, and I certainly didn't say we're ready to print wedding invitations, so cut out that happy dance!" She looked around to see if they were attracting attention, but for now, they seemed to be alone in the store.

"Ah, come on, Leo. You know you can tell me. I'm not the enemy here."

That much was true. Jenny had always seemed like the quintessential small-town girl to her. The horizon of her experience ended at the city limits. But she didn't seem upset at the thought of Holly and her dating. In fact, she seemed pleased, and Leo hadn't expected that.

She rubbed her neck. "I know. Don't take it personally, but if you're in the limelight all the time, you learn to keep your private life private."

"Don't worry." Jenny waved a package of cookies. "I won't say a word. I'm just glad Holly has finally found someone."

Leo swallowed against the sudden lump in her throat. Not knowing what to say, she just watched as Jenny scanned the rest of her items.

For once, she was glad when another customer came up behind her and asked for an autograph and a picture.

When he was busy checking out the photo Jenny had snapped on his cell phone, she quickly put her bagged groceries into the cart and pushed them to the door.

"Enjoy your picnic!" Jenny called after her.

"Uh, thanks." Leo stumbled to her rental car and shook her head to clear it. What a surreal experience. She felt as if she'd stepped into the Twilight Zone.

Maybe Holly had been right. Maybe people in this town could change— at least some of them. Too bad her father wasn't among them.

Leo found her parents in the living room, where her mother was helping her father put together a puzzle. It looked as if it was going to be a violin with a rose resting across the strings.

Every time she saw her father like this, helpless and wheelchair-bound, she had to look away. Rough emotions clutched at her insides, but she didn't want to focus on them long enough to identify what exactly she was feeling. "Mom? Do you mind if I take over your kitchen for a while?"

Her mother looked up with wide eyes. "You want to cook?"

"Hey, I made breakfast several times since I've been back. I'm not that bad of a cook. Besides, I just want to prepare some…uh, snacks."

"Of course. Go ahead and let me know if you need any help."

"I can manage, thanks." At least she hoped so. Her area of expertise was the concert stage, not the kitchen, but she was determined to give it her best.

An hour later, as Leo was putting a lid on the bowl of potato salad, her mother peeked into the kitchen, looking as if she expected to find a battlefield.

But Leo had cleaned up as she went, not wanting to create even more work for her already-stressed mother.

"Oh. That looks wonderful." Her mother entered the kitchen and watched Leo pierce mozzarella balls and cherry tomatoes onto skewers. "Is this…um, for you and…and Holly?"

Wow. Leo put the skewers aside and turned. Was the Fair Oaks rumor mill working so quickly, or had her mother suspected all along? Or maybe she thought it was just a picnic between friends. Her mother's powers of denial had always been impressive. If she didn't want to deal with something, she ignored it so completely that it ceased to exist.

"Yes," Leo said carefully.

"That's…nice," her mother said, just as carefully.

This was one thing that definitely hadn't changed. They were still tiptoeing around each other and the topic of Leo's sexual orientation. She heaved a sigh.

Her mother cleared her throat but then didn't say anything. Instead, she turned toward the counter, away from Leo, took a cherry tomato, and slid it on another skewer, followed by a mozzarella ball.

So the conversation was over, and the topic would be ignored—again. Leo wasn't sure if she should be relieved or angry. She popped a tomato into her mouth and chewed forcefully. "You don't need to help, you know?"

"I don't mind. We barely spend any time together, so this," her mother waved her hand in a circle that included Leo, herself, and the kitchen, "is nice."

It was true, Leo had to admit, if only to herself. Since she'd been back, she had spent more time with Holly than with her parents. Maybe she should make more of an effort to patch up her relationship with them, but being with Holly was so much easier. Despite their differences, they seemed to understand each other in a way that she could never hope to achieve with her parents.

Her mother put the finished skewer into the container with the ones Leo had already done. She studied them as if they held the answers to all the secrets of the universe—or at least the winning lottery numbers. "So… Holly and you…?" She peeked at Leo, then back at the skewers. "Are you friends or…?"

"We're dating," Leo said.

Her mother turned and leaned against the counter as if she needed the support.

Leo braced herself for what was to come.

"She's a wonderful girl, you know?"

"She's a woman, Mom. We both are. We're not teenagers, and this is not a phase that we'll grow out of."

"I…I know. I've known it for a while now, and I'm okay with it." Her mother glanced at the floor. "Not overjoyed, mind you, but okay. Holly really is a wonderful g…woman."

Now it was Leo's turn to lean against the counter for support as her knees seemed to transform into overcooked spaghetti. She opened her mouth, but it took a while before she could make her vocal cords work. "You're okay with it…with me being gay?"

Her mother nodded. "Having Holly around…getting to know her really helped. Her entire family is very supportive of her. I think Holly telling everyone about her…that she's gay, it brought them even closer, and it occurred to me that's how it should have been with us too."

"Why…why didn't you say anything?"

"When?" Her mother looked at her with damp eyes. "When was I supposed to say anything? You called so seldom that I didn't want to take the chance of making you stop altogether by bringing it up."

Leo folded her arms across her churning stomach. Her mother had worked through her issues, and she had missed it—would have kept missing it…if not for her father's stroke. "What…what about Dad? Does he…? Is he…okay with it too?"

"Why don't you ask him yourself?" her mother said.

She shook her head. "You know I could never talk to him. Certainly not now. The few times he tried to talk to me, he either insulted me or I didn't understand a word."

"Maybe you need to try harder."

Now they were back on familiar territory—that gentle reproach in her mother's voice was something she had heard a lot in the past. "I tried, Mom. You know that. I tried so hard to live up to his expectations…" She flicked a bit of lettuce from the sandwiches into the sink. "I spent my entire childhood doing nothing else. But whatever I did, it was never good enough. I was never good enough. I'm done trying."

"Leontyne…" Her mother stepped closer and reached for her hand.

Leo pulled away. "No, Mom. Thank you for accepting me. It means a lot. But I can't let him run my life. I need to be my own person, not a carbon copy of him."

Her mother smiled, but it was full of sadness, not joy. "Then maybe you should stop being just as stubborn as he is." Without another word, she walked out of the kitchen.

Leo stared after her. *Damn.* Her mother had changed too. In the past, she had never talked to her like this. She had been the peacekeeper of the family, gently mediating between Leo and her father, but never voicing an opinion or, God forbid, criticizing her husband in any way.

Now she had done both, and Leo had no idea what to do with it.

The Velcro made a ripping sound as Holly removed the blood pressure cuff from Gil's arm. She smoothed down the sleeve of his T-shirt before jotting down the numbers. "Hmm. Your blood pressure is a little high today."

He craned his neck to see the numbers. "Die?" he asked with a twinkle in his eyes.

She smiled. At times like this, when his sense of humor shone through, he reminded her of Leo. "No, you're not going to die. It's not dangerously high, just something to keep an eye on. You probably just had too much excitement."

He snorted and waved his good hand toward the stereo and the view from the window, which were his main entertainment.

She'd been talking about the fact that Leo was back home, but he seemed as determined to ignore the elephant in the room as his daughter was.

"I'll call the doctor, and we'll have him come in and take a look at you tomorrow, okay? Maybe your meds need to be adjusted." She put the blood pressure cuff back into its case. "How about a nap now?"

When he nodded, she helped him transfer from his wheelchair to the bed. It was too warm for the covers, so she tugged a thin sheet over him, more for comfort than warmth. "Sleep tight. I'll see you tomorrow with the doc—and pictures of the puppies and kittens."

Her shift was over, so by the time he woke, she would be long gone.

When she reached the door, he said, "Hol...Holly?"

She blinked and turned around. He rarely used names. For some reason, they seemed harder to access for him than other words. Apparently, the promised photos of the puppies and kittens had motivated him to try harder. "Yes?"

"Um...please. No." He shook his head in frustration. "Uh...thanks."

She smiled at him from across the room. That wasn't a word he used often either. "You're very welcome. See you tomorrow."

She left the room and went in search of Sharon to hand over the baby-monitor receiver and give her a short report. Noises came from the kitchen, so she headed that way.

But instead of Sharon, it was Leo who was slicing a mango and some strawberries.

Holly paused in the doorway and watched her for a minute.

Leo walked back and forth between the counter and the sink to wash more fruit. Each step looked as if she were dancing. Holly had never cared much for Leo's overly provocative music videos, but this...this she could watch forever.

Sunlight streaming in through the kitchen window made Leo's honey-blonde hair shine like gold. It was tied back into a loose ponytail so it wouldn't get in the way while she worked.

Her long fingers, which had flowed over the piano keys so gracefully, handled the knife in a slightly awkward way that told Holly she didn't spend much time in the kitchen. Well, she had mentioned a nutritionist, so maybe she had a personal chef too.

Holly struggled against the impulse to join her in the kitchen, guide her hands, and show her how it was done.

Stop it. What she needed to do was tell Leo she had thought about it all day yesterday and had reconsidered. Their lives were too different, so they were unlikely to find happiness together—not that Leo was looking for long-term happiness with her. It was better to end it now, before Holly got any more involved.

Leo turned, and their gazes met immediately. An almost shy smile spread over Leo's face and crinkled the edges of her olive-green eyes, so unlike the fake, sexy grin she flashed on TV.

Holly's heart gave a little stutter.

"Hey." Leo ran both palms down her jean shorts, then combed her fingers through her disheveled hair. "Is your shift over?"

"Yes. As soon as I find your mom for our handover. If you have a minute afterward…" Holly forced herself to continue, speaking through the lump in her throat. "I'd like to talk to you."

"Of course. I'd love to spend some time with you. In fact… I got a little surprise for you." A hint of a flush covered Leo's cheeks as she pointed to a large basket full of Tupperware containers. "I thought we could have a picnic."

"You prepared a picnic?"

"Yes. I thought it might be nicer than taking you to a restaurant. More privacy. Um, not that we need privacy for anything, of course, but it's nicer to talk at the creek and all."

Aww. She was cute when she got all flustered and started to ramble. Holly couldn't stop the tiny smile tugging at her lips.

"All I need to do is finish the fruit salad and we can go. So, what do you say? Are you in the mood? Uh, for a picnic, I mean." Leo's blush deepened, and she looked at Holly like one of the puppies hoping for a treat.

God, how could she tell her it was not a good idea now, after Leo had gone to all this trouble and was looking at her with this hopeful expression? She couldn't resist that look from one of the puppies, and she certainly couldn't say no when Leo wore it either.

Well, she could have that conversation with her during the picnic. Leo was right, after all—there was more privacy at the creek.

"All right," she finally said. "You put the finishing touches on the fruit salad, and I'll go find your mom."

They strolled along the path in silence. Leo shifted the handle of the picnic basket to the bend of her other arm, freeing the one closest to Holly, and took her hand.

The move startled Holly, and she couldn't hide a tiny flinch.

Leo immediately let go. "I'm sorry. I didn't mean to—"

"No. No. It's okay. Really. It just surprised me for a moment." Holly reached for her hand and held it firmly, not letting her pull away again, even as she scolded herself for it. Conflicting desires wrestled each other for several seconds; then she bargained with herself: she would allow herself to enjoy these last few moments with Leo. But once they reached their spot at the creek...

"Are you sure?" Leo asked.

"I like holding hands." She entwined their fingers. The rasp of the calluses on Leo's fingertips against her knuckles tickled a little, making her smile. "I'm just not used to it. I've never held anyone's hand, at least not here in Fair Oaks. Ash didn't want to draw attention."

Leo let out a low growl. "You know, the longer I'm back, the more I start to wonder what I ever saw in her."

The protective fire in Leo's eyes made her feel good. "She has her good sides too. She's intelligent and independent and has a great sense of humor."

"True. But the same could be said about you...and so much more." Leo squeezed her fingers. "So, what else do you like, besides holding hands, I mean?"

Holly peeked over and met Leo's gaze. "I like hugs." She hummed a little at the thought of embracing Leo, burying her face against her shoulder, and breathing in her scent. Another voice in her head screamed at her, *Stop talking like this! You wanted to break things off, remember, not give her pointers!* But Leo's hand felt good in hers, so she allowed herself a moment of fantasizing. "I also like backrubs and cuddling and soft caresses."

Golden sparks seemed to light up Leo's irises. "Hmm, I like that too. What about kissing? What we did up on the roof...you liked that, right?"

"Kissing is fine." She allowed herself to fantasize about kissing Leo for a moment or two and felt her cheeks grow hot. "Actually, it's more than fine." While it might have been a sexual act for some people, she enjoyed it on an entirely sensual level—at least most of the time.

Leo stopped in the middle of the path and studied her. "But?"

Holly sighed. "Sometimes, it's hard for me to enjoy it."

"Why?"

"With the right partner, I could kiss for hours, but I know it doesn't work like that for allosexual people."

"Allosexual?"

Holly looked left and right, making sure they were still alone in the park. "Someone like you. Someone who isn't asexual. You're used to kissing leading to something…well, more, and I can't fully relax into it if I know any kind of affection will inevitably lead to sex."

"It won't," Leo said.

If only it were that simple. It was tempting, so very tempting to let herself believe it, but Holly knew better.

They started walking again.

Before she could find the courage to break things off, the bench in the middle of the park came into view. Someone was sitting on it.

"Hi, Mr. Gillespie," Holly said to the old man enjoying the sun. "Nice day, isn't it?"

Mr. Gillespie didn't answer, too occupied staring at their entwined fingers.

Leo didn't let go, clearly not ashamed to be seen with her. "Downright beautiful," she added with a hint of defiance.

Finally, Mr. Gillespie inclined his head in a grudging nod. "Yeah, it kinda is."

They walked on until they came to their spot at the edge of the park, out of sight of Mr. Gillespie. While Leo spread a blanket over the flat rock next to the creek, Holly stood frozen at the realization that they already had a place they considered *their spot*.

Leo tugged Holly down next to her in the middle of the blanket and began to unpack and open containers. Soon, they were surrounded by tomato-mozzarella skewers, grapes, different cheeses, olives, potato salad, fruit salad, French bread, BLT sandwiches, scones, and cookies.

"I think I have everything the heart desires." Leo presented her bounty with a proud sweep of her hand. "What would you like?"

That was a loaded question. Her heart desired more than what was offered on this blanket. *Do it. Do it now.* "Leo…"

"Look, I even have LGBTA sandwiches." Leo held out one of the BLT sandwiches.

For a moment, Holly let herself be distracted from the inevitable. "You mean BLT sandwiches, right?"

"Nope. This is a LGBTA sandwich. It's got lettuce, garlic mayo, bacon, tomato, and avocado slices. I wanted to make it an LGBTQIA sandwich, but I couldn't find any ingredients starting with Q or I." Leo shrugged. "But at least it's got the A, so it's an asexual-inclusive sandwich."

Holly took the sandwich, but the giant lump in her throat prevented her from taking a bite. Why the heck did Leo have to be so adorable right now? She already felt like an ass for changing her mind about them.

Leo's cell phone started to ring.

Should she be angry or relieved at the interruption, which gave her a few more minutes before she had to break it off? Holly wasn't sure.

Leo pulled the cell phone from the back pocket of her jean shorts and glanced at the display. A scowl appeared on her face. "It's my manager—again. He thinks I'll come back sooner if he keeps nagging me every day."

"Go ahead. Take the call."

But Leo rejected the call and put the cell phone away. "No. It's not important. I'll call him back later."

If circumstances had been different—if the two of them had been different—Leo might have been the perfect woman for her.

"So, where were we?" Leo held up a bottle of wine. "I hope you like red."

Holly pinched the bridge of her nose between her thumb and index finger. She couldn't wait any longer, or she might lose her nerve. "I think we should talk."

A wrinkle appeared between Leo's brows. She put the bottle of wine down. "What's wrong?"

"I don't think this is going to work."

Leo swept her gaze over the blanket. The wrinkle on her forehead deepened.

"I'm not talking about the picnic," Holly said. "I'm talking about us. I'm sorry, Leo. I know I agreed to date you, but I've thought about it and I don't think it would work."

Leo looked as if Holly had thrown the sandwich in her face. The joy had gone out of her eyes, like a light being turned off. "Why? I thought you liked me…liked spending time with me."

Her expression was stony, but the tiny tremor in her voice really got to Holly. "I do. I really do, but that's the problem. If I'm not careful, I could easily develop feelings for you." Admitting it made her feel like a knight who had taken off all armor and dropped her shield in the middle of battle. "But in a week or two, you'll be gone, back to New York or some other big city."

Leo didn't say anything for quite some time. She stared out over the creek. "You…you could come with me," she said after a while, her voice very quiet and a bit scratchy.

Holly swallowed. She hadn't expected that. Then she shook her head. It wasn't a realistic offer. "I don't think I'm made for the big city. Even if I were, we're not at that point in our relationship yet."

"How are we supposed to ever get there if you break it off now?" Leo massaged her forehead. "Listen, I don't have all of the answers. All I know is that I really like you, and I want to spend more time with you. Where does that leave us?"

"I don't know. There's just so much working against us. Even without the long-distance thing, relationships between allosexuals and asexual people rarely work out."

"Some do. I came across people in one of the forums who say they're very happy together."

"Yeah. It can happen. But these couples are in a very different position than we are. They don't live in different cities…and different worlds. Those couples are fully committed to making it work." She forced herself to look Leo in the eyes. "You don't honestly expect me to believe that you are too, after just one kiss, do you?"

Leo stared at her, then glanced away. "Um…"

Holly hadn't expected her to say *yes*. She wouldn't have believed her if she had.

"Well, technically, it was two kisses," Leo mumbled.

156

"You really think that makes much of a difference in our situation? You know, sometimes..." Holly squeezed her eyes shut but then opened them again and forced herself to face the truth, no matter how much it hurt. "Sometimes, I can't help thinking that maybe the reason you're so eager to spend time with me is to avoid having to deal with your father."

Leo plopped onto her ass from her kneeling position as if Holly had slapped her. "Jesus, Holly. Is that really what you think?" She looked so hurt that an urge to pull her into her arms and hold her overcame Holly.

She fought it. "I'm not sure what to think anymore. I've never met anyone like you. You're so...so understanding...so willing to embrace my asexuality."

"I wasn't aware that's a bad thing," Leo said.

"It's not. But...maybe it's just my own insecurities talking, but...a part of me can't help wondering if you're welcoming my asexuality because if there's no sex, it won't be a real relationship, so it will be easier to walk away from me...from us, when the time comes."

Leo grabbed the nearest object—the bottle of red—and hurled it away. Instead of shattering on the rocks, it splashed into the water and disappeared from view. "Just because I'm not asexual doesn't mean sex is what makes a relationship real for me. I've had sex with people without it meaning anything. Why wouldn't the opposite be possible?"

"It is for me, but..."

Leo jumped up. "You know what? Maybe you're right. It wouldn't work. Enjoy the picnic. I need a fucking drink, and the only alcohol I brought is in the creek." She stormed away before Holly could answer.

Chapter 14

LEO STOMPED PAST MR. GILLESPIE, WHO still sat on the bench. Her earlier comment to him about what a beautiful day it was now seemed like a cruel joke. She thought about just going home, but she wasn't in the mood to face her mother's inevitable questions, so she continued on to the bar and grill.

She hadn't even reached it when her phone rang.

It was Saul again.

"Not now," she said without a greeting.

"This is getting ridiculous, Jenna."

No, what was ridiculous was him insisting on calling her by her stage name. "I said not now."

"It's been nearly four weeks. *Four weeks!*"

"So what? I haven't taken one goddamn vacation in a dozen years."

"So what?" Saul repeated, his voice an incredulous squeak. "The record execs are getting impatient. Your fans probably think you're in rehab. It's only a matter of time until the paparazzi find you in your little hideaway town. And the producers of *A Star is Born* will pick another judge if you don't sign the contract soon."

Leo paused in front of the bar's door, and the memory of how she had run into Holly the last time she had stood there washed over her. "I don't care about the execs or the paparazzi or that contract," she said slowly, emphasizing every word. "I need this time away. I need it, Saul."

He took an audible breath. "One more week. That's all I can give you. I need you in Manhattan next Friday to meet with the guys from Clio Records."

How weird. She hadn't wanted to stay in Fair Oaks for more than a few days, but now the thought of going back was just as unappealing. But what reason did she have to stay? Holly had just dumped her, and her parents would be fine without her. She would make sure they had everything they needed before she left. "All right. E-mail me the plane ticket, and I'll be there."

Without waiting for a reply, she ended the call, pushed the door open, and marched up to the bar.

Two middle-aged men who looked familiar sat at the end of the bar, but she ignored them as she climbed onto one of the stools.

Chris put the glass he'd been polishing away and came over to her.

Oh great. Of all the people tending bar at Johnny's, it had to be the man who had a crush on Holly.

He didn't look any more pleased to see her than she was to see him. "What can I get you?" he asked without even a hint of a welcoming smile or an attempt at small talk.

All the better. She wasn't in the mood to talk to anyone. What did one order after getting dumped on the first real date? She'd never been in this situation before. Heck, she had barely even dated. She was too busy with her career and too disillusioned with love to waste much time on it.

With Holly, it hadn't felt like a waste of time.

Forget her. "I'll take a shot of Johnnie Walker." It was the first thing that came to mind. After all, she was in a bar called Johnny's.

Chris turned and reached for one of the liquor bottles lined up like soldiers behind the bar.

When he placed the drink in front of her, she took it and drained the glass in one big gulp. A trail of fire burned all the way from the back of her throat to the pit of her stomach, adding to the acid that already pooled there. She gasped and grimaced. A hard-drinking pop star she wasn't. *Bah.* She smacked her lips and shook herself. The stuff tasted awful.

Chris nodded down at the empty glass, his expression not any warmer than before. "Want another?"

She hesitated. *Come on. You know this is stupid.* It wouldn't help. All it would do was prove that Holly was right about her avoiding dealing with her problems. "No, thanks. But how about a Boulevard Wheat and a sandwich or something?" She hadn't eaten since this morning, and drinking on an empty stomach was not a good idea.

He nodded. "Coming right up."

Someone tapped her on the shoulder.

Leo swiveled around on her barstool, prepared for someone who wanted an autograph.

Instead, Ethan, the younger of Holly's brothers, stood before her. He climbed onto the stool next to hers without waiting for an invitation. "Hey, Leo. I saw you head in from across the street and thought I'd say hi."

"Hi," she murmured. Couldn't she even get drunk in peace? Now she had to look at him, and damn if his eyes weren't the same clear blue as Holly's.

Chris set down the beer in front of Leo. "You want one too?" he asked Ethan.

"Sure." He grinned, which dimpled his cheeks in a way that made him resemble his sister even more. "You know what they say about drinking alone. Slippery slope and all that. Can't let a friend do that."

It didn't take long for Chris to return with Ethan's beer and a BLT for Leo.

Of all the sandwiches on the menu, he had to bring her this one. She wondered what had happened to the picnic sandwiches. Was Holly still at the creek, enjoying them alone?

No. She knew Holly better than that. No way could she enjoy the picnic after their argument. The thought of Holly sitting there, alone and sad, made her lose her appetite. She pushed the sandwich over to Ethan. "Here. Take it, if you want. I'm not hungry after all."

"Really? Yum." Ethan didn't have to be asked twice. He grabbed the sandwich, took a big bite, and chewed. "So," he said as he paused for a swig of beer, "you're dating my sister now."

If she hadn't handed over her sandwich, she might have choked on it. She glared at Ethan, then at Chris, who was suddenly all ears, pretending to wipe down the bar in front of them so he could listen in.

"Did she tell you that?" Leo asked.

Ethan grinned. "Oh no. Holly's pretty secretive when it comes to things like that. But she didn't have to. It's a small town."

"A small town with a big mouth," Leo grumbled.

His grin turned into a frown. "You don't want people to know?"

"It's not that. It's just…complicated. We're…we're no longer dating."

For the first time since she had stepped into the bar, Chris smiled.

Leo huffed. *Don't think you stand a chance now, buddy, just because I'm out of the running.*

Ethan thumped his beer back onto the bar top. "You dumped her? Was it because…because of her…because she didn't want to…?" He stopped himself and glared at Chris, who was still hovering nearby. "Hey, man, why don't you go restock the bottles over there or something?" He waved toward the other end of the bar.

Chris took his rag and trudged off.

"No," Leo said, a little too loudly. She lowered her voice and repeated, "No. It wasn't because of that."

"Why, then? My sister is a great catch. I admit I wouldn't necessarily want to be in a relationship with someone who…well, you know. But Holly is really—"

"Jesus, would you just stop it? I didn't dump her. She dumped me. And even if I had, it wouldn't be because of…that, okay? Why does everyone keep making such a big deal of it?"

He blinked. "It's not for you?"

"I don't know. I didn't even have time to find out before she dumped me." She gulped down half her beer. "And that's the last I want to say on this topic. I'd rather not talk about it, especially with one of her brothers."

"Fine with me," Ethan said. "It's not that I'm keen on this type of conversation. Normally, Zack is the one who's responsible for the if-you-hurt-my-sister-I'll-break-your-legs talks."

Leo hadn't wanted to talk about Holly anymore, but now she couldn't help being curious. "I can't imagine he had to have that kind of talk very often, did he?" Holly seemed like the type of woman who could take care of herself, and as far as Leo knew, she had only ever had three relationships in her life—one of which no one knew about.

"Just once, I think. When she came home for spring break her senior year of nursing school, she brought her girlfriend with her." He wrinkled his nose. "Dana."

"I take it you didn't like her?" Leo stole a fry from his plate.

"We really tried to give her a chance. Well, Zack and me mostly." Ethan took another bite of sandwich. "Mom and Dad were still hung up on the fact that she was with a woman. The way she treated Holly didn't help."

A swift wave of protectiveness surged through her. "What did she do?"

He chewed and shrugged, taking much too long to answer for Leo's liking. "It was more what she didn't do. Sometimes, she was all lovey-dovey, but other times, she was about as warm toward Holly as a frozen mackerel."

Leo remembered what Holly had told her about Dana—that they had been fighting about Holly's lack of desire for her all the time. *Damn.* Dana had probably given her the cold shoulder and withdrawn any affection whenever Holly hadn't wanted to sleep with her.

Was that what she thought Leo would do if they got involved? The thought hurt and made her angry and sad all at the same time.

She gulped down the rest of her beer while Ethan hadn't even finished half of his.

"You okay?" he asked.

"Yeah. But I think it's time to go home." She put enough money for the sandwich and their beers on the bar. "If you see your sister, tell her…"

"Tell her what?" He waited, his beer halfway to his mouth.

Leo shook her head. "Nothing." She had to stop avoiding direct conversations. Whatever she wanted to say to Holly, she had to do it herself. If she ever figured out what to say.

Holly didn't know how long she sat there, just staring at the bend in the path where Leo had disappeared. Her ears buzzed, and it wasn't from the gurgling of the creek next to her.

Finally, she lowered her gaze to the picnic Leo had so lovingly prepared. Her eyes started to burn, and for a moment, she wanted to toss it all after the wine, into the creek. But she knew she couldn't bring herself to do that. Neither would she let herself curl up into a ball in the middle of all the food.

She had done what needed to be done. It would be better in the long run, even if it didn't feel that way at the moment.

Now she needed to move on with her life, starting with figuring out what to do with this food. She slid her fingers over every container as she put them back into the basket. God, Leo had put so much thought into this. There was even the smoked Gouda she liked so much. How had Leo found out about it?

Stop it. You're just torturing yourself.

She packed up the rest of the picnic, then slid off her sandals and waded into the creek, hoping to locate the bottle of wine. But she couldn't find it and gave up the search after a few minutes. It was gone. *Like Leo.*

Ignoring her morose thoughts and her wet feet, she put her sandals back on and climbed over the rocks, back to the path. She gave Mr. Gillespie a nod in passing but marched on instead of stopping to chat, the basket tightly gripped in both hands.

What was she supposed to do with it? Return it to Leo?

She had a feeling that wouldn't go over too well. Eating whatever she could wasn't an option either because the mere thought of food made her stomach churn. But she didn't want Leo's picnic to spoil.

Finally, she decided to take it to her mother's. Ethan and Zack and their kids stopped by almost every day, and with that hungry brood around, no food ever went to waste.

Holly had a key, so she let herself in. Some days, she still expected her father to greet her when she stepped into the house. God, what she wouldn't give to be able to sink into one of his warm embraces right now. Leo didn't appreciate what a blessing it was to still have her father around.

Would you finally stop thinking about her?

"That was fast," her mother said behind her.

Holly jumped and whirled, clutching the basket to her chest. "Mom! I didn't know you were home. I was just about to leave a note."

Her mother came closer. "No grumpy cats to deal with today, so we closed on time for once. But what are you doing here?"

"I, um, brought some food for the kids." Holly held up the basket.

"Leftovers from the picnic with Leontyne?"

"How…how do you know?"

"A little birdie told me." Her mother put on a mysterious smile but couldn't keep it up. "Okay, it was Phil Eads. He came in with his Rottweiler mix earlier and said he heard Leontyne and Jenny talk about it in the store. So, how did it go?"

"Um, well..." Holly followed her mother to the kitchen, where she put down the basket.

"She and you...is it serious between the two of you?" Her mother's eyes shone. "Is that why you were talking about happy endings the other day?"

"It won't work out." Saying it out loud was harder than she had expected.

"Why wouldn't it? Is it because she's a pop star?" her mother asked. "I admit that had me a little worried too, but then I figured she's still Gilbert and Sharon's daughter, you know? The little girl who got a rock stuck in her nose when she was three."

Holly managed a small smile. "That's not it. I mean, it's part of it." She rubbed her face with both hands. "Leo will go back to New York and her career soon."

Her mother pulled out two chairs in the breakfast nook, pressed her down onto one, and took a seat on the other. "But you knew that before you agreed to go on a date with her, didn't you?"

"Yeah, but—"

"So there has to be something about her that made you say yes anyway."

"I..." Holly put her elbows on the table, leaned her forehead into her palms, and buried her fingers in her hair. "I didn't think it through."

"Well, there usually isn't much thinking going on when you're in love... or at least in lust." The corners of her mother's mouth curled into an amused smile.

It certainly hadn't been Holly's libido that had overwhelmed her common sense. *But I don't think I'm in love with Leo either...am I? More like a little crush, right? Okay, a pretty big one.*

"Why not try a long-distance relationship?" her mother asked. "I know they're not easy, but they can work out. Your father lived in Kansas City when we met."

"That's hardly a long-distance relationship."

Her mother shrugged. "If you're yearning to be together, even a hundred miles feel like a long distance. Why not give it a try? There's not exactly a wide choice of lesbians in Fair Oaks. The only one I know is Ms. Voerster, and she's eighty-one."

"Ms. Voerster?" Holly nearly burst out laughing despite her gloomy mood. "What makes you think she's a lesbian?"

"She's got one of those rainbow-flag stickers on her bumper."

"She probably just thinks they're nice and colorful and has no idea what they mean."

"Well, she might not be a lesbian, but you are. And that means if you don't want to be alone for the rest of your life, you'll have to take a risk on someone from out of town at some point." She studied Holly with an intense motherly gaze. "Doesn't it?"

Holly bent her head and rubbed her neck with one hand. "I don't know, Mom. In my experience, taking risks doesn't pay off."

Her mother reached across the table and took her free hand. "Who hurt you so much?" It came out thickly, as if she could barely speak because she was so overwhelmed.

Holly shook her head. "It's not—"

"It was Dana, wasn't it? You haven't brought anyone home since her. God, Holly, I'm so sorry we weren't there for you back then."

"You were."

"Not the way we should have been. But we weren't ready, and then your father…the accident happened and…"

Holly squeezed her mother's hands with both of hers. "It's okay."

"No, it's not. Why don't you ever talk to me about this part of your life? We talk about everything else. Why not this too?"

"Because…because there's nothing to talk about."

"That might have been true before Leontyne came back." Her mother sent her an imploring gaze. "Honey, I know I wasn't exactly a PFLAG mother of the year at first, but I'm really trying."

"I know, Mom. It's not because I don't trust you. It's just complicated."

Her mother sighed. "All right. Just know that I'm here for you whenever you want to talk."

"Thanks, Mom. Maybe another time." As she rose to give her mother a hug, a thought crossed her mind. Was she doing what she had accused Leo of doing? Was she coming up with every excuse under the sun to avoid a serious conversation with her mother?

The sun was slowly setting by the time Leo made it home. She had hoped to escape to her room without anyone in the house seeing her, but as soon as she opened the door, her mother stepped out of the kitchen. "Back from your picnic so soon?"

"Yeah." She didn't want to lie, but neither did she want to discuss the reasons.

Thankfully, her mother didn't push.

"Is Holly on baby-monitor duty tonight?" Leo asked.

"No. Didn't she mention it during the picnic? It's my turn to keep an eye on him."

At least that meant she didn't have to see Holly tonight. She walked past her mother to the stairs but then did a double take. Boy, her mother looked like shit. Constant worry had engraved lines on her face, and she moved as if she was bone-tired. Had she lost more weight recently, or had she looked like this for the past four weeks and Leo just hadn't noticed?

Damn. It hurt to admit it, but Holly had been right. Not about her spending time with Holly just so she could avoid dealing with her father. She honestly liked Holly and enjoyed every minute they spent together. But there was a kernel of truth in what she'd said. Leo *had* avoided dealing with her father—with both of her parents, really.

Just one more week in Fair Oaks, then she'd be gone for good. At least for the next few years, if her track record held up.

Just seven more days to prove Holly wrong.

But it was hard. She opened her mouth, closed it, and opened it again.

"Yes?" her mother said. "What is it?"

"I..." She licked her lips. Her gaze flicked to the stairs leading to her room. *No.* She squared her shoulders. "I can take over the night shift tonight, if you want."

Her mother stared at her as if she had said she were pregnant with triplets. "You...you want to...keep an eye on your father?"

Leo shrugged as casually as possible, pretending it was no big deal, but she sensed that she wasn't pulling it off. "Yeah. Why not?"

"You don't have to do that."

"Yes," Leo said, her voice wavering a little. "I think I do."

Her mother crossed the distance between them faster than Leo had thought her capable of. She threw her arms around Leo and squeezed tightly. "Thank you," she whispered against her shoulder. "Thank you for trying."

Leo laughed shakily and held her for a moment. "Don't thank me yet. Dad and I might end up killing each other, leaving you to deal with the bodies."

Her mother giggled, sounding giddy and nervous at the same time. "That's a risk I'll gladly take if only…"

She didn't finish her sentence, but the weight of her expectations settled heavily on Leo's shoulders nonetheless.

After another moment, they both let go and stepped back.

Leo cleared her throat. "So, what do I do? On night shift, I mean."

"Thanks to his occupational therapist, your dad has gotten pretty good at handling most things himself. You'll need to help him to the bathroom and back, but he can wash up by himself if you push him up to the sink."

Phew. At least that would spare them both some embarrassment. "That's it?"

"Make sure he brushes his teeth. That's a little hard for him with his left hand."

"Okay." *I can do that. I think.*

"Oh, and take his blood sugar before he goes to sleep. Do you remember how?"

Her father had suffered from diabetes all of his life, so Leo had watched him prick his finger and measure his blood sugar level a thousand times. She nodded. "What about the insulin?"

"He's got a pump now, so no more injections. Are you sure you want to do this? I could easily—"

"No, it's okay. You go get some rest. I'll handle things down here."

"Are you sure?" her mother asked again.

Leo forced a smile. "You know what I said about you having to deal with our bodies was a joke, right?"

A faint smile ghosted across her mother's tense face. "All right. I know you'll take good care of him. Give me a minute to say good night, then he's all yours."

It didn't take long until she returned. She raised up on her tiptoes, kissed Leo's cheek, and then climbed the stairs.

Leo watched her take each step slowly, as if she either didn't have enough energy to walk any faster or was still hesitant to leave her alone with him.

When the bedroom door clicked closed behind her mother, Leo straightened and rubbed her damp palms against each other. All right. Now she had to put her money where her mouth was.

Her legs felt like rubber as she walked toward her father's room. God, she hadn't been this nervous before her concert at Madison Square Garden. *Calm down. It's just your father.* But that thought didn't calm her nerves any more than the thought of a lion waiting behind that door would. She gave herself a mental kick and knocked.

A grunt came from inside the room.

She took it to mean "please come in" and opened the door. As she entered, she realized how little time she had spent in this room during the past four weeks—another indication that Holly had been right.

Her father was in his wheelchair, in front of his stereo, flipping through a stack of CDs. He didn't stop or look up when she came in.

"Time for bed," she said. *Wow. That was weird.* He had said the same to her a thousand times when she'd been a child. This role reversal would take some getting used to.

He put the CDs down, turned, and craned his neck. "Um…Mom?"

For a moment, she thought he was confusing her with his long-dead mother, but Holly had assured her that his memory wasn't affected. He was asking for her mom, not his own.

She walked over and swiveled his wheelchair so he was facing her. "Didn't she tell you? I'll be helping you tonight."

He glowered at her. "No."

Why did he have to make this so hard on her? She folded her arms across her chest. "It's me or handling everything yourself. Mom needs some rest."

They faced each other in a silent stare-down.

Knowing her father, they would still be here without either of them giving in when the sun rose, so Leo grabbed the handles of his wheelchair and pushed him toward the bathroom.

He let out a growl. "Drunk."

She stopped. Her hands slid off the wheelchair handles. "What?"

"Drunk," he repeated more clearly and put his good hand on the wheel so she couldn't keep pushing.

Damn. That man was like a human alcohol detector. He'd been the same on prom night, when she had come home tipsy and babbling about kissing Ash. But that had been fourteen years ago. She was no longer that smitten girl, and she wasn't drunk.

She circled the wheelchair to glare at him. "Can you stop with the holier-than-thou attitude for once? I'm an adult, and all I had was one beer and a shot. Not all pop stars are alcoholics and drug addicts, you know?"

He said nothing, but at least he took his hand off the wheel.

She pushed him through the sliding door and into the bathroom. Her parents had used some of the money she had sent them to turn the half bath into a full bathroom with a walk-in shower, and she'd had a new sink installed shortly after returning home. It was lower than the old one, providing easy access from the wheelchair. The toilet seat was elevated, and safety handles covered the walls next to it, so he could get in and out of his wheelchair on his own.

She parked his chair close to the toilet. "Um, do you want some help?"

He firmly shook his head.

"All right. I'll be right outside. Call me when you're done, and I'll help you wash up."

"Stop," he said before she could reach the door.

She turned. "Yes?"

"Stop," he said again.

"I did stop. I'm not doing a thing."

"Stop." He gestured at the wheelchair in sweeping, impatient motions. "Put stop."

What the hell was he trying to tell her? Once again, they were staring at each other, unable to communicate. *Story of my life.*

"Stop," he repeated, nearly shouting now, as if speaking louder would help her understand. He drummed his good hand against the armrest.

Sweat started to pool along her spine. Was this how parents felt when their toddler threw a tantrum? She just hoped her mother didn't hear this ruckus and hurry downstairs to make sure they weren't really killing each other. "I don't understand what...oh!"

Shit. She had forgotten to set the brake on the wheelchair. With burning cheeks, she bent and did it. "Sorry," she mumbled and ducked out of the bathroom as fast as possible.

Outside, she buried her face in her hands. *God.* How did Holly do this every day? She, herself, sure as hell wasn't cut out to be a nurse.

No wonder her mother looked exhausted. Taking care of him three or four nights a week wasn't any less stressful than a world tour with a concert every other day. She leaned against the wall and listened to the sounds drifting through the door, which she'd left ajar.

The toilet flushed, then he groaned and she heard him shuffle across the tiles on one leg, probably dragging himself back into the wheelchair.

"Do you need some help?" she called.

"No," he grunted out.

A frustrated growl echoed through the tiled room.

"Dad?" She peeked into the bathroom.

He had somehow managed to get back into the wheelchair and to take off his shirt, but now he was struggling to unlock the brakes.

She squeezed past him and unlocked them. Ignoring his scowl, she pushed him over to the sink and squeezed out a bit of toothpaste for him.

He sent her a glare in the mirror before starting to brush his teeth. It looked like a chore with his left hand, and he took the toothbrush out of his mouth after less than a minute.

"Three minutes," she said. Again that feeling of role reversal swept over her. "Remember how you used to play a three-minute song for me when I was learning to brush my teeth on my own?" She hadn't thought about it in many years.

He stopped glaring. For a second, his expression softened; then he frowned and put the toothbrush back into his mouth.

Finally, he was done.

She waited while he washed his face and hands, and then she returned him to his room. This time, she even remembered to set the brake when she parked the wheelchair next to the bed.

With a little help from her, he struggled out of his shorts, slid into bed, and exhaled, looking as relieved as Leo felt.

Now she just had to take his blood sugar, and they'd be done. She got the blood sugar kit from his bedside table and unzipped it. The device was a new one, not the one she was familiar with from her teenage years, but she figured it would work the same.

She inserted a test strip into the glucometer and watched its screen light up before setting it aside. Gently, she pressed the lancing device against the side of her father's finger, where it was less sensitive. A leathery pad covered its tip, not quite like her thicker guitar calluses, but still very familiar. She had watched these hands play the violin and the piano more often than she could count. Now, he would likely never play again. Without warning, a wave of grief and compassion swept over her. She sat there, clutching his finger and biting her lip.

"Press," her father said.

"Yeah, I know." She pressed the button.

The needle shot out and pricked his finger. He didn't flinch.

For a second, she stared at the drop of dark red blood on his fingertip before holding it against the test strip jutting out of the blood sugar device.

They stared down at the small display.

It seemed to take forever until the result popped up.

"One hundred and seven." She blew out a breath. That meant his blood sugar level was just fine, and she didn't need to call her mother—or, worse, Holly—to ask for help.

She wrapped the used test strip in a tissue, zipped the blood sugar kit up, and put it back on the bedside table. Everything was done now, but something inside her urged her not to go. Not without trying to talk to him.

But when she turned back toward him, he had closed his eyes, either because he was exhausted or as a signal that he didn't want to talk.

Okay. She had tried her best. It obviously wasn't meant to be.

Really? a voice in her head piped up, sounding very much like Holly's. *You're giving up this easily?*

She hovered at his bedside. "Dad?" she said quietly. "Can we talk?"

He opened his eyes and waved at his head with a grimace.

"Yeah, I know you can't talk very well. But can you listen?"

He sighed, pulled himself up a little with the use of the triangle dangling down from above his hospital bed, and gestured toward his wheelchair. "Seat."

Her heart pounded wildly, as if she were facing a firing squad, not merely her father. She plopped down into the wheelchair and sat there for quite some time, searching for the right words. After all these years, where should she start? Finally, she decided to keep it short because she didn't have the nerve to draw this out. "I know you had my entire life mapped out before I could even talk—Juilliard, getting a bachelor of music, playing in a symphony, maybe marrying a fellow musician and raising the next generation of little Mozarts."

He gave her a look that clearly said "What's wrong with that?"

"Nothing's wrong with that," she answered. "It's a fine goal—but not for me. I'm not you, Dad. I'm not straight, and I'm not into classical music. I want different things. But just because they're different doesn't mean they're worse than what you want for me. Can you accept that?"

His eyebrows lowered. He reached out his good hand from beneath the thin sheet, gripped Leo's left hand, and rasped his thumb over her fingertips. "Gentle," he said with a dismissive shake of his head. "Uh, no." He stared off to the side as he obviously searched for the right word. "Soft."

Leo looked down at their hands. Slowly, she zeroed in on her fingertips. The calluses on her fretting hand had gotten soft because she hadn't played the guitar in the past four weeks. "Um, yeah, I'm taking a break from playing right now. What does that have to do with what I just said?"

"Not…um, know…the…um, want."

Leo ran the words backward and forward to figure out what he meant. Finally, it clicked. "You mean I don't know what I want?"

He nodded firmly. "You, uh, know…you play."

"If I knew, I would play?"

Another nod. He held her gaze, his chin raised in a silent challenge.

Her first instinct was to argue with him or storm out. But that would be just more of the same—avoiding a serious conversation. As much as she hated to admit it, she knew, deep down, that he was right. She wasn't playing her guitar anymore, because it was a symbol of her career, which she wasn't sure she wanted anymore.

Damn. That insight wasn't what she had wanted to get from this conversation. She tried to roll the wheelchair closer to the bed, but the brakes were set, so it didn't move. With a grunt, she shoved it over to the spot she wanted.

"Okay. I might not know what exactly I want, but I know what I don't want. I don't want to play the violin. I don't want to join a symphony. I don't want to marry some guy." *I don't want to be here* had been part of the list up until a few weeks ago, but now she wasn't so sure any longer.

"Fine." He waved his hand dismissively and turned his head away.

"No, Dad." She jumped up and moved around the bed and into his line of sight so he was forced to look at her. "It's not fine with you at all, is it? Come on. At least admit it. You never had a problem stuffing your opinion down my throat in the past."

Again, he turned his head to the other side—but this time, not before Leo had glimpsed the look in his eyes. It wasn't anger or resentment, as she had expected. Frustration was a big part of it, sure, but what she had seen was mostly something else.

She knew that look. She had recently seen it on Holly's face when they had argued. Hurt. Dejection. Resignation. Fear of being hurt again.

Was it possible…? Had he thought she was rejecting him—as a father, a musician, a teacher, and a man—when she had declared that she didn't want the things he valued most in life, his music and his family?

She crossed back to the other side of the bed.

He closed his eyes. "Sleep."

"In a second. Please, Dad, look at me."

He huffed out a breath but opened his eyes.

She perched on the side of his bed. "You know that this…me being a lesbian and not wanting to become a violinist…has nothing to do with you, don't you?"

He stared at her with a stony expression, but something in his eyes flickered.

"Being gay isn't a choice, Dad. It has nothing to do with rebelling against you or rejecting you or not wanting to be like you. It's the way I am, and there's nothing I—or you—can do to change it."

"Music?" he said, his tone challenging.

"Yeah, okay, that was a choice. But pop is still music."

Her father lifted one brow.

Leo had to think of the way Holly had explained asexuality to her, using her chocolate metaphor, and both of them agreeing that white chocolate wasn't chocolate at all. Apparently, her father felt the same way about pop music.

"It is," she said firmly. "I'm a musician, just like you are. Think about it this way: I could have become a porn star."

His brow arched even higher.

"All right. Maybe not a porn star. I could have become a waitress, a hairdresser, or a mechanic. But I didn't. I chose to be a pop singer. Is that really so bad? It still gives us something in common. We both love music. Can't that be a start?"

He lifted the shoulder on his good side in a semi-shrug.

That was all she was going to get after pouring her heart out? She gave him an incredulous stare.

Just when she was about to get up and walk out, he cleared his throat and labored to get out a word. "Women." He waved back and forth between them, and a ghost of a smile darted across his usually stoic face, lending it a much softer appearance. "Two…two, uh, things."

God, what wouldn't she give for a translator. "I don't understand."

The lines on his forehead deepened. He repeated the motion with his hand. "Two things. Mu…music. Women."

"You…?" Her breath caught. Was he pointing out the two things they had in common—music and women? She stared at him. Was she imagining things, or had he just cracked a joke about her sexual orientation—not a homophobic one, but a joke that hinted at acceptance?

The corner of his mouth twitched.

Unbelievable. He had been joking. Her strict, overbearing father had joked about her sexual orientation as something that might unite them instead of stand between them. *Jesus Christ!*

Laughter bubbled up from deep inside of her. She pressed a hand to her mouth and realized what she was struggling to hold back wasn't laughter— it was a sob that wanted to escape her chest.

Don't. This might be a beginning, but it was too fragile to burden it with tears.

She fisted a handful of the sheet and took several calming breaths to get herself back under control.

"Fine?" he asked, and for an instant, she saw the gentleness that he had sometimes shown her when she'd been a little girl and he had guided her hands over the strings of the violin.

She inhaled and exhaled again. "Yeah. I'm fine. Are you really okay with me being a lesbian? With me being…everything I am?"

"Not…don't, um, like. Don't…change." He gave that half shrug again.

She nodded her understanding—he didn't particularly like it but accepted that he couldn't change it. *Guess it's a start.* It was certainly more than she had ever expected to hear from him.

When she got up from the bed, she felt as if she could float out of the room. A decades-old weight was finally starting to lift off her chest. She stood next to his bed and peered down at him for several moments, wanting to say something but not knowing what. That must be what he felt when he struggled for words. Finally, she gave up and instead bent to kiss his cheek.

He put on a gruff expression, but his gaze was soft. It followed her to the door, where she turned and looked back at him.

They nodded at each other; then he pulled the sheet higher and closed his eyes.

"Good night," she said softly.

Blowing out a shuddery breath, she picked up the baby-monitor receiver and tiptoed out. The first thing that went through her mind was that she wanted to call Holly and tell her everything.

But things between them were over. Were they even still friends? Did she want to be, after she had opened herself up, only to get dumped?

It was a moot point anyway. She didn't have Holly's number. *Hell, how's that possible?* They had shared a lot of very intimate information but not their phone numbers?

Instead of trudging upstairs and brooding over Holly and the unceremonious end of their relationship, she resolved to do something that she had avoided for the past month: unpacking her suitcase, even if it was only for another week.

Chapter 15

BIRDSONG AND THE PALE LIGHT of dawn woke Leo.

She had slept fitfully, tossing and turning with thoughts of Holly. Their argument at the creek played through her mind on a loop. Finally, she had fallen asleep about two hours ago.

Unlike Leo, her father seemed to have slept peacefully. There hadn't even been the slightest peep through the receiver of the baby monitor.

Well, at least that part of her life had taken a turn for the better after she had gathered the courage to have a conversation with her father. Maybe she and Holly could do the same. She would leave in just another week, and she didn't want their last few days together to end with them not talking. Truth be told, she didn't want them to end at all. She wanted to get to know Holly better.

Maybe she could surprise her with breakfast to make up for the picnic she had abandoned yesterday, and they could talk and clear the air between them. At the very least, she wanted to tell Holly that she'd been right about one of the two things she'd said at the creek—and dead wrong about the other.

With that thought in mind, she climbed out of bed before sunrise.

A rooster crowed somewhere in town as she made her way downstairs. She grinned at herself. Now she was getting up with the roosters. If she stayed here much longer, there was no telling what other local habits she would take up.

The house was quiet, so her mother was probably still asleep. She really must have been exhausted.

Leo opened her father's bedroom door a few inches and peeked inside. He was still asleep too.

She started to withdraw, but something made her pause. Something was…off. Goose bumps rose on her arms, and the tiny hairs stood on end.

It took her a moment to figure out what had triggered her sixth sense: Her father was breathing weirdly—deep, but much too fast for peaceful sleep. As she watched, his breathing slowed and became shallow…and then it just stopped.

Panic flooded her. "Dad!" She rushed into the room.

Before she reached him, he started breathing again.

Her knees went weak with relief. "Jesus, don't scare me like that." She shook his shoulder to wake him.

He didn't move; just his chest continued to rise and fall in a slowing pattern.

"Dad!" She shook him again. "Please, please, wake up!"

Nothing.

Phone. Call 911. She fumbled around on his bedside table but found only the baby monitor and his blood sugar kit. In a burst of speed, she took the stairs three at a time. "Mom," she shouted at the top of her lungs. "Wake up! It's Dad! We need an ambulance!"

Not waiting to see if her mother would wake up, she snatched up her phone. Her hands shook so much that she could barely dial 911.

As the phone rang, she raced back downstairs, to her father's side.

For a second, his chest seemed to have stopped moving, but then the fast, deep breaths started again.

She gasped for breath along with him.

"911. What's your emergency?" the dispatcher said in a calm, practiced tone.

"It's my father. I…I can't wake him, and he's breathing weirdly. I need you to send someone—now!"

"Calm down, ma'am."

Calm down? How could she calm down when her father was…? She swallowed and refused to even think it.

"Can you confirm your location, ma'am?"

She rattled off her parents' address, hoping she wasn't getting it wrong in her blind panic. "Hurry, please!"

"Okay. Help is on the way," the dispatcher said. "I'll stay on the line with you until the ambulance arrives."

Her mother stumbled into the room in her nightgown. "Oh God, Gilbert!" She hurried to his side. "What happened?"

"I-I don't know. He was like this when I came in."

Every second ticked by painfully slow as they stared down at him, unable to help.

Tires crunched over the gravel outside. *The ambulance!* She pressed the phone into her mother's hand, rushed through the hall, and tore open the door.

But it wasn't an ambulance parked in the driveway—it was a red Jeep.

Holly! Leo nearly sank to her knees. Holly was a nurse; she could help. The cold prickle of sweat along her back slowly receded. Holly was here. Everything would be okay.

Holly parked her Jeep in the driveway and grabbed the paper bag with the scones. Now that she was here, she wasn't so sure that showing up this early had been a good idea. Leo was probably still asleep, and even if she wasn't, what was there to say?

Nothing had changed after all. They still lived in different states and still had different expectations in a relationship.

That doesn't mean we can't be friends. Even though she'd convinced herself it was better not to try a relationship with her, she didn't want to lose Leo entirely. It wasn't that she didn't have other friends—she did—and she loved spending time with them. But that couldn't compare to what she had felt when she had climbed up onto the roof with Leo, dangled her feet in the creek with her, or snuck into the kitchen for a glass of milk and some middle-of-the-night conversation. She wanted more of this feeling, whatever it was…and she wanted to apologize.

She had hurt Leo with her back-and-forth of emotions and actions, first kissing her and agreeing to date her and then telling her she'd changed her mind. The memory of the look on Leo's face down at the creek had kept her up all night.

With a lump in her throat, she got out of the Jeep and closed the driver's side door. Before she took the first step toward the house, she realized that the front door stood open and someone was on the porch.

Leo.

Their gazes met across the car's roof.

A hesitant smile tugged on Holly's lips. It spread across her face as Leo rushed toward her. Apparently, Leo wasn't just willing to talk; she had obviously missed Holly too.

But Leo wasn't smiling. Her eyes were wide with panic. "Holly! It's my dad. He's not waking up!" She grabbed her hand and pulled Holly after her into the house.

Holly dropped the bag of scones onto the hall table, praying with all her might that this emergency wasn't what she thought it was. She gently nudged Sharon aside and shook Gil's shoulder.

Nothing. Not even a moan from him.

Oh God, Gil. For a moment, panic threatened to grip her, but then her training took over. "Have you called 911?"

Leo nodded. "They're on their way." She took the phone from her mother and lifted it to her ear. "Holly's here. My father's nurse. Yeah, she's already doing that."

While Leo and Sharon anxiously hovered next to her, Holly bent over him and checked his blood pressure, his heart rate, and his pupils. One of them was dilated, and his breathing pattern indicated Cheyne-Stokes respiration. *Damn, damn, damn. That's so not good.*

She reached for the blood glucose meter on the bedside table.

"You think it's low blood sugar?" Leo asked.

Holly had a feeling it was something else, but she didn't want to worry them unnecessarily. "It's worth checking. Could you get me another pillow?" She wanted to raise his torso a little to make sure he didn't aspirate on his own saliva. It would also give Leo something to do while they waited for the ambulance.

Leo rushed off.

Just as Holly was about to take his blood sugar, the sound of sirens grew louder and then stopped in the driveway.

Sharon ran to let them in.

Seconds later, she returned with the two EMTs. Leo trailed after them, pillow in hand.

Holly blew out a breath. She knew them both. Gil would be in good hands.

She gave them Gil's vitals, then stepped out of the way and joined Leo and Sharon at the foot of the bed. Quietly, she slid her hand into Leo's.

Her fingers were damp, and she clutched Holly's fingers tightly, as if holding on for dear life.

"Looks like a stroke to me," Holly said to the EMTs. "He's had two already, one last year, the other three months ago."

With efficient movements, the EMTs repeated her checks. Vickie, the female EMT, attached EKG patches to Gil's chest and hooked him up to a cardiac monitor, while her colleague clipped a pulse oximeter to his finger and measured his blood glucose. It was a little on the low side but not low enough to make him lose consciousness.

"How long has he been like this?" Vickie asked.

Holly looked at Leo.

"I don't know. He was like this when I tried to wake him a few minutes ago." Leo glanced at her wrist, but she wasn't wearing a watch. "He seemed just fine last night when I put him to bed around nine, and I didn't hear anything from him all night."

Leo had put him to bed and kept an eye on the baby monitor? Holly stared at her for a moment. But it didn't matter right now. More important was the fact that he hadn't woken her once during the night. "He usually has to get up at least once during the night," she said to the EMTs.

They traded knowing gazes before lifting Gil onto a gurney and strapping him into place. Within seconds, they had wheeled him out and through the open doors of the waiting ambulance.

Sharon, Leo, and Holly hurried after them.

"Can one of us ride with him?" Leo called, still clutching Holly's hand while wrapping her free arm around her mother.

Vickie shook her head. "We'll probably end up airlifting him to Saint Luke's."

Saint Luke's. The hospital had a first-class stroke unit. So they were thinking what Holly was thinking. If this was a massive stroke, as she suspected, the local hospital couldn't do much for him, and the window of opportunity for a clot-busting drug was rapidly closing. They had to act fast, and taking a family member with them would only slow them down.

She wrapped one arm around Leo's waist and made eye contact with Vickie. "We'll meet you there. You still have my number?"

Vickie nodded.

"Let me know where you are taking him as soon as you know."

"Will do." Seconds later, the ambulance doors closed behind her, and the ambulance sped down the street, sirens blaring and lights flashing.

Leo stood in the middle of the driveway and stared after them as if she still hadn't grasped what had happened.

Holly gently chafed Leo's hand between both of hers. Now that the ambulance with Gil had left, she slowly shifted out of nurse mode. Her knees started to tremble.

Leo turned to face her. The numb expression on her face gave way to fear. "He seemed fine last night. I swear he... Oh God, what if he...?"

"He'll be fine," Sharon whispered like a mantra. "He'll be fine." Then she burst into tears.

The three of them came together for a desperate group hug in the middle of the driveway. Leo's trim body, which normally exuded such confidence, now trembled and felt fragile against her. With one hand, Holly rubbed circles over her back until she felt the tense muscles relax a little.

"Come on," she finally said. "Let's get you two inside."

Still holding on to each other, with Leo in the middle, they made their way to the house.

Chapter 16

IN LEO'S EXPERIENCE, HOSPITAL WAITING rooms were the same all over the western world, and the one in Saint Luke's emergency room was no different—same hard plastic chairs, same smell of disinfectant and cleaner, same sense of fear and sorrow.

Leo peered over at Holly, who sat next to her, still holding her hand. Had she been sitting in a waiting room like this after her father's accident too? Did this remind her of that horrible day?

But if Holly was thinking of the past, she gave no indication of it. Her attention was firmly on Leo. "Want me to get you a coffee or something from the vending machine?" She looked from Leo to her mother.

Both shook their heads.

"No, thanks." The last thing Leo needed was for the caffeine to make her even more jittery. She could barely sit still as it was. For the fifth time in as many minutes, she glanced up to the large wall clock, whose hands seemed to barely move. Why was no one coming to let them know what was happening? A CT scan shouldn't take this long, should it?

She wished someone would turn off the television mounted in the corner. Some soap opera played with the sound off, ignored by the handful of people in the waiting room.

Her mother's shoes squeaked on the linoleum as she paced back and forth.

Leo leaned forward and put her elbows on her thighs without letting go of Holly's hand. It was her lifeline in all this chaos. "I'm sorry about… about before." She wasn't sure why she was thinking about it now, but the words bubbled out of her. "I don't want you to think I'm a person who throws things if she doesn't get what she wants. That's not who I am."

"I know." Holly caressed her fingers with her thumb. Her forearm rested on Leo's thigh next to her arm. "I was just as much to blame. But it's not important right now. Let's focus on your father, okay?"

For a moment, Leo wanted to lift her hand to her mouth and press a kiss to her palm. She was so insanely grateful to Holly that there were no words for it.

"I didn't hear him," she whispered. "Last night. I never heard him. What if he called for me or screamed out and I just...I slept through it?"

"Look at me." Holly tugged on her hand until Leo raised her gaze to her eyes. "You did nothing wrong. It could have happened on any other night when your mother or I kept an eye on him, and we wouldn't have heard a thing either. None of this is your fault. None. Do you hear me?"

Leo nodded, but a few what-ifs still clung to her mind like stubborn cobwebs. It would take some time until she could shake off the last remainder of doubt.

A scrub-clad doctor pushed through the set of swinging doors. His gaze swept over the people in the waiting room. "Mrs. Blake?"

Her mother stopped pacing—even seemed to stop breathing. "That's me. How is he?"

Leo shot to her feet.

Holly jumped up with her, their fingers still linked.

The doctor cleared his throat. "As you probably guessed, your husband suffered another stroke."

"But he'll be fine, right?" Leo's mother asked. "He's survived two strokes already. He'll make it through this one too...right?"

"Mrs. Blake... This one was much worse than the others. There's substantial swelling in his brain, and it's putting pressure on the brain stem—the part of the brain that regulates important life functions such as his breathing and heart rate." He cut himself off as if realizing they were too overwhelmed to grasp all the details. "We don't expect him to recover from that."

"N-not recover?" Leo's mother stammered. "What does that mean? Will he die?"

"I'm sorry. We're doing all we can, but the odds of survival are very remote. You should prepare for the worst. I don't think he has long."

Leo swayed, feeling as if he had punched her. She gripped Holly's hand to stay upright.

Her mother burst into sobs, grabbed Leo in a desperate hug, and buried her face against her shoulder. Warm tears soaked Leo's shirt.

She let go of Holly and wrapped both arms around her mother.

The doctor met her gaze over her mother's head. His face was a professional mask, but compassion shone in his eyes. "We'll be sending him up to the stroke unit in a minute. You can stay with him if you want to."

Leo couldn't speak, but Holly did it for her. "Thank you. We'd like that."

The door swung shut behind the doctor, but his words continued to echo through Leo's mind. *I don't think he has long.* She pressed her hand to her mouth. *He will die. Oh God, he will die.*

Her father's hospital room looked like the bridge of a spaceship. A large monitor dominated the space at the head of his bed, and Leo couldn't look away from the green and white lines moving across the screen in a hypnotizing pattern. Constantly changing numbers were displayed next to them, but they meant little to her.

A breathing tube was taped to her father's mouth, but there was none of the hissing, pumping, and beeping she had expected. This wasn't like the scenes she had seen on TV at all. An eerie silence filled the room, interrupted every now and then by the shrill alarm of a monitor in one of the other rooms.

Leo almost wished for more sounds, anything to distract her from the unmoving figure in the bed. Her mother was talking to him, stroking his pale face around the breathing tube, and kissing his forehead, but he never reacted.

This was what she'd expected when she had first gotten her mother's call, four weeks ago. Now, after she had talked to her father just last night, it caught her unawares. Part of her still couldn't grasp that the patient lying motionless beneath the white hospital blanket was him.

The only thing that felt real was Holly's presence. Since there were only two visitor's chairs, she stood behind Leo like a guardian angel, one hand on Leo's shoulder. "You can hold his hand if you want," Holly whispered to her.

Leo glanced back at her.

Holly gave her an encouraging nod.

A clip was attached to his finger on the right, measuring the oxygen in his blood or something, and her mother had a careful grasp on that hand, so Leo took hold of the other. Somehow, she had expected his skin to be warm, as it had always been, but now it was cool against her own. A shiver went through her.

Holly rubbed her shoulder, sending a bit of warmth back into her.

Grateful, Leo reached up with her other hand and put it on Holly's for a moment. She sat very still, watching his shrunken face. When was the last time she had held his hand like this? Had she ever? She must have, as a child, but she couldn't remember.

Her mother slid her chair closer to the bed and reached across his lap for Leo's other hand.

Leo let go of Holly's hand to hold her mother's.

Her fingers were warm, especially in comparison to his. Tears trickled down her mother's face, but she didn't reach up to wipe them away. One, then another dripped onto the stark white sheet.

Leo's heart went out to her mother, but no tears came for her. This was all too surreal. She didn't even know what time of day it was or how long they had been in here. The blinds on the large window were down, shutting out the rest of the world. It might as well have ceased to exist for all she knew.

"If you want, you could play him some music," Holly said quietly.

Grateful for anything that would interrupt the awful silence, Leo fumbled her cell phone from her pocket and searched for Pachelbel's "Canon in D."

Soon, the low, soothing strains of violins filled the room.

She sat there for what felt like hours but could easily have been minutes. Her father's hand in hers seemed to become cooler, and the numbers on the monitor fell slowly but steadily.

"Dad," she heard her own voice croak out, as if that could call him back from where he was going.

A muscle twitched in his face.

Had he heard her?

"Dad?" she tried again.

Wasn't it ironic? Except for last night, they hadn't talked in fourteen years, and she hadn't wanted to, and now she longed for a single word or sign of recognition from him.

She watched him so intently that she jumped when the blood pressure cuff buzzed. For a moment, she had thought his arm was moving. But when the blood pressure cuff deflated, all went still.

"We're here," she whispered anyway.

Her mother gripped her hand more tightly, and Holly's fingers fanned out over her shoulder as if trying to soak up her pain.

A piercing alarm from the monitor interrupted the peaceful ebb and flow of the violins.

Even though Leo had known this would happen at some point, panic swept through her. She wanted to run to the door and call for help, but her mother didn't let go.

Rapid footfalls approached, and a nurse came in, followed by a doctor. Neither asked any questions. One of them turned off the shrill alarm while the other switched off the ventilator before murmuring "sorry for your loss" and quietly leaving the room.

Leo's mother buried her face against her husband's unmoving chest and wept.

Slowly, as if any jarring movement would disturb his peace, Leo slid her hand out of her father's and turned off the music on her phone. When silence fell, she latched on to Holly's hand, hoping she would keep her afloat in a sea of pain and grief.

Later, she couldn't have said how long they stayed with her dad, what words they exchanged with the hospital staff, or how they got back home. The only thing she knew was that Holly stayed by her side through it all.

Chapter 17

I T FELT STRANGE NOT TO check on Gil last thing in the evening. She had been his nurse for a year and a half and had shared his home for months. He'd been grumpy for most of that time, but never in a mean way. Somehow, she had come to like him and his curmudgeon ways. She would miss him.

She stood in the doorway of his room and stared at the empty bed for quite some time. Finally, she wiped her eyes, gave herself a mental nudge, and went in to pick up the empty wrappers and other trash the EMTs had left behind.

Technically, her job as his nurse had ended, and she was free to go home, but she didn't consider it for even a second. Not before she had made sure Leo was okay—or at least as okay as she was going to get today.

She put the remainder of the food the neighbors and the members of Gil's church choir had brought over into the fridge and tiptoed upstairs.

A quick glance into Sharon's room showed her that she was asleep. The sleeping pill Holly had given her must have finally kicked in. Sharon had cried all the way home. By the time they had entered the house, she'd been so exhausted that Holly and Leo nearly had to carry her upstairs, yet she had still been too agitated to settle down.

Holly quietly closed the door and continued on to Leo's room.

No answer came to her knock. Hesitantly, she opened the door a few inches and peeked in.

Leo's room was empty. For a second, fear surged through her veins. Had Leo gotten into her car and driven off, not knowing where she was going, just away from the empty bedroom downstairs and the memories it evoked?

But then a light breeze brushed her cheek. The dormer window stood open. Holly knew instantly where Leo had gone.

She crossed the room, climbed onto the desk chair, and stepped out onto the roof. Once her eyes had adapted to the darkness, she spread her arms to both sides and balanced along the roof. When she rounded the chimney, she could make out a shadowy figure huddling against the bricks.

Leo.

She sat with her arms wrapped tightly around her knees and stared out over the town. Holly wasn't sure she actually saw any of it.

"Hey," she said softly as she approached so she wouldn't startle her.

Leo didn't flinch, almost as if she had expected Holly to show up on the roof. Or maybe she had just heard her climb up.

Holly settled next to her. They sat with their shoulders pressing into each other, neither of them speaking. She wanted to ask if Leo was okay but held back. Of course Leo wasn't okay. Who would be after a day like this?

While Holly turned her head to study her, Leo continued to stare straight ahead. When they had been in the hospital, Leo hadn't cried a single tear, not even right after her father had died. But now tears trembled on her lashes. It had been the same for Holly after her own father's accident. She had held herself together for her mother and had only fallen apart after Sasha had taken her home.

Leo sniffed and brushed the tears away with an abrupt movement, as if she was annoyed at herself for allowing that display of emotion.

Holly wrapped one arm around her. "It's okay to cry and be sad, Leo. Let it out."

Leo stiffened. "I don't need to…" she started to mumble, but the tears were already falling, much too fast now to brush them all away.

Holly's eyes grew damp too. "It's okay," she said again.

With a groan, Leo buried her face against Holly's shoulder. Tears soaked into the fabric of Holly's shirt. Leo made no sound as she cried, but her body shook with silent sobs.

"God," she got out, even as she cried, "what is this? I don't normally…"

"Shhh." Holly slid her fingers into Leo's hair to keep her face against her shoulder and bent to kiss the top of her head. "This wasn't a normal day."

Finally, the shaking and the tears stopped. Leo hiccuped once and took a shuddery breath before lifting her face off Holly's shoulder.

Her eyes were puffy; her nose was red and her hair a tangled mess. She blew her nose on a tissue, ran the back of her hand over both cheeks, and gave Holly a weak smile. "If my fans could see me now... Sexy, right?"

Holly regarded her seriously. "I don't care how sexy you are. I just care about how you are here." She gently touched her fingertips to Leo's chest, right over her heart.

For a second, Leo looked as if she might start to cry again. Instead, she put her hand on Holly's and pressed it to her chest. "Thank you for everything you did today. I don't know how I would have survived all of it without you. I was in no shape to drive us to Kansas City and back without crashing."

"Of course you weren't. I wasn't either when my dad...when we got the call from the hospital." It had been five years, but right now, Holly felt raw, as if it had happened only a few hours ago.

"That's different," Leo said. "You and your father...you were close, right?"

Holly nodded and smiled, trying to hang on to the good memories, not the bad ones. "I was the quintessential daddy's girl."

"That's just it. It was never like that between my father and me. We never got along. I really don't know why..." Her voice wobbled. "...why it's hitting me like this."

"He was your father," Holly said, as if that explained it all. To her, it did. She turned her hand and intertwined their fingers. "And maybe it's hitting you like this *because* you never got along. You're grieving not just for your father, but also for all the lost opportunities. It's gotta be tough to know you'll never get the chance to settle things between you."

Leo slid her knees away from her chest, stretched out her legs, and put their hands down on her thigh. She studied their linked fingers for a while before looking up. "We did, you know? Settle things between us. Well, kind of."

"You did?"

Leo nodded. "After what you said to me at the creek…about me wanting to spend time with you only so I didn't have to deal with my dad…"

"I shouldn't have said that or that you were okay with no sex only so it would be easy to walk away." Truth be told, she'd been grabbing at straws, trying to find reasons to keep her distance so she wouldn't end up getting her heart broken.

"No, you were right."

A stab went through Holly's chest, but she forced herself not to react.

But apparently, Leo knew her well enough by now to sense how much that had hurt. She tipped up Holly's chin with her free hand so their gazes met. "I didn't mean it like that. I love spending time with you, just because…because you're you. You get me. You see me—the real me."

The pain in Holly's chest was replaced by warmth. They looked into each other's eyes.

Leo cleared her throat. "What I meant is that you were right about me avoiding having to deal with my father. I knew it all along, but I was content not to think about it or do anything about it. What you said at the creek…that really hurt."

Holly bowed her head, unable to look her in the eyes. "I'm sorry."

Leo squeezed her hand in silent acknowledgment. "At least it kicked my butt in gear and forced me to face the past. To face my dad. So when I got back home, I offered to take over the night shift."

"How did that go?"

Leo covered her eyes with her free hand. For a moment, Holly thought she might be hiding renewed tears, but then Leo chuckled. "God, I might be the world's most inept nurse. Dad got pretty frustrated with me. He is… was not the most patient man."

"So unlike his daughter," Holly said with a smile.

Leo grimaced. "Who threw a bottle of wine and stormed off instead of staying and talking it out. Yeah, maybe he and I really do have something in common. That's where our awkward conversation ended up last night— Dad pointing out that we have two things in common."

Holly gave her a questioning gaze.

"Music," Leo said. "And women."

Gil had really said that? "Wow, that's—"

Leo sighed. "I know it's not much."

"No, no, that's great. For a man like your father, that's a huge concession."

"It is. It didn't magically erase all the problems between us, but I thought…I thought maybe it could be a new beginning. And now…" She raised her empty palm skyward as if trying to reach for something that would forever escape her grasp.

"Sometimes, that beginning is all that counts, and you'll have to trust that it would have been the start to something great, even though you can't be sure of it. It's still a good thing that you got to share that with him."

Leo seemed to think about it for several seconds, then she slowly nodded and turned to look at Holly.

"What?" Holly squirmed a little under that intense gaze.

"I'm just wondering whether that's true about us—you and me—too. Maybe we should have that kind of trust too and just…try."

"Are you really up for that discussion now?" Holly wasn't. All she wanted right now was to hold Leo and take away her pain. Rejecting her a second time was impossible tonight. *Because you don't want to hurt her…or because you want to say yes to whatever she's offering?*

"You're right. Add awful timing to the list of things my father and I have in common."

Holly shook her head. "You talked and found some common ground just in time…" She bit her lip. "I'd say that's pretty good timing."

Leo wrapped her other hand around Holly's and gave a gentle squeeze.

Again, their gazes connected.

Holly swallowed. She had to get Leo off the roof, out of this emotionally charged atmosphere, before she could do something stupid. *Like kiss her.* It surprised her how much she wanted to do that.

Leo looked away first. "Is Mom still sleeping?"

"Yes. I gave her something so she could sleep through the night." She got up, carefully balancing on the roof, and pulled Leo up with her by their joined hands. "And now I'll take you to bed too. Uh, I mean…"

"Relax. I know what you mean."

They climbed back to the window, with Holly leading the way, and slipped into the room.

"Are you going home?" Leo asked. "Or will you sleep in your…in the guest room?"

It didn't sound like a casual question. There was need behind it. Holly studied Leo's face, which was still a little puffy from crying. "Where do you want me to sleep?"

Leo's shoulders lifted and fell under a deep breath. "I want you to stay. But not over there." She waved toward the guest room and lifted her gaze to Holly's eyes. "I want you to sleep with me."

Holly's mouth was as dry as a bag of sawdust.

"Uh, I mean, sleep," Leo added hastily. "Just sleep. I…I don't want to be alone tonight. But if it would make you uncomfortable…"

The tremor of vulnerability in her voice made Holly's heart melt. She couldn't say no—and she didn't want to. "No, it doesn't. Come on. Let's get ready for bed."

She tried to make it sound casual, as if it were something she did every day, but Leo seemed to look right through her.

"Are you sure?"

Holly nodded. "I'm sure. Do you want the bathroom first?"

"No, you go ahead."

As Holly passed her on the way to the door, she squeezed her hand. Amazing how naturally little touches like that came.

She went into the guest room to get her pajamas before stepping into the bathroom. Her hands were a little unsteady as she slid out of her clothes and turned on the water in the shower.

There was no reason to be nervous, she told herself. Nothing would happen. Leo was grieving.

But maybe that wasn't what made her so nervous. Okay, not *just* that. Sleeping with someone—just sleeping—was pretty intimate for her, especially in a bed as narrow as the one in Leo's childhood room. There was no way to avoid touching, being in some kind of contact all night. Would she be able to sleep like this?

She wasn't used to it. She and Dana hadn't lived together, and she'd never been eager to have sleepovers because she knew they came with certain expectations. Maybe that was part of why she had been so willing to enter into a relationship with Ash, who was so deeply closeted that she rarely risked staying over or having Holly stay the entire night.

"Holly?" Leo called through the closed door. "You okay?"

"Uh, yeah, I'm fine. I'll be right out." She hadn't realized how long she'd been in the shower. Hurriedly, she shut off the water, toweled off, and put on her pajamas.

A cloud of steam followed her as she opened the door to Leo's bedroom. "It's all yours."

Leo's gaze swept over the thin straps of her pajama top before veering away. "Are you really okay with this?" She waved her hand toward the bed.

"Leo..." She stepped closer until she could take Leo's hand and feel her body heat. "If we're doing this..." She paused, suddenly not sure if she was talking just about sleeping in the same bed tonight or about giving a relationship a chance.

"If we're doing this...?" Leo prompted.

Holly gave herself a mental kick to unfreeze her brain. "You'll have to trust me that when I say I'm okay with something, I am okay with it." That didn't mean she wasn't nervous, of course.

"Okay." Leo nodded. "I'll try to do that from now on."

From now on... She was definitely talking about more than just tonight, wasn't she?

Holly stared at Leo's retreating back. When the bathroom door clicked shut behind her, she told herself to stop overthinking things and slid beneath the covers.

The sheets smelled of Leo, and so did the pillow. She pressed her face against it, breathed in deeply through her nose, and closed her eyes. *Mmm.* She couldn't say what it was that Leo smelled of, maybe almond soap and a faint trace of perfume. Whatever it was, it was nice. Very nice.

The water in the bathroom cut off.

Either that had been the quickest shower in the history of mankind, or Holly had lost track of time while she had immersed herself in Leo's scent. Her cheeks burned.

The bathroom door opened, and Leo stepped out in a pair of cute, pink boxer shorts and a white tank top. The damp ends of her hair brushed her nearly bare shoulders, and Holly drank in the sight of her smooth skin and long legs.

Before Leo could once again ask if it was okay, Holly held up the covers, inviting her to slide into bed beside her.

Leo crawled into bed, and Holly settled the covers over them.

They lay on their sides, facing each other, not touching, but with just a few inches of space between them.

When Leo reached out a hand, Holly didn't flinch away. She wanted Leo to touch her, to establish a connection.

Instead, Leo reached across her and flicked off the lamp on the bedside table, throwing the room into darkness. Only a bit of silvery moonlight filtered in through the window they had left open.

A wave of disappointment swept over Holly as Leo's hand dropped back to the bed. At the same time, she couldn't help smiling at herself and her own eagerness. Only twenty-four hours ago, she had wanted to keep her distance from Leo. What had happened to that resolution?

Slowly, careful not to brush against Leo's body in the darkness, she turned around. The rustling of the covers indicated that Leo was doing the same, so now they were lying with their backs toward each other.

Holly lay with her eyes open, listening to Leo's breathing. If one of them turned around in her sleep during the night, they'd practically be on top of each other.

"Holly?" Leo's voice, sounding almost like that of a child, broke the silence. The mattress shifted as she rolled over, onto her other side. "C-can I...?" Her hand tentatively brushed Holly's shoulder blade.

Instead of answering, Holly rolled onto her back and opened her arms.

Leo cuddled up immediately, one arm wrapped around Holly's middle. She fit her face into the curve of Holly's neck. Her hair fanned out across Holly's shoulder and tickled her skin.

"Your heart is pounding," Leo whispered into the darkness. "Are you okay?"

"I'm fine. Besides, this is about making sure *you* are okay." She tried to make out Leo's features in the pale moonlight. "Are you?"

When Leo sighed, her breath washed over Holly's neck, making her heart beat even faster. "I will be." She shifted a little closer still, nestled their bodies together, and carefully settled her leg across Holly's thighs.

As different as they were—Leo tall and slim, Holly curvy and shorter—they fit against each other perfectly. It was a completely new and yet strangely familiar feeling.

Leo hummed against her neck. "God, Holly. You have no idea how good this feels."

"It feels really good to me too."

"It does?" Leo asked quietly.

Holly nodded. "Oh yeah."

"Good. I don't want this to be just about what I need."

Wow. How could she have ever thought Leo was a spoiled, egocentric superstar? She slid her fingers into Leo's slightly wavy hair and started to caress her scalp.

Leo let out a sound that resembled a purr. Her eyes fell closed, her lashes fluttering like the wings of a butterfly against Holly's skin.

Holly tightened her hold. She wanted to hug this moment close forever. How could anyone think that anything could be more intimate than this?

"Holly?" Leo's voice was already tinged with sleep.

"Hmm?"

"Thank you."

"You're welcome," Holly said, but she could tell that Leo had already fallen asleep in her arms.

Holly tenderly trailed her fingers through her hair and held her while she slept until she finally drifted off too.

Leo floated awake from the most amazing dream she'd had in years. She lay there with her eyes closed, trying to hang on to it for as long as she could. Then, as her brain became fully awake, she realized that it wasn't a dream. She was still cuddled up to Holly, as if they hadn't moved an inch the entire night. Maybe they hadn't. Instead of tossing and turning with thoughts of her father all night as she had expected, she had slept peacefully.

At that thought, it all came flooding back with the force of a tsunami. *Dad!* Her body stiffened in Holly's gentle embrace. A cascade of images from yesterday hailed down on her—her father lying motionless in his bed, the sound of his harsh breathing and then the awful silence, the ambulance doors closing behind him, and the piercing sound of the monitor in the hospital.

New tears burned in her eyes, but she forced them back. Her throat still felt raw from last night's crying. Boy, that had been unexpected. Grief had moved in like fog, creeping up on her. The only thing that had chased away the swathes of mist had been Holly's presence.

Leo clung to her and let Holly's steady heartbeat beneath her ear soothe the jagged edges of sadness piercing her chest. In a little bit, she would get up and check on her mother, but first, she wanted a few more minutes in this quiet haven with Holly.

She lifted her head off Holly's chest and watched her sleep. Holly's full lips were slightly parted, and her auburn lashes threw shadows onto her cheeks in the soft orange light of sunrise. Her hair was mussed, and Leo's fingers itched to reach out and smooth it back into place.

Tenderness filled her, almost like an ache.

As if sensing her perusal, Holly stirred against her and, still half asleep, snuggled even closer. It took another minute before her eyes blinked open. She stared at Leo for a few seconds, as if she couldn't figure out what they were doing in bed together, then the corners of her mouth tipped up into a smile. "Good morning." Her voice was husky with sleep.

Simply adorable. Leo smiled back. "Good morning."

Holly yawned and stretched beneath her, and Leo suddenly became aware of where exactly Holly's leg rested—right between hers.

She bit back a groan and struggled against the urge to press even closer.

Holly reached up with one hand and ran her fingers through Leo's hair while she studied her with a concerned gaze. "How are you feeling?"

Leo fought to sum up the chaotic mix of emotions running through her. *Sad, surreal, happy, embarrassed, and a little aroused.* "I'm okay."

Holly gave a tiny tug on Leo's hair and looked at her skeptically.

"Really," Leo said. "It could be a lot worse." *Without you here.* Reluctantly, she rolled to the side, away from temptation. "What happens now?"

"You should probably help your mother with the funeral arrangements."

Reality hit her as if someone had poured a bucket of ice-cold water over her head, reminding her that there was a world full of problems beyond this cuddly, warm bed. She sighed. "Yeah."

"I can help too, if you want."

The cold receded a little. "Don't you have to work?" That was what she had meant when she had asked her what would happen now—with Holly... with them. "I mean, you're not our...uh, my father's nurse anymore, so won't the agency send you somewhere else?"

The thought felt wrong. Four weeks ago, she had viewed Holly as an intruder and wondered what she was doing in her parents' home, but now

Holly seemed to belong there. Imagining the house without her father *and* without Holly sent a shiver through her.

"Eventually," Holly said. "But it's Saturday, so I'm not working."

Romancing Holly by taking her casket shopping hadn't been part of Leo's plan, but she felt ill-equipped to handle it all on her own. Was it wrong to lean on her so much? She had never relied on anyone, at least not for emotional support. Why change now?

Because she could, she realized. For once in her life, someone stood by her without expecting anything in return—and Leo wanted to let her.

"If you really don't mind…"

"I really don't," Holly said firmly. "You don't have to go through this alone, okay?"

Tears welled up unexpectedly. "Thank you," Leo croaked out.

They came together in a tight embrace in the middle of the bed.

"You're welcome," Holly whispered against her temple.

Leo slumped into the passenger seat of Holly's Jeep and pressed the balls of her hands to her closed eyes. Who knew that making funeral arrangements was so exhausting? When her grandparents had died, she hadn't helped with anything beyond ordering the nicest wreath money could buy, but now she had to take care of everything.

Her mother wasn't up to making any of the decisions—selecting a casket, picking out the clothes her father would wear, taking care of the obituary, and choosing which music would be played during the visitation and the funeral. The to-do list seemed endless.

"Home?" Holly asked from the driver's seat of her Jeep that was parked in front of the funeral home.

"Not yet."

"Leo, you have to take a break and eat something." Holly reached across the middle console and put her hand on Leo's leg for a moment.

The touch raised Leo from her emotional stupor. She opened her eyes and turned her head toward Holly. "I will. But there's one more thing I need to do first. Can you drop me off at Ashley's flower shop? I need to order the flower arrangements for the funeral."

"I don't need to drop you off. I can come in with you."

Leo shook her head. Holly had helped her so much already. There was no need to put her through talking about flowers with Ashley. Surely Ash's denial of their relationship still stung. "Thanks, but I'll be fine on my own for this one. Maybe you should go home. Your family is probably wondering where you disappeared to."

"Probably. But how will you get home?"

"I'll just walk. It's not that far, and I could use some fresh air to clear my head."

Holly hesitated. "All right," she finally said but didn't look happy. She took her hand off Leo's leg, put the car into drive, and pulled away from the curb.

Two minutes later, they were parked in front of Ash's flower shop.

Holly shut off the engine. "Are you sure you don't want me to come in with you?"

Leo wasn't, but she nodded anyway. "Will I see you…?" She cut herself off before she could add the *later*, not wanting to take it for granted that Holly would return to the house. "Will you come to the funeral?"

"The funeral?" Holly echoed. "You will see me later, when I come by to check on your mother."

Part of the tension inside of Leo eased. She smiled at Holly. "Just on my mother?"

Holly mirrored the smile. "Well, since I'll be there already, I might as well look in on you too."

Their gazes held across the middle console. Leo felt as if strings were growing between them, tying them to each other and tugging her forward, toward Holly.

Holly leaned across the middle console too, making Leo's heart pound with anticipation. When their lips were just inches apart, Holly paused, shook her head as if at herself, and then hastily retreated to her side of the car.

What…? No, don't go! everything in Leo screamed out.

"I, um… See you later," Holly croaked out.

Still staring at Holly's mouth, Leo licked her lips and tried to get herself back under control. As much as she wanted to kiss her, Holly was right. They hadn't resolved anything between them, and besides, this wasn't the time or the place. "See you later." Reluctantly, she climbed out of the Jeep and closed the door.

They looked at each other through the glass of the side window. Neither made a move to part ways.

Get a grip. Just because Holly wasn't going to accompany her was no reason to act as if she were heading into a war zone, not a flower shop.

Holly gave her an encouraging nod and a wave before starting the Jeep and pulling away.

When her taillights had disappeared in the distance, Leo squared her tense shoulders and entered the flower shop.

The bell over the door tinkled. Moist air engulfed her, heavy with the scent of roses, orchids, and other flowers that Leo couldn't identify.

There was no one in the store.

"I'll be right there," Ash's voice came from a back room. The sound of a radio playing drifted over from the same direction.

Leo stuffed her hands into her pants pockets and looked around. A large refrigerated glass case took up one wall, while the others were lined with metal buckets and vases full of flowers in all colors of the rainbow.

Apparently, Ashley had done well for herself.

A minute later, Ash emerged from the back room in a green florist's apron. "How may I—?" She froze. "Leo!"

Leo shifted on the balls of her feet. "Hi."

Her gaze never leaving Leo's, Ash rounded the counter. "I heard about your father. I'm so sorry." She wiped her hands on her apron and then wrapped her arms around Leo.

For a second, Leo stood ramrod straight before lifting her arms to return the embrace. The heady scent of Opium swirled around her, triggering memories of high school. It had been Ash's signature fragrance even fourteen years ago. Back then, Leo had always thought the perfume aptly named because it had been like a drug for her. She had lived for one of the rare but warm hugs from Ash.

Now all it did was make her think of the way it had felt to be wrapped in Holly's arms all night. Apparently, Opium was no longer her drug of choice. She much preferred Holly's lighter, more subtle scent.

"Thanks," she mumbled when they let go of each other. "I'm here for, um, flowers. For the casket."

Something shifted on Ash's face, from a friend offering comfort to professional florist. "Of course. Did you have anything particular in mind?"

Leo lifted her hands and then dropped them. "I don't have the slightest idea about flower arrangements for a funeral."

"Lucky for you, I do," Ash said with a soft smile. "Let's see... Did your father have a flower he liked?"

"I don't think so."

"What about his favorite color?"

Jeez, this was embarrassing. She didn't know the answer to any of these questions. Maybe she should call her mother. But then she decided not to. Her mother had been the one to take care of her father for many months; now it was her turn. "Um, blue, I think." At least that was the color of the tie he wore most often.

"Blue. We can work with that. What about these delphinium?" Ash walked around the store and pulled out flowers with long stalks, their blue blooms encircling the stem. "We could weave in white carnations or maybe lilies or orchids." She added the flowers she had mentioned and held them out for Leo to see. "What do you think?"

Leo tried to decide whether her father would have liked the arrangement. Had he even liked flowers? Finally, she decided that it didn't matter. He was no longer here to see it, so the flowers were more for her mother than for him. "Looks good to me."

"So, when will the funeral be?" Ash asked.

"Monday at ten."

"I'll make sure the casket spray is at the funeral home in time." Ash put the flowers she had pulled out back into their buckets. "Do you want me to arrange flowers for the altar and boutonnieres for the pallbearers too?"

Leo had no idea what boutonnieres even were, so she nodded. "Yes, please. Just bill me for everything."

Ash shook her head. "No bill. I won't charge you for a thing."

"Ash, you can't—"

"We're still friends, aren't we?"

Were they? Leo wasn't sure. Ash paying for the flowers seemed odd, definitely beyond the status of their relationship. "You're friends with most people in town. If you did this for everyone..."

"You're not everyone, Leo. We were best friends."

"Yeah, but this is your business. You need to make a living, and I can imagine that it's not easy to stay afloat in such a small town."

"I'm doing great," Ash said.

"Well, I'm not exactly a starving artist either. I can afford to pay for the flowers, you know?"

"This isn't about money. Let me do this for you and your father."

Leo hesitated. Since she had left Fair Oaks, she had learned that most seemingly selfless favors like that came with a hefty price tag later. People always wanted something in return, even when they pretended otherwise. But maybe it wasn't always this way. It wasn't with Holly.

"Thank you," she finally said. "That's very generous of you."

Ash reached out and squeezed her arm. "If there's anything else I can do for you…*anything* at all…"

There was something in her voice and in her eyes that made Leo wonder if that offer included a far more personal form of comfort than flowers. To her own surprise, she wasn't tempted to find out.

"Thanks. Will I see you at the funeral?" With Ashley, she meant the question exactly as she had asked it, not hoping for an earlier time to see her.

Ash's hand was still on her arm. "I'll be there."

"See you on Monday, then." Gently, Leo freed herself of Ash's grip and walked to the door without looking back.

Holly walked into her house and went straight to her laptop, which she had left on the couch on Thursday evening. It felt like weeks, not barely two days ago, and she hadn't fully processed everything that had happened since then.

As soon as her laptop was open, she clicked on the Skype icon in the task bar and logged in.

Meg should be back from her business trip by now, but that didn't mean she was hanging out online.

Please be home. Please be home.

She scrolled through her online contacts. A green tick was displayed next to Meg's avatar, indicating that she was online.

Yes! Hopefully, Meg would be by her computer. She clicked on the contact and then on the call icon.

On the second ring, Meg's smiling face popped up on her laptop screen. Her hair, which was always carefully spiked, stuck to her head on one side.

Normally, Holly would have teased her friend about losing the battle with her hairbrush, but "normal" had gone out of the window the moment Leo had returned to Fair Oaks.

"Hi, Nerdy Nurse," Meg said.

Holly didn't bother with pleasantries. "I did something really stupid," she blurted out.

Meg groaned. "God, please don't tell me you got back together with that closeted flower girl!"

"What? No. It has nothing to do with her."

"Phew." Meg wiped imaginary sweat off her brow. "What is it, then?"

How could she sum up what had happened during the last few days? "Leo's father died yesterday, and I got her down from the roof and then I slept with her, and now I don't—"

"Wait a minute!" If she were a cartoon character, Meg's eyes would have bulged out of their sockets. "You did *what?*"

Holly mentally reviewed what she had just said. "Oh. Oh no. No, not like that. We slept—just slept—in the same bed. She didn't want to be alone, and I...I wanted to be there for her in whatever way she needed."

"And Leo would be...who? Jeez, Holly, I go on a business trip for two weeks, and I don't know what's what in your life anymore." Meg waved her arm like a drowning person wanting someone to throw her a lifeline. "Catch me up, please. Leo...Is that the woman who owns the bakery?"

"Bakery? No, that's my friend Sasha. Leo is..." Holly stopped herself. Should she really tell Meg? Well, she trusted her, and it wasn't as if Leo's full name was a big secret. It was even on Wikipedia. Still, she fixed a gaze on Meg that would have terrified a hardened criminal. "This has to stay between you and me, okay? You can't tell a soul."

Meg's eyes widened. "Not even Jo?"

"Um, you can tell her, but no one else. And tell Jo to keep quiet about it too."

"O-kay." Meg drew out the word carefully. "Now I'm almost afraid of what you have to tell me. I don't have to sell a kidney to bail you out of jail or something like that, do I?"

Holly shook her head. "It's not a kidney thing. It's more of a heart thing."

"You're in love with this mysterious Leo?" Meg's voice came out in a squeak.

"No, no, no. Not love." It wasn't…couldn't be, right? Not this fast. "But…"

Meg held up both hands. "I really think you should start at the beginning. Who is this Leo? Does she live in Fair Oaks?"

"No, and that's part of the problem. She…" Holly lowered her voice, even though no one could overhear her. "Her full name is Leontyne Jenna Blake. She is—"

"Holy fucking unicorn!" Meg screamed so loudly that Holly turned down the volume on the laptop and shushed her. "Jenna Blake? *The* Jenna Blake?"

"The one and only."

Meg inflated her cheeks and then blew out a breath. "So you and Jenna Blake are…?"

"Not me and Jenna. Me and Leo."

A blur of motion filled the screen as Meg waved her hand. "So you and Leo are…? You became close? Like, romantically close?"

Holly bit her lip and nodded.

"Wow." Meg sank against the back of her chair. "How did that happen?"

"I have no idea. I didn't even like her when she first got here. I thought… Well, I assumed a lot of stupid things about her. But once we got past that, we started spending time together." Holly took a deep breath and told her everything that had happened between her and Leo in the past four weeks—their argument in the rain-pelted Jeep, the evening at the bar with the gang, going on runs and getting scones together, nearly cuddling on the bed while watching *Central Precinct*, taking Leo to see the puppies and kittens, playing the piano together, and climbing up to Leo's secret spot on the roof.

She couldn't help smiling through most of her story. These were all happy memories, she realized—the happiest she had made in some time.

When she came to the point where she had told Leo they couldn't be together, all she could think of was the look in Leo's eyes. It reflected the pain she felt herself.

"Then her father died, and everything else took a backseat," she finally ended her story.

"Understandably. Is she okay?"

"I hope she will be," Holly said.

"Are *you* okay?"

Holly ran her fingers through her hair. It didn't help to sort out her chaotic thoughts. "Yeah. Kind of. It's just a lot to process."

"Hell yeah! I never thought you'd get involved with Jenna Blake!"

"We're not involved. Not really. Like I just said, I ended it before…" *Before what? Before she could hurt me?* She put that thought aside for now. "And she's not Jenna to me. She's different, Meg. Different than how I thought she'd be. Different than Dana and Ash. She's smart, considerate, funny, and generous." Holly realized she was babbling and snapped her mouth shut.

"Does she know?"

The question didn't need a qualifier. Not between them. "Yes. I told her when she first asked me out. Didn't I mention it?"

"Nope. Apparently, you skipped the interesting part," Meg said. "So, how did she react?"

Holly sighed. "You know how it goes. They tell you they are fine with it…until they aren't and start to resent you."

"Is that what happened—or what you assume will happen?"

"It's what I *know* would happen if I got involved with her," Holly said. "It happened with Dana and Ashley too."

"You just said she's different from them."

Trust Meg to beat her with her own words. "I thought you of all people would tell me it's not worth the heartbreak and that I'm fine on my own."

Meg gave her an impish grin. "Nah. If you want the stay-away-from-her speech, you've come to the wrong person. Jo always calls me the most romantic aromantic in the world." The grin faded away, and she studied Holly with an earnest expression. "Seriously, though, the way you talk about her, it makes me think there's something there. Why don't you give it a chance?"

"Because it won't work."

"And you know that how?"

"We're too different. I'm ace; she isn't. I'm a nurse; she's a superstar. I live in Fair Oaks; she lives in New York. Do I need to go on?"

Meg snorted. "You think you're an unlikely pair? I've got you beat by a country mile."

"Um, you do?"

"Sure! Hello?" Meg pointed at herself. "Aromantic, asexual, a total chatterbox, and as Irish as a pint of Guinness." She waved her hand toward where Holly knew Jo's room was. "Romantic, not on the ace spectrum, taciturn, and Mexican American. How's that for differences?"

All true, and yet her friends just seemed to fit into each other's lives so perfectly. "Yeah, but it's not the same."

"Why? Because our relationship is not romantic, so it can't possibly be as important?" A look of hurt flashed across Meg's face.

"No," Holly said hastily. "No, of course not. I'm sorry, Mordin. You know I don't believe that at all. I just… Ugh. I don't know. This situation has me all messed up." She scrubbed both hands over her face and then dropped them to her lap.

Meg's expression softened. She leaned closer to the webcam. "When I asked Jo if she wanted to be my queerplatonic partner, I was scared out of my mind. I thought she would think it was weird or not real or something. Even when she said yes, I kept doubting her…doubting us. I thought she'd leave me as soon as she met a hot woman who could fall in love with her. I never thought it would work in the long run." Her grin reached from one ear to the other. "Now look at us. Five years later and we couldn't be happier. In fact…we'll start looking at houses on Monday. We want to buy something in the burbs."

"Wow, Meg! That's great." Holly beamed at her friend. "I'm so happy for you guys."

"Thanks." Even the less-than-stellar quality of their Skype connection couldn't hide that Meg was flushed with happiness. Her eyes shone.

In moments like this, Holly struggled to understand how her friends could insist they were not a traditional couple and that while they loved each other, they weren't in love. It helped her understand how people who weren't asexual themselves often had a hard time understanding her sexual orientation.

In the end, it didn't matter whether she fully understood it or not, as long as it worked for her friends—and it clearly did. But what did that mean for her and Leo?

"So," she finally said, "what's your advice, Dear Abby?"

Meg laughed. "Why do people keep asking the aromantic for relationship advice?"

"Because you're so good at it."

A snort escaped Meg. "I take my wisdom from video games."

"Oh, that reminds me." Holly reached for the card she kept on the coffee table, ready to send out in time for Meg's birthday next week. "I got you the autograph you wanted."

Meg rubbed her hands together. "Great. I wanted to ask you about it, but with my business trip and all, I forgot."

Holly opened the card and held it into the camera. "Can you read it?"

Meg's forehead furrowed in concentration as she leaned toward the screen. "Happy birthday and many butterfly kisses," she read out loud and wrinkled her nose. "Not that I want those. You can have them."

A blush made Holly's cheeks burn as the memory of the two kisses she had shared with Leo flashed through her—and nearly kissing her again earlier, in the Jeep. If she had ever needed proof that sensual attraction existed, she had it now. Not kissing someone had never been so hard, but she couldn't keep giving Leo mixed signals, or she would hurt her even more.

"Oooh!" Meg let out a wolf whistle. "Looks like you already did! You really did skip the interesting parts of your tale."

"Read the PS," Holly said in a stern tone and raised the card to the webcam again to hide her blush.

"PS," Meg read what was below Leo's signature, "Triss is way cooler than Yen." She huffed. "Ha! I take it back. Don't get involved with her. She clearly has no taste in women."

"Hey, she likes *me*," Holly protested.

Meg sobered. "Okay, she has no taste in *fictional* women. But if she's still interested in you after finding out you won't jump into bed with her and after you tried to discourage her at every turn, I think you've got a winner on your hands and should give her a chance. That's my sage advice."

Could she be right? Part of Holly latched on to that bit of hope and didn't want to let go, but another part was still afraid to get hurt again.

She glanced at the clock in the task bar. Leo had probably ordered the flower arrangements by now and was back home. "I should go check on her."

"Yeah, you do that. Keep me up to date on how you two are doing, okay?"

"Will do. And Meg? Thank you."

Meg grinned. "You can thank me by not throwing the bridal bouquet in my direction at your wedding."

"Wedding?" Holly spluttered. "There'll be no wedding."

Still grinning, Meg waved and ended the call.

Chapter 18

ALL THIS TIME, LEO HAD avoided her father, but now she found herself just as uncomfortable around her mother and wanting to do the same. They sat next to each other on the porch swing without saying a word.

When she had gotten back from the flower shop, her mother had already been out here, as if she couldn't stand to be in the empty house by herself. How would she handle it once Leo went back to New York?

The thought made Leo feel guilty, and she resented that. She had worked hard to build her own life and to become successful. Her mother wouldn't expect her to give that up…would she?

"Do you remember when you were a little girl?" her mother interrupted the silence. "You and your father would sit out here for hours and sing together. It was so cute that every neighbor who passed by stopped and listened."

Leo hadn't thought of that in years, probably decades. If she focused, she could still hear her father's voice. Back then, he had always let her pick the songs they would sing instead of trying to force his music preferences on her. He had sung along even to nursery rhymes like "Itsy Bitsy Spider"—complete with the hand motions—and he hadn't cared whether the neighbors had seen him do it.

What had happened to that man to turn him into the strict father she had known as a teenager?

"I can't believe he's gone," her mother whispered, as if speaking any louder would really make it true.

Leo didn't know what to say, so she reached over and put her hand on her mother's arm.

She instantly covered Leo's hand with her own. "I'm so glad you came home and got to see him before…" She pressed her lips together and fell silent.

"Yeah," Leo said, "me too. We talked a little, you know? The night before he… It wasn't overly affectionate or anything like that, but I think we mended some bridges."

"Oh, honey!" Her mother squeezed Leo's fingers with unexpected strength. "You don't know how much I hoped that would happen. I know your father wasn't always great at showing it, but I know it meant a lot to him that you came and took the time to stay so long."

"Did he say that?" Leo asked.

"Well, not in as many words. You know talking was a struggle for him after the second stroke."

"What about before?" Leo couldn't help asking. "Did he talk to you about me? About what he thought of my music and my sexual orientation?"

Her mother patted her hand. "You know how your father was."

"No, actually, the longer I'm here, the more I find I don't." Her jaw felt stiff with tension. "I didn't even know his favorite flower when I ordered the casket spray."

"Lily," her mother said. "It is…was the lily."

Just like hers. But, of course, her mother wouldn't know that. "Why didn't you ever call?" The question surprised even her. She hadn't planned on asking that. She hadn't even been aware that it had been on her mind.

"I…I'm sorry," her mother choked out. "Please don't think I ever forgot about you." She blinked away another tear, this time one that might be for Leo, for them, instead of for her husband.

Adding to her mom's pain made Leo want to take back her question, but at the same time she knew they needed to finally talk about it. "Then why didn't you call?" she repeated her question more softly.

"I was never sure you wanted me to. You were so focused on your new life and didn't seem to want any reminders of who you were before."

Was that really how it had been…how she had been? Leo wanted to dismiss it, but she remembered all too well how hard she had worked those first few years, how focused she had been on getting a record deal, then on recording her debut album and promoting it. There had been space for nothing else in her life.

"Maybe you're right," she finally said, "at least at the beginning. But why didn't you call me when he had his first stroke…and then the one in May?" She swallowed down the lump of emotion in her throat so she could continue. "Didn't it occur to you that I'd want to know?" Maybe now, just twenty-four hours after her father's death, wasn't the right moment to have this conversation, but Leo realized the question had gnawed at her for quite some time, and her mother had never really answered her when she'd asked it the first time.

"Of course it did. I wanted to call you the minute it happened. Please believe me." Her mother's eyes swam in tears. "But your father was a proud man. He didn't want you to see him like that—weak and helpless. Only when he was out of the hospital and had worked with his therapists for a while did he finally give in and allow me to call."

His damn pride… Leo bit the inside of her cheek until she tasted the coppery tang of blood. "Allow you?" she forced out, her voice rough. She had always hated the way her mother went along with whatever her father wanted, as if she were unable to make her own decisions. When her father had told Leo he wouldn't tolerate her "lifestyle," her mother had just stood by. She struggled to tone down her anger. "What about what you wanted? Couldn't you call me anyway?"

Her mother firmly shook her head. "No, Leontyne. I couldn't, no matter how much I wanted to. If I didn't respect his wishes in this one thing, he would have never forgiven me." She wiped away her tears and looked at Leo, scrutinizing her so closely as if searching for answers in her very soul. "Will you?" she whispered.

Before Leo could grasp the meaning of her question, her mother continued hastily, as if she was afraid of what Leo would say. "I know your father and I…we weren't always the best parents, but we were still your parents, and we loved you." She choked back a sob. "I love you."

Sudden tears burned in Leo's eyes, and she wiped at them with jerky movements. Part of her wanted to hide behind that armor of resentment that had protected her so far. It would make going back to New York a lot easier. But the other part knew that she was ready for a new beginning. Why else would she have come home and hung around for four weeks, even though her mother and Holly had her father's care well in hand and there wasn't much for her to do?

Now she only had one parent left, and she would be damned if she destroyed what relationship they had by clinging to the same stupid pride her father had.

"I...I forgive you, and...and I love you too." She had said it for her mother's sake, but as soon as it was out, she realized that it was true and that saying it had a freeing effect on her too.

New tears streamed down her mother's cheeks. Sobbing, she sank into Leo's arms.

Leo held her, very awkwardly at first, but as the minutes ticked by, she relaxed a little.

"Thank you," her mother whispered into her shoulder.

"It wasn't all your fault, you know?" She could admit that to her mother and herself now.

Somehow, her mother managed to shake her head while still having her face pressed to Leo's shoulder. "It was. I don't blame you for leaving home as soon as you could. We were—"

"Shhh." As good as it felt to hear those words, they wouldn't help them move forward. "What's done is done. Let's focus on doing better in the future."

Her mother moved back and blew her nose with a handkerchief that had the initials of Leo's father. A ghost of a smile tugged on her lips, looking almost surreal on her tear-streaked face. "I'd love to think you got that maturity from me, but I think you came by it all on your own."

Maturity? Leo nearly laughed. Hanging out at home for four weeks without talking to either of her parents didn't seem very mature to her. "I think I inherited a few things from you and Dad too." Not all of them good, but she'd need to work on that.

They sat in silence for a while, softly rocking back and forth on the porch swing.

"There's one more thing I need to ask of you," her mother said. "It would have meant so much to your father."

Instantly, Leo tensed.

Her mother looked at her through watery eyes. "Would you give the eulogy?"

That was the last thing Leo had expected. Her stomach rose up in her throat. "Me?"

Her mother nodded.

"Why me?"

"You are his daughter."

It was similar to what Holly had said to her last night, up on the roof, as if that simple statement said it all. But it wasn't that easy for her. "I wouldn't know what to say."

Her mother patted her hand. "It'll come to you. You write such beautiful lyrics. I know you'll come up with something that's just right."

She knows my songs…and she thinks they're beautiful? Leo gaped at her before remembering what they were talking about. Her mother might like some of her songs, but she didn't know the whole truth—that she hadn't written anything and certainly not anything beautiful in years. She opened her mouth to say so, then closed it again. This wasn't the time to burden her mother with her career problems.

"Please," her mother said. "I think this is important. Not just for your father, but for you too. It'll give you a chance to reflect on his life and maybe get some closure."

Acid roiled in her stomach. "I'll think about it." That was all she could promise for now, and her mother luckily didn't press for more.

Holly's red Jeep swung into the driveway.

Leo's stomach stopped its theatrics and settled down…at least for the few seconds before Holly climbed out from behind the wheel, and then butterflies started to swarm.

Their gazes met across the driveway.

Leo wanted to run toward her and throw herself into Holly's arms as if they had been through a decade-long exile instead of being apart for less than two hours. *Ridiculous,* she told herself. It was probably just one of the stages of grief that heightened her emotions. But whatever it was, she was damn glad to see her.

As Holly crossed the driveway toward the house, she immediately zeroed in on Leo. She looked emotionally drained, but her eyes were dry. Was that a good or a bad thing?

At the base of the three steps leading up to the house, Holly paused and looked up at mother and daughter, not wanting to interrupt if they were having a moment, finally talking.

Before she could say anything, Sharon gave her a shaky smile. "Hi, Holly. Thank you for going with Leontyne to the funeral home. I..." She dabbed her eyes. "I couldn't."

Holly climbed the three steps and gave her a smile. "You're welcome. If you need anything, my family and I are always just a phone call away."

Sharon nodded and got up. "Thank you. I'll go make dinner."

"You don't need to do that," Leo said. "The entire town brought over enough food to last us the rest of the year. And if you're in the mood for something else, I can make it."

Sharon patted her shoulder and moved past her. "I know, but it'll give me something to do." Instead of walking past Holly, she engulfed her in a hug. "I'm so glad you're there for Leontyne," she whispered.

Before Holly could think of an answer, the screen door closed behind her, leaving Holly and Leo alone.

"What was that about?" Leo tilted her head and nodded to where her mother had disappeared.

"She was just...thanking me."

When Leo patted the now-empty space next to her, she took a seat. The porch swing was large enough for three, yet they both scooted toward the middle and sat with their bodies touching from their shoulders to their bare knees. Feeling Leo against her like this was incredibly nice. It could become an addiction, if she let it.

"How are you?" she asked quietly.

For a moment, Leo looked as if she would put her off with an "I'm okay," but then she said instead, "My mother wants me to give the eulogy."

Wow. Getting up there in front of half of the town when everything inside her was still so raw... Holly hadn't been able to do that at her father's funeral. She had left it to her brother Zack. "If you don't want to do it, I could help you find someone else."

Leo shifted even closer and used her feet to set the porch swing in motion as if she needed a few moments to think about it. "Thanks. But I think I'll do it. My dad and I, we missed so many moments we could have had together. I don't want to look back and have even more regrets about something I didn't do, just because I was afraid to put myself out there."

Holly swallowed. She knew Leo was talking about her relationship with her father, but the words fit her and Leo too. Holly certainly had a lot of regrets, especially about hurting Leo. "That's very brave."

Leo turned her head and looked at her, those olive-green eyes turbulent and intense.

Was she thinking about the same thing?

"I'm sorry I wasn't as brave," Holly said quietly. "I wanted to believe in you...in us, and a part of me really does. It's just..." She fell silent, unsure if this was really the time and place to bring it up. Leo had enough on her plate right now.

"I know I should focus on the funeral right now, but I feel like everything is slipping through my fingers if I don't hold on to it." Leo stopped and cleared her throat. "I think we will regret it too if we don't give this...give us a try. I don't want to pressure you into anything you don't want, and if you honestly think we're better off as friends, I'll have to accept that, but I'd really like to try because I think you're wonderful and everything I want in a woman."

Her words made Holly's heart sing, but at the same time she couldn't quite trust them yet. "Except for being asexual," she murmured and stared off into space.

Leo gently touched her fingers to her cheek and directed Holly's head around to look at her. "No," she said forcefully. "That's not what I said or what I thought. You're great, just the way you are."

"I know you believe that...at least for now." Holly struggled to keep her voice from trembling. "But you're a passionate woman, Leo. I hear it in your music and see it in everything you do. At some point, you'll want more. You'll want that passion with me, and I can't give it, and then you'll start to resent me, and that would break my heart." She pressed her hand to her chest because she could already sense that pain, and now she had made herself even more vulnerable by speaking so openly.

"I'm not saying it will always be easy, but why would I resent you for something that is a part of you?"

"I…I don't know, but that's the way it's always been." All the bitterness and the hurt that had accumulated deep inside of her over the years chose that moment to rise up. "If I don't put out—"

"Put out? Jesus, Holly!" Leo took both of her hands and clutched them almost painfully tight. "Listen to me. I'll say this only once, and if you still think it's not worth taking the risk, I'll leave you be. Relationships are hard—not just for asexual people. I've never been able to make any of mine work. Want to know why?"

Her throat was choked with emotion, so Holly only nodded, clinging to Leo's every word and to her hands.

"Once I became famous, women started flocking to me like moths to a flame," Leo said. "They didn't hesitate to jump into bed with me or even to move into my condo."

A fierce stab went through Holly's chest. *Great.* Now she could add jealousy to the chaotic mix of emotions swirling through her.

Leo stroked her hands as if she could sense it. "But not one of them could separate Leo from Jenna. They loved me for my fame, my money, my pop-star sex appeal, but not for who I am, deep inside. So, in a way, your sexual orientation is a good thing for me." She paused as if contemplating what she had just said, then nodded in confirmation. "Your asexuality makes you see beyond all that surface stuff."

Hope trickled through her. Did Leo really see her asexuality that way—as something positive? "Well, I happen to think that most of us aces are pretty awesome, but there are a few superficial, money-grubbing assholes among us too, you know?" She forced a smile, trying for a bit of levity because the emotions bouncing back and forth between them were almost too intense to stand.

"Yeah, but not you," Leo said with unshakable conviction. "You appreciate me for me, not for my body or my fame. You see *me*."

"I do," Holly whispered. *Jesus.* They had kissed exactly twice, and yet here they were, sounding as if they were proposing marriage. It was crazy—and it felt completely right.

"I see you too. And I want to see more of you." Leo gave a lopsided grin. "And that's not an allusion to wanting to see you naked." She sobered. "But if that's not what you want…"

Holly sucked in a lungful of air. This was it. Either she had to follow Meg's advice and put her heart on the line…or she had to let Leo go for good. *Come on. Be brave.* "I want it. I want *us*."

A huge grin spread across Leo's face, making her even more beautiful.

Holly was still afraid, mainly of not being enough for Leo, but that look on Leo's face made it worth the risk.

"Oh God, Holly. Thank you." Leo lifted one of Holly's hands to her mouth and kissed her open palm while staring into her eyes. "C-can I…? Can I kiss you?"

Holly loved the way Leo had not just assumed it would be okay because they had agreed to try a relationship. Again, her voice deserted her, so she leaned toward Leo and kissed her instead.

Leo sighed against her lips. Her mouth was soft and warm and incredibly tender.

Holly sank into the kiss and forgot everything else for a while. It had been so long since she'd last been able to do that, just enjoy a kiss, without a part of her keeping watch for the moment she had to break it off before her partner would want more.

Leo's hands didn't start to wander. Instead, her fingers entwined with Holly's own so Holly could fully relax into the kiss. God, she could kiss Leo forever.

The creaking of the screen door made them move apart.

Leo's mother leaned in the doorway and looked back and forth between them. "Um, I'm sorry. I didn't mean to…um…"

"It's okay." Holly tried to pull her hand from Leo's grasp, but Leo wouldn't let go. Apparently, she didn't intend to hide their relationship from her mother. *Not that that's even possible, seeing as she just caught us kissing.* Holly stifled a giggle that wanted to bubble from her chest. Was it wrong to feel so happy so soon after Gil's death?

"I forgot to ask if you'd like to have dinner with us." Sharon directed her words at Holly. "Are you staying the night again?"

Again… So Sharon knew that she hadn't gone home last night. She didn't seem upset about it. Did she assume Holly had slept in the guest room?

Holly turned her head to direct a questioning gaze at Leo. Did she want her to stay?

Leo gave her the same questioning look.

"I'd like that," Holly said, more to Leo than to Sharon.

Judging by Leo's smile, that was the answer she had hoped for.

"Good," Sharon said. "I'm making tuna casserole, your favorite." She ducked back inside, and the screen door banged shut behind her.

"I think she likes you better than me," Leo murmured.

"Nah. So, what's your favorite dinner food?"

"Not sure I have one. I'm more of a dessert kind of woman."

"Really?"

Leo nodded. "Yeah. For example, I could really go for another kiss right now."

"Hmm…" Holly pretended to think about it. "But if you get that kiss right now, before dinner, it isn't dessert, is it?"

"Then I declare kisses my favorite dinner and tuna casserole my favorite dessert." Leo gave her a dazzling smile. "Does that work?"

In the past, kissing and anything that might head into sexual territory had been a serious thing for her. Now she was surprised how much she enjoyed their playfulness. "We'll make it work." She hoped that would be true for so much more than just their dessert.

Then she stopped thinking and leaned toward Leo to enjoy her new favorite dinner.

The floorboards in the upstairs hall creaked beneath Leo's feet as she shifted her weight and watched her mother and Holly tightly embrace in front of her mom's bedroom door.

Was it just her, or was this a little weird?

Fourteen years ago, her parents would have kicked any girlfriend she brought home out of the house—and Leo along with her. Hell, that was practically what they had done when they had found out she was gay. Now her mother was clinging to Holly, acting as if she were a beloved daughter-in-law.

Watching them together—watching Holly made her smile. Holly was so sweet, warm, and genuine, and Leo couldn't help admiring her. At the same time, it made her a little jealous because her own interaction with her mother didn't have that ease. There was too much history between them.

Finally, her mother let go of Holly and walked up to Leo. Grief and loneliness were reflected in her eyes.

She would have to climb into her cold, empty bed with only her memories to keep her company while Leo would get to cuddle up to Holly all night—that was, if Holly was okay with doing that again.

A wave of compassion overcame Leo, and it didn't feel so awkward to wrap her arms around her mother and hold her close.

Her mother clung to her as if she never wanted to let go. Finally, she dropped her arms with an audible sigh.

"Are you sure you don't want a sleeping pill?" Holly asked.

"I'm sure. I don't want to rely on them too much."

"Mom, I don't think another night or two will hurt any," Leo said.

Her mother shook her head. "Thanks, but I'll be fine. I'm exhausted, so I'll fall asleep eventually."

Leo gave up. Apparently, she hadn't inherited her stubbornness just from her father.

"If you change your mind, come get me any time." Holly pointed at the door to Leo's room.

So they would share a bed again. It was almost a bit silly how relieved Leo felt at that thought.

"I will." Her mom kissed them both on the cheek and then went into her room. The door clicked shut behind her.

They faced each other in the otherwise empty hall.

"So…" they said at the same time and then smiled at each other.

"Want to have the bathroom first?" Leo asked.

"Yes. Thanks. I'll hurry. You must be pretty exhausted too."

"Kind of." She was, but at the same time, she knew she was too wired to sleep.

They took turns showering, and when Leo stepped out of the bathroom, Holly was already snuggled into bed. *God, I could get used to seeing that every night.* Her steps faltered. *Whoa! Every night? Don't put the cart before the horse.*

Holly lifted the edge of the covers up for her, and Leo slipped into bed beside her. Drawn in by Holly's warmth, she moved closer and wrapped one arm around her. "Is this okay?"

"Very." Holly put one arm around her too.

Their bodies came together in the middle of the bed, Leo's face snuggled into the crook of Holly's shoulder and her leg across Holly's thighs.

They both let out a hum and then a chuckle.

"Does the Asexual Headquarters award you a toaster oven if you convert a certain quota of women into cuddle bugs?" Leo asked without lifting her head from its comfy space. "Because I've got to tell you, you're well on your way with me."

The warm body beneath hers shook as Holly laughed. "If they do, I'm nowhere near the quota. You are my first. Converted cuddle bug, I mean."

Now Leo lifted her head to stare at her. "Really?"

"Yeah. With my other partners, it was more them trying to convert me." Holly's voice vibrated as if she was struggling to hold back a sigh.

Leo slid up in bed a little, dipped her head down, and whispered against Holly's lips, "Fools." *Goddamn fools.* She gave her a soft kiss.

Holly slid her fingers into Leo's hair and returned the kiss. At first, it was just a brush of their lips against each other—a simple, almost chaste contact, yet it felt as if Leo was finally coming home.

Then Holly tentatively opened her mouth and touched her tongue to Leo's bottom lip.

Oh Jesus. Pleasure surged along Leo's nerves. She parted her own lips and eased her tongue forward to caress Holly's with gentle, almost careful strokes.

After a moment, Holly melted against her.

Leo angled her head so she could explore even more of her. *God, silk and fire.* Heat twisted low in her belly. Holly's fingers against her scalp and the glide of her tongue against Leo's felt so incredible that she couldn't help moaning.

Holly went still against her.

Dazed, Leo broke the kiss and blinked down at her.

Holly looked away. "Sorry, I…"

"Hey." She caressed Holly's face with her fingertips until she made eye contact. "It was a kiss. A very nice one, but nothing more. Just because it didn't leave me, um, unaffected doesn't mean I'm up for anything more. Even sexual people don't want to be sexual all the time. You can relax." She smiled. "Really."

Holly brought her own hands up to Leo's face too and brushed strands of hair behind her ears, all the while looking into her eyes. "Okay," she whispered and pulled her back down for another kiss.

Again, Holly was the one to deepen the kiss, and Leo kept pace with her, grateful that they weren't going too fast. This slow, unhurried exploration was exactly what she needed right now.

When they pulled back several minutes later, Leo was breathless—not so much because of what they had shared physically, but because of the emotions it evoked. Her gaze clung to the blue of Holly's eyes, which were watching her as if she were hypnotized. She gently caressed Holly's cheek with the back of her fingers, then turned her hand around and cupped her cheek in her open palm. "Good night."

It wasn't that she was tired, but she wanted to signal Holly that she wasn't waiting for anything else to happen tonight.

Holly leaned her face into Leo's touch. Her eyes fluttered shut before blinking open again. A slow smile tugged on her lips as if she had received Leo's message. "Good night," she whispered, sounding a little out of breath too.

So she hadn't been entirely unaffected by their kiss either, even though it might not have been the same effect that she had experienced. The thought made Leo grin. She reached across Holly to flick off the lamp on the bedside table and then turned on her side.

Immediately, Holly spooned up against her back and fit her body around Leo's.

With a contented hum, Leo pulled Holly's arm more tightly around herself, flattened their palms against her upper chest with her hand covering Holly's, and closed her eyes. Even if she might not be able to sleep, she would be happy to spend the night like this.

Holly woke with a start. Her eyes fluttered open. It was still pitch-dark in the room, which meant dawn hadn't broken and she could cuddle up to Leo and go back to sleep.

Drowsily, she reached out, expecting to find warm skin, but encountered only cold sheets instead.

What the…? She sat up. Had Leo gotten up to use the bathroom? "Leo?" she called out quietly so as not to disturb Sharon, who slept next door.

No answer came from the bathroom, and no band of light seeped in from under the door.

A prickle of worry ran down her spine. She shook off the lingering effects of sleep and climbed out of bed to search for her missing bedmate.

The dormer window was closed, so clearly, Leo hadn't climbed out onto the roof.

In her pajamas, she tiptoed downstairs, not bothering to turn on a light so she wouldn't wake Sharon.

A glimmer of light falling into the hall from the kitchen guided her. She paused in the doorway to let her eyes adjust to the sudden brightness. Once they did, she could make out Leo sitting at the breakfast bar, a glass of milk and a notepad in front of her.

Was she working on a new song? Holly watched her without announcing her presence, not wanting to interrupt in case Leo really was composing—or maybe she just enjoyed watching her while Leo felt unobserved.

Leo sat with one of her long legs up, her bare foot half-tucked beneath her on the seat. Her tank top revealed plenty of her smooth skin. She fiddled with a pen, every now and then reaching up with her other hand to tuck a strand of her honey-blonde hair behind her ear.

So beautiful. Holly loved how strength and vulnerability combined in her features and her body.

Whatever Leo was working on, it wasn't going too well. Crumpled-up pages surrounded her, and the top sheet of the notepad was empty except for a ring of condensation from the glass of milk.

Before Holly could decide whether to announce herself or to let her be, Leo looked up, as if sensing her gaze. Her tense features relaxed into a smile. "Hey. I didn't mean to wake you."

"You didn't," Holly said. "I just…" *Couldn't sleep without you?* "I woke up, and you weren't there. Are you okay?"

"Yeah. Just couldn't sleep, so I thought I might as well get up and work on the eulogy."

Holly crossed the kitchen and climbed onto a stool next to her. "How is it going?"

Leo sighed. "Not good. You're supposed to come up with something inspiring and uplifting, right?"

"Well, that's what Zack tried to do for my father's eulogy."

"Everything I've written so far," Leo indicated the ripped-out sheets of paper strewn around her, "was about as uplifting as bankruptcy or flatulence. Completely lame. I might have written Grammy-winning song lyrics, but I can't write this." She dropped her pen on the empty notepad.

Holly slid her stool closer and reached up to massage Leo's shoulders. The muscles felt like rocks under her hands.

Groaning, Leo leaned into the touch, and Holly would have bet money that her eyes were fluttering closed. After a while, the tension in her shoulders eased a little, and she turned around to face Holly. "Thank you." She took Holly's hands and pressed a kiss to each one.

"I know it's hard," Holly said quietly. "Especially knowing you'll have to read it in front of the whole town."

Leo shook her head. "That's not it. I'm used to having an audience. I would gladly get up in front of a thousand people if I had anything to say."

Holly looked from the long, slender fingers that still held hers up to Leo's eyes. "How did you do it when you wrote 'Odd One Out'?"

"I don't know." Leo shrugged. "I just…did it. I just let everything I felt about my childhood pour out onto the paper."

"Then maybe that's what you should do with the eulogy. Don't think about it too much. Just speak from the heart. But not now. You need to get some sleep first." She slid off the stool and pulled Leo up too.

Hand in hand, they climbed the stairs, stopped in front of Sharon's door, and peeked in on her. It felt strangely as if they were a married couple checking on their kids.

That thought made Holly chuckle, and she quickly closed the door so Sharon wouldn't hear her.

"What is it?" Leo asked.

"Nothing." It had been a completely crazy thought, especially since they hadn't talked about the future at all. She definitely needed to get some sleep too. But first she wanted to hold Leo and maybe give her a head rub until she fell asleep.

Chapter 19

AFTER SPENDING EVERY MINUTE OF the past two days with Leo, it felt weird to leave her behind on Sunday, but Holly's mother would have killed her if she hadn't shown up for dinner with the family. None of them had missed a Sunday since their father had died.

She had pondered asking her mother if she could bring two guests. No one would have batted an eye since they often had friends join them, but Sharon didn't feel up to the lively family setting, and Leo didn't want to leave her mother.

When Holly saw what was for dinner, she was glad she had come.

Zack barely waited until everyone was sitting at the table before he pounced on the ham balls. He gobbled one down almost straight from the pan. "Oh shit. That's hot," he mumbled around a mouthful but still reached for a second.

"Serves you right," their mother said. "Let them cool down a little."

Holly heaped scalloped potatoes on her plate and took the bowl of carrots her sister-in-law handed her.

"How are Sharon and Leontyne doing?" her mother asked from the head of the table.

"They're hanging in there, but tomorrow is going to be tough."

Her mother stared right through the bowls on the table, as if remembering a day five years in the past. "Once the funeral is over, it's going to get better. At least it's sinking in, and then you can really start to grieve. We're all going to be there to show our support, right?"

Zack and Ethan and their wives nodded.

"It's nice of you to keep looking after Sharon," Lisa said to Holly, who paused with her fork halfway to her mouth.

Damn. She hadn't told her family about her and Leo yet, so apparently, her sister-in-law now assumed she was over at the Blakes' because she'd been Gil's nurse. Holly hesitated. Should she really tell them now? Or would it be better to wait?

Wait for what? For the funeral to be over…or for either of you to fuck up and ruin what you have? She put her fork down. *You can't keep thinking like that.* If she wanted their relationship to work, she had to believe in it—starting right now.

"I'm not over there as a nurse," she said loudly so she would be heard over the background noise of conversation, cutlery on plates, and Noah pretending the carrot on his fork was a tractor. "Leo and I… We're together. As in, a couple."

Zack took another ham ball and grinned at her. "Does that mean we get to fly on her private jet and stay on some Caribbean island for your wedding?"

"She doesn't own a private jet," Holly said, choosing to ignore the other part of his question.

"Oh, honey!" Her mother jumped up, hurried to Holly's end of the table, and hugged her. "That's wonderful news!"

Holly sank into her mother's warm embrace, aware how lucky she was to have a family who took this as good news. "Thank you. And thanks for talking me into giving the long-distance thing a chance."

Her nieces and nephews rushed her for a hug too, even though most of them were too young to really understand what was going on. But Holly was happy to accept their hugs anyway. She ignored the fact that some of their hands were sticky from the brown-sugar glaze on the ham balls.

"I thought you dumped her?" Ethan said when everyone had settled back down.

Holly stared at him. How the heck did he know that? Sometimes, the very effective Fair Oaks rumor mill amazed her. "Who said I did?"

"Leo."

"Leo?" Holly echoed. "When was that?"

"Thursday, I think. She was crying into her beer at Johnny's."

Holly's stomach plummeted. "Crying?"

"Not literally. More like sulking." Ethan shrugged. "But she said it wasn't because..." He flicked his gaze to the other members of the family. "Because of you being...um, unique. She said that wasn't a problem for her. Cool, hmm?"

Their mother frowned. "What's that supposed to mean? Of course your sister is unique. Why would that be a problem for Leontyne?"

Holly glared at her brother. *Great.* Now he had gotten her in trouble. Maybe she finally needed to have that conversation with her mother. "There is no problem, Mom. I'll explain it later." Coming out to her entire family in one big swoop was a bit much for her, especially with the kids right there, listening in.

She spent the rest of dinner picking at her food. Normally, she loved ham balls as much as everyone else in her family, but suddenly, every bite sat in her stomach like lumps of chalk—and tasted about the same.

Her mother eyed her the entire time but didn't say anything until Zack, Ethan, and their families had said their goodbyes.

Holly rinsed the last of the dishes while her mother packed leftovers for her to take to Sharon and Leo.

"So," her mother said as she clicked the last container shut, "what was Ethan talking about earlier?"

Holly closed the dishwasher, leaned against it, and wiped her damp palms on her shorts. Why was this so hard? She wasn't a teenager anymore, and even if she were, her mother would hardly kick her out of the house for *not* sleeping with someone. The thought made her giggle almost hysterically.

Her mother eyed her. "It's nothing bad, is it?"

"No. It's not," she said firmly. "It's just something about me that I want you to know."

Her mom steered her over to the breakfast nook and had her take a seat. "What is it? Is this the secret that you never talked about? And don't bother saying you're not keeping secrets. I know there's something you keep to yourself."

"It's not exactly a secret, but...yeah. I'm not ashamed of it. It's just unusual and hard to understand." Holly gripped the small table between them with both hands and looked her mother in the eyes. "Mom, I'm asexual."

Somehow, it didn't have the same oomph as *Mom, I'm gay,* she thought wryly—and it didn't get the same reaction.

Her mother furrowed her brow until she looked like one of the bassets she treated. "What do you mean?"

Holly took a deep breath. "It means that I'm not attracted to people. Not sexually, at least."

"Not attracted to people?" Her mother's eyes widened. "You don't expect me to believe that you're one of the people they showed on TV? The ones who are attracted to their rubber plants or something."

"What?" A startled laugh escaped her. "No, Mom. That's not what it means. I'm not attracted to anyone...or anything. I never have been."

"But...but...I don't understand. You've been with Dana."

"Yes, but..." Holly cleared her throat. Talking about this with her mother was awkward. "I never experienced a strong desire to sleep with her."

Her mother nibbled her lip. "Have you seen a doctor? Maybe there's something wrong with your hormones."

Holly sighed. She should have expected a medical explanation from her mother, the vet. "No, Mom. My hormones are fine."

"And you're sure it wasn't just Dana who couldn't...um, who wasn't right for you?"

Holly shook her head. "I've been with other people, and it was the same. It's not them. It's me. This is my sexual orientation, just like being straight is yours."

The lines on her mother's forehead deepened. "I thought you were a lesbian?"

"I am," Holly said. "At least I still identify that way. Being a lesbian isn't only about sex. It's also about who you fall in love with...about who you want to date and kiss and build a life with. I think Leo is absolutely beautiful. I could stare at her forever, and I love holding her and kissing her, but that doesn't make me want to...um, get horizontal with her."

"Then it's more like a friendship?"

"No, Mom. What Leo and I have isn't platonic. There's so much more to a relationship that makes it different from a friendship, not only sex. Just because I'm not eager to sleep with her doesn't mean that I don't love her." She pressed both hands to her mouth. Had she really just said that, and…had she meant it? She breathed in and out deeply. *Yes,* she admitted to herself. They had only been together for a very short time, but that didn't stop the feelings from being there—or from being real.

A careful smile replaced her mother's frown. "You do?"

Her heart thudded in her throat, so Holly couldn't speak. She just nodded.

"Does Leontyne know?" her mother asked.

Holly shook her head. "I only now admitted it to myself."

"That you're…what did you call it…asexual?"

"No. I've known that for years. I just wasn't ready to tell you. I meant that I only now admitted to myself that I love her. But she does know that I'm asexual."

"So that was what your brother was hinting at?" her mother asked. "That she doesn't mind you not wanting to sleep with her?"

Holly nodded while her mind was busy repeating that last phrase. *Not wanting to sleep with her…* That wasn't exactly what being asexual meant, although it did boil down to this for most aces. But it would probably overwhelm her mother if she tried to explain the finer nuances of sexual attraction right now.

Her mother let out a deep sigh. "If you feel this is the way you are, then I'll accept it. It just makes me a bit sad to think that you're missing out on such a wonderful aspect of a relationship. Your father and I—"

Holly slapped her hands over her ears. "Lalalalala. I really don't want to hear about this."

Her mother laughed. "Okay, okay. No details. But it's still something wonderful that I would have wanted for you."

"Wonderful by *your* standards," Holly said. "Do you ever feel like you're missing out by not eating broccoli?"

Her mom wrinkled her nose and shook herself as if smelling something foul. "Why would I? You know I hate broccoli."

"See? It's not that I hate sex, but I wouldn't seek it out, and I certainly don't feel like I'm missing out on anything." She made eye contact. "Please don't judge me by your standards or think my relationship is any less normal or important."

Her mother stared down at her folded hands on the table, then back up. Finally, she nodded once. "You're right. I don't understand it, but I accept it."

That was it? She had agonized for years over whether and how to tell her mother, fearing she might not understand, and now her mother just accepted it?

Holly struggled to speak through the lump in her throat. "When was the last time I told you how much I love and appreciate you?"

The laugh lines around her mother's mouth deepened, and her eyes shone. "Earlier, when you came in and smelled the ham balls."

They laughed together.

Then her mother sobered. "I just want you to be happy—by your standards, not mine."

With tears in her eyes, Holly got up and rounded the table for another hug. "I'm getting there," she whispered into her mom's shoulder.

Leo sat in the front pew of the church, next to her mother.

When the organist began to play Pachelbel's "Canon in D," her mother's silent tears turned into all-out sobs.

Leo wrapped one arm around her and bowed her head. If only she had picked another piece of music… But maybe it wasn't the music that had made her mother cry. Maybe it was that her father had played the organ in this very church every Sunday for more than thirty years.

Finally, the organ faded away, and the minister began his homily.

The words rushed by Leo without her grasping their meaning. All she could do was stare at the casket at the end of the central aisle. The mahogany shone in the sunlight streaming through the stained-glass windows. Her father lay on the white satin in the starched shirt and tie he had always worn to church. Part of her still couldn't believe that this was him, that she would never again be able to talk to him. Now, in death, he looked softer, more approachable than he had when he had been alive.

Leo hoped that meant he had made peace with his life before he had died.

The minister started to read from the Bible. When he was done, it would be her turn.

She shifted on the pew. Why did they have to be so hard? She resisted the urge to bounce her knee up and down while she waited for her turn to speak. Her hand repeatedly slid to the folded piece of paper in the chest pocket of her blazer, just to make sure it was still there.

Finally, the minister wrapped up his reading. "Leontyne, Gilbert's daughter, has some words she would like to share with us."

Suddenly, Leo wanted nothing more than to keep sitting on the uncomfortable pew. She squeezed her mother's arm, got up, and walked over to the lectern to the right of the altar.

She took out her notes, slowly unfolded them, and smoothed out the pages before laying her speech on the lectern. The microphone was a little too low, so she reached out and adjusted it to her height. She must have stood in front of a microphone a few thousand times during her career, but never had her fingers been this unsteady.

Slowly, she looked up and out over the casket at the crowd of black-clad people.

The church was filled to capacity. A few people even stood at the back of the church because every seat was taken. Everyone in town had known her father, and now they were all staring at her, waiting for what she would have to say.

She searched out Holly's face in the sea of people. There she was, sitting with her family. Last night, during the visitation at the funeral home, Holly had been by her side, helping her through it all, and when Holly now gave her an encouraging nod, Leo nodded back. She could do this.

Her gaze zeroed in on the slightly wrinkled notes. She had labored over them all day yesterday, but they hadn't gotten any better. They sounded more like the introduction of a keynote speaker at a conference than a eulogy for her father.

Holly made eye contact and mimed crumpling up her notes and tossing them aside. She mouthed something, and Leo could guess what it was. *Speak from the heart,* Holly had told her.

She's right. Anything was better than this impersonal speech. After she had finally found the courage to talk—to really talk—to her father that last night, this felt like a step back.

She folded the pages and put them back into her pocket.

Holly smiled at her, thawing that frozen feeling that had overcome Leo.

She leaned in to the microphone and did what she had done with "Odd One Out": she just let everything pour out. "I had a speech prepared, but a very wise woman told me to speak from the heart, so I think I'll try that instead."

An approving murmur went through the audience. Well, they didn't know yet what she was about to say.

"First, thank you all for being here today. I think it would have made my father proud to see how many people came to honor him. For the last two days, I tried to find the right words to do the same—to honor him with this eulogy. After all, that's what giving a eulogy is all about: talking about the traits of the deceased that you admired and sharing some happy memories, right?" She let her gaze sweep over the pews.

Several people in the front rows nodded.

"Right. And I wish I could stand here and do that, but I feel like I hardly knew him at all."

Someone in the back of the church cleared their throat.

Leo clutched the sides of the lectern with both hands and continued. "You see, my father and I hadn't talked in fourteen years. Even when I went home for my grandmother's funeral, we sat next to each other in this very pew," she nodded toward where her mother sat, "like we were complete strangers. In many ways, that's what we were. We never understood each other, even before my father had the second stroke and could hardly talk anymore."

She kept her gaze on Holly while she spoke, without glancing toward her mother. If she saw a look of disapproval on her mother's face, she wouldn't be able to finish this—and she needed to.

"Truth be told, I didn't try very hard. I thought I already knew how every conversation with him would end: with us going our separate ways in anger. So while I've been home for four weeks, I didn't spend much of that time with him, and he seemed to prefer it that way."

It felt strange to stand up here and say that, almost as if she were talking about someone else. Her face and mouth were so stiff that she could hardly form the words.

"It wasn't until the night before he died that we finally talked, and I started to remember all the good things about him that I had forgotten. His integrity and strong work ethic. His sharp mind and his tenacity. If he made a promise, he always followed through, no matter what, and he expected the same of others. He taught me the value of hard work and to stand up for what I believe in...even if he didn't always like my beliefs. I discovered that we had more in common than I had thought. Not just our passion for music, but the way we dealt with problems—by avoiding them."

She tried a smile, but her lips didn't cooperate. "We avoided talking for fourteen years. We almost waited too long. I nearly missed my last chance to talk to him. I would have never known a lot of his attitudes toward me had changed over the years."

Her eyes burned, so she reached up to wipe across them with her thumb and forefinger. She stared at the tears on her fingertips. God, this was hard. "Don't make the same mistake. Don't leave too much unsaid. Tell the people in your life how much they mean to you before they're gone."

More words wanted to come, but they all tangled up somewhere between her chest and her mouth, so she finally gave up and stepped down from the podium.

On the way back to her seat, she touched her fingers to her father's casket. The smooth mahogany beneath her fingertips grounded her a little. She took several deep breaths and slid back into the pew without glancing at anyone.

What would her mother say? Airing their dirty family laundry in front of half the town certainly wasn't what she'd had in mind when she had asked Leo to deliver the eulogy.

A handkerchief appeared in her line of vision.

Leo took it and blew her nose before reluctantly turning her head.

Her mother was smiling at her, even with tears in her eyes.

Smiling! Leo stared.

"Thank you," her mother whispered and took Leo's hand.

"But...but that wasn't exactly what he would have wanted me to..."

Her mother squeezed her hand, interrupting her. "Sometimes, it's not about what you want; it's about what you need. He needed to hear that years ago. All three of us did. And maybe some of them," she tilted her head toward the people in the pews behind them, "did too."

The opening notes of the organ amplified around them, and everyone stood to sing a hymn.

Leo didn't let go of her mother's hand as she rose too.

The rest of the service passed in a blur. Before Leo knew it, they were following behind the hearse to the cemetery.

Again, she barely heard a word of the minister's prayer.

The sun beat down from a cloudless, blue sky. Leo stood next to the open grave, which was surrounded by countless wreaths and flower arrangements. Ashley had picked lilies for the casket spray, she realized only now.

The minister nodded at them to come forward.

Her mother's hand trembled as she placed a rose on the closed casket, but Leo's was strangely steady. What she had said in the church had been her farewell to her father, not this flower.

One of her father's colleagues played a mournful melody on the violin as the casket was lowered into the ground.

When the minister finished with "ashes to ashes, dust to dust" and dropped a handful of earth onto the top of the casket, her mother clutched Leo's arm painfully tight, and Leo gently rubbed her hand.

When the last notes faded away and the violinist lowered his instrument, a very familiar sound interrupted the sudden silence: the click of a camera shutter.

Leo looked up.

Two paparazzi stood at the edge of the cemetery, half hidden behind a stand of trees. Another had stalked closer, clad in black so he would fit in with the mourners. Several black SUVs with dark-tinted windows were parked along the gate.

As the press vultures continued to snap picture after picture, Leo clenched her hands into fists. For the first time, she really understood how helpless her father must have felt after his stroke.

God, she had been a fool to reject Saul's offer to send PR people and security guards for the funeral. She hadn't wanted the pack of babysitters that guided and guarded her career to intrude into her life in Fair Oaks, and she had assumed she wouldn't need them. So far, the press either hadn't found her, or they had something more interesting to report.

She should have known they would want to cash in on pictures of a mourning Jenna Blake.

"Oh my God!" Her mother gasped. "What are they doing? They're taking photos—here?"

Leo gritted her teeth. "Not much is sacred for them."

Instead of dispersing now that the funeral was over, the townspeople crowded around Leo and her mother, shielding her from the paparazzi.

The rapid-fire click-click-click of cameras ended abruptly as a very determined Holly, followed by her brothers, Travis, Jenny, Ash, Chris, and several others, marched toward them.

Leo's eyes stung with tears. She had expected the people of Fair Oaks to rat her out to the press the day of her arrival in town, but not only had they not given her away, now they were closing ranks and standing up to protect her.

Hidden behind her circle of human shields, she couldn't see what was going on at the other side of the cemetery, but a minute later, the black SUVs pulled away and sped down the street as if the devil were chasing them.

Holly pushed through the crowd to get to Leo. Her blue eyes were lit up with righteous fury but then gentled when they turned onto Leo. "You okay?"

Leo could only nod.

"Don't worry." Zack gave her a pat on the shoulder. "They won't be back."

"I know." Leo sighed. "Why would they? They've already got the shots they were after."

"No, they didn't." Grinning broadly, Zack held up an SD card.

Next to him, Travis presented two more.

Leo gaped at them. "How did you...?"

"You don't want to know." Zack straightened his tie, which had become askew.

"You didn't hit them, did you?" Not that they didn't deserve it, but she didn't need headlines such as *Violence at Superstar's Dad's Funeral.*

"No," Holly said quickly. "It was Sasha who got them to hand over the SD cards."

"Sasha?" Leo blinked over at Holly's friend.

"Well," Sasha said, "I told them I'm a police officer and that if they weren't gone within three seconds—without the SD cards—they'd get to enjoy the hospitality of our local jail for a week while I came up with some creative charges and lost the paperwork a few times."

Leo stared at her. "You bake scones for a living." Fantastic scones, but still...

Sasha smiled and shrugged. "But they don't know that."

With a shaking hand, Leo pocketed the three SD cards. Maybe without knowing it, Sasha had found the only thing that could stop the paparazzi: the threat of being stuck in some backwoods county jail while their deadlines were ticking away and other paparazzi were out there, making boatloads of money on celebrity photos.

"Thank you," she got out, her voice rough. It wouldn't keep the paparazzi away for good; she knew that from experience. But it meant the world to her that the townspeople had stood up for her, and maybe it would make the press vultures more careful about where they took photos.

Holly put a hand on her shoulder. "Come on. Let's get back to the church. The lunch they prepared for us should be about ready."

Still surrounded by half the population of Fair Oaks, Leo and her mother made their way back to the car. Apparently, she hadn't just misjudged her parents; she had also misjudged the entire town.

Chapter 20

"WHAT IS THIS?" LEO HELD up the world's ugliest bow tie pinched between her thumb and index finger.

Her mother looked up at the pile of things she was going through. A laugh exploded from her, a sound that had been rare since her husband had died two weeks ago. "That's the bow tie your father wore on our first date. I didn't know he kept it."

Leo eyed the green-dotted thing. "It's a miracle you went out with him a second time. Wow. To think that my very existence was almost thwarted by a bow tie."

"Thank God it wasn't." Holly leaned across the to-be-discarded box and gave Leo a gentle kiss.

Leo hummed against her lips. The open affection Holly showed her was like a constant ray of sunshine that lit up her days.

"So," Leo said when Holly had turned back toward her stack, "where does it go?" She dangled the bow tie over the box of things to be thrown away.

"Don't you dare!" Her mother tapped the box to her right. "It's a keeper."

Leo groaned playfully and reached into the drawer to continue going through her father's things. Maybe because most of his possessions had to do with music, notes kept swirling through her mind, coming together to form snatches of a melody.

Before she could decide whether she was ready to listen or should chase it away with a shake of her head, her cell phone rang, drowning out the melody in her mind. She pulled it out of her pocket and glanced at the display.

It was her manager.

She had wondered when he would call—and what she would say once he did.

"Sorry." She looked from her mother to Holly. "I have to take it. It's Saul."

"Go ahead," her mother said with a smile. "I'll use the distraction to make sure the bow tie doesn't end up in the wrong box."

Leo chuckled, handed over the bow tie, and accepted the call. "Hi, Saul."

"Hi, Jenna. How are you doing?"

How strange. For a moment, she hadn't realized he was talking to her. She hadn't been Jenna in six weeks. "A little better every day," she said, looking at her mother, who slid her fingers over the bow tie in a gentle caress before placing it in the box of things to keep.

"That's great. Um, listen, I don't want to be indelicate, but…when are you flying back home?"

Home… That term didn't seem to fit New York anymore. But then, where was home? It couldn't be Fair Oaks, could it? She had fought so hard to escape the town.

She stepped out of her father's room and pulled the door closed behind her so her mother wouldn't hear. "I don't know yet. It's only been two weeks."

"But you've been gone for six weeks. That's a lifetime in the music industry; you know that."

"Yeah, I know, but I can't just run off. I still need to take care of a few things here, like handling the insurance companies, taking care of financial matters, and sorting through his things."

"I'll send someone to do it," Saul said. "Don't you worry about a thing. I'll hire the best financial adviser in all of—"

"No, Saul." Leo paced to the kitchen and back. "No. This isn't a problem you can solve by throwing money at it." It was what Holly had told her on that first day—and she'd been right. "My mother doesn't need a financial adviser. She needs her daughter."

Saul's teeth were audibly grinding together. "For how much longer?" he finally got out.

"I don't know. A week…a month… I really don't know. Grief doesn't exactly stick to a timetable, you know?"

"I'm aware of that. Please don't think I'm unsympathetic, Jenna, but people here need you too. You've got obligations."

"Frankly, they don't hold a candle to the obligations I have here." If she was honest, it wasn't just her obligations that kept her in Fair Oaks. There was also Holly.

Saul huffed out a sigh. "I'll see what I can do to hold them all off for a little longer. But at some point, you'll have to come back."

"I know. Thanks, Saul." She ended the call.

When she took a step toward her father's room, her mother stood in the doorway. Her expression made it clear that she had overheard at least part of the phone call.

"Mom…"

"It's okay if you fly back." Her mother's voice was soft but somehow still managed to hold a firm undertone that revealed how much she meant it. "I know you have been gone for much too long already."

"You need me here," Leo said.

Her mother patted her arm. "I'll be fine. I have Holly and the rest of town looking after me. Right?" She glanced behind her.

Holly stepped up to her and put both hands on her shoulders in a silent gesture of support. She nodded but didn't look Leo in the eyes.

"Maybe," Leo said, her voice a little scratchy, "I need to be here for myself too."

A smile creased her mother's face, and Holly looked at Leo for the first time since the conversation about her leaving had started. Amazing what warmth those blue eyes could exude.

Leo got caught in that gentle gaze.

"Then stay," her mother said. "I'm always happy to have you home for however long I can get you."

Holly whispered something under her breath. Had it been "me too"?

Her mother wiped at her eyes before turning around. "Come on, girls," she said over her shoulder. "Let's get back to work."

Leo followed her back into her father's room and went through the rest of the drawer.

At first, she had thought he had shoved that bow tie into the top drawer and then forgotten about it, but then she pulled out programs of his first concerts, a broken violin string, her grandparents' wedding picture, and tickets to movies her parents had seen together more than thirty-five years ago.

While the rest of her father's things were all practical—clothes, books, his sheet music, and neatly sorted bank statements—this drawer obviously held all the things of sentimental value.

Who knew her father had a nostalgic side?

She carefully put everything into the "keepers" box.

The last item left in the drawer, stored at the very bottom, was some sort of photo album. She pulled it out. There was no year or any other kind of label on it. She opened it to the first page. Not a single photo. Instead…

She gasped.

Staring back at her was a grainy black-and-white version of herself—or rather of Jenna Blake. Her father had obviously cut out a short newspaper article about her very first concert after leaving Fair Oaks. The headline said, *Hometown girl opening for New York band Reckless.*

She held her breath as she turned the page, then the next one.

The album documented every stage of her career—her early attempts to get a foot in the door by playing at festivals and open mics, reviews of her debut album, a photo of her holding up her first Grammy Award, her picture on the cover of *Rolling Stone,* and a music critic's opinion on her first number-one single, in which her father had highlighted the words *stellar breath control* and *flawless technique.* He had even found a short press release announcing that she had signed with Clio Records.

Holly stepped next to her and touched her elbow. "What is it? You look a little pale all of a sudden."

Leo couldn't speak, so she just held out the album.

Holly took it and flipped through it.

Leo's mother joined them, and they looked through her father's Jenna Blake collection together.

Once she had studied each page a second time, Leo finally found her voice. "Did you know about this?"

Her mother shook her head. "I had no idea. I never even mentioned your career around the house because I always thought…"

"Yeah, me too. I thought I was a total disappointment to him."

"You weren't." Holly gently tapped the album. "This is proof. He was proud of you and everything you achieved."

Leo still stared down at the pages, which blurred before her eyes. Why hadn't he ever told her? Why let her assume he was disappointed in her all these years?

She would probably never get an answer to these questions, and that hurt like a thorn that had dug in beneath her skin.

As if sensing it, Holly stroked her forearm and up to her shoulder.

She gave Holly a shaky smile. Finding the album was still a good thing. She slid her fingers over the open page and then closed the album.

But when she put it into the "keepers" box, her mother took it back out. "No. That doesn't go there."

"It doesn't?"

Her mother shook her head and pressed the album into her hands. "It belongs to you."

A sudden onslaught of grief and joy rose from deep inside of Leo and poured out of her in the form of tears. She pressed the album to her chest as if it could hold back the flood of emotions.

Her mother and Holly held her, forming a human huddle of comfort.

After a second, Leo stopped trying to get a grip and just let the tears come. When they finally dried up, she blew her nose. *Wow.* She had thought she was done crying for her father, but it had felt strangely freeing.

"Let's stop for today," her mother said. "I'm in the mood for baked potato soup and a BLT."

"You want to cook? Now?"

"No. I want to invite my two favorite girls…women to lunch at Ruth's Diner."

Leo stared at her. Her mother hadn't wanted to leave the house in the past two weeks. Apparently, she was ready to head out into the world again, and her appetite had returned too. Maybe this had been a freeing experience for her as well.

"What about the paparazzi?" Leo asked. A few of them were still in town, even though they hadn't dared come too close. If they had taken any photos, it had been through telephoto lenses.

Her mother shrugged. "I don't think a photo of three women having lunch is what they're looking for. They're probably after inheritance battles, grief-induced benders, and illegitimate half siblings suddenly showing up."

Leo gave her a surprised look. "Since when did you become an expert on the tabloids?"

A hint of red entered her mother's cheeks. "Well, I might not have started an album like your father, but I followed your career too."

Leo's mouth went dry. "You did?"

Her mother nodded. "So, shall we?"

Gently, Leo put the album down and nodded.

Her mom hooked her right arm through Leo's and the left through Holly's and dragged them toward the door.

Leo threw a glance over her shoulder, back at the album, before allowing herself to be led out of the house.

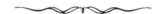

A few days later, Leo was in the middle of slicing an avocado for an LGBTA sandwich—Holly's new favorite lunch—when she realized she was humming. A melody floated around in her head.

She paused and cocked her head to listen. It sounded strangely familiar. For a moment, she thought it might be a ballad she had recently heard on the radio.

No. It was the elusive melody that had popped into her head a few days ago, the way it had often happened in the past, back when she had still written her own music.

Now she was ready to open herself up to the melody and the emotions that came with it.

She dropped the knife, wiped her hands on a dish towel, and rushed upstairs, all the while humming the melody so she wouldn't lose it.

Her guitar had sat untouched in her old room for the past six weeks, but now her fingers itched for it. God, how wonderful it was to get that feeling back!

She knelt down in front of her battered case, which she had kept out of sight in one corner of the room. Carefully, she lifted out her guitar and touched the place where the gloss had worn off around the sound hole. It wasn't the guitar she used during concerts. This was her very first guitar.

Her father had bought it for her after weeks of begging, and it had been one of the few things she had taken with her when she'd left Fair Oaks.

She settled her fingers into the familiar positions. As soon as she felt the fretboard beneath her fingertips, she realized how much she had missed this.

Sitting cross-legged on the floor, she tuned the guitar, tinkered with the chord progression for the intro, and then grabbed the nearest piece of paper to work on the lyrics to fit the tune.

The first two verses and the chorus came to her with amazing ease, pouring from her mind as if she were merely taking dictation. If songwriting had always been like that, she would never have stopped.

Some time later, she paused and shook out her hands. Her calluses had softened after weeks of not playing, and now her fingertips stung from the strings, but she welcomed the pain. It seemed to deepen the elation coursing through her.

She stared at the pages she had written. From the chaos of words and notes on the paper, a love song stared back at her.

Wasn't that what she had wanted to get away from?

But this wasn't one of the streamlined, commercial songs about love. She hadn't written it to land another number-one hit; she had written it to express her feelings. This one came straight from her heart.

It hit her with the force of a rock star smashing his Les Paul at the end of a concert. She was in love with Holly!

Her offer of "no commitment, let's just enjoy each other's company while I'm here" wasn't all she wanted anymore. She didn't want to give up what they had once she left. She wanted to share her life with Holly.

Pen and paper slid from her fingers. It had been ages since she had truly been in love, and even then, there had always remained a speck of doubt about whether she was appreciated for herself or for her fame and money. With Holly, everything was different.

Somehow, they had to find a way to make it work, even if she didn't have any idea yet as to how.

A car door slammed in the driveway.

Leo looked up as if awakening from a deep trance. That couldn't be Holly already, could it? She glanced at her wristwatch. Jesus, it was after one already!

The key Leo's mother had given Holly jangled in the front door. "Leo? Sharon?" Holly called from the hall. "I hope you didn't cook. I brought pizza."

Leo chuckled to herself. Well, that was a good thing since the LGBTA sandwiches sat half-prepared on the kitchen counter. She put the guitar on the bed, got up, and hurried downstairs to greet the woman she was in love with.

Wow. That sounded surreal—and great. She could only hope that Holly would return her feelings once she told her.

Holly paused in the hall with the warm pizza box in her hands.

Upstairs, a door creaked open, and then Leo nearly skipped toward her. Her cheeks were a little flushed, and her olive-green eyes seemed to shine from within.

God, it was good to see her so happy, whatever had caused it. Holly smiled reflexively.

"Hey, you. What are you up to?" She leaned across the pizza box to kiss Leo hello. As always, she could have gotten lost in the sensual feeling of Leo's lips against hers, but this time, Leo broke the kiss after a few seconds.

"Come with me." She held out her hand, palm up.

Holly let go of the pizza box with one hand. As soon as she entwined her fingers with Leo's, she was dragged toward the stairs. "Um, the pizza is getting cold."

"We'll reheat it in a minute." Leo detoured to the kitchen, took the pizza box from Holly, and put it on the counter. "But first, there's something I've got to show you."

"All right." Holly followed her upstairs. "Where's your mom, by the way?"

"Over at the neighbors'. Knowing her, she'll be gone for a while. We've got the house all to ourselves."

"And the pizza."

Leo flashed a grin over her shoulder. "Are you, by any chance, hungry?"

"Let's just say I doubt there'll be leftovers. Whatever you want to show me, it'd better be quick, or I'll start nibbling on you." After the words were out, it occurred to her how sexual they might sound to Leo. Sometimes, when she said things like this, Leo stared at her with this heavy-lidded gaze, as if she wanted to devour her. It was strange to know Leo was experiencing something Holly never would. Her fantasies, if she had them, always stopped at kissing.

"Don't worry," Leo said. "I just want to play you something; then you can eat."

Holly pulled them to a stop in the upstairs hall. "Play? You're playing your guitar?"

Leo nodded, beaming as if she had won another Grammy. "Yeah. And not just that. I'm working on a song. My muse seems to be back."

"Oh, Leo. That's wonderful."

They came together in a tight embrace. Leo's body, pressed to hers, seemed to vibrate with excitement.

Maybe it was part nervousness too, Holly realized when they finally continued to Leo's room. The hand holding hers was damp.

"Please keep in mind that it's a work in progress, okay?" Leo closed the door behind them. "I've got the first two verses and the chorus so far, but I want a third verse, and the lyrics need a bit more work in a couple of places where I might have one syllable too many, so…"

Amazing. Leo must have performed a thousand concerts throughout her career, but now, about to play a new song with just Holly there to listen, she seemed as nervous as if she had never performed in front of an audience.

Holly lifted Leo's hand to her mouth and kissed it. "I'm sure I'll love it."

"I hope you will," Leo said in a whisper. She directed Holly to sit on the bed and then picked up her guitar.

Holly leaned forward to give her and the new song her full attention.

Within the first few notes, she could sense that this song was different from Leo's last album. It wasn't a polished piece designed to appeal to the masses; it was a return to Leo's musical roots—powerful, raw, and full of emotions.

At any other time, she might have watched the graceful way Leo's fingers moved along the instrument. But right now she couldn't take her gaze off Leo's face. Her expression was completely open and vulnerable, as if she was baring her very soul as she sang out the lyrics, and her smoky, emotion-filled voice made goose bumps rise all over Holly's body.

What used to be a place to hide
Is now a spot to be truly me.
With just the stars as our guide
I'm finally free.

Feels like home for the very first time,
Up on the roof.
No fame,
No game,
It's just us here,
Up on the roof.

You listen to my words and hear my soul
And you hold me all night.
With you I feel whole.
Everything feels finally right.

Holly's breath caught. The song…it was about them, about what Leo felt for her—trust and comfort and, if she wasn't mistaken, love. Her heart drummed against her ribs, outpacing the gentle rhythm of the song.

When the last notes faded away, Leo lowered the guitar. She licked her lips and slowly raised her gaze to meet Holly's. "What do you think?"

Holly slid off the bed to kneel on the floor in front of Leo. With the guitar still between them, she wrapped her arms around her as well as she could.

"It's beautiful," she whispered.

"Yeah? So you don't think the lyrics are a bit too…I don't know… mushy?"

Holly firmly shook her head. "I love them." She sucked in a lungful of air. *Say it.* "And I love you too."

Leo stared and then blinked.

Oh God! Had she misinterpreted the message of the song? She started to slide her hands off Leo's shoulders. "Shit. I shouldn't have… The song and the look in your eyes… I thought…"

Leo put the guitar on the floor and threw her arms around Holly, stopping her retreat. "No, no, don't go. I should have taken my own advice and told you what I felt days, hell, weeks ago, but I guess I wasn't ready to face it, and now it poured out in a song."

Holly held her breath and gazed into her eyes. "So you…?"

"I love you," Leo said, emphasizing every word as if they were part of a magic spell.

Giddiness swept through Holly, so strong it left her weak. She threw herself at Leo, toppling them both to the floor, where they lay laughing and kissing and whispering it again and again.

Leo's heart beat fast beneath hers, and her hands ran from Holly's shoulders to her hips and back as if she needed to touch her to convince herself that this was real.

"I know it's pretty fast," Leo said when they came up for air. "But with my dad and being back home, everything feels sped up, more compressed and intense somehow. Like dog years compared to human years, you know?"

"Yeah, it feels that way for me too." Holly laughed at the comparison and swiped a strand of hair behind Leo's ear. It was as if hearing Leo's song had pulled the stopper that had bottled her emotions, and now she couldn't stop beaming at her. Was it possible to feel drunk on love? A lot still had to be resolved, but for now, she wanted to enjoy this feeling.

Just as she was about to bend down and kiss Leo again, the front door creaked open and Sharon's voice drifted up the stairs, "Leo? Holly?"

Holly let her forehead sink against Leo's.

"Next time, we go to your place," Leo grumbled.

"We can't leave your mom alone in the house yet." But truth be told, she couldn't wait to spend more time with Leo either, just the two of them.

Reluctantly, Holly got to her feet and held out her hand to pull Leo up too. "Come on. Let's go warm up the pizza."

As they walked to the door, Holly remembered something. "You never told me what you're going to call the song."

"I was thinking maybe 'Up on the Roof.' Like the line in the chorus."

"I like it. But isn't there a song with that title already?"

Leo rubbed her chin. "Damn. You're right. How about 'Holly's Song'?"

"Uh…wow…I…" Having Leo name the song for her was so special, she didn't know what to say.

Leo studied her. "Unless you don't want to make our relationship quite so public yet."

Holly smiled. "I want to shout it from the rooftops." She pulled Leo to a stop at the top of the stairs and kissed her. "Speaking of rooftops and the chorus... If you let your mother hear that song, she'll know it wasn't a squirrel up on the roof."

Leo laughed. "I think she already suspects the squirrels were a little larger than normal...quite a bit larger."

With one hand on her hip, Holly gave her a playful glare. "Are you calling me fat?"

Leo trailed her hand over Holly's other hip in a gentle caress. "Nope. I like my squirrels just like this."

"Squirrels, plural?"

"Squirrel, singular," Leo said, all playfulness gone.

"Hey, you two." Her mother stood at the bottom of the stairs. "What's with all that talk about squirrels?"

They looked at each other and laughed before descending the stairs.

"Nothing, Mom. Nothing squirrelly going on at all."

Chapter 21

LEO HAD KNOWN SHE LIKED women, not men, since she had been thirteen. In the nearly twenty years since then, she had, for some reason, never bought flowers for any of the women she had dated. Jewelry, perfume, bottles of wine, sure. Once, she had even gone overboard and bought a car for one of her girlfriends.

She would give Holly the world if she allowed it, but she had a feeling that if she tried to woo her with expensive gifts, Holly would probably tell her she was crazy.

But she still deserved something to let her know how much Leo loved her and how much her constant support throughout the past three weeks had meant to her. Instead of returning to work full-time, Holly had requested part-time work for a while. So now she had taken over some of the patients of a colleague who was on maternity leave and checked on Ms. Voerster and other elderly residents of Fair Oaks several times a day. That left her free to spend her afternoons and evenings with Leo.

And nights.

Whenever Holly stayed over, which was three or four times a week, they cuddled all night, and the kisses they shared were breathtaking. Holly seemed to enjoy it very much, but it never went any further, and Leo was fine with that.

What kind of flower would say "I love you," "I accept you," and "I'm so grateful, I could fall to my knees and build a shrine to you" all at the same time?

For the second time this month, Leo stood in front of Ashley's flower shop. The bell above the door jingled, and the scent of soil and fresh flowers surrounded her as she entered, reminding her of the last time she'd been there. It had been less than three weeks ago, but so much had happened since.

"I'll be right with you," Ashley called from the back room.

Leo turned toward the card rack next to the cash register. Some of the cards said "thank you," others "I love you," but none of them were good enough to express exactly what Leo was feeling.

Ashley stepped out of the back room. A warm smile crossed her face when she saw Leo. "Oh hi, Leo. How are you doing?"

"I'm fine," Leo said and, to her surprise, found that it was true. The wounds of the past were still there, but they were starting to heal. "How are you?"

"Pretty good. The shop's keeping me busy."

"I can imagine. Thanks again for arranging the flowers for Dad's funeral. Everyone said they were beautiful, and Mom loved the lilies you put into the casket spray."

Ash glanced down, coloring a little beneath the praise. "I'm glad to hear that. So, what can I do for you?"

"I need a bouquet."

"Something for your mother? Maybe some white daisies and some purple and pink carnations to cheer her up?"

"Uh, actually…" *Damn.* Getting flowers for Holly from Holly's ex had been a dumb idea. But now she was here, and she refused to hide their relationship the way Ash had done. "You know what? I need two bouquets. Getting flowers for my mom is also a good idea. Let's go with the daisies and the carnations."

Ashley pulled flowers from several buckets around the shop, trimmed the stems, and artfully arranged them. She kept glancing up at Leo as she worked.

Leo gave her a questioning gaze. "What is it?"

"Um, nothing. I just… You look good."

What the hell…? Was it just a sincere compliment between friends, or was it something more? Leo ran one hand through her hair. "Uh, thanks."

In the silence that followed, Ash held the bouquet out to Leo for her approval, which Leo gave with a nod.

Tissue paper rustled as Ash tore it from a roll and wrapped it around the flowers. She extended the bouquet toward Leo but then kept hold of it so they both ended up clasping the flowers from either side. "You know," she said so quietly that Leo had to strain to hear her, "back then...on prom night...when you kissed me...I was afraid."

Leo nearly dropped the bouquet. She hadn't expected Ash to ever bring it up. "Of me?"

"No. Not of you. Never of you. Just...of my own feelings and what they might mean."

A roaring sound started in Leo's ears. She swayed a little. "So you..." She smacked her dry lips. "You had feelings for me? Back then?"

Staring down at the flowers, Ash nodded.

This was what Ash should have told her fourteen years ago, when Leo had searched her out the day after the prom to let her know she was leaving and to talk about the kiss. Why did no one ever talk to her—really, openly talk?

"Then why didn't you tell me?" Leo asked. "You let me believe that I was the only one who felt anything."

"I never meant to hurt you. I just wasn't ready to deal with it."

"And now you are?" Judging by how Ash had treated Holly during dinner with the gang, she found that hard to believe.

Ash peered up at her. Was there a hint of hope, of expectation in her eyes? "Yes. I think I am. So, I was wondering... Maybe you'd like to...I don't know...have coffee with me sometime?"

Leo clutched the flower stems. *Wow. Just...wow.* That question would have meant the world to her fourteen years ago, but now it left her with a bitter taste in her mouth.

When the silence stretched between them, Ash looked away. "Oh. I see. There's someone in New York."

"No. Not in New York." God, Ashley seemed to be the only person left in Fair Oaks who hadn't yet heard that she and Holly were dating. Or maybe she had thought it was just a rumor. "But I do have a special someone."

Ash paled. "It's not...not Holly, right?"

Something in her tone—as if Leo couldn't possibly date someone like Holly—made her bristle. She stood up straighter and looked Ashley square in the eyes. "Yes, it is."

"Oh, Leo." Ash let out a long sigh and put a hand on Leo's. "You have no idea what you're in for."

Leo pulled her hand away. "In for?"

"Didn't she tell you about her...um, issues?"

For a second, Leo could only stare, open-mouthed. Then anger bubbled up so fierce and hot that she thought steam would come out of her ears. She struggled not to beat Ash with the bouquet. "Issues?"

"Oh. So she didn't mention that she's...um...?"

"If you mean that she's asexual, yes, she did. But the only one with issues here is you!"

"Leo, please. Don't be like that. I just want you to be happy."

"Who said I'm not happy with Holly?"

Ash opened her mouth to answer, but Leo interrupted her with a forceful shake of her head. "You know what? Save it. Just because you didn't appreciate what you had with Holly doesn't mean I'll make the same mistake."

"You don't understand."

"No, you're the one who doesn't understand." Leo fought not to raise her voice. "And how could you? You can barely accept your own sexual orientation, so how are you supposed to accept Holly's?"

A tear ran down Ashley's face. "That's not fair."

Leo gritted her teeth and restrained herself from further discussion. "What do I owe you for the flowers?" She jerked her head toward them.

Ashley stammered out an amount.

Leo slammed two bills onto the counter and stormed out without saying goodbye or waiting for her change. Only when she was halfway to her car did she realize that she hadn't gotten flowers for Holly. Well, she would have to find another way to show Holly how much she loved and appreciated her, because she wasn't setting foot in Ash's shop again anytime soon.

She jerked the driver's side door open and set the bouquet onto the passenger seat. "Issues, my ass!"

When Leo glanced at her wristwatch, sweat started to bead on her forehead, even though she wasn't the one lugging a large mattress up a set of stairs. "Come on, guys. She'll be here any second. I'll give you a hundred bucks each if you make it out of here within the next five minutes."

The two delivery men exchanged a glance and doubled their efforts.

Within four minutes, the new mattress was in place.

Leo signed for it on the clipboard one of them held out to her before she paid them and herded them back downstairs and out the door.

Just as they climbed into their van, Holly's red Jeep came down the street. She waited until the van had backed out before she pulled into the driveway.

Damn. Somehow, nothing was going right this week. First her aborted attempt to buy Holly flowers and now this.

When Holly climbed out of the Jeep, Leo forgot about the possibly ruined surprise for a moment. Unlike when she had worked for Leo's father, Holly was now wearing scrubs.

Leo had never thought of scrubs as hot, but with Holly wearing them, they were damn sexy. Or was it *asexy* in Holly's case? The thought made her smile.

She crossed the driveway to greet Holly with a warm hug and a kiss, and they walked back to the house hand in hand.

"What was that?" Holly pointed over her shoulder with her thumb. Her lips curled into a smile. "You're not cheating on me with a couple of burly guys, are you?"

"Damn, you caught me. I thought with you working and Mom on a grocery run to St. Joe, it would be a good time for a threesome."

Holly's smile faded away. She closed the front door behind them and turned toward Leo with a serious expression. "Is that something you'd ever do?"

"A threesome with two guys?" Leo shook her head. "Nope. I'm not interested in men, even if my manager sometimes tries to sell me as bi."

"I wasn't talking about threesomes, just…I don't know…maybe having an open relationship."

Leo gaped at her. Where the hell was that coming from? "Is that really what you want?"

Holly stared at the top of her sneakers. "No. But I know other mixed-orientation couples handle it that way."

"Mixed-orientation couples?"

"Yeah. You know…where one partner is asexual and the other isn't."

"Well, there's one problem with that approach: the thought of sleeping with someone else has about this much appeal to me." Leo pressed her thumb and index finger together to indicate zero. "I've never tried an open relationship, and I certainly don't want to start now."

A long breath escaped Holly, and a shadow lifted off her face.

"Holly…" Leo tugged on her hand to get her to look at her. "What's going on? Why offer something that would hurt you?"

Holly's gaze flicked up to meet hers. "Because I want you to be happy."

"*You* make me happy," Leo said firmly. "I don't want or need anyone else."

Moisture gathered in Holly's eyes.

Leo pulled her into her arms. "Next time doubts like that start to creep up, just tell me. I don't want you to think for a second that you're not enough for me." She held Holly at arm's length so she could look into her eyes. "Okay?"

Holly nodded and nibbled her bottom lip as if she needed to process that thought.

Tenderly, Leo guided her even closer and kissed her. "So, want to find out what the burly guys were really doing here?" When Holly nodded, she led her upstairs.

"Don't tell me you put a piano upstairs," Holly said.

Leo chuckled. "No. Better than a piano. More comfy, at least." Slowly, she opened the door to her old room to reveal the new queen-size bed that had taken the place of her single bed. She had planned to put nice sheets on it, but the mattress had been delivered later than expected, so now it lay on the bed frame, completely bare.

Holly stood in the doorway and stared at the bed. "Wow."

Was that a good wow or a bad wow? Leo searched her face. "It's in no way meant to pressure you into anything. I just thought this would be more comfortable."

"I bet it will be. I love being close to you, but your old bed wasn't meant for two people. I can't wait to try out the new one. Thank you." She tugged

Leo close by their entwined fingers, cupped her face with her free hand, and brought their lips together for a leisurely exploration.

The kiss started out tender rather than steamy, but then Holly surprised her with a playful lick and a nibble on her bottom lip.

Jesus! Every bone in Leo's body seemed to liquefy. She wrapped both arms around Holly to keep herself upright.

Holly's hands came to rest on her hips, her fingers splayed tantalizingly close to the upper curve of her butt.

That warm contact and the slide of Holly's tongue against her own made her body tingle from head to toe, and she couldn't suppress a moan.

It took conscious effort to keep her hands on Holly's back instead of letting them explore her tempting body. God, she ached to touch her, to let her fingers slide over the gentle curve of her hips or up to her full breasts.

"I'm not going to break if you touch me," Holly murmured against her lips as if reading her thoughts.

But maybe I will. She couldn't resist the invitation, though. Slowly, giving Holly every opportunity to stop her, she slipped one hand beneath her scrub top and stroked the satiny soft skin of her back.

Holly hummed against her lips and mirrored the move, pulling the T-shirt from Leo's shorts and letting her fingers caress every inch, from Leo's hips to the clasp of her bra and back down. "So soft," she whispered, then tilted her head and pressed a kiss to the side of Leo's neck.

Leo gasped and pressed Holly closer with both hands. Did Holly have any idea what she was doing to her? Something inside of her felt close to spiraling out of control. While she knew sex wasn't on the table, her body obviously hadn't gotten the message.

"Uh, Holly. I…" She struggled to form words despite the haze of desire in her brain. "I think I need a shower." *A cold one.*

Holly's hands lingered against her hips for another second, as if she was reluctant to let go. "Now?"

Leo nodded. "Um, yeah. I'm a little sweaty. I mean, I…I was helping the delivery guys with the bed earlier, so I, um, worked up a sweat." Her body protested as she forced herself to pull away and marched to the bathroom.

Once inside, she softly closed the door, leaned against it, and exhaled. *Je-sus!* Was this what it would be like?

So what if it is? You're not a hormone-driven teenager who can't control her urges.

But they existed, as the none-too-subtle pressure between her legs told her in no uncertain terms. She loved Holly; she knew that, but was she ready to give up sex for good?

It's a little late for that question, isn't it? She had already made that decision when she'd realized she was in love with Holly. But she had underestimated how hard it would be to ignore her desire in situations like this. Could she really go through with it, not just now but for the rest of her life?

She pressed both palms against the door and took several deep breaths. *Yes,* she decided. If that was what it took to build a life with Holly, she would learn to live without sex. There were other forms of intimacy and other expressions of love she could share with Holly, and when it came to orgasms, she could take care of that herself.

Yeah. Like, right now. She stripped off her T-shirt and bra and dropped them to the floor, followed by her shorts and underwear. It probably wouldn't take much.

Holly stretched out on the bare mattress with a happy grin and folded her arms behind her head as she dreamily stared up at the sloped ceiling.

Kissing Leo and touching her lips to the soft skin of her neck had been so sensual, so intimate. She wanted...no, needed to be close to Leo.

But what about what Leo needs? The old surge of guilt coursed through her. She knew their make-out session had turned Leo on. The little gasps and moans that had escaped her and the way her body had trembled against Holly's had made it pretty obvious. Holly wished so badly she could give her the experience of having her desire returned, but she couldn't. There wasn't a doubt in her mind that she loved Leo in every way she could—and that her love was returned unconditionally.

Leo didn't expect her to change or to have sex with her. Relief from those pressures emboldened her to contemplate doing things she had never expected she'd want to do for someone—including having sex. A part of her was even curious about what it would be like with Leo and about what new insights into her partner it would give her.

Maybe it would be different with Leo, just as their relationship so far had been different from Holly's previous ones. With Leo, she might be able to experience sexual intimacy without being expected to feel things that were impossible for her or to change her very identity.

She glanced at the alarm clock on the bedside table. Leo had been in there for some time. Holly strained to make out what was going on behind the closed bathroom door, but the only thing she could hear from across the room was the patter of water.

"Leo?" she called. "You okay?"

If there was an answer, she couldn't hear it through the closed door.

She got up from the bed, went to the door, and opened it a few inches without peeking inside. Just as she started to repeat her question, a strangled moan drifted over from the shower.

They both gasped.

Holly's cheeks burned. *Oh God. Is she...touching herself?*

"Jesus, Holly! You can't just barge in like this!"

"Sorry, sorry! I just... Sorry!" Hastily, Holly closed the door and backed away to the other side of the room. *Stupid, stupid, stupid!* Of course Leo would need to take care of herself after the kisses and caresses they had shared, but it hadn't even crossed Holly's mind. She shook her head at herself and started to pace.

Should she hide out in the kitchen until Leo had finished in the bathroom? More heat shot into her cheeks. *Well, not finished, finished.* At least she didn't think Leo would be in the mood to continue masturbating after being caught.

Finally, she decided against fleeing downstairs. If she and Leo didn't learn to be honest with each other about their needs and communicate openly, their relationship didn't stand a chance.

After a few minutes, the bathroom door slowly crept open, and Leo peeked out, her cheeks flushed either from the hot water or from embarrassment.

Or because she just had an orgasm, Holly's mind helpfully supplied. A part of her even felt a little curious about how Leo would look in the throes of passion.

Leo stepped into the bedroom. The clothes she had worn earlier stuck to her skin as if she had dressed hastily, without thoroughly drying herself off. She shuffled her bare feet.

"I'm sorry, Leo." Holly was the first to break the silence. "I shouldn't have barged in like that."

Leo rubbed her neck, then looked up. "No, I'm sorry. I didn't mean to yell at you. I was just embarrassed."

"Embarrassed?" Holly echoed. Pushing away her own embarrassment, she marched over to Leo and took her hand. "Leo, you never made me feel like my sexual orientation is something to be ashamed of."

"It's not," Leo said.

The fierceness in her tone made Holly love her even more.

"And neither is yours. I don't want you to feel bad about being sexually attracted to me. You don't have to hide it from me. It's okay if kissing me, touching me…and being touched in return arouses you. It's also okay if you want to do something about it. In fact…" She gave herself a mental nudge. Leo wouldn't take the initiative; she knew that. She was too afraid to pressure Holly into something she didn't want—and Holly did want it, even if it wasn't the same way or for the same reasons Leo wanted it. Just bringing Leo pleasure would please her too. "I wouldn't mind lending you a hand every now and then."

Leo plopped down onto the bed as if her knees had given out. "No, Holly. I don't expect that of you. I admit it's not always easy knowing you don't crave me the same way I desire you, but that's my issue, not yours. Love and sex are two different things. I get that."

"If lots of love would automatically mean lots of sex, you'd have to give up your career because I'd never let you out of this bed again."

"My fans might complain, but I certainly wouldn't." Leo grinned but then added with a softer smile, "Not that I'm complaining about lots of cuddles either. You don't need to prove anything to me."

Holly sat next to her and again took her hand. She traced the heart line in Leo's palm with her thumb. "I know. I'm not trying to prove anything. I just want to make you feel as happy and accepted as you make me feel, and that includes showing you that I know your sexual orientation is an important part of who you are."

But Leo was still shaking her head. "You do. We don't need sex for that."

"Jeez, that's a first." Holly nudged her a little. "I never had to talk any of my partners into having sex."

They laughed along with each other, and it eased the tension in the room considerably.

"See?" Leo said. "This is intimacy too. Sharing a moment like this. Laughing with each other. Talking." She returned the tender caress of Holly's palm. "Cuddling. Being intimate doesn't require sex. I learned that from you."

Holly's heart seemed to expand in her chest. She blinked back tears. No one had ever gotten her and what was important to her like this. For the first time, she had hope that a relationship with someone who wasn't asexual could work out.

"Really, Holly," Leo continued, "I would be perfectly happy to…um, take care of myself."

"Perfectly happy?" Holly arched her eyebrows.

"Okay, maybe not perfectly happy, but it would be okay." Leo looked her in the eyes. "I don't want you to have to lie back and think of England."

Holly chuckled. "I'm American, not British."

Not even a shadow of a smile ghosted across Leo's features. Her gaze was intense. "Still, it would kill me to know you're forcing yourself to do something you detest, just for my sake."

"I told you sex isn't like that for me. I don't crave it, but under the right circumstances, my body likes it just fine."

"You…you do?" Leo's lashes fluttered rapidly. "Now I'm confused. I thought…"

The look of utter puzzlement on her face made Holly smile. "Human sexuality—or asexuality—is pretty complex. I'm not sexually attracted to anyone up here." She tapped her own forehead. "But down there," she waved at her lap, "my body works the same as yours. It doesn't for all asexual people. Some never experience arousal, but others do have a libido. It's just not directed at anyone."

A line carved itself between Leo's brows. "I'm not sure I understand."

Holly leaned up and kissed the still-furrowed forehead. She had never talked about it in so much detail, so for a moment, she thought about the best way to explain. "Would you say you're attracted to yourself?"

Leo chuckled nervously. "I know people think I'm a conceited superstar, but...no. That would be weird."

"But when you touch yourself, you still get aroused, right?"

A lovely red color crept up Leo's neck. "Uh, right."

"Why?"

"Why?" Leo echoed.

"Yeah. If you're not attracted to yourself, why would you get aroused?"

Leo rubbed her chin. "Because...because...I guess the physical stimulation just feels good."

Holly nodded. "It's the same for some asexual people."

"Oh. Now I get it. I think. So you...? Do you...?" Leo flicked her gaze toward the bathroom. Then she covered her face with her free hand. "God! When I first found out about asexuality, I promised myself I wouldn't ask such stupid stuff."

Smiling, Holly drew Leo's hand away from her face. "It's okay. I'm not too happy when strangers think it's perfectly fine to ask me that, but I don't mind talking about it with you." She tried to be matter-of-fact about it as she added, "The answer is yes. I do masturbate every now and then. It's not even really a sexual thing for me."

"Not sexual?" Leo scratched her head. "Far be it from me to tell you what you are and aren't experiencing, but how can it not be sexual?"

"Earlier, when you were, um, in the shower...what were you thinking about?"

Leo's cheeks flushed an even deeper red. "Are you sure you want to know?"

"Yes. Leo, I'm not some naive virgin." Holly quirked a smile. "You don't have to protect me from anything sexual. I'm fine talking about this."

"Okay." Leo swallowed audibly but then lifted her gaze to meet Holly's. "You," she said quietly. "I was thinking about you. About what it would feel like to have you touch me...all over." Her naturally smoky voice went even more raspy on the last two words.

It was a strange experience to have the intense heat in Leo's eyes directed at her. Somehow, it felt empowering and humbling at the same time. While she might not understand fully how it would be to desire someone so urgently, she vowed to never take advantage or make Leo feel bad about it.

She cleared her throat and forced her thoughts back into their original direction. "See, that's the difference between you and me. When I masturbate, I don't think about anything."

Leo opened her eyes wide. "Nothing at all?"

"Well, sometimes, my thoughts wander, but not to anything sexual. I don't fantasize about other people or picture myself in a sexual situation. Mostly, I think about how it feels. It's just something that relaxes me after a stressful day and makes me feel good or helps me go to sleep more easily."

"Ah. I get that. I think it's the same for people who aren't asexual. Sometimes, I masturbate for reasons other than the hottest woman on earth turning me on, you know?"

They smiled at each other.

Holly was so relieved that she felt like climbing up on the roof, spreading her arms wide, and shouting something *Titanic*-esque. It meant so much to her that they could talk about this and even joke about their differences a little.

"So are you trying to say that sex is a little like that for you too?" Leo asked.

Holly nodded. "If I can get into the right head space, it can be. I'll never feel the urgent need to ravish you or be ravished by you, but I can still enjoy the sensations."

Leo stretched out on the bed and stared up at the ceiling. "Too bad no one has invented something that allows us to inhabit each other's brain for an hour. I'd love to experience making love in your special asexy way."

She made it sound so positive that Holly had to blink back tears.

"Maybe it's a good thing that we can't," Holly said. "Inhabiting your sexy brain would probably blow my fuses."

Leo chuckled.

Holly kicked off her sneakers and curled her body around Leo's on the bed. "But there are other ways to experience making love the asexy way." She put her hand on Leo's flat belly and looked into her eyes. "If you want."

The muscles beneath her palm tensed and quivered. Leo covered Holly's hand with her own, trapping it against her body and preventing her from moving it either higher or lower. "You really don't have to—"

"I know. I want to. Do you?"

Leo's pupils were so large that her eyes looked black rather than green. "Yes," she whispered.

With one hand next to Leo on the bed, Holly leaned down to kiss her.

Before their lips could touch, Leo stopped her with a hand on her shoulder. "But not now."

Holly stared at her. Leo's belly muscles were tense beneath her hand; her cheeks were flushed and her pupils dilated. Why would she say she didn't want it when her body obviously did?

"Not on a bare bed, with you still in your scrubs, while my mother could return at any time," Leo added. "You said you needed to get into the right head space, right?"

Holly nodded.

"Then I don't think a spontaneous quickie would work for you, and it's not what I want for our first time either. I want it to be special—for both of us."

For a moment, Holly thought she might cry. "Thank you," she whispered.

Leo shook her head and reached up to tenderly stroke Holly's cheek. "No need to thank me."

This was almost too good to be true, but Holly tried to trust it. She cuddled up to Leo with a contented sigh.

"So…" Leo slid her fingers through Holly's short hair and rubbed tender circles along her temples. "Want to keep talking about sex a little? I'd really like to find out more about how I can make sure it's good for you."

"If you tell me in return how to make you feel good too," Holly said.

"I can sum that up in two sentences. I'm not a fan of S-M or anal sex, but pretty much everything else is fair game."

Holly pressed a kiss to Leo's lips but kept it chaste, not wanting to be a tease. "That was one sentence, not two. Tell me more."

Leo hesitated.

"There's no need to be embarrassed." Holly stroked her cheek. "What is it? Bondage? Dirty talk? Role-playing?"

"No, nothing like that. I like to be seduced, maybe even teased a little. To let the anticipation build slowly until I can't stand it any longer." Leo's face flushed, and a low moan escaped her as she obviously imagined a

260

scenario like that. "God, that would be hot." She searched Holly's face. "Is that going to be a problem?"

"A problem? Heck, no! That's the nicest part of sex for me, just being able to caress and kiss you all over, without immediately having to...you know. My past partners often got so frustrated when I wouldn't..."

Leo kissed her softly. "I won't. That's half of the fun for me too."

Oh, wow. Maybe they weren't completely incompatible when it came to sex after all. "But you'll have to tell me when you've had enough and need some...um, relief, because I won't always know the right moment."

"Don't worry," Leo said with a little laugh. "I will definitely let you know." She continued to slide her fingers through Holly's hair. "So, what else went wrong for you in the past? I don't want to accidentally do something you're not comfortable with."

Holly mentally flipped through her inventory of unpleasant experiences. "One thing that never worked for me was when my partners initiated a back rub, cuddling, or kissing in the hopes that it would naturally escalate into sex. That never happens for me, so it always left them disappointed. If you want sex, it's better to just ask for it."

"Hmm." Leo's brow furrowed. "I'm not sure I want to do that. Won't it make you feel pressured?"

"I don't think so. With you, I'm comfortable saying no...or maybe sometimes yes *and* no."

Leo gave her a helpless look. "What do you mean?"

"Sometimes, I might be happy to touch you, but I might not always want to be touched...that way in return."

Leo rolled over so they were side-by-side. "I admit that will be a little weird. I would feel like a selfish ass if I expected you to pleasure me without getting anything out of it."

"Who says I'm not getting anything out of it? I'm in it for the intimacy, not the orgasm. But if you want to give me something in return, how about a nice massage or some cuddling? It could be part of foreplay for you and something to just enjoy for me." She tilted her head. "Orgasm for you, cuddlegasm for me. Would that work for you?"

Leo's eyes glazed over for a second at the mention of *orgasm*, making Holly laugh.

God, she's cute. It was freeing to realize she didn't feel threatened by Leo's sexual desires at all.

"It'll take some adjusting, but we'll make it work," Leo said. It sounded like a vow.

They hugged each other tightly in the middle of the bed.

Holly pressed her face to the warm cotton covering Leo's shoulder, kissed the firm flesh beneath, and breathed in Leo's scent.

Leo slid her hand beneath Holly's scrub shirt and caressed her back in long strokes.

Holly melted against her. With Leo, she could relax and enjoy a caress like this fully, knowing it wouldn't be turned into anything else. She wanted this moment to last forever.

But all too soon, a key jangled in the front door and steps sounded in the hall downstairs. "Leontyne? Holly?" Sharon's voice drifted up to them. "Can someone come help me with the groceries?"

Leo groaned. "I'll go help." She powered herself up on one arm, ready to climb off the bed.

But Holly pulled her back for a moment. "Wait."

Instantly, Leo sank back against her. "What is it?"

"I…" Unexpected tears burned in Holly's eyes. "I just want to tell you how much I love you and how much it means to me that we could have this conversation."

Leo's features softened. She framed Holly's face with both of her hands. "I love you too, and this conversation helped me as much as it did you."

Hand in hand, they crawled out of bed. As they descended the stairs, Leo leaned over and whispered, "Try not to look so ridiculously happy, or my mother will think we did the dirty."

After a few moments of trying to rein in her grin, Holly gave up. She stole a glance at Leo and nudged her with her elbow. "You're looking pretty happy yourself."

Leo laughed. "True. Let Mom think whatever she wants."

Leo opened the door to Johnny's Bar and Grill with one hand while keeping hold of Holly's hand with the other.

But before she could step through, Holly pulled her to a stop by their joined hands. "You know they're going to tease us mercilessly if we walk in like this, right?" She nodded down at their hands.

"I don't care." Leo searched her face. "Do you?"

Holly smiled. "No. I just wanted to make sure you know what you're in for."

Still standing in the open door, Leo leaned forward to kiss her before stepping inside. "Thanks."

Just like the first time she had met with her former classmates at the bar, a chorus of shouts erupted from the corner booth.

This time, however, the commotion wasn't because of her—it was because of *them*.

Travis wolf-whistled as they walked in hand in hand. "I knew it! I told Jenny I gave it four weeks before the two of you started—"

Jenny put her hand on his mouth, muffling the rest of his words, but Leo had a feeling it wouldn't have been something G-rated like *dating*.

"Why are we friends with him, again?" she whispered to Holly.

"Because he's going to stop with the asshole comments right now and buy us a beer to apologize," Holly answered, loud enough for everyone to hear. "Right, Travis?"

With his mouth still covered by his wife's hand, Travis nodded.

Leo stared at Holly for a moment, then a grin broke out on her face. She loved the way Holly didn't take shit from anyone.

Everyone slid to the left on the horseshoe-shaped booth to make room for them, and they squeezed in next to Zack.

Leo let her gaze drift over her former classmates. Finally, it came to rest on Chris, who sat at the other end of the booth and stared into his beer, a scowl on his face. *Oh Christ.* She hoped he wouldn't start behaving like an ass too, just because he had a crush the size of Missouri on Holly.

"Where's Ash?" Holly asked.

"She said she can't make it tonight," Zack said.

She was probably still hurt or angry after Leo had told her off last week. Leo stood by what she had said, but maybe she could have said it a little more calmly. She hadn't realized how angry she was with Ash until that moment, not only for letting her think her teenage crush had gone unreturned but also for treating Holly like her dirty little secret.

263

"But look who I talked into joining us." Zack waved to someone who had just entered the bar.

Leo slid her arm across the back of the booth as she turned, settling it around Holly's shoulders.

Sasha walked toward them, her height drawing the attention of the people hanging out at the bar. She didn't seem to notice as she folded her frame into the booth next to Chris.

Holly let out a playful gasp and pressed her hand to her chest. "Be still my heart! Sasha Peterson in a bar!"

"I'd go to plenty of bars if I didn't have to get up at four every day, unlike the rest of you slackers," Sasha said.

Everyone laughed.

Leo realized that she'd never had that type of gentle ribbing between friends who knew each other well.

The waitress came over, and they ordered a round of beer and chips and salsa for everyone to share.

Just as Leo had taken the first sip of her Boulevard Wheat, someone stepped up to their table. She looked up.

It was a brunette who looked barely old enough to be in a bar. "I hate to interrupt, but I was wondering if I could get an autograph." She held out a napkin.

Automatically, Leo slid her pop-star mask into place—a smile that was friendly but also slightly aloof.

Holly tensed next to her and turned as if trying to block Leo from view.

But before either of them could say anything, Chris leaned forward. "Can't you see that she's having dinner with friends? There's a time and a place for autographs. This isn't it."

Leo stared at him. He was the last person she had expected to defend her.

The young woman stammered an apology.

"If you're still here when I leave, I'll stop by on my way out and give you an autograph, okay?" Leo said.

With an eager nod, the brunette headed back to the bar.

Leo held out her beer bottle. "Thanks, Chris."

He clinked his bottle against hers without saying anything.

After interruptions like this, it was usually impossible for Leo to relax and go back to being herself, but with Holly's warmth against her side and the conversation and jokes at the table continuing as if nothing had happened, she managed to slowly shed the layers until she was just Leo again.

Finally, Sasha tucked a bill beneath her empty beer bottle. "I'm outta here, guys."

"What? You turn into a pumpkin if you're not in bed by ten?" Travis asked.

"It was the coach that turned into a pumpkin, not Cinderella." Sasha got up.

Leo exchanged a glance with Holly, who nodded. "We'll walk you home."

Towering over all of them, Sasha flashed a grin. "It's just a few steps to my apartment above the bakery."

Leo shrugged and slid out of the booth anyway. She wanted some time alone with Holly before the evening ended.

Travis laughed. "Don't you get it, Sash? 'Walk you home' is code for—"

Zack threw his coaster at him. "Shut up, Travis."

"Night, guys."

They made their way to the door, with Leo stopping at the bar to sign an autograph for the young woman, who, apparently, had passed the time by drinking way too much. She let out a happy screech, threw her arms around Leo, and kissed her cheek.

Leo withdrew as quickly as possible. As they stepped out onto the street, she peered over at Holly to see if she would get jealous.

"I think we need to get you a sign or a T-shirt or something," Holly said with an amused grin. "One that says *no kissing*."

"No kissing?" Leo drawled, lowering her voice an octave. "Are you sure about that?"

"Well, the fine print would say *unless you're Holly Drummond*."

"Mmm, I like that fine print." They stopped beneath a streetlamp to share a kiss.

"Now I know what 'walk you home' is code for." Sasha laughed.

Chapter 22

Content disclaimer
This chapter includes a sex scene.
If you'd rather not read sexually explicit content,
please skip ahead to chapter 23.

WITH HER FINGER HOVERING OVER the track pad of her laptop, Holly glanced over at Leo to see if she was ready. When she caught her smoothing down an errant strand of hair, she giggled and gave her a loving nudge. "Stop preening. Meg is ace too. She doesn't care how your hair looks."

"What? Are you saying aces can't appreciate nice-looking hair?"

"Oh, we can, but Meg really couldn't care less."

Leo shrugged. "I just want to make a good impression. I know she's one of your closest friends."

Holly wrapped one arm around her waist and kissed her. "Don't worry. She'll love you. Not half as much as I do, of course."

Leo stopped fussing with her hair and returned the kiss.

The melody announcing an incoming Skype call interrupted them. Apparently, Meg didn't want to wait for them to call her. Maybe she was as nervous as Leo was.

Holly clicked to accept the call.

Meg's smiling face appeared on the laptop screen. When she saw herself in the little Skype window, she reached up to adjust her hair.

Leo nudged Holly. "See?" she whispered. "She cares."

"Yeah, yeah." Holly nudged her back before turning her attention to the screen. "Hi, Meg."

"Hi." Meg waved energetically and then looked at something offscreen. "Come on, Jo. They're here."

Jo dropped onto a seat next to her and pressed a mug into her hands. "Hi," she said in the direction of the webcam.

"Leo, these are my friends Meg and Jo. Guys, this is Leo." Holly leaned in to Leo until their shoulders touched.

Meg laughed. "I know. I've seen her on TV."

"Oh." Heat crept up Holly's neck. Most of the time, she forgot that Leo was a celebrity. To her, she was just Leo. "Of course."

"Thanks for the card and the autograph," Meg said before the moment of silence could become awkward. "I really appreciated it."

"The PS too?" Leo asked with a teasing grin.

"Yeah, well, I'll forgive you for that." Meg waved her hand like a queen pardoning a prisoner. "I hear falling in love can cloud your judgment."

The small window in the corner of the main screen showed Leo arching her eyebrows.

"I didn't tell her that," Holly said quickly.

Meg snorted. "Oh please. You're both head over heels. It's as obvious as the fact that Yen is way cooler than Triss. That's why I encouraged you to give it a chance."

"You did?" Leo asked. "In that case, I forgive you for your lapse in good taste regarding Triss and Yen."

The two laughed, and Holly beamed along with them. Only now did she realize that she'd been a little nervous about this first meeting too. She wanted her friends and Leo to like each other, and apparently, they were off to a good start.

"So, how did the two of you meet Holly?" Leo asked.

Holly covered her face with both hands. "Oh no. Not that story."

Meg let out an evil chuckle. "Well, she asked for it, and far be it from me to deny her."

"Wait, now I remember. Didn't you say you met on Tumblr?" Leo gave Holly a puzzled look. "How's that embarrassing?"

"I left a comment on one of her Tumblr posts...and it had a typo that caught Meg's attention."

"And that of about a million people all over the Internet," Meg quipped with a grin.

Leo's gaze flicked back and forth between Holly and the screen. "Must have been some typo. What was it?"

Meg opened her eyes dramatically wide. "She called me aromatic."

"It was that damn autocorrect," Holly grumbled. "I typed in *aromantic*, and it corrected it to *aromatic*."

"Well," Jo said, speaking up for the first time, "since I'm doing the laundry in this house, I can tell you that you weren't completely wrong about her being aromatic either. At least not when it comes to her socks. They are—"

Meg covered Jo's mouth with her hand. "Excuse us for a moment. I have to go beat up my partner here." But instead, she merely tousled Jo's hair.

When their call ended about ten minutes later, Holly and Leo leaned back on the couch and grinned at each other.

"That went well," Holly said.

Leo tilted her head. "You didn't think it would?"

"No, I thought they would like you. I mean, what's not to like, right?" She smiled.

"Exactly."

They chuckled.

"But you never know with Jo." Holly swung her legs onto the couch and settled them on Leo's lap. "She's usually not a people person, but she warmed right up to you."

"I like them," Leo said. "Have you made many friends online?"

"A few. Dana and I got to a point where things were so bad that I spent a lot of time online, asking other aces and their allosexual partners for advice." A sigh escaped her. "Not that it saved our relationship." Needing the closeness, she sat up and slid forward, which put her nearly in Leo's lap.

Leo pulled her more firmly onto her lap and held her securely. She played with the embroidered design on the back of Holly's jean shorts. Basically, she was almost caressing her butt, and Holly found that she didn't mind at all. In fact, it was nice, and so was the feeling of skin on skin, since they were both wearing shorts.

"If you ever feel that things between us aren't going well, promise me that you'll talk to me instead of people on the Internet, okay?" Leo said.

"I don't think we'll ever get to that point. But yeah, I promise." She ducked her head and rubbed her nose against Leo's, liking that, for once, she was the taller one. "I'm not squishing you, am I?"

"Not at all. I like you here." Leo nuzzled her face against Holly's throat and continued to speak with her lips close to her skin. "You know…I had no idea how complex relationships could be. Meeting you and your friends really opened my mind and made me see nuances that I wasn't aware of before."

Speechless, Holly looked down at her. No one had ever made her feel so good about herself. The urge to make Leo feel just as good thrummed through her veins. "Leo?" Her voice trembled a little, but it wasn't fear, only an overload of emotions. "Do you…do you want to make love?"

Leo went still beneath her. "N-now?"

"Why not? I've got the day off tomorrow, and you told your mother you might sleep over at my place, didn't you?"

"Yeah, but I didn't have an ulterior motive when I said that. I just thought we might stay up late, playing some games on the Xbox."

"So you'd rather play video games?" Holly asked with a smile.

"Hell, no! I'd much rather make love to you. But if you want to stop at any time, just say the word. It would really be okay."

"I know. This is what I want. Will you trust me?"

Leo looked her in the eyes. "Yes."

Holly climbed off Leo's lap and held out her hand, palm up.

When Leo reached for it, her fingers were shaking.

Somehow, it was soothing to know she wasn't the only one who was nervous. They held each other's hand tightly as Holly led her to the bedroom and pulled back the covers. She flicked on the lamp on the bedside table and turned off the overhead light, leaving a more intimate glow.

For several moments, they stood next to the bed without moving, gazing deeply into each other's eyes.

Where to start? It had been years since Holly had been with anyone, and back then, she hadn't known herself and her needs very well, so her partners had always taken the lead. But with Leo, she wanted things to be different. She didn't want to have to lie back and think of England, as Leo had put it.

Getting both of them naked might be a good first step. "C-can I...?" She pointed at Leo's T-shirt.

"Whatever you want," Leo answered.

Holly stepped closer until she could sense Leo's body heat. Barely breathing, she tugged the T-shirt from the front of Leo's jean shorts. As she pulled it up, her fingers grazed the warm skin of Leo's belly.

Leo's breath hitched, but she willingly lifted her arms and let Holly pull the shirt up over her head.

The soft light of the lamp made her skin glow with a golden shimmer.

Holly couldn't resist feathering her fingertips along her shoulder and down her arm until she could entwine their fingers.

Leo lifted her hand to her mouth and kissed it. "Yours too?"

In the past, Holly had always preferred undressing herself, needing that bit of control, but now she nodded.

Leo's pulse beat visibly in her neck as she reached for the edge of Holly's shirt. She kept eye contact as she pulled it up, interrupting it only for the moment when she pulled the shirt over her head, then her gaze was back on Holly's.

The shirt fluttered to the floor.

Leo traced her collarbone with a single finger and then touched her face. "Bras too?"

Holly leaned her cheek into Leo's palm and nodded.

When they reached around each other, their nearly bare torsos brushed. Leo sucked in an audible breath, and Holly shivered at the intimate feeling. Both fumbled a bit with the clasp of the other's bra. The cups of Leo's bra fell away first.

"Hey," Leo protested with a smile. "I'm supposed to be the one who's better at this."

Holly looked into her eyes. "You're not supposed to be anything. Not with me. No expectations, okay? Just you and me."

"I'd like that very much," Leo murmured. She touched her lips to Holly's in a gentle kiss.

When the kiss ended and they moved back a little, Holly's bra, which had been trapped between their bodies, dropped to the floor too.

"Shorts next?" Leo asked.

Holly nodded. She couldn't resist sliding her hands over the soft skin of Leo's outer thighs as she helped her out of her jean shorts.

Then it was her turn.

Leo's fingers trembled a little as she opened the button on Holly's shorts. Slowly, looking into Holly's eyes, she slid down the zipper and then guided the shorts down her legs.

Cool air flowed over Holly's nearly bare body as she stood in front of Leo in just her panties. Goose bumps broke out all over her skin.

Leo's heated gaze roamed over her, lingering on her breasts and her hips. "Wow," she murmured and then swallowed audibly and lifted her gaze back to Holly's face. "You're beautiful." Her voice was rough and tender at the same time. "Very beautiful."

Encouraged by those words, Holly slid her panties down her legs.

Leo mumbled something that sounded like, "God, give me self-control," which made Holly blush and giggle. Leo's lips quirked up into an answering smile.

Holly relaxed a little. It was good to see that they could laugh with each other and didn't need to be so serious.

She reached out a hand and caressed Leo's panty-clad hip. "I want to see all of you too."

Leo didn't hesitate to fulfill that wish. Within seconds, her panties fell to the floor.

Holly couldn't help staring. She knew Leo was beautiful, but this... The low light of the lamp made her hair gleam like gold. Several strands cascaded down onto the smooth skin of her shoulders and brushed the upper slope of her small, firm breasts. Holly's gaze took in the flat planes of her belly and lingered on her long legs. There wasn't a doubt in her mind that she was looking at the most beautiful woman in the world—and, more importantly, the woman she loved.

"What do you feel when you look at me like this?" Leo asked. Her cheeks had flushed beneath Holly's gaze, and her voice had become even huskier.

"It makes me want to touch you." Not necessarily in a sexual way, but it could include that without making her uncomfortable.

"You can do whatever you want to." Slowly, Leo framed Holly's face with her hands, brought their mouths together, and kissed her—just a tender contact, with only her fingers and lips touching Holly.

With a sigh, Holly sank into the kiss. She slid her fingers into Leo's hair and pulled her closer until their bodies touched all along their lengths. The feeling of Leo's bare skin against her own was so intimate that it made her head spin.

Leo moaned into her mouth and deepened the kiss. Heat radiated off her skin. Finally, she broke the kiss with a gasp and looked into Holly's eyes. Without breaking eye contact, she guided her onto the bed and slid onto the mattress next to her. "Would you be comfortable lying on your belly, even if you can't see what I'm doing?"

"Um, what?" That was the last thing Holly had expected. "I mean, yes, I would be comfortable doing that, but…"

"Then roll over," Leo whispered. She smiled and cradled Holly's cheek in her warm palm. "Orgasm for me, cuddlegasm for you. That's what you said would work for you, right?"

Raw emotions burned in the back of Holly's throat. It meant the world to her that Leo put her needs over whatever she herself might want. Too choked up to speak, she rolled over onto her belly.

Leo cuddled against her side, one breast warm against Holly's arm. "Mmm, you feel good," she whispered into Holly's ear.

Her warm breath made goose bumps rise all over Holly's body again.

Leo supported herself on one elbow next to her and trailed her fingertips along Holly's back. She drew tiny circles around each ridge of her spine, one by one.

The calluses on her fingers tickled a little, making the corners of Holly's lips twitch up into a smile.

Leo took her time, mapping every inch of Holly's back with her hands. She swirled her fingertips around the contours of Holly's shoulder blades before moving lower. Her fingers followed the arc of Holly's ribs, but each caress stopped short of the outer edge of her breasts.

"Is this okay?" Leo asked.

"Very okay." Holly sighed in contentment. Her eyes fluttered shut.

Leo's caresses trailed down her body and lingered in the dip of her waist.

"The curve of your hips is so beautiful." Leo slid her fingertips down Holly's sensitive side and then over one hip in a whisperlike touch. "Makes me wish I was a painter, not a singer."

Holly nearly melted under Leo's touch and her honest admiration.

On the small of her back, Leo paused and began a gentle massage before trailing her hand down over Holly's butt and down her leg until she reached her calves. She kneaded each one tenderly and then started to slide her fingers back up Holly's leg.

Trusting Leo not to dip toward the inside of her thigh, Holly relaxed beneath her touch.

Leo made several languid sweeps of her body, from her shoulders to her ankles, until Holly felt heavy with pleasure yet strangely light at the same time.

When Leo retraced her route up her back again, Holly pressed her forehead into the pillow to expose her neck.

Leo chuckled. "Are you trying to tell me something?"

"Wouldn't want you to forget the best places," Holly murmured into the pillow.

"Best places, hmm?" Leo's voice was laced with amusement and affection. She slid her fingers up along either side of Holly's spine, half massaging, half caressing. When she reached her neck, she gentled her touch. Her short nails rasped over Holly's skin and teased the tiny hairs on her neck. Soft strands of hair fanned over Holly's shoulder blades, tickling her skin, as Leo leaned over her and ducked down her head. Her bare breasts brushed Holly's back, making her shiver.

Then Leo's warm lips pressed a kiss to the nape of her neck.

A moan escaped Holly.

"You like this?" Leo whispered, her breath warm on Holly's ear.

"Mmm, yes." It was the most sensual experience of her life, and she could enjoy it for what it was.

"Good. I like it too. Very..." She kissed behind Holly's right ear. "Very..." And then the left. "Much." She feathered a string of kisses all over her neck. "Did you cuddlegasm yet? Or is it caressgasm, in this case?"

Holly smiled into her pillow and then turned her head a little so she could answer. "I've had neither." She didn't want this wonderful experience to end. "I've got lots and lots of stamina, you know?"

The sound of Leo's laughter flowed over her. "Lucky for you, I do too." She shifted a little and swung one leg to the other side of Holly's body so she was straddling her, her weight on her knees, not on Holly. "This okay?"

"Yes," Holly whispered.

Leo sat up a little more. The curly hair at the apex of her thighs tickled Holly's butt, but Leo didn't try to rub her center against her. Instead, she focused fully on Holly's pleasure.

Using both hands, she followed the lines of Holly's shoulders with her fingertips, out to her upper arms, and then traced along the sensitive inside of her forearms until she found Holly's hands, which were lying palm down beneath the pillow. She entwined their fingers and gently lifted Holly's arms to the sides, her own arms parallel to Holly's and her breasts pressed against her back. Leo's lips trailed tender kisses along the side of her neck.

Their position left Holly completely vulnerable, and it surprised her how much she enjoyed it. A sound of approval hummed from her throat. It felt like being covered by Leo's love. She tilted her head a little more to give Leo unlimited access to her neck.

Leo smiled against her skin and placed a string of gentle nibbles and kisses down her neck. She nuzzled a sensitive spot below Holly's ear; then her weight disappeared from Holly's back. "Turn over," she whispered.

Holly did, so they were lying side by side.

Their gazes connected, and then their lips brushed. They separated for a moment before meeting again in a firmer, more passionate contact.

Finally able to touch, Holly wrapped her arms around Leo and trailed her hands over the smooth planes of her back.

Leo moaned into the kiss, and a fine tremor ran through her body, reminding Holly that this wasn't just pure sensual bliss for her partner.

Gently, she guided Leo onto her back and started her own explorations.

Leo lay still, her fingers splayed wide against the mattress, as if she needed to brace herself for what was to come.

Holly caressed Leo's flushed cheek. "Don't hold back, okay? I want you to enjoy this, so stop worrying about me and just…feel."

Leo swallowed and nodded.

Alternately using the back of her hand and her fingertips, Holly stroked the long arms that always held her so tenderly. When she reached the bend of her elbow, she slid down in bed and added her lips to the exploration. The skin on the inside of Leo's forearm was a shade or two lighter than the outside. It shone like alabaster in the light of the lamp on the bedside table.

She guided one of Leo's hands up so she could kiss the open palm and then nibbled on her index finger.

A long, breathy moan escaped Leo.

That was sexual for her? Interesting. To test her new discovery, she slid the tip of Leo's middle finger into her mouth and tasted her salty skin.

Another moan and the pulse in Leo's wrist throbbed beneath Holly's fingers. Leo stared up at her. The green of her eyes formed thin rings around her enlarged pupils.

Wow. Holly had been a little afraid that seeing Leo in the throes of passion would make her feel disconnected from her, because she was getting into a zone where Holly had no way of following. Usually, this was the point when things started to feel surreal for her, as if she was watching someone else while the analytical part of her brain tried to figure out what she should do next.

But now she found that she was mostly fascinated by how easily Leo responded to her touches. She tried to stay in the moment and focus on emotions, not merely motions.

She moved back a little and skimmed her lips over the elegant arc of Leo's collarbone, then kissed the hollow at the base of her throat.

Leo encouraged her with little gasps, moans, and hums.

Goose bumps rose beneath Holly's lips as she trailed them up Leo's neck, and Holly made a game out of trying to kiss them away. In between kisses, she lifted her head and glanced at Leo's flushed face to see how she reacted to each touch.

Leo seemed to struggle to keep her eyes open.

Holly pressed her lips to the warm spot below Leo's ear, where she caught faint traces of Leo's perfume. She inhaled deeply, enjoying the scent and the heat of her skin.

Leo's pulse thudded beneath her mouth as Holly trailed careful little nibbles down the other side of her neck.

A light sheen of perspiration made the valley between her breasts feel like silk beneath her fingertips. Holly idly ran her fingers back and forth. *Mmm, nice.* She could have done this forever, but she knew this was foreplay for Leo, not the main course, so she tilted her head down and nuzzled her cheek against Leo's breast.

So warm and soft…

Leo's chest quickly rose and fell beneath her, and both of her hands took a firm grip on the sheets.

For Holly, stroking Leo's shoulder was as pleasing as stroking her breast, but for Leo, there was definitely a difference.

Let's see… She watched Leo's face as she experimentally smoothed her thumb over one of her nipples. It instantly hardened beneath her touch.

A low, hungry sound escaped Leo. "C-can you…?" Her voice cracked. "Do you want to…do that again?"

The reactions she could cause in her partner were amazing. She smiled. "Of course. Or do you want me to kiss it?"

"Yes. Either. Both."

Holly cradled one breast in her hand and placed slow kisses all around its slope, then closer to its center. Gently, she tasted it, fascinated by the contrast between the satiny soft skin and the hard nipple. What would Leo do if she sucked it a little?

She got the answer to her question when Leo arched up against her and let go of the sheet with one hand to bury her fingers in Holly's hair and hold her to her breast.

Holly smiled around the nipple in her mouth. Now that she had found out what Leo liked, she tried more of the same to find the best way to bring Leo pleasure.

Tiny tremors ran through Leo as Holly flicked her tongue over the nipple. Her hips shifted against Holly's, and her fingers played restlessly with her hair. She didn't try to urge her on, though, but let her explore at her own pace.

Holly spent a long time loving one breast before switching to the other. In between kisses and licks, she glanced up at Leo's face.

Each time, Leo looked back at her through heavy-lidded eyes, her cheeks flushed and her lips slightly parted.

Finally, she let go of Holly's hair and dropped her hand back to the mattress like a wrestler tapping the mat to signal surrender. "Please." She panted out the single word. The flush on her cheeks had spread to her entire body, and need simmered in her eyes.

Holly pressed a kiss to her lips and then slid her hand over Leo's tense belly, down to the inside of her thigh. How soft the skin there was. For a moment, she forgot what she'd been about to do until Leo moaned out another "please."

The helpless need in her voice made a wave of protectiveness crest over Holly. She slipped her hand between Leo's thighs and started to stroke her. At first, it was a little awkward. That familiar disconnected feeling threatened to rise.

But then she looked up and saw the open, vulnerable expression and the look of pleasure on Leo's face. She had put that there, just by touching her this way. It amazed her and made her feel good about what she was doing.

Leo rolled her head back and forth on the pillow. "So good."

"Yeah?"

Leo nodded frantically, as if now beyond speech. A groan tore from her chest. She let go of the sheets and gripped Holly's hips with both hands, arching up toward her.

Fascinated by how out of control Leo was getting, Holly matched her rhythm.

"Holly!" Leo slid her fingers up, dug them into Holly's shoulders, and pulled her down, guiding their mouths together in a deep kiss.

Everything was moving a little fast for Holly now. She couldn't keep up. But it didn't matter since Leo set the pace for them both.

After only a few seconds, Leo tore her mouth away and surged upward, clutching Holly to her.

Holly's breath caught at how beautiful Leo looked as she strained against her. Her head was thrown back in abandon, the muscles in her neck corded.

She choked out Holly's name before stiffening against her; then she collapsed back onto the bed with a ragged gasp. "Holly," she murmured. "God, Holly."

She looked all flushed and soft, as if her limbs were too heavy to move even an inch, and all Holly wanted was to hold her close—so she did. She curled against Leo's side and rained down tender kisses on her closed eyelids and her flushed cheeks before settling her head on her sweat-dampened chest. Leo's heart drummed a fast beat beneath her ear.

God, she loved seeing her so satisfied, loved knowing that she could do this for her. Seeing Leo come had been fascinating too, but this—holding her afterward—was simply amazing.

"My limbs seem to have turned into overcooked spaghetti," Leo murmured, "but I'll be as good as new in a minute. So if you want…"

Holly kissed her. "No. Not today. This was perfect for me."

"Mmhm. For me too." Leo lifted her head and kissed her, reconnecting. Holly hummed into the kiss.

When it ended, Leo searched her face. "Was it really okay for you?"

Holly brushed damp strands of hair out of Leo's eyes. "More than okay. What you did for me… No one has ever made love to me that way. Even if it didn't end with me having an orgasm, that's what it was for me—lovemaking."

"I know. It felt wonderful to touch you like that." Leo gave her a dreamy smile. "But what about the rest?" She reached for the hand that Holly had used to touch her, lifted it to her mouth, and kissed it. "Was that okay too?"

"Yes," Holly answered without hesitation. "You looked so beautiful that I nearly forgot what I was doing."

Leo laughed, her voice still raspy. "Oh yeah. I could tell when you suddenly explored my inner thigh in great detail."

Holly blushed all the way down to her toes. Since she was naked, they could both see it. "Your skin is very soft there," she said in her defense and trailed her fingers over that soft spot.

Leo sucked in a breath and covered Holly's hand on her thigh with her own, stilling it. "Unless you're up for a second round, you better find another soft spot to caress."

"Oh." Holly smiled sheepishly and moved her hand to Leo's belly. "Better?"

"Perfect." She wrapped both arms around Holly and held her close. Slowly, her breathing returned to normal, and her heartbeat beneath Holly's ear slowed to a steadier pace.

Holly snagged the covers that had slid to the bottom of the bed with her toes and dragged them up until she could reach them with her hand.

Leo laughed at her acrobatics. "What are you doing?"

"Covering us." She pulled the covers up over their cooling bodies.

"Holly?" Leo's voice was already drowsy, as if she was beginning to fall asleep.

"Hmm?"

"I love you." Leo's lashes fluttered closed, and her breathing turned into the slow rhythm of sleep.

Smiling, Holly reached past her and flicked off the light before settling back against Leo's side, one arm and one leg hooked around her. "I love you too," she whispered into the darkness. It was wonderful to lie here and hold Leo close without feeling the resentment or the loneliness that usually followed sexual encounters for her.

She knew there might be days when things didn't go as well and their needs would be just too different. But no matter what, she trusted that they would always find ways to compromise and make each other feel loved in some way.

With a butterfly kiss to Leo's shoulder, she closed her eyes and followed her into the realm of dreams.

Chapter 23

LEO SLOWLY DRIFTED INTO WAKEFULNESS. The first thing she became aware of was the warm body pressed to hers from behind. Holly's knees were tucked behind hers, her groin snugly fitted to Leo's bottom, and her naked breasts pressed against Leo's back. One foot rested between Leo's ankles, and her arm was draped around her waist.

Once, when Leo had awakened during the night, they had been in the exact same position, as if they had slept like that all night.

She lay still and listened to Holly's even breaths, enjoying their closeness and the feel of Holly's bare skin against hers.

Flashes of last night replayed through her mind: Holly bending down to kiss her breast, her breathy moan when Leo had kissed the nape of her neck, the look of wonder on her face as she brought Leo pleasure. God, what a night. She couldn't stop smiling. Not because she'd had great sex—okay, not *just* because she'd had great sex—but because they had managed to make it a good experience for them both.

Holly murmured something incomprehensible in her sleep. Leo thought it might have been her name.

She couldn't resist rolling over to watch her sleep, careful not to dislodge Holly's arm around her in the process.

Streaks of morning sunlight bathed Holly's face in a golden hue and glinted off her auburn hair, which was tousled from the many times Leo had run her hands through it last night. One hand rested beneath her chin, and her face was relaxed in deep slumber.

The sheet had slipped down to her waist some time during the night, and now Leo drank in the curves of her body and the glow of her skin.

As if sensing her attention, Holly mumbled something and tightened her hold on Leo.

With a hum, Leo cuddled closer and kept watching her face from just inches away.

Finally, Holly blinked open her eyes. A smile curled her lips as their gazes connected. Without saying anything, she trailed her fingers along Leo's jaw and to the corner of her mouth. Her fingertips rested there as she bridged the few inches of space between them and kissed her, caressing Leo's lips with her own.

"Good morning," she whispered when the kiss ended. She yawned and stretched like a lazy cat. Her soft skin brushed along Leo's in a sensual slide.

Leo struggled to bite back a moan. Her "good morning" came out much raspier than intended. *Get a grip.* She'd woken up next to Holly several times by now, but never naked. Never after a night of lovemaking. "Is this okay?" She nodded down at their entwined bodies. "The naked cuddling, I mean."

"Very okay." Holly splayed her fingers across Leo's back as if soaking up the feeling of her skin and let out a contented sigh. "I could stay like this all day."

Very aware of the leg between her own, Leo cuddled closer. "Hmm, me too. Anything else you'd like to do today?" She ran a finger up Holly's side, enjoying the goose bumps that rose beneath her touch. "Maybe something a little more..." Her voice dropped a register. "...active?"

"How about some Xbox?"

Leo paused with her finger near the edge of Holly's breast and stared at her. "Xbox?" she echoed.

Her eyes half-closed and a peaceful expression on her face, Holly nodded. "Meg sent me a game that I think you might like."

With Holly's naked body pressed against hers, she could barely think of anything but how amazing last night had been.

Yeah, it was amazing, but it didn't change who Holly is. She's still ace. A surge of love tightened Leo's throat. *My ace.*

"But if you're not in the mood..." Holly added.

Leo burst out laughing.

Holly opened her eyes more fully and gave her a puzzled look. "What's so funny about video games?"

"Nothing." Leo trailed her fingers through Holly's tousled hair. "Just thinking about how much I love you."

Holly went still against her, and a slow smile brought out her dimples. "I love you too." She kissed her tenderly. Then her smile turned into a challenging grin. "But that doesn't explain why you were laughing." She dug her fingers into Leo's bare side, tickling her. "Tell me!"

They laughed and wrestled playfully. The sheet tightened around their calves, chaining them to each other.

Leo squirmed and halfheartedly tried to get away. "Sex," she cried out breathlessly. "Sex and video games."

Holly stopped. The tickling turned into absentminded caresses. "Huh?"

"That's what made me laugh—the way our brains are wired. You were thinking about video games, and I was thinking about making love."

"Oh." Holly blinked once; then she slapped her own forehead and laughed too. Finally, she sobered, placed one palm along Leo's face, and looked into her eyes. "Well, if you want to, we can—"

Leo interrupted her with a soft kiss. "I appreciate the offer." She kissed her again, this time a little more deeply, just enough to show her that she was still desired. "But I'll need my energy to kick your ass at Xbox."

They looked into each other's eyes, and a silent understanding passed between them.

"Later," Holly said, her voice a little hoarse. "First, I need more cuddle time."

With twin sighs, they settled back into each other's arms.

Leo's eyes drifted closed. *Sex and video games,* she thought with a smile. It would make for a cool song title.

A week later, Leo leaned back on the couch and playfully wiggled her toes against Holly's thighs as she tried another chord progression for the chorus she was working on.

Without looking up from her novel, Holly started a one-handed foot massage that had Leo sigh in contentment and put down her guitar to enjoy it more fully.

Holly looked up. "Hey, why did you stop playing? That song was starting to sound really nice." She hummed the chorus in the adorably off-key way that always made Leo smile.

"I love you." Saying those three words had never come easily to Leo, and she wasn't using them lightly now either, but with Holly she found herself thinking it—and saying it—at the most surprising times.

A glow from within lit up Holly's face, transforming her features from cute to breathtaking. Her gaze went soft. "I love you too." She tugged on Leo's big toe, and the tender smile grew into a teasing grin. "Even if there's a hole in your sock."

Leo craned her neck to see it. "There is?"

"Mm-hm." Holly tickled the bit of skin peeking out through the hole.

Leo's foot twitched. "Yeah, well, musical geniuses work better with some ventilation."

"Oh yeah?" Holly tickled a path up Leo's leg and found the sensitive spot behind her knee.

Leo giggled and squirmed but didn't withdraw. It was so wonderful to see how comfortable Holly had become with these little playful touches.

"Why are you even wearing socks in the middle of summer?" Holly asked. "You'd think you were the one with the ugly crooked toes."

"Hey, I love your crooked toes."

They looked at each other, knowing Leo was talking about much more than Holly's toes.

The ringing of a phone from the kitchen interrupted the moment.

"Leontyne?" Her mother called from the same direction. "That's yours. It's your manager calling—again."

"On a Sunday?" Holly muttered. "Doesn't he keep normal office hours? I'm beginning to really dislike that man."

Just as Leo was about to get up from her comfy spot next to Holly, her mother entered the living room and held out the ringing phone to her. "Me too," she said to Holly. "He'd do anything to get Leontyne back to New York. Sometimes, I wonder if he was the one who told the paparazzi where to find her."

Leo's stomach churned. Saul wouldn't do that…would he? In the past, she never would have doubted him, but now she no longer had that kind of trust. *Yeah. And that should tell you it's time for a change.*

"I wouldn't put it past him," Holly muttered. At the mention of Leo returning to New York, her face had gone carefully blank.

By now, Leo knew that look: Holly put it on whenever she didn't want to broadcast her feelings. It was probably something she had learned as a nurse. She put a hand on Holly's knee and rubbed gently. "Don't worry. I think this time he's calling because of something else."

But she knew Holly would continue to worry. She did too whenever she thought about her inevitable return to New York. At some point, she wouldn't be able to postpone it anymore. But that day wouldn't be today.

She let the call go to voice mail, even though she was eager to find out what Saul thought of the two songs she had recorded on her laptop and then sent to him.

"You could have taken the call," Holly said. "I have to get going anyway. I'm running low on clean clothes because I spent all week playing video games with a certain someone, so I need to do some laundry before we meet for dinner at Mom's."

They grinned at each other; then Leo shook her head and said, "Nah, that's fine. I'll call him back later."

Holly got up from the couch and bent to kiss Leo goodbye.

"You can kiss me anytime," Leo said before their lips were about to meet, "but just to let you know, I fully intend to walk you to your car."

Holly smiled and kissed her anyway.

It had been a nice surprise how comfortable she was with public displays of affection.

When they pulled apart, Holly hugged Leo's mom goodbye. "You're coming to dinner too, right?"

"If you're sure that the two of you wouldn't rather be alone…"

"Alone?" Holly laughed. "My mom, my brothers, their wives, and their four kids will be there. Maybe a cousin or two or one of my brothers' friends too. My mom will be glad to have someone her age to help her reign over the chaos."

Leo's mother smiled. "Then I'll gladly come. Tell Beth I'll bring an apple pie."

"Will do," Holly said. "Thank you."

Leo took her hand and walked her to the Jeep.

Holly unlocked it and opened the driver's side door but didn't get in immediately. Instead, they stood facing each other, their fingers tightly entangled.

Every time they separated, even if just for a few hours, Leo was more reluctant to let her go. They really had to figure out what to do about the future, because one thing Leo knew for sure: whatever happened in her life, she wanted to share it with Holly.

One of their neighbors walked past and waved to them. "Hi, Holly. Morning, Leontyne. How's your mom?"

How amazing. If someone recognized her on the street in New York, they usually started jumping up and down, screaming hysterically, or they rooted around for a piece of paper for her to sign. She sometimes encountered fans here in Fair Oaks too, but most of the people in town didn't make a big deal of her presence.

"She's hanging in there, keeping busy making apple pies," Leo answered.

"We'll start harvesting our Jonagold next week. I'll have Jack bring her a basket. They're great for pies." The neighbor waved again and walked on.

Holly smiled. "You're still not used to it, are you?"

"Hmm?" Leo turned her gaze from where she had stared after the neighbor.

"You're used to people going gaga over your very presence. Do you miss it?" Holly asked softly.

Leo didn't have to think about it. "Not at all. As a teenager, I used to daydream about being famous, the fans going crazy when I climb out of my limousine in some fancy designer dress or something..." She gave a self-deprecating smile.

"That's so not you," Holly said.

"No, it isn't. But I didn't know that back then."

"Well..." Holly lifted up on her tiptoes and gave her another sweet kiss. "You won't need a designer dress to have dinner with my family. But putting on a different pair of socks before you come over might be a good idea, musical genius."

Chuckling, Leo watched her climb behind the wheel of the Jeep. Neither let go of the other's hand.

They smiled at each other for several seconds. Then their hands slid apart, and Holly closed the driver's side door.

Leo stood in the driveway and waved until the Jeep disappeared down the street.

"So, dinner with your in-laws," her mother said when Leo returned to the living room. "Are you nervous?"

It hadn't occurred to Leo that she had reason to be, but now that her mother said it, something started to flutter in her stomach. "Um, you think I should be? It's no big deal, right? Holly's had dinner with us dozens of times."

"That's hardly the same. Holly had dinner with your father and me several times a week before you came home. But Beth hasn't had much of a chance to get to know the woman who's in love with her daughter."

"Beth has known me since I was knee-high to a grasshopper."

"She knew you back then, when you were a little girl and then a teenager, but she doesn't know the woman you've become. It would only be natural if she was a bit skeptical. What woman would like her daughter to date a rock star?"

"Pop star," Leo mumbled.

"You know what I mean. If I were her, I'd want to know what your intentions are."

Leo gulped and plopped down onto the couch. That sounded as if she might be in for a maternal interrogation. "Gee, thanks, Mom. Now I am nervous."

Her mother laughed. "I'm sure it'll be a lovely dinner."

The cell phone rang again, and Saul's name flashed across the display.

"I'll get started on that apple pie." Her mother left the living room.

Once she was alone, Leo accepted the call and skipped the usual pleasantries. "What did you think?"

"Um, I assume you mean the songs you sent me?"

"Yes, what else? Come on, Saul. Don't make me wait." She bounced on the couch once. "What did you think?"

He cleared his throat. "They're good."

"Really?" She sank against the back of the sofa. Somehow, she had expected him to talk her out of trying something new—or, rather, into returning to her old style—no matter how good the songs might be.

"Yeah. I mean…technically. But, Jenna, they're not what we're looking for."

She should have known there was a *but* involved. Leo gritted her teeth. "We?"

"Well, the label. They want something…flashier."

"To hell with what they want. What about what *I* want?"

"What do you want?" He sounded as if he was just humoring her.

Leo struggled not to raise her voice. "I want to let my music speak for itself. No more high-tech shows, costumes that barely cover a thing, or music videos that would make a sex worker blush!"

"Jenna, please. You know that's not enough nowadays, especially not with the younger crowd. Good voices are a dime a dozen. If you want to be successful, you've got to deliver the full package. You know what they say: sex sells."

A sudden calm came over her. "You know what? Sex is overrated. And so is money. I made enough to last me a lifetime. If I'm not at the top of the charts all the time, I can live with that. I want to go back to making music, Saul. Real music."

"But the label execs won't—"

The calm dissipated like fog under the burning sun. She jumped up. "Enough! You work for me, not for the label!"

Saul breathed in and out audibly, as if she were a child trying his patience. "Yes, I do. Which is why I'm trying to save your career."

"Who says my career needs saving?"

"I do. The label does. And the producers of *A Star is Born* do. They know a sinking star when they see one."

"Sinking star? Oh, come on! I'm sick and tired of that you're-on-the-brink-of-losing-everything routine! You pull that shit every time I'm not doing what you want." She had avoided dealing with her dissatisfaction long enough. Now she was done with keeping the status quo out of fear or indecisiveness.

"What *I* want?" Saul huffed. "I'm doing what's best for *you!*"

"And you think you know what that is, without even asking me?"

"Of course I do! I've been your manager for a dozen years, and your career only took off once you hired me! With my help, you achieved everything you dreamed of—and now you're destroying all that hard work!"

Leo took a deep breath so she wouldn't yell at him. "You're right. I achieved my dream, and I'm grateful for your help. But you know what?

Now that I'm living it, my dream is feeling more and more like a nightmare. I hung in there for a long time, thinking it might change, that it was just stress. But if my time back in Fair Oaks has taught me one thing, it's that I've got to face the truth. It's time to make new dreams."

"New dreams. Yeah. You'll have to, because the old ones are slipping through your fingers." His tone cut like steel. "The producers of *A Star is Born* just told me they hired someone else to be a judge on the show."

Maybe he thought the shock of hearing that would be the slap in the face that would make her see reason, but it wasn't even a blip on Leo's emotional radar. "That was your dream, not mine. I was never eager to tell a couple of wannabes that they can't sing to save their lives." If she wanted off-key singing, Holly could do it much cuter.

"Do you have any idea what ratings that show—?"

Long-pent-up anger bubbled up inside of her. "Fuck the ratings! From now on, I'm doing what I want."

"You'll regret it. When the label drops you like a hot potato and your fans forget who you even are, you'll wish you'd stuck with it."

"Maybe." Leo gave a one-shouldered shrug with the phone still pressed to her ear. "But then at least it will have been my choice. I can't go on like this, Saul. Either I start making my own decisions, or I'll retire on the spot."

"At thirty-two?" He snorted. "That's ridiculous."

"No, you know what's ridiculous? You talking to me as if you were footing my paycheck, not the other way around. I'm done with how you are running my career. Either you support me in this, or we go our separate ways."

He sucked in a breath. "You can't just—"

"I can and I will," she said, her calm voice a counterpoint to his yelling. "So, what's it gonna be?"

"You're crazy if you think for a minute that you'll—"

"Goodbye, Saul. I'll make sure you get your last paycheck. And Saul? If I ever find out that you were the one who told the paparazzi where to find me, I'll make sure no one else in the music industry will ever hire you again." She ended the call before he could answer. There was nothing left to say.

As silence spread through the living room, she slowly began to grasp what she had just done.

She'd fired her manager of twelve years, the man who'd been a big part of her success. She might have just ruined her career.

Oh God. Her knees gave out, so she plopped down onto the couch. *Holy cow! I did it. I really did it.*

It was crazy and terrifying, but it also felt freeing, as if she had thrown off shackles that she had worn for so long that she'd forgotten they were there. She had fulfilled the contractual obligations to Clio Records when she'd wrapped up her world tour, so now she was free. No one could force her to return to New York if that wasn't what she wanted.

So, what did she want?

The first thing that popped into her mind wasn't her music. Instead, images of Holly rose from deep inside of her—images of walking hand in hand along the creek, of Holly smiling at her as they lay in bed, talking and cuddling, and of the peace she had felt when they had hung out on the couch earlier, with Holly reading and her composing a new song.

That's what I want. She had no idea what the future would bring when it came to her career, but she knew with a certainty that left no room for doubts that she wanted a life with Holly. *Now the question is: how do I get it?*

Holly slid the bookmark between the pages of her novel and put it on the bedside table. The book was good, but she couldn't focus on its plot. The empty spot in bed next to her was too distracting.

At breakfast, Leo had told her that she had an important appointment today and that it might be pretty late by the time she got back. That was when Holly had decided she might as well sleep in her own bed for a change. Now she regretted that decision as she imagined how nice it would feel to slip into bed with Leo, cuddle close, and let her heartbeat and her wonderful scent lull her to sleep.

Jesus, get a grip. It's just one night. What are you going to do when she flies back to New York or goes on a year-long world tour?

A chill slid over her, even though it was a pleasant seventy-two degrees in her bedroom. She and Leo had avoided talking about it, but they both knew the day would come when they had to go their separate ways.

Or you could go with her. Nurses are needed everywhere, even in New York.

The thought made her heart pound with part fear, part excitement. Except for the four years when she'd been away at college, she had lived in Fair Oaks her entire life. She loved it here—being around her family and the people she'd grown up with, working with long-term patients she came to care about.

How would she deal with the anonymity of a big city like New York and the constant change of patients in a large hospital?

Maybe she could find work as a home-health-care nurse.

Of course, Leo might say that she didn't have to work at all since she made more than enough money for the two of them. But she loved her work and didn't want to give it up. While she loved Leo even more, she didn't think that giving up her job would be good for their relationship either. She wanted them to be equals.

The ringing of her cell phone interrupted her thoughts.

When she saw the name on the display, she smiled. *Leo!*

She decided then and there that she would tell her about the option of her coming to New York with her—just throw it out there and see what Leo would think. They might be moving a little fast, but she had a feeling Leo would like the suggestion.

Her finger felt a little unsteady as she swiped to accept the call. "Hey there."

"What are you wearing?" Leo asked.

Holly chuckled. "You're not, by any chance, trying to have phone sex with an asexual woman, are you?"

Leo's laughter trickled through the line. "No. I'm trying to find out if the aforementioned woman is still dressed so she can come open the door."

"Open the...?" Holly's breath caught. "Where are you?"

"In front of your house," Leo said, a big grin in her voice.

Holly jumped out of bed, almost getting her feet tangled in the covers in her haste to get to the door. Seconds later, she threw it open.

Leo leaned against her father's car, which she was driving now, cell phone at her ear. Her blonde hair was tousled, as if she'd repeatedly run her hand through it. She exuded an energy that seemed to make the air around her crackle.

Holly hesitated, not sure what it was—excitement or nervousness. "Hi," she said, then realized that she was still talking into the phone. She put it away and repeated, "Hi. All done with your appointment?"

Without moving away from the car, Leo put her phone away as well and nodded. "Just came back. There's something I have to tell you, and I didn't want to wait until tomorrow."

"I've got something to tell you too." Holly paused and took a second to study Leo more closely.

Leo's expression was so serious that it could only mean one thing: her appointment had been with her manager, who had flown all the way to Missouri to drag her back to New York, and now she had come to tell Holly she was leaving. Surely she would want Holly to come with her, right? The thought of living apart and not seeing Leo every day caused an almost physical ache, and she was sure it wasn't a one-sided feeling.

Still, her knees started to tremble, so she leaned against the doorjamb. "You met with Saul, didn't you?"

"Saul?" Leo shook her head. "No. And I won't be getting any more phone calls from him either."

Because Saul would finally get what he wanted—Leo back in New York—or was there another explanation? "Why not?"

"Because I fired him."

Holly gripped the doorframe. "You fired him? Why didn't you tell me sooner?"

"It just happened yesterday, even though it was a long time coming. We just don't want the same things anymore."

Holly swallowed. "What is it that you want?"

"For one thing, I want to write music like 'Odd One Out' or 'Holly's Song.' I don't know if my record label will go for it, but if they don't, I could easily finance it myself. That way, I would have full creative control."

"Oh, Leo. That would be fantastic!" Something in Leo's expression told her that wasn't all. "There's more, isn't there?"

Leo nodded. "I also want to give Chance a good home."

"You want to give Chance a good home?" Holly repeated as if that would help her understand.

An affectionate smile spread across Leo's face. "Are you going to repeat everything I say?"

"Sorry. My brain can't keep up. Who or what is Chance?"

Now Leo stepped to the side, opened the back door, and pulled a cat carrier from the car. "This is Chance."

Holly rushed over and peeked through the bars.

Big yellow eyes stared back at her from a furry face.

"Aww. You got yourself a kitten? Is it one of Happy's little ones?"

"No. I mean…yes, he's one of Happy's kittens. But I didn't get him for me—I got him for *us*."

"For us?" A thrill of hope spiraled through her. She stared at Leo, just as wide-eyed as the kitten. "Does this mean you want me to come to New York with you?"

"No."

Holly waited for her to go on, her heart hammering and her mouth dry.

"Because I'm not going back to New York," Leo added. "I'm not going anywhere."

"But what about your music?"

Leo shrugged and grinned. "I always thought someone should build a recording studio in Fair Oaks. Might as well be me."

"But…but…you don't like it here. You said it's claustrophobic."

"It's endearing," Leo corrected, as Holly had many weeks ago. "In my mind, I made it into this horrible place full of nosy, narrow-minded people. It took coming back to realize that there's also a lot of positive things that I had forgotten about. I like the slower pace here and that I can be just Leo. And you are here. I like that most of all."

"Leo?" Holly's voice quivered as she struggled to hold back either tears or giddy laughter—she wasn't sure which.

"Yeah?"

"You'd better put that cat carrier down."

Leo looked back and forth between the kitten and her. "Um, why?"

"Because I'm about to jump you."

Leo laughed—loud, happy, and unrestrained. "Who needs New York when I've got you right here?"

Then neither of them said anything else, because Leo put the carrier down, and Holly threw herself into her arms and kissed her with all the love in her heart.

It was a high-pitched *mew* that pulled them apart minutes later.

They leaned their foreheads together.

"I think someone is feeling a little neglected," Leo whispered against Holly's lips.

"He'd better get used to it because I intend to do this…" She kissed Leo again, but this time just for a few seconds. "…any chance I get."

"Any chance." Leo laughed. "See, I named him well. Because there'll be lots and lots of chances." She rained kisses down on Holly's face before she picked up the cat carrier by its handle and slid her free hand into Holly's.

Holly felt as if she were floating rather than walking into the house. Having Leo here, knowing she would stay, was more than she had ever dreamed possible.

Once inside, Leo lifted the kitten out of the carrier and nuzzled her cheek against its soft-looking fur for a moment.

Aww. The two were so cute together that Holly nearly melted. "You didn't happen to get a litter box for him too, did you?"

"It's all in the trunk." Leo pointed to where she'd parked the car. "Your mother gave me a list of things I'd need for a cat."

Holly stared at her. "My mother knew about this? That you're staying? She didn't say a word when we all had dinner together yesterday."

"I asked her when I helped with the dishes and you were busy cleaning up the mess your nephew made in the living room."

"So, what did she say?" Holly asked.

"That we'll have to have Chance neutered in about two months, and that she expects me to be there for it." Leo grinned. "I think it's her way of telling me I'd better stick around and not play fast and loose with her daughter's heart."

"And you will? Stick around, I mean." Holly still couldn't believe it.

"I will," Leo said. "I'll probably have to travel and give a concert or an interview every now and then, but I won't do big tours anymore. Let other singers do it. I've been on the road for long enough."

Could it really be so easy? Holly felt a little faint with happiness, so she pulled Leo over to the couch.

They snuggled together on the middle cushion and watched Chance explore his new home.

"So," Leo said after a while, "what was it that you wanted to tell me earlier?"

"Hmm?" Holly leaned her head on Leo's shoulder.

"You said you had something to tell me too."

"Oh. That." She chuckled. "Great minds think alike. I was about to offer that I move to New York with you."

Leo stared at her. "You would have moved away from Fair Oaks? For me?"

"For us." Holly lifted her head off Leo's shoulder. "The offer is still on the table if you'd rather do it that way."

"Hell, no! Your mother would use her evil vet tools on me." Leo laughed but then sobered and looked into Holly's eyes. "I'm exactly where I want to be."

Drawn in by the loving look in Leo's eyes, Holly leaned toward her for a kiss.

Chance chose that moment to leap for the laptop power cord dangling off the edge of the couch. When he couldn't reach it, he tried to climb Holly's leg.

Leo saved her by gently picking him up before he could use his claws. "There goes your peace and quiet. Are you sure you're ready for this?" She nodded down at the kitten batting at a strand of her hair.

Holly grinned. "Who needs peace and quiet when I can have the two of you?"

They beamed at each other and then leaned across Chance to share a kiss—the first of many kitten-supervised kisses.

Epilogue

One year later

LEO'S FINGERS SHOOK AS SHE clicked on the refresh button on her laptop's browser. "Oh God, it's up!"

Her voice, louder than intended, made Chance look up from the catnap he was taking at the foot of the bed. He gave them a disgruntled glare before rolling into a no-longer-tiny ball and going back to sleep.

Instantly, Holly wrapped her arms around Leo from behind and pulled her back against her tank-top-clad body. "Want me to take a look and tell you?"

Leo shook her head. "Let's read it together." With Holly's warmth surrounding her, it wasn't quite so scary. Holly loved her music—and, more importantly, loved her; that was all that mattered.

They held on to the laptop together while Leo scrolled to the beginning of the review and then read it out loud.

Jenna Blake has just released her first independently produced album. The twelve tracks have been written and recorded in the studio the Grammy-winning artist built in her Missouri hometown last year.

That wasn't quite true. Most of the songs had been written in the living room of the small house they now rented together, with Holly next to her on the couch. But the press didn't need to know that. The media attention she had garnered when she had announced her own recording label had been bad enough.

If you haven't bought a copy of the aptly named album, Perfect Rhythm, *get one ASAP.*

Fans of her last album might not like this one as much, but this reviewer actually thought it was superior in every way— beautiful melodies, profound lyrics, and Jenna's smoky voice that effortlessly glides through octaves. With songs like "In the Rain," "Sex and Video Games," "Holly's Song," and "When Our Hearts Collide," you'll have a hard time deciding which is your favorite.

Blake has always been one of the most technically sound singers in pop music, but she has been criticized for focusing too much on showy elements and not enough on emotion. Well, this album will definitely silence those critics. She has put her heart and soul into this album, and it shows. Five stars out of five.

Leo's voice cracked on the last word. She swiveled her head around to face Holly. "She liked it."

"She *loved* it. I told you so."

"You did." Holly had believed in her from the very start. Whenever Leo had struggled to reinvent herself as an artist and a brand, she'd been there to encourage her.

Leo closed the laptop and set it on the floor so she could lie down and take Holly into her arms. "Thank you," she whispered into Holly's ear.

Holly combed her fingers through Leo's hair. "Anytime."

They lay cuddled together for several minutes while the reviewer's words echoed through Leo's mind, making her beam. Life was so good that she felt a little drunk on it. There was only one thing that would make it even more perfect.

"The concerts in New York, Boston, and Chicago are coming up next month," Leo said.

Holly slipped her hand beneath Leo's shirt and stroked her back. "Don't worry. They'll love the new songs too."

That wasn't what made Leo's body vibrate with renewed nervousness. "Will you come with me? I know you probably won't be able to come to all three, but how about at least Chicago? Someone has to protect me from all the bra-throwing fans who don't get that 'Sex and Video Games' isn't an invitation."

"All the bra-throwing fans?" Holly arched her brows. "Didn't you say you don't have any wild groupie stories to tell?"

"Oh, so you paid attention to what I said, even back then? Jealous?" Leo asked in a teasing tone.

Holly's expression was serious. "A little."

Leo rolled around so she could lean over Holly on one elbow and look into her eyes. "There's no need. You know that, right? All the wild groupie sex in the world could never compare to what we have. Not even close." She put emphasis on every word.

In reply, Holly pulled her down and kissed her. "For me neither."

Leo nibbled on Holly's bottom lip. "So, will you come to Chicago? We could even meet up with Meg and Jo while we're there."

"That would be great. Can we get them tickets to the concert?"

"Sure. I could get them all-access passes. In exchange for...some information."

Holly cocked her head. "What information?"

"Well..." Leo swallowed. "They bought a house last year, didn't they? Maybe they could give us some pointers."

Holly stared up at her. "You mean...?"

Leo nodded. "I love living here with you. But I'd really like us to have something that is ours. Something a little bigger, with a guest room and—"

Holly let out a cry that made Chance jump off the bed and stalk out of the bedroom in search of a quieter napping spot. Ignoring him, Holly wrapped her legs around Leo, rolled them around so she was on top, and let her lips wander over every inch of her face.

Among kisses and happy laughter, Leo gasped out, "So that's a yes?"

"Yes, yes, yes." Holly punctuated each affirmation with another kiss. She looked down at her. "Were there ever any doubts about what my answer would be?"

Leo shrugged. "Well, you really like this little house..."

"Not half as much as I love you. And having a house of our own, you and me together...that would be wonderful." A dreamy look appeared on Holly's face. "Maybe we could even soundproof one of the rooms."

A blush crawled up Leo's chest. "I hardly think I'm that loud...am I?"

Holly laughed. "Loud enough to make poor Chance hide beneath the couch last night. But I wasn't talking about our bedroom. I meant we could have a music room. Maybe move in your father's piano, if it's all right with your mom." She paused and stroked Leo's face. "Unless you aren't ready for that."

A year ago, Leo couldn't have imagined it. The piano held too many memories of the past. But now it held new ones too, including sitting on the piano bench with Holly, playing together. "I'm ready."

With Holly by her side, she was ready for anything life could throw at her.

Author's Note

As Holly said in the story: Human sexuality is pretty complex, and so is asexuality. Asexual people are a diverse group. Some experience romantic attraction, like Holly; some don't, like Holly's friend Meg. Some can enjoy sex with a partner they love under the right circumstances; some are indifferent toward sex; and others are repulsed by the thought of it.

There's such a broad range of perspectives and experiences on the ace spectrum that it's impossible for one character to represent all asexual people. That's why it's so important to have more books about ace-spectrum characters.

When I first became aware of asexuality, there wasn't a single romance novel involving a homoromantic asexual woman. That's why I wrote *Perfect Rhythm*—to make non-asexual readers more aware of this sexual orientation and to help make ace-spectrum readers feel a little less alone. I hope I achieved what I set out to do.

Thank you for reading *Perfect Rhythm*.

Jae

About Jae

Jae grew up amidst the vineyards of southern Germany. She spent her childhood with her nose buried in a book, earning her the nickname *professor*. The writing bug bit her at the age of eleven. Since 2006, she has been writing mostly in English.

She used to work as a psychologist but gave up her day job in 2013 to become a full-time writer and a part-time editor. As far as she's concerned, it's the best job in the world.

When she's not writing, she likes to spend her time reading, indulging her ice cream and office supply addictions, and watching way too many crime shows.

CONNECT WITH JAE

E-mail her at: jae@jae-fiction.com
Visit her website: jae-fiction.com
Like her on Facebook: facebook.com/JaeAuthor
Follow her on Twitter: @jaefiction

Other Books from Ylva Publishing

www.ylva-publishing.com

Something in the Wine

Jae

ISBN: 978-3-95533-793-3
Length: 302 pages (100,000 words)

All her life, Annie suffered through her brother's practical jokes. He sets her up on a blind date with lesbian winemaker Drew, even knowing Annie is straight. Annie and Drew turn the tables on him by pretending to fall in love.

But what starts as a revenge plan turns their lives upside down as the lines between pretending and reality begin to blur.

Fragile

Eve Francis

ISBN: 978-3-95533-482-6
Length: 318 pages (103,000 words)

College graduate Carly Rogers is forced to live back at home with her mother and sister until she finds a real job. Life isn't shaping up as expected, but meeting Ashley begins to change that. After many late night talks and the start of a book club, the two women begin a romance. When a past medical condition threatens Ashley, Carly wonders if their future together will always be this fragile.

A Story of Now
(A Story of Now Series – Book 1)

Emily O'Beirne

ISBN: 978-3-95533-348-5
Length: pages: 388 pages (140,000 words)

Nineteen-year-old Claire knows she needs a life. And new friends. Too sassy for her own good, she doesn't make friends easily anymore. And she has no clue where to start on the whole life front. At first, Robbie and Mia seem the least likely people to help her find it. But in a turbulent time, Claire finds new friends, a new self, and, with the warm, brilliant Mia, a whole new set of feelings.

The Light of the World

Ellen Simpson

ISBN: 978-3-95533-507-6
Length: 378 pages (107,000 words)

Confronted with a mystery upon her grandmother's death, Eva delves into the rich and complicated history of a woman who hid far more than a long-lost-love from the world. Darkness is lurking behind every corner, and someone is looking for the key to her grandmother's secrets; the light of the world.

Coming from Ylva Publishing

www.ylva-publishing.com

The Brutal Truth

Lee Winter

Australian crime reporter Maddie Grey is out of her depth in New York, miserable, and secretly drawn to her powerful, twice-married, media mogul boss, Elena Bartell, who eats failing newspapers for breakfast. As work takes them to Australia, Maddie is goaded into a brief, seemingly harmless bet with her enigmatic boss—where they have to tell the complete truth to each other. It backfires catastrophically. A lesbian romance about the lies we tell ourselves.

Perfect Rhythm
© 2017 by Jae

ISBN: 978-3-95533-862-6

Also available as e-book.

Published by Ylva Publishing, legal entity of Ylva Verlag, e.Kfr.

Ylva Verlag, e.Kfr.
Owner: Astrid Ohletz
Am Kirschgarten 2
65830 Kriftel
Germany

www.ylva-publishing.com

First edition: 2017

Credits
Edited by Lee Winter & Michelle Aguilar
Proofread by Louisa Villeneuve
Cover Design and Print Layout by Streetlight Graphics

"When Our Hearts Collide"
(Companion song to *Perfect Rhythm*)
Written and performed by Mariah Glasscock
© 2017 by Mariah Glasscock